Praise for S

'Suspenseful, claustropho
turns than a blac
Katy Brent, author of *How to Kill Men and Get Away With It*

'A fast-paced tale of revenge where no one can be trusted,
all set against a glamorous snowy backdrop and
with some brilliant twists. Loved it.'
Catherine Cooper, bestselling author of *The Chalet*

'A tense and twisty thriller that keeps you guessing.'
Nikki Smith, author of *The Beach Party*

'A clever, slick and chilling read, I found myself glued to the
pages and suspicious of everyone right up to the heart-racing
denouement. Clarke is at the top of her game!'
A.A. Chaudhuri, author of *The Final Party*

'An explosive revenge thriller packed with enough twists and
turns to leave you breathless – I love it!'
Mira Shah, author of *Her*

'A pacy, chilling, claustrophobic thriller … revenge,
suspense, tension and some completely unexpected
twists thrown in for *après ski* … I devoured it!'
Diane Jeffrey, author of *The Other Couple*

'A lightning-paced thriller about revenge and keeping your
enemies close.'
Woman's Own

'An intensely gripping thriller, with astute characterisation,
a cleverly woven plot that keeps you guessing all the way,
and a story that is both suspenseful and moving.
A hugely satisfying read.'
Philippa East, author of *Little White Lies*

'A gripping read, exposing the dark lies at the heart of a supposedly perfect life. Pacy, with well-drawn characters you care about. The perfect thriller!'
Louise Mumford, author of *The Hotel*

'An incredibly tense psychological thriller that grips you from the very first page. The suspense is utterly breathtaking.'
Victoria Dowd, author of *The Smart Woman's Guide to Murder*

'A carefully crafted, clever novel with plenty of twists, suspense and red herrings. A sparkling and satisfying read.'
Diane Jeffrey, author of *The Silent Friend*

'A dark and clever thriller that kept me turning the pages late into the night.'
Sophie Flynn, author of *All My Lies*

SARAH CLARKE is a writer living in South West London with her husband, children, and stubbornly cheerful cockapoo. Over fifteen years, Sarah has built a successful career as a marketing copywriter. When her youngest child started secondary school, she joined the Faber Academy Writing A Novel course to learn the craft of writing psychological thrillers. Sarah graduated in 2019 and joined HQ Digital two years later.

Also by Sarah Clarke

A Mother Never Lies
Every Little Secret
My Perfect Friend
The Ski Trip
The Night She Dies

Someone in the Water

SARAH CLARKE

H Q

ONE PLACE. MANY STORIES

HQ
An imprint of HarperCollins*Publishers* Ltd
1 London Bridge Street
London SE1 9GF

www.harpercollins.co.uk

HarperCollins*Publishers*
Macken House, 39/40 Mayor Street Upper,
Dublin 1 D01 C9W8
This edition 2025

1
First published in Great Britain by HQ,
an imprint of HarperCollins*Publishers* Ltd 2025

Copyright © Sarah Clarke 2025

Sarah Clarke asserts the moral right to be identified as the author of this work.
A catalogue record for this book is available from the British Library.

ISBN: 9780008725600

This novel is entirely a work of fiction. The names, characters and incidents
portrayed in it are the work of the author's imagination. Any resemblance to
actual persons, living or dead, events or localities is entirely coincidental.

All rights reserved. No part of this publication may be reproduced, stored
in a retrieval system, or transmitted, in any form or by any means,
electronic, mechanical, photocopying, recording or otherwise,
without the prior permission of the publishers.

Without limiting the author's and publisher's exclusive rights, any unauthorised
use of this publication to train generative artificial intelligence (AI) technologies
is expressly prohibited. HarperCollins also exercise their rights under Article
4(3) of the Digital Single Market Directive 2019/790 and expressly reserve this
publication from the text and data mining exception.

Printed and bound in the UK using 100% Renewable
Electricity by CPI Group (UK) Ltd

MIX
Paper | Supporting
responsible forestry
FSC
www.fsc.org
FSC™ C007454

This book contains FSC™ certified paper and other controlled sources
to ensure responsible forest management.

For more information visit: www.harpercollins.co.uk/green

For
the San Lu 1998 crew

Author's Note

In my twenties, I spent four months working at a hotel in Corsica. I fell in love with the island – its mix of Caribbean-style beaches, lush vegetation and snowcapped mountains – and when I became an author, I knew I wanted to write a book set there. But when I began researching Corsican history and culture, I had no idea of the riches I would uncover. Or how perfect Corsica would prove to be as the backdrop for a dark psychological thriller.

In *Someone in the Water*, you will be introduced to the mazzeri legend. While the book is a work of fiction, the mazzeri legend is a real, and deeply rooted, part of Corsica's mystical culture, and it reflects the island's history of invasion and passionate commitment to independence over centuries. While I do take some slight poetic licence with the details, I have tried to portray the legend authentically, and I thought it would be helpful to provide this context before you start reading.

I hope you enjoy discovering all of Corsica's secrets as much as I have.

Prologue

1st August 2025

It's dark.

More than dark. Pure, perfect blackness, the type that makes you wonder if you really exist. Whether you might be floating in space, or some other unknown dimension.

A noise pulls Lola back to the room. Rustling.

She imagines rats scurrying across the floor.

Spiders crawling.

She closes her eyes, feels the slow trickle of salty tears down her face.

Why didn't she listen? Trust her mum's judgement?

In her black hole, the images come for her. Dead strangers. Grieving mothers. Wild animals being chased through forests by hooded warriors.

A faceless killer.

And him.

There's that noise again but coming from a different direction. Or is it a different noise? Rustling, yes, but louder now, like a person.

'Hello?' she calls out, her voice breaking in that one word. 'Who's there?'

2025

Frankie

25th July

I pull at the zip. Grumble out a swear word when the slider doesn't budge, the teeth of the zipper straining but refusing to meet. But it's not my holdall's fault that it won't close. It's me, overfilling it, too worried about overlooking something that I'll need while I'm away. I sigh, remove one of my jumpers – it's July after all, I don't need five – and finally the bag zips shut.

My phone buzzes in the back pocket of my shorts. I feel a jolt of panic as I pull it out, but it's only my mum. 'Hey, Mum.'

'Hi, love. How's the packing going?'

'Yeah, fine.' I eye the jumper, wonder whether I should lay it between the bag's handles, just in case. 'I'm leaving soon though. Nothing to hang around here for.'

'So Lola got off okay then?'

This is why I've got nothing to stay for, but it's also the reason I panicked when my phone rang. Imagining my daughter in trouble, even though she's currently about thirty thousand feet in the air, somewhere over France probably. With her phone on airplane mode.

'Yeah, I checked online, and the plane left about half an hour ago. Ayia Napa is two hours ahead, so it'll be four o'clock in the afternoon by the time they land.'

'Just in time for a fun night out then.'

'Yeah, I'm not sure I need reminding of that.'

Mum chuckles. 'They're good girls. They'll be fine. And you can't hold on to them forever, however much you want to. I still remember dropping you at the airport when you were eighteen, how nervous I felt, and you were going away for months, not weeks. And without any besties to watch your back.'

'And look how that turned out.'

The words spill out before I can stop them, and I have to blink to keep the tears away. Twenty-one years on, and I'm still a mess. Although that's not fair. Yes, for the first two years after that terrible summer, I wasn't sure I'd find a way to survive. But gradually things improved. And now it's only at this time of year, the two anniversaries, when those memories threaten to smother me again.

'Lola is going on holiday with her friends,' Mum says softly. 'They will have a fantastic time, and then come home in one piece. I promise.'

'Yeah, you're right. Thanks, Mum.' I try to take deep breaths, but quietly, so that Mum doesn't pick up on my anxiety – she's had more than enough of that to deal with over the years.

'And you'll keep an eye on your phone, just in case Lola can't get hold of me?' I continue. I can't trust my behaviour at this time of year, which is why I go away by myself, to somewhere remote, so that no one I love is exposed to it. We've been following this routine for fourteen years now, so both Lola and Mum are used to it. But Lola has never been out of the country during this period before. I hate to think that she might need me, and I won't be there for her. But I know there's no better stand-in than my mum.

'Of course. I'm used to being here for her at this time of year, aren't I? And I guess this will be my last rodeo as her responsible adult with her eighteenth birthday only days away,' she adds, her voice turning wistful.

I ride the crashing wave of guilt that is so familiar now. All those childhood birthdays I've not been here for. And now it's too late to ever make amends. 'I owe you a lot,' I say quietly.

'She's my granddaughter. You're my daughter. I do it because I love you both; you don't owe me anything.'

When I found out I was pregnant with Lola, I thought it was a sign. After two years of nightmares, delusions, and insomnia – peppered with drinking binges and topped off with a four-week stay on a psychiatric ward – I felt I'd been given a second chance at life. I'd only hooked up with Lola's father that once – a free-spirited traveller from New Zealand's South Island on a global journey of discovery (his words) – and I had no plans to ask him to stick around to help. But a baby. An amazing, innocent new life. I stopped the booze, the pills, the partying with people I barely knew. I moved out of London and back to my childhood home in Southbourne on the south coast, took up yoga, and rediscovered my love of the sea. And I slept. Blissful eight-hour periods when my brain stayed quiet.

But then the sonographer at my twenty-week scan told me that Lola's due date was 31st July. It was a cruel joke by some higher power I don't believe in, but it still sent me spiralling.

I told myself over and over that it was just a coincidence, that there was no way my baby's upcoming birth could possibly be connected to what happened in a different country three years earlier. But as the date got closer, and I got bigger, my hormones raged, and the nightmares returned with a vengeance. And with them their trusted companion, insomnia.

My beautiful, thoughtful Lola held on for one extra day – her birthday is the 1st of August – and at the time I hoped that would be enough. But it wasn't. And three years later, on Lola's third birthday, I was reminded just how tight a vice those memories held me in.

7

'And anyway,' Mum continues, 'I'm sure Lola won't need either of us. I've transferred three hundred pounds into her Revolut account as an early birthday present, so hopefully there'll be a gushing message of gratitude, but otherwise I doubt we'll hear from her. She won't be short of money, and those girls are all smart cookies.'

I try to soak up Mum's reasoning. Because she's right. Lola is with her three best friends, girls who have been in and out of each other's houses and lives since primary school. They'll look out for each other. And she deserves to have a holiday after working so hard at her A levels, much harder than I did – although in my defence, I had only buried my dad two months before my exams started.

'What would I do without you?' I whisper.

'The feeling is mutual, my love. So you go away, do whatever you need, safe in the knowledge that Lola will be having the best time ever without you, and I'll have my phone by my side the whole time.'

I catch my reflection in my bedroom mirror and notice that I'm smiling. Which is as it should be. Lola has had to spend her birthday with my mum since she turned four, never quite understanding why I wasn't there to celebrate with them. This is the first time we're going to be apart on her terms. 'Thanks, Mum. You know, I really think you'd make more money as a therapist.'

'And I think I'd be the one needing therapy if anyone dragged me away from my workshop,' she counters, making my smile widen even more.

We say our goodbyes and I lug my holdall down the stairs. It's ten forty-five. I have access to the rental cottage in the New Forest from eleven o'clock this morning.

And maybe the sooner this purgatory starts, the quicker it will be over.

Frankie

25th July

I drive slowly through town, checking for potential hazards, cyclists weaving in and out of the traffic, tourists scooting past each other on the pavements. When I hit the A337, heading north away from the coast, I speed up, but stay under the sixty-mile-an-hour limit. Of course Lola isn't in the car with me today, and thanks to taking a sleeping pill at three this morning, I slept for a solid four hours last night, so I'm feeling rested enough. But some memories run too deep.

Being the mother of a newborn is much more than exhausting. It removes every morsel of energy from your muscles, bones, brain, and eyes. Which means, in the first few months after Lola was born, I finally felt normal. This state of fatigue that had become so familiar to me during the summer months, was suddenly being experienced by my new friends at antenatal classes. And that sense of belonging gave me hope that I could turn the tide on my insomnia.

But it wasn't to be.

Lola was slow to sleep through the night – perhaps she could

9

sense me twitching and fidgeting in the room next door – so I was still living the tired mum routine on her first birthday. But by the time she turned two, she was a better sleeper than me. We spent her birthday at the beach in Southbourne. It was a beautifully sunny day, so it should have been idyllic, but the warm sand proved too comforting and I dropped off. My mum was with us – thank God – so when Lola waddled to the water's edge, Mum was there to whisk her to safety. But I was left with the guilt of knowing I hadn't protected my daughter.

Mum didn't come to the play zone with us on Lola's third birthday. There'd been a storm the week before, taking a load of windsurfers by surprise, and Mum was too busy fixing ripped sails in her workshop. So when my head drooped on the drive home after a couple of hours' climbing through inflatable tunnels, there was no one to shake me awake. And when the car veered into a field, not even Lola's calls of 'Mumma' could drag me back to consciousness.

I hit a tree and flipped the car. The airbags saved us, and neither Lola nor I was physically hurt. But I still spent three weeks in hospital, on the psychiatric ward. With the trauma of 'what might have been' rocketing around my brain, I couldn't stop my mouth from gabbling about being possessed by an evil spirit, and the doctors deemed me a risk to myself and others.

From that point on, for the two weeks when the worst of my insomnia hits, around the anniversary of those two tragedies, I have left Lola with my mum. Not being with her on her birthday has been a heart-wrenching sacrifice, but always worth it to keep her safe.

I turn the radio on – Bruno Mars' 'Just the Way You Are' – and look out of the window. There's a burst of deep purple heather spreading over dark green shrubs and two wild ponies are grazing in the distance. Lola and I moved to Lymington twelve years ago, when I got a job at the local college, and it's one of the things I love most about this area. Being in a coastal town one minute, and deep into English countryside the next. Lymington is surrounded by the New Forest, and I drive deeper into the woodland until I reach the hamlet of Linwood. I spot the dirt track from the rental company's website description and crawl down it at a snail's pace. The further I go, the more isolated it becomes, and the better I feel. Finally, I reach a narrow gate and park up on the verge. The name of the accommodation is inscribed on a wooden plaque – The Wolf Den – and it makes me shudder. But I knew this when I booked, and I'm not going to let a name put me off.

I find the padlock code on my phone, then open the gate and appraise my home for the next fortnight. It's a converted shipping container on the edge of a field, its location so isolated that the owners have installed a roll-top bath outside on the deck. In different circumstances, it would make a beautiful romantic getaway. But for me, it's a refuge. A place where I can mutter nonsense about evil spirits, and no one will hear me.

I head back to my car and open the boot. I grab the holdall and a handful of canvases. It takes three more trips to unload everything – food for a fortnight, paints and brushes, laptop and speaker – and another half hour to find a place for them all in the small living area. When I'm done, I make a cup of tea and sink into one of the two sheepskin-lined bucket chairs on the deck. Beyond the small garden, there are fields, trees, fences, and more fields. Not a single human being. It's perfect.

But I still can't relax.

I pull my phone out of my pocket and stare at my home screen. Lola is smiling broadly, tendrils of dark, wet hair framing her face, a medal around her neck, and a proud expression on her face. The photo was taken last summer. Lola had just won a local windsurfing competition and was feeling justifiably pleased with herself.

It's not surprising that Lola is a natural on the water. The beach has been a big part of her childhood, just like it was for me, and

11

my mother before that. Mum turned sixty-three last year and she still takes a windsurf board out when there's a stable cross-shore wind. And except for two years when I was too scared to go near the sea, I've been a lifelong fan too. Mum has made sure that windsurfing is Lola's first passion, but she's also a talented sailor, swimmer and water-skier.

I run a finger over the cool glass, then swipe upwards to bring it to life. I click into WhatsApp and finds Lola's name. When she left yesterday evening to stay at Tamsyn's ahead of their early morning trip to the airport, I hugged her tightly, but then whispered in her ear that it might be better if she phoned her Grams rather than me if she needed anything while she was away. And I can still see her expression now, as she drew away from me, the mix of sadness and resignation on her face.

My eyes fill with tears at the memory. It feels like such an impossible choice. I hate the thought of Lola seeing me at my lowest – sleep-deprived, grief-stricken, talking about murderous mythical legends as though they're real. But I know that in protecting myself, I'm rejecting her. Year after year. What kind of mother does that?

Lola is two thousand miles away in Cyprus. There's no chance of me physically hurting her like I almost did when she was three. And Lola hardly ever calls me anymore – it's always messages or voice notes. If I stick to typing rather than talking, surely I won't lose my sanity so deeply that I actually write any of the crazy nonsense that I've allowed to slip out of my mouth in the past?

My hand hovers over the chat function, my mind frozen with indecision. But then I push my hair away from my face, drop my thumbs onto the screen, and type.

Hey, hope you had a good flight.
Just to say, what I said about contacting Grams,
ignore it

I'd love for you to keep in touch with me.
And I can't wait to hear all your holiday gossip
Love you, Mum xx

Frankie

25th July

I tip my head to one side and assess the canvas. I don't often paint landscapes, but the view from this place is so stunning that it has inspired me to give it a go. I don't think my new watercolour will win any awards, but I'm grateful for how it has distracted me this afternoon, and I like the sense of tranquillity that the painting radiates. Especially when I know it's the calm before the storm.

My stomach growls, and I remember that I haven't eaten since breakfast. I take a pasta ready meal out of the fridge and put it in the microwave. As I wait for it to heat up, I start making the familiar deals with myself.

If I don't force sleep, the nightmares won't come.

If I accept the insomnia, my body will find a way to rest when it needs.

If I give my imagination an outlet by painting the mazzeri, I won't start to believe they're real.

The microwave pings. I slide the pasta onto a plate and take it outside. The sun is setting, wispy clouds lit up orange against the darkening blue sky. I sink into the soft bucket chair and watch dusk float towards night as I chew. By the time I've finished my meal, the sun has disappeared over the horizon, so I take my plate back inside and open up Spotify on my laptop.

Five minutes later, I'm back behind my easel with a fresh canvas resting on its ledge. Music spills out of the portable speaker. I always listen to the same playlist when I hide away from the world every summer. Coldplay's 'Clocks'. Black Eyed Peas' 'Where Is the Love?' Kelis' 'Milkshake'. Hits that take me back twenty-one years, like an act of self-harm.

I haven't heard from Lola since I sent her that message, but I can't let myself worry about that. She'll be in a bar by now, I imagine, or maybe a nightclub, drinking and dancing with Tamsyn, Martha, and Ruby. Four girls enjoying their post-college summer holiday without a care in the world. Just as I thought it would be for me that same summer.

I turn up the volume and focus on the white square in front of me.

And I paint. Scenes that I have grown to hate, but that seem to live inside me. Corsican mountains at night, cedar and fir trees glowing in the moonlight. Spiky white asphodels – known by the locals in Corsica as flowers of the dead. Red deer hiding in the shadows, golden eagles roosting on rocky ledges with watchful eyes. And men with hoods, their faces obscured, prowling through the undergrowth with weapons.

The mazzeri dream hunters.

I would never let my students paint onto canvas without a sketch to follow, but this is more about survival than art. Exposure therapy maybe. The mazzeri story is a mythical legend distinct to Corsica, the island where my dad was born, and where I spent that terrible summer, and for centuries it was considered as real as Catholicism by the locals. Of course it's not real – all myths are just stories – but that doesn't make the dreams any less scary. As I have discovered for myself. Especially when … but no, I won't go there tonight.

15

At around 3 a.m., my eyelids start to grow heavy, but instinctively I know it's too early to lie down. That if I try to sleep, my brain will fill up with a toxic merging of real memories and crazy fantasies. I need to finish the painting first and be so tired that I can barely stand. At that point, if I help things along with a sleeping pill, I'll black out rather than sleep, and the nightmares should stay away.

Two hours later, with dawn rising, the picture is finished. I stand back to study it. Art was my favourite subject at school, and I was good at it, but it wasn't a passion, not when I had the beach as my playground. But that changed during my first stay in hospital in London. Art therapy was offered every other day, and after my first session, I found myself waiting impatiently for the next time I could pick up a paintbrush. When I was discharged, Mum encouraged me to keep going with it, so I signed up for lessons at Putney Art School. It wasn't meant to lead to a career, but my teacher, Becky, said I had great potential. And that stuck with me.

I couldn't become an art teacher the conventional way because I didn't have a university degree, but I got a job as a part-time art assistant in a private school in Bournemouth when Lola was two and slowly worked my way up. I started a full-time position at Lymington college three years later, and now it seems my decade and a half of experience counts for more than a piece of paper, because I teach art to both sixth-form students and adults on evening courses.

With the sun sneaking over the horizon, I finally turn away from the easel and walk inside. I've been standing up for nearly nine hours and my legs are exhausted, so I grab my laptop from the table and lower into the small, plump sofa.

When I first started painting these pictures, I would throw the canvases away at the end of my stay. But they're expensive and it always felt like such a waste, so after a few years, I set up a small online business, and called it Imitating Art. I got a business email address and bank account, and only put my initials on the paintings, so they couldn't be linked to me. Then I signed up with Artfinder and Etsy. Gradually the sales crept up, and by 2016 I was even making a small profit.

A couple of years later, I was interviewed – anonymously, I made sure of that – by an obscure online art magazine, and soon after, an art dealer got in touch via the website. Nick Daniels. He told me that he specialises in Corsican art and had come across Imitating Art via the article. He said that he loved my paintings, and that he could sell them for a lot more than I was charging.

My relationship with these pictures is complex – fear, yes, but intimacy too, and veiled pride – and I couldn't help feeling flattered by his compliments. I gave him the following summer's stock as a trial, and over the next few months, a steady stream of transfers began arriving in my business bank account. It was proper money too – enough for Lola and me to go on our first overseas holiday – and Nick Daniels has been selling my mazzeri paintings ever since.

I don't know much about him – in fact, Nick might even be short for Nicola, although I've always sensed that it's a man – but we've built up a weird kind of friendship over the years. Nick is the only person I'm in regular contact with while I'm away on these sabbaticals from normal life, so I have to really concentrate on not appearing crazy when I'm dog-tired from lack of sleep, or wired from too many pills. I know I've let my mask slip on a couple of occasions, confided secrets even my mum doesn't know, but I tell myself it doesn't matter, because he's got no idea who I am.

I open a new Imitating Art email and add his address. The first one is always the most nerve-racking – the chance he's lost interest in my paintings over the year – and I can feel my heart rate tick up as I type.

Hey, hope you're well.
It's that time again. I have another picture for you

and there'll be more over the next couple of weeks.
Are you still interested?

Even though it's six in the morning, an email comes back almost instantly.

Ah, my favourite mystery client returns!
And I hope you're joking? Your paintings are amongst my most popular sellers – people particularly love the anonymity element (thank you, Banksy!) They're going for over a grand each now, so you can expect a boost to your bank balance too. If you can confirm that you'll send them to the same storage facility, I'll arrange collection.
Good to have you back online.

Relief and shame penetrate my tired body. It's good to hear from Nick again, and to know my pictures are selling well. But the growing price makes me feel uncomfortable. Like it's blood money, even though that makes no sense. Maybe I'll donate it to charity this year. Share it between the RNLI and the Samaritans.

I send a quick acknowledgement – there'll be time for longer emails over the next few days – then close my laptop. I lay my head on the table and stare at the view. It's going to be another sunny day here. But not as hot as it will be in Ayia Napa. I guess Lola will still be in bed now, sleeping off the excesses of her first night out.

I hope it's not giving her nightmares.

Lola

25th July

Lola wipes the sweat off her forehead and drains the last of her water. The sun is pounding down, there's no shade, and she's got a killer headache. But she's got no choice except to wait. She thinks about her girls, whether they've made it to the beach yet, if they're missing her.

And can't help wondering if she should have gone to Ayia Napa with them after all.

She remembers their expressions when she first revealed her plans, three months ago when they were booking the trip. At first, they were disappointed – the four of them have been mates since primary school and were all looking forward to their first holiday together as adults, with no parents or teachers setting the rules. But when Lola explained her reasons, her need to find out what's behind her mum's insomnia, why it gets so bad in the summer that she disappears over Lola's birthday every year, that disappointment had morphed into understanding, even admiration.

Lola adjusts the straps on her backpack and checks the time on her phone – again. When she looked at the bus timetable on the airport website, straight after she booked her flight to Corsica, it said that there was a bus to Porto Vecchio every hour, and that it takes forty minutes to get to the town centre. No advance booking was required, and it accepted Apple Pay. It was supposed to be a simple journey. But she's been waiting for over two hours now and nothing has appeared. How can public transport from an international airport be so non-existent?

'You want cab, miss?'

Lola eyes the man with crooked teeth smiling at her from the dusty silver people carrier. 'No thanks. I'm getting the bus.' Porto Vecchio is over twenty kilometres away, and while she's noticed that Grams has put three hundred pounds in her account – which was a nice surprise – she's not squandering her limited supply of cash on private transport. After all, she doesn't know how the next nine days are going to play out.

'No more buses today,' the driver says. 'Where you going? I take you.'

Lola bites her cheek and considers her options. He could be lying about the buses to get her fare, but it is five o'clock now – she can't believe she's spent most of the afternoon pointlessly standing here – and if he's right, she's screwed. Even the airport shuts at night. 'How much to Porto Vecchio?'

'Twenty euros.'

Lola sighs. 'Fine.' She opens the back door, climbs inside, and immediately decides it was a good call. The air conditioning is blasting cold air, and even the sticky plastic seating is a relief after standing for hours.

The driver swings onto the road and looks at her through the rear-view mirror. 'What hotel, miss?'

'Umm,' Lola murmurs, scrolling through her phone for the booking reference. 'It's an Airbnb, not a hotel. Hang on, I've got the address.' As she says the street name in badly accented French, she watches the cab driver's expression change and her belly tightens.

When she first planned this trip, she envisaged staying at Hotel Paoli, the hotel where her mum worked when she was eighteen – literally retracing her mum's steps to try to get to the bottom of what happened to her there. But that plan imploded when she checked the prices. Even with the money she's been saving from helping out at Grams' windsurf repair workshop every Sunday, the swanky hotel with beach frontage was way out of her budget.

And, it turned out, so were all the other hotels to a lesser or greater degree. So she changed tack and booked a room in someone's home via Airbnb instead – and has been wondering ever since whether she's about to step into a serial killer's lair. So the cab driver's reaction isn't a good sign.

At least she gambled and only booked for three nights, even though her flight back to the UK isn't until next Sunday – the same day the girls fly back from Cyprus. She figured that if she liked it, she'd offer cash for the final week, and if not, she'd have three days to find something better. Okay, so there's also the thing that she's been daydreaming about – the owner of Hotel Paoli giving her a massive discount as soon as he hears who her mum is. But that wasn't the driving force behind her decision. She's not that naïve.

'I know it,' the driver says, nodding. 'But it's not a good neighbourhood. You know, my brother-in-law has small hotel. It's on the edge of town, away from the beach, but very safe area. He might have a room. I can call him?' He points at a phone nestled in a cradle by the aircon unit.

'Thanks, but I'm good.' Lola can't read the driver's face now, whether there's genuine concern on it or the recognition of opportunity, but as soon as the words are out, his warning taps at her skull again – *not a good neighbourhood*. She thinks about her mum. She knows that something happened to her in Corsica that scarred her for life, and here Lola is, risking moving in with a serial killer. Is she even crazier than her mum?

The driver nods and shrugs like it's no skin off his nose, then turns his gaze back to the road. Fifteen minutes later, they take a left turn at a roundabout signposted Porto Vecchio. The sign is vandalised with small dents and graffiti, like most of the others she's seen, but the roads are lined with luscious trees – a strange mix of oaks, firs, and palm trees – and there's a beautiful mountain range rising in the distance. Lola can't quite work out whether Corsica is a sunny beach resort or a rugged wilderness.

Eventually they reach the town with its narrow streets, and brightly coloured residential blocks. As the cab driver turns left onto the coast road, Lola stares at the marina with its line of sparkling white boats, and it reminds her of home. She thinks about Grams busy in her workshop, her mum fighting her private demons in some mystery location, because why the hell should her only daughter be trusted with the address. Neither of them knows that Lola's in Corsica, but she doesn't feel guilty. If her mum can have secrets, disappear every year, so can she.

The car follows the coast road for another five minutes, then heads inland again. There's a mix of patches of scrubland and big apartment blocks. Originally white, but greying now, and decorated with cracks that span out like tree roots. The cab driver takes a few more turns and then parks up outside one of the buildings that all look the same. He twists to face her. 'This is it. Happy holidays.'

'*Merci*,' Lola mumbles, embarrassed by how much her hands are shaking as she gives him twenty euros. Then she hoists her backpack onto her shoulder, slides out of the car, and walks towards the front door with her heart pumping.

Lola

25th July

Lola pushes the half-eaten basket of fries away and tries not to cry. When she first knocked on the door of her Airbnb, she thought things would be all right after all. Okay, the views weren't as pretty as the parts of Porto Vecchio she'd seen from the cab window, but what could she expect for forty euros a night? And the woman who answered her knock – Celine – had a kind face and bright eyes, and she bustled with the efficiency of someone who'd welcomed new guests many times before. The room was small, but the bed was comfy, and even though she had to share the bathroom with Celine's family, it was clean, and everything worked.

But then Celine's husband and grown-up son turned up – loud, leery, and smelling of fish, sweat and beer – and Lola suddenly wanted to be anywhere else.

The town is busy with holidaymakers, but under the black sky, their drunken laughter sounds threatening. About an hour ago her resolve dipped low enough for her to contact her girlfriends in Ayia Napa. She sent them a long voice note, hoping they'd lift her spirits back up. But their response did the opposite. With barely concealed terror in their voices, they told her to call her mum. That her safety was more important than any secret mission.

She's not calling her. Partly because she's too proud, but mainly because she's scared of what her mum's reaction might be.

Even though he died before she was born, Lola has always known that her grandfather, Grams' husband, was Corsican, and that her surname – Torre – is a common Corsican family name. But when she asked if they could go there on holiday when she was eleven, her mum point-blank refused. She blamed the cost, which made sense at the time – they had never holidayed outside the UK back then – but when her mum got a bonus at work a few years later, she still wouldn't agree to a trip to Corsica, and took Lola skiing instead. For years Lola couldn't understand why her mum didn't want to find out more about her heritage.

And then, in February, she found the answer by accident.

She was at work. It was still winter, and there weren't many windsurf sails to fix, so Grams asked her to clear up the workshop. There was an old wardrobe in the back corner, and she decided to start there. As well as a bunch of ancient windsurf equipment, there was a cardboard box full of memorabilia. She found a few photos of herself from when she was little and got sucked in. Then a while later, she came across a thin pile of postcards held together by a dry and faded rubber band that snapped when she wriggled it off.

There were five postcards from a place called Porto Vecchio in Corsica. And each of them was from her mum to Grams. They were dated from June to August 2004 and kept in order. The first was of a hotel with a beautiful beach, the name Hotel Paoli written in cursive script at the bottom, and on the other side her mum had written:

This is where I work. Amazing, isn't it?! And I've made a new friend – Izzy – who's awesome. I miss you, but I'm really loving it out here. I hope you're coping okay without me.

The next three postcards weren't quite as effusive, but her mum still seemed to be enjoying herself. Then Lola read the final postcard, dated 1st August 2004, her birthday. And the words made her skin crawl.

The last three days have been the worst of my life
I am a monster
I need to come home
I will never forgive myself for this

Lola put the postcards back in the cardboard box and shoved it to the corner of the wardrobe. But she couldn't wipe those words from her mind. She knew her mum wasn't a monster, but clearly something had happened that summer, and her mum had never forgiven herself for it. The insomnia, her mum's mental health challenges, her annual disappearances – it seemed to have all started in Corsica in 2004.

Lola knew that if she confronted her mum, she would be met with either silence or lies. And that the only way to get the truth was to unearth it herself. And then maybe, just maybe, she could use that knowledge to fix her mum. When Tamsyn suggested a girls' holiday to Ayia Napa after their A levels, it gave Lola the perfect cover story.

Except it doesn't feel so perfect anymore.

Lola slips off the high stool and leaves the café. She hovers on the pavement for a moment, but she can't put it off forever, so she reluctantly turns north and starts walking back towards her Airbnb. Hopefully she can slip into her room without being noticed, although whether she'll sleep or not with no lock on her door is a different matter. Perhaps getting a taste of her mum's insomnia on this trip would be poetic.

It's quieter off the main drag, which makes Lola nervous. But night-time can do that – even when she's at home in Lymington – so she tries to bat the feeling away. As she follows the route back, the roads get narrower until she's walking down one not much wider than an alleyway, with only a street lamp at either end. She quickens her pace. But then jolts to a stop when she sees the shadow of a man in the distance.

He's leaning against the grey concrete wall of a house. Smoking a cigarette. Lola senses him staring at her, but is he really? She's automatically labelling him as a threat, but he might just be chilling out in front of his own house. She's the foreigner here, not him.

She says a silent prayer and starts walking again. She can't pretend she's not scared – her blood is pumping in her ears – but she'll pass him in ten or so steps.

He's wearing a hoodie, she notices as she gets closer, and the hood is pulled low over his brow. The rest of his face is obscured by a mask.

And then he steps out in front of her.

She half gasps, half screams, but there's no one around to hear. She takes a step backwards, but he moves forward, his face inches from hers, his hot breath seeping through the mask.

'Gimme your phone,' he says, holding his hand out, his voice gruff and muffled.

His skin is tanned, rough. His arm is thin and sinewy. Lola stares at it. 'What?'

'Give me your fucking phone,' he repeats, more slowly. 'And money. You got money?' He has an accent, but Lola can't place it. 'Now,' he demands. 'I have a knife; I'll cut you.'

Lola's eyes dart left and right, but no one is coming to help her. What is she going to do without a phone?

But she can't fight him.

With trembling fingers, she drops her phone, her lifeline, into his hands. But he doesn't leave.

'And money? I'll search you,' he threatens.

26

Lola's face crumples. 'I don't have any,' she whispers. And it's true. She pays for everything on Apple Pay.

'Bullshit!' he hisses. 'What's in there?' He points at her middle.

Lola follows the direction of his finger. She's been wearing the belt bag for so long that she'd forgotten she had it on. Her tummy clenches as she remembers her mum giving her fifty euros. *I want to see that back, but have it in case of emergencies.* She has just lied to a thief, a mugger. What will he do to her now?

'I forgot,' she blurts out. 'I'm sorry!'

'Give me the bag,' he orders.

'No, I can't …'

He shoves her in the shoulder. She stumbles backwards.

'Give me the fucking bag!'

She has no choice. She fumbles with the clip, tears smarting her eyes. She hears the click of the belt opening, but so does he, because he reaches out and snatches it, scratching her arm with his jagged fingernail. He holds her gaze for a split second, and then he's gone.

She stares after him, feels the trickle of blood run down her arm. Then a delayed panic kicks in, and she turns and runs. Not towards the room she has rented, where her backpack is, but to the beach. It's always been her favourite place. And she needs it now. Somewhere to steady her.

Because that man hasn't only taken her money and phone.

The key to her accommodation is in that belt bag.

And so is her passport.

Lola

26th July

Lola's eyelids twitch as light seeps through. She opens one eye, then the other. The sun is rising over a hill in the distance and its rays are splayed out like the spokes of a wheel. She shivers, partly with the cold, but partly with anticipation of the heat she knows the sun will bring. Heat her body is craving after a night spent curled up in the sand.

She pushes to sitting, her muscles stiff and aching, and turns her head towards the sea. Ripples flow slowly towards the shore, barely even frothing before they disappear back into the sparkling blue water. Daylight, sunshine, it makes everything seem better. But it isn't really. She still doesn't have a phone, or a passport, or any money. The cut on her arm is stinging, her backpack is lying on a stranger's bed at the wrong end of town, and her mum thinks she's in Ayia Napa with her friends.

When Lola arrived at the beach last night, she didn't plan to stay. She just couldn't go back to that apartment straight away and explain her missing key, not to those men with beer on their breath, not after being mugged only one street over. It's stupid to think that an expanse of sand with no lights or walls could feel safer than a bedroom she has paid for, but in that moment, it was the only place she wanted to be. Although the beach has always been Lola's happy place. Which is probably why, when the adrenaline finally settled and her body sagged, she could curl into a ball, burrow into the sand, and fall asleep.

There's movement to Lola's right and she turns to watch a woman in a navy-blue swimsuit make a beeline for the water's edge. She's wearing a swim cap and goggles. Lola doesn't know what time it is – for years she has relied on her phone for that kind of information – but it feels early. When the swimmer reaches a yellow buoy thirty metres out, she turns ninety degrees and starts swimming parallel to the shoreline, back and forth, length after length. Lola finds the sight of the woman calming, and by the time she returns to shore, Lola has made a decision.

She waits for the woman to dry herself down, then walks over to her.

'Excuse me, do you speak English?'

The swimmer looks Lola up and down. Lola waits to be judged for her dishevelled appearance, but the woman's face softens. 'Sure,' she says in an Irish accent. 'Can I help you out with anything?'

'Do you have a phone I could borrow?'

The woman hesitates, just as Lola would have done if the conversation was reversed. A stranger asking for one of her most private things. 'You don't have your own then?' she finally asks.

'I did, but I was mugged last night,' Lola explains, trying to keep the emotion out of her voice.

The woman's expression transforms. 'Oh my God, that's awful. I'm Amy. And of course you can borrow my phone. Come on, my gear's over there.' She points to a large palm tree near the beach entrance with a bag resting against its trunk. As they walk towards it, Amy starts looking around. 'Who are you here with? Do they know what's happened to you?'

'No, I'm … Can I call my mum?' Lola asks, shifting the

29

conversation. 'She's in England but I can get her to call me straight back.'

'Listen, you can call Timbuktu if it means getting the help you need. I would offer to come to the police station with you, but we're leaving today, just getting one last swim in before it's back to Dublin with its freezing water and constant drizzle.'

'Oh sorry, I'll be quick,' Lola says, reaching for Amy's proffered phone. When her mum demanded that Lola memorise her phone number a few years ago, Lola thought she was catastrophising. But now she's grateful. She listens to it ring, then her heart sinks when it clicks into voicemail. She waits for the beep and starts talking. 'Mum, it's me. Listen. Something's happened. I'm okay, well, kind of. But I don't have my phone. A lady lent me hers, to call you, but she can't stay long. I guess it's early in the UK, you're probably still asleep. But if you get this soon, can you call me?'

Amy gives her a sympathetic look. 'Do you want to try someone else?'

Lola shakes her head. None of her friends, not even her Grams, catastrophise like her mum does, so she doesn't know anyone else's number.

'How about we go to the beach café for a coffee and try again in a bit?' Amy says. 'I'm good for another half an hour or so, and you look like you need warming up even more than I do.'

Lola smiles her gratitude, but inside she's flailing. What happens if her mum doesn't pick up in half an hour either? When Lola left home on Friday, her mum told her not to call her. But yesterday, she changed her mind. She always goes weird around this time – she calls it her insomnia winning the battle over her sanity. It's why she takes herself off every year, to save Lola from seeing it. What if she has flipped out too badly to notice Lola's voicemail?

An hour later, Lola promises Amy that she has a plan B for about the twelfth time, and demands that Amy go back to her husband who, by the sound of his messages, is getting increasingly worried that they're going to miss their flight home. Amy sighs, still conflicted, but then gives Lola a tight hug, pushes forward a napkin scrawled with her number, and runs in the direction of the road.

Once she's out of sight, Lola lets her smile sag. She has called her mum six times on Amy's phone and has left two voicemails. It's not even eight o'clock in the UK, so her mum has every right to still be asleep. But she supposedly can't sleep – that's why she goes AWOL every summer – and aren't mums meant to have a sixth sense when their kid is in trouble?

Not that it matters anymore. Now that Amy has left with the phone, her mum can't call her back anyway.

Lola pushes out of the café chair and straightens up. She needs to go back to the apartment. Explain about the stolen key. Hopefully Celine will let Lola use her phone and her mum will pick up this time.

Forty minutes later, Lola knocks on the apartment door. She took a longer way back so that she could avoid the narrowest streets, but there was no shade on the main roads, and she's beginning to wish she'd chosen a more hydrating drink than coffee. And said yes when Amy offered to buy her some breakfast. After only managing half a basket of fries for supper, she's starving, and she still has no money. When there's no answer, she knocks again. And again. It takes a full five minutes before Lola finally accepts that no one is home.

She closes her eyes and leans her clammy forehead against the cool wall. She doesn't want to cry. She thought she was doing the right thing, coming to Corsica, finding out what happened to her mum so that she can understand her better, help her overcome her demons. But everything has gone wrong so far. And she doesn't know anyone here.

Except.

Lola pushes away from the wall, stares at the scuffed paintwork.

There is one thing she knows. Not a person, but a place. Hotel Paoli. Twenty-one years is a long time, but not a lifetime. And the purpose of this trip has always been reliant on someone remembering Frankie Torre. Lola thinks about her daydream – the welcome with open arms, the heavily discounted hotel room – and heads back outside.

Frankie

26th July

There's shouting. Silhouettes of men. I stare into the distance, but I can't make out where the sea ends, and the night sky begins. The only clue comes from the weak moonlight, drifting between clouds, streaking the water. I shift my gaze closer. Who is on the beach with me? They're both silent, sleeping. But I can't see their faces. Now I can hear a distant droning sound. Is that a boat?

I jerk awake. Blink. My neck is twisted and stiff, my cheek stuck to the tabletop. Sunlight floods through the window, and my laptop screen is black in front of me – asleep or out of power. I'm in The Wolf Den, I remember. And the droning noise is my phone buzzing. I grab it, arch my back to sit up.

'Hello?' I say, my voice thick with sleep.

'Mum? Thank God! Why did you take so long to answer?'

Lola is in trouble. That is as clear as an air-raid siren blaring in my ears. I suck in a breath and hold it as I swipe the mouse on my laptop to bring it to life. It's connected to my phone – something Lola set up for me – and it lists six missed calls and two voicemails from a mobile number I don't recognise. The missed calls were all made between six thirty and seven thirty, and I curse my body, my mind, for keeping me awake all night and then sending me into the deepest sleep at dawn.

'I'm … I'm sorry, I'm here now,' I stutter. 'But what's happened? Why aren't you calling from your own phone?'

'I was mugged last night,' Lola says, her voice jittery. 'He didn't hurt me, but he took my phone, and my belt bag, which had my money and passport inside, and my room key. I slept on the beach, and—'

'You slept on the beach?' I interrupt, my pitch rising. 'Why didn't you go back to your apartment? Where are your friends?'

There's a long silence on the other end of the phone. I become aware of my own breathing. Like a rush of wind. 'Lola?'

'I'm not in Ayia Napa with the others,' she finally whispers.

Something heavy drops into my belly and my spine curves. 'What? Where are you?'

'I'm in Corsica.'

I gasp. I can't help it. I think I might have a panic attack, but I mustn't. I need to stay in control. I push myself out of the chair and stride outside. The deck is already bathed in sunshine, and I try to use the brightness to steady me.

'Mum? Are you okay?'

'What are you doing there?' I ask, managing to keep my voice steady, which is a miracle.

'Um, I'm sorry, I wanted to find out more about where Grandpa came from. But you knew that, didn't you? I've been asking to come here for years.'

I close my eyes. 'I told you before,' I say, slowly, with as much authority as I can muster. 'I have no interest in going to Corsica, and neither should you.'

'But that's not true.'

Her words are spoken quietly, but they hit like a slap.

'What do you mean?' I ask carefully.

34

'I know that you spent time in Corsica,' she says. 'In the summer of 2004. That you worked at Hotel Paoli.'

'No,' I whisper. Not a denial, just horror that she has found out. 'How do you know?'

'I found some postcards in Grams' workshop.'

For a second, I'm back there – sitting on my bed, scrawling a postcard to my mum, Izzy doing a handstand against the wall as she waits for me to finish. I shake the image away. 'You need to come home,' I say, silently pleading that Mum destroyed that final postcard, that Lola doesn't know how my time in Corsica ended. 'You can't stay there.'

'I know something really bad happened to you here.'

My face crumples and I sink down until my legs reach the warm decking. 'Please, Lola. You don't know anything, not really. If you come home, I can explain.'

Lola sniffs, and I suddenly realise that she's crying too. 'I want to, Mum,' she whispers. 'After everything that's happened. But how can I? I don't have my phone, my passport, any money. My backpack is at the Airbnb, but no one is answering the door. And I'm scared to keep going back to that neighbourhood on my own after what happened last night. I don't know what to do.'

Neither do I. The urge to get Lola out of Corsica is so powerful that I can't think straight. What are you supposed to do if you lose your passport? Is there a British consulate in Corsica? How can I get money to Lola if she can't access her accounts?

Then I open my eyes as another thought jolts in. 'If you're not at your accommodation, where are you? And whose phone are you using?' I check the small screen. 'The number looks like a landline?'

Maybe it's the silence. Or maybe it's true that mothers and daughters can communicate without speech. But either way, I know where Lola is calling from before she says the words. Although when they crash out of her mouth, I'm still not ready for them.

'I'm at Hotel Paoli, Mum.'

'And who … who let you use the phone?'

'The lady behind reception. She's English. Anna. She said she remembered you.'

I scrape my lip with my teeth until I taste blood. Anna. Of course she remembers me. People hold on much tighter to the bad memories. And nothing could be worse than what happened that summer. But I can't let Lola hear about it from Anna, or her husband Raphael. It doesn't surprise me that they still run the hotel – it's a family business, and family loyalty is everything in Corsica – but I never thought I'd have to worry about keeping Lola away from them.

'Did she say anything else?'

'Like what?'

I lick blood off my lip. 'Have you spoken to the police? Reported the mugging?'

'No. I … I don't know how. I don't know where the police station is.' Lola suddenly sounds so young, a child trying to navigate an adult world.

Just how I felt all those years ago.

I close my eyes and remember. Sitting in a hard plastic chair, opposite that police officer with his bushy moustache and withering expression. Being forced to relive the worst moment of my life, only forty-eight hours after the tragic incident that I thought would hold that title forever. Will Lola have to go to the same place? Sit in the same chair?

'Maybe Anna could take me. She wants to help.'

'I'm coming out to Corsica.' The words are out before my brain catches up. But it's the right decision. It doesn't matter that I'm petrified about going back – protecting Lola comes first. But from what? I shake the stupid mystical fears from my head.

'Really?'

'It's not fair for you to deal with this on your own. I'll get a flight out as soon as I can. And if Anna wants to help, see if you can stay at the hotel until I arrive … but please, don't talk to anyone.'

'What happened here, Mum? What are you so scared of?'

My head is throbbing, and my eyes sting with tears. 'I'll explain everything when I get there,' I lie.

2004

Frankie

16th March

I pluck at my newly cropped hair – an impulsive decision, but I don't regret it – and stare out to sea. I'm surrounded by the soft hum of respectful conversation, the clink of spoons against teacups, but I shut it out. I've got nothing against these people, these mourners, but I'm not in the mood for making small talk today. Mum thought I should invite some of my own friends, that I might need their support, but I prefer to do this by myself.

I pick a sausage roll off the buffet table and walk out onto the terrace, my gaze low to avoid accidental eye contact. I lean on the balustrade and let the coastal breeze whip against my cheeks as I chew. The sky is bleached blue, and the sea a greenish shade of grey. The beach is quiet, the weather not yet warm enough for crowds, and the gulls swoop and cry uninhibited. It's chilly, so I pull the unfamiliar black jacket tighter around my chest. I got it from a charity shop, and it feels like a straitjacket compared to the slouchy jeans and sweatshirts I usually wear.

But this view relaxes me. I have always lived in Southbourne, and the beach, with the sea beyond it, is my home. Mum works there every day, repairing windsurf sails and boards in a workshop facing the beach. And before he got sick, my dad had a second-hand powerboat that he tinkered with whenever he could get away from his job as an electrician. And it's where I come after school, at the weekend, during school holidays. A trip to the beach – to work, play, eat, study, be.

'Hey, love.'

I turn at the sound of Mum's voice, but then pause. There's a man with her who I don't recognise. His hair is silvery and cropped short, and his blue eyes look out of place against the deep tan on his face. I find the polite voice that I always use with strangers. 'Hello.'

'Frankie, I want you to meet Salvo. He's come all the way from Corsica to pay his respects to your dad. Isn't that kind of him?'

'Hello, Francesca, it's wonderful to meet you, and Debra.' Salvo shifts his gaze back to my mum for a moment, then refocuses on me. 'I'm sorry that Pascal has been taken from you both, and much too soon.'

I nod, and smile, because Mum's right, it is kind of him. But I wonder why he has come. My dad always claimed to be proud of his Corsican roots, but he never spoke about friends from his home country, or had any visitors from there. He didn't talk about his childhood much at all, but then he wasn't a big talker in general, and I never thought to ask.

'How did you know my dad?'

'We grew up together, in Sartène,' Salvo says, in his accented English. 'I moved away as a teenager, but we still saw each other often enough. Your father always wanted to get away, to explore the world. I thought he was crazy at the time – we lived on such a beautiful island, so why leave it? But now I'm glad that he followed his dreams.' His smile fades. 'I only wish I'd got to meet up with Pascal before he died. We lost touch for many years, but he wrote to me after finding out he was ill. We exchanged lots of letters after that, and I always hoped to visit.'

42

'I'm sorry you didn't get the chance,' Mum says softly. 'But it was quick when it came. He was ill for two years, but the end still took us by surprise, didn't it, Frankie?'

Again, my mum's showing how incredible she is. She's the one who's lost her husband, but her instinct is to console this man who hasn't seen him in decades. Incredible but also, somehow, irritating. It makes me want to say no, I wasn't surprised. That actually I expected Dad to die every day after he broke the news about the cancer spreading to his liver. And maybe even before then. When I found out it wasn't normal for your dad to be eighteen years older than your mum, and what that could mean. But I would never admit the other part – that I was sometimes disappointed when he was still alive at bedtime because I'd have to wake up the next morning feeling the exact same way.

But maybe this is just grief making me unkind. Or guilt that I don't feel sad enough. I loved my dad of course, but he was always so aloof. The only times I came close to feeling a proper bond with him were on the nights when he put me to bed. He'd tell me stories about Corsican folklore and mythical creatures, and I would listen, rapt, pretending not to be scared. And never letting on how difficult it was to get to sleep afterwards.

'That is kind of you to say, but please, don't give my regret a moment's thought.' Salvo takes my mum's hand and cups it in both of his. 'You have your own grief to deal with, and that's more than enough.'

I stare at Salvo. It's as though he's read my thoughts. Either that, or he's just a decent human being.

'Debra?' A voice floats over from inside the café-cum-restaurant-cum-wake venue. It's my mum's sister, Aunty Emma. 'Oliver and Jess are heading off now. I thought you might want to say goodbye?'

'Excuse me,' Mum says, squeezing my arm as she backs away. 'Duty calls.'

I turn back to look at the sea, suddenly awkward. I sense Salvo lean on the balustrade beside me and match my movements.

'Pascal said that you're a natural on the water. Windsurfer, water-skier, sailor.'

My breath catches at the thought of my father boasting about me. 'Well, I have my parents to thank for that. But yeah, I love the sea.'

'Me too,' Salvo says. 'But I'm more of a fisherman these days.'

'I didn't think Sartène was on the coast?' I suddenly worry that I'm making a fool of myself, that my geography is off, but Salvo nods.

'Yes, that's right. But I live in Porto Vecchio now, which is on the south-east coast of the island. My mother and aunt opened a café together decades ago. It's been through a few changes since then and it's been a hotel for the last few years. I run it with my son.'

'That sounds cool.'

He chuckles, and it's a nice sound. 'Cool, yes. I suppose it is,' he says. 'You should come out. We have a full water sports programme.'

'Maybe.' It takes a lot of effort to sound non-committal. A hotel with water sports on the Mediterranean Sea is my idea of heaven, but it is also expensive. And money is not something we've ever had too much of in our family. Fixing windsurf sails and rewiring homes are not exactly money-spinners.

'What about this summer?'

'Oh thanks, but I'm planning on working,' I explain. 'My exams finish in May, and then I'm going to find a job. Mum wants me to go to university in September, but I'm not sure. I think I'd prefer to go travelling for a while. Maybe I'll come to Corsica then.'

'It sounds like you've inherited your father's wanderlust.'

I consider that. I'm so used to being compared to my mum, even though I have my dad's dark colouring, that Salvo's words sound strange. But it makes sense that I'd inherit some of my dad's traits too. Salvo describes him as an explorer, a dreamer, which is so different from the quiet, serious man I remember. Maybe

44

I didn't really know him at all. I push away from the balustrade and turn towards Salvo. 'It looks that way, I guess.'

'Well, maybe you could start in Corsica instead. Do you have any water sports qualifications?'

'I teach water-skiing in the summer holidays. I have my level-two instructor award.' I first water-skied behind my dad's boat when I was four, and I fell in love with the sport instantly. From that point on, if the water was flat and we had enough spare cash for fuel, we went out.

'And a powerboat licence?'

'Of course.'

'Well, would you like to come and work for me? At Hotel Paoli? Our season starts in May, but the water sports don't get busy until June. You could come out after your exams, earn some money and get a taste of travelling at the same time.'

'That's very generous of you.' I shift my eyeline back out to sea. Why am I hesitating? This man is offering me a dream job, a chance to be on the water every day without having to pull on a wetsuit or shiver in summer rain. Is this about not wanting to abandon Mum? Or am I scared of leaving the only place I've ever known?

'Talk to your mum,' Salvo says. 'It would be an honour to help Pascal's daughter out, and to get to know you a little more, but I don't want to drag you away from Debra if she's not comfortable with it.' He slips his hand inside his suit jacket and pulls out a tan leather wallet. I worry for a second that he's going to give me money – sympathy cash – but he hands me a business card. 'But I think you'll love it, and if I've learned one thing in my sixty years, Francesca, it's that we should seize opportunities when they present themselves. Because we don't know what's around the corner.'

Frankie

25th May

The woman behind the desk tips her head to one side and smiles. 'I'm guessing you're the new water-ski instructor.'

'Yes, that's right. Frankie Torre.'

'That's a very Corsica name,' she observes. She looks like a model – tall and willowy with long limbs and sweeping blonde hair – but there's something uncertain about her expression, like she's not sure she fits in.

'My dad's Corsican. Was Corsican,' I correct.

She gives her head a tiny shake. 'Sorry, yes, I knew that. Salvo told me that they were childhood friends. And now you've come to discover your roots.' She smiles, but it doesn't reach her eyes. Then she takes a deep breath. 'Anyway, I'm Anna, Salvo's daughter-in-law. I would take you down to the waterfront myself, but I'm sure Raphael will want to do the honours, if you don't mind waiting a minute.'

I nod and drop my backpack. It's filled to capacity (and beyond) and it lands on the terracotta tiles with a thud. 'So you're English?' I don't know why I say it as a question when the answer is so obvious.

'Yes.' Anna looks sad for a moment, but then smiles again, like smiling is her default expression. Maybe that's what working on a hotel reception does to you. 'I did the opposite of your dad, moved to Corsica seven years ago and never left. The plan was to find myself, but I found Raphael and well, you can't fight love, can you?'

'I guess not,' I say. Although I've never had a serious boyfriend so I'm not really the best person to ask. But at least it explains who Raphael is. 'And you run the hotel together? With Salvo?'

'Kind of, yes. This place has been in Raphael's family for a couple of generations, but it has grown over the years. Salvo has taken more of a back seat since we turned it into a hotel and Raphael runs the show these days. Well, we run it together. We're a team.'

Anna's smile definitely looks false now and the sight makes me feel tense. The reality of being away from home for four months, in a strange country, sharing a room with someone I don't know, is proving harder to get excited about than I expected, even with Mum's blessing.

Footsteps sound in the corridor and a man appears at the double doors to the reception. 'Are you Frankie? I'm Raphael, great to meet you.'

Raphael has what I think of as classic Corsican looks. Dark hair swept back, brown eyes, tanned skin, a strong, square jaw. Good-looking, which explains the model-like wife. 'You too,' I say.

'And you've met Anna? That's good. If you have any practical needs like fresh bedsheets, and so on, you can ask her.'

I turn towards Anna in time to see her smile fade a fraction.

'I guess you'd like to meet the waterfront team next?' Raphael continues. 'If you're not too tired from your flight? My condolences, by the way. I never met your father, but Salvo spoke very highly of him.'

To my horror, my eyes prickle. Man, I need to toughen up. I

blink, try one of Anna's smiles. 'Thank you, and yes, I'd love to meet them.'

Raphael nods, then turns, and I grab my backpack and follow. We pass a restaurant area, then step outside onto a terrace. We walk past the swimming pool, and a long bar, onto a rolling lawn sprinkled with sun loungers. When we reach the beach, I feel an urge to take my trainers off – feel soft sand between my toes – but Raphael doesn't slow down.

The water sports area is at the far end of the beach. There are two catamarans and six Lasers, plus a rack of windsurf boards with brightly coloured sails hung up close by, all good brands and new-looking. My nervousness fades at the familiar sight. In the summer months, I spend every spare hour doing some kind of water sport back home, but summers are short in the UK, and I don't have that many spare hours. The thought of doing this all day, every day, for four months, is awesome.

A girl with loose honey-blonde curls tied up high on her head is leaning over one of the catamarans, tightening the ropes.

'Izzy, do you have a moment?' Raphael asks.

The girl straightens and turns. Her face softens. 'Sure.'

'This is Frankie. The new water-ski instructor we've hired to help Dom. Can you show her around?'

'Of course. *Salut*, Frankie.'

'Um, *salut*,' I say, wishing Dad had taught me at least some basic French. Being half Corsican and only getting a D in French GCSE is embarrassing.

Izzy smiles. 'Don't worry. I spent three years in London, so my English is pretty much perfect.'

I smile back in relief. 'Are you from Corsica originally?'

'Oh, no, I'm French,' Izzy explains. 'From Nice on the south coast – that's where I learned to sail. But I came to Corsica on holiday when I was little a couple of times, and I do love it here.' Izzy turns back to Raphael. 'Leave Frankie with me. I'll introduce her to the others.'

He thanks her, then lifts his hand in a short wave and walks back up the beach. I watch a young boy – maybe four or five – run over to him and reach for his hand.

'That's Patrick,' Izzy says, noticing me looking. 'Raphael and Anna's son. Sweet kid. Shame about his mum, pointless Anna, the classic brainless beauty.' Izzy pulls a face and giggles. 'And there's Raphael's dad – Salvo,' Izzy goes on. 'He lives here too, with his wife, Rosa. She's nice enough, but he's one of those gnarly old Corsican men who hates everyone – tourists, the French, the Italians, ignorant young people – so worth steering clear of. Anyway, come on.' Izzy reaches for my arm. 'Guests have lunch between one and three, so the team are chilling out in the hut at the moment.'

As we walk past a row of buoyancy aids hanging up to dry, I wonder why I didn't come to Salvo's defence, or at least tell Izzy about him knowing my dad, and him giving me this job. I feel disloyal, but there's something about Izzy, an intoxicating warmth, that makes me reluctant to disagree with her. And it's not like I know him, after all.

We reach a beach hut and Izzy gestures for me to walk inside. There's a makeshift reception desk on one side, and a wide doorway, but there are no windows, and the sudden darkness blinds me. By the time my eyes have adjusted to the gloom, four bodies have unfurled from a pile of cushions on the floor.

'Guys, this is Frankie. Dom, she's here to show you up behind a boat.'

'Ha, no chance,' a guy says, taking a step forward and reaching out his hand. He's tall and broad with wavy light brown hair and dimples in his cheeks. 'Although thank fuck I've got someone to help me hoist the kids out of the water when they stack it on those little skis,' he goes on. 'I'm sure I've lost a few of them this week.'

'Sadly, I doubt he's joking,' says a girl with strong shoulders and iron-straight ash-blonde hair, pushing herself forward. 'I'm Harriet, senior sailing instructor.'

I recognise Harriet's type straight away and feel the gnawing anxiety return. Private school, sailing in the Caribbean every Christmas, and Salcombe or Sandbanks over the summer. Rarely seen out of Helly Hansen clothes. Harriet gives my hand a firm shake, and I try to match her strength. I can hold my own on the water; I just need to learn to do it on dry land too.

'Hey, I'm Archie,' another guy says in a Scottish accent. 'I teach windsurfing with Jack.' Archie is tall and lean, with freckly skin and longish red hair that he curls around his ears.

'And I'm Jack.'

I turn towards the last voice and try not to let my eyes widen with awe. Jack is a tanned version of Brad Pitt with a peroxide-blonde buzz cut and sea blue eyes. He's not wearing a T-shirt, and his chest is broad and impossibly smooth. 'Hello, I'm Frankie,' I say, then wince – Izzy has already introduced me – and Jack's smirk doesn't make me feel any better.

'Don't mind Jack,' Archie continues. 'He's a man of few words.'

'Unless you slate his precious Spurs,' Dom adds with feeling.

'Luckily Frankie's got me to look out for her,' Izzy says, hanging her arm over my shoulder. 'Now come on, let me show you our room. I hope you don't mind sharing with me. Harriet took the single room, didn't you, *mon amie*?'

'Well, I am the senior sailing instructor,' Harriet says.

'I'm happy to share,' I say, my instinct to appease kicking in.

Izzy smiles, then winks at me, as though she was just winding Harriet up. 'Great, let's go.'

With Izzy's arm still slung over my shoulder, I feel myself lean into her and a warm sense of anticipation rolls through me. Beach, sunshine, water sports, and new friends. Dom, my water-ski partner, Izzy my new roommate, and Jack, the best-looking guy I've ever met.

I don't know what I was worrying about. This summer is going to be epic.

Frankie

13th June

'Remember what I said!' I shout above the idling engine. 'Knees tucked into your chest, arms straight, and let the boat pull you up. You have totally got this; I believe in you!'

During my first week at Hotel Paoli, I thought my job was to turn every guest into a proficient water-skier. I threw technical terms at them, pointed out their faults, forgot to smile. Then Dom reminded me that everyone was on holiday, and that my only objective is to make sure the guests have fun, so now I'm dishing out these inspirational quotes like sweets at a kids' party.

Liam is our last guest of the day, a thickset police officer from Manchester on holiday with his fiancée who is watching from the beach, armed with a camera. Satisfied that his body is vaguely in the right position, I twist back in the driver's seat and slowly push on the throttle. There's always two of us in the boat – one driving, one spotting – so I can rely on Dom to tell me if Liam face-plants at any point. But the roar of triumph floating over my shoulder is enough of a clue that he's finally made it out of the water – that and the drag caused by his fourteen-stone weight.

I nose the boat out to sea, making sure to stay away from the swimming area, and clear of the last two Pico sailing boats slowly tacking their way to shore in the dying wind.

When I get close to the edge of the bay area, where the sea is rougher, I curve back in a wide turn. This is always the trickiest part for a beginner skier – being thrust unaware into a slingshot manoeuvre – but Liam clings on, brute strength coming to his aid, and makes it onto the straight again. When I guide him towards the beach ten minutes later – Dom hollering at him to drop the rope – Liam looks exhausted but elated. Another happy guest with a story to tell at dinner. I acknowledge his fist pump with a wave, and then watch with mild relief as he drops his buoyancy aid into the container of fresh water and trudges up the beach towards his whooping fiancée. I've been on the go since seven o'clock this morning and I'm looking forward to an evening chilling out.

I hope Izzy is thinking the same. I've only known her for three weeks, and she's eight years older than me, but I already feel like we've been friends forever. Maybe it's the intensity of living and working together, or maybe I've been lucky enough to find a kindred spirit a thousand miles from home, but I already can't imagine our friendship stopping when the summer ends.

I haven't got as close to the rest of the waterfront team yet. Izzy warned me that they can be cliquey, and they do seem to give her the cold shoulder a lot of the time. It makes me feel uncomfortable – and confused – because she's so lovely. But they're nice enough to me. Dom is the entertainer in the group, which veers between amusing and annoying depending on my mood. Harriet hasn't dropped her superiority act but loosens up after a couple of Long Island ice teas, our favourite cocktail. I have a lot of time for Archie – he's warm and funny, but with a vulnerable edge too – and it's still too early to know about Jack, although that might be because I turn into a nervous wreck whenever he's around.

'Jeez, my back is shot,' Dom says, pulling in the rope, then leaning back with an exaggerated grimace. 'How about we swap: you carry the skis and stuff back to the hut, and I'll moor up the boat?'

'Not on your life,' I say, shaking my head. In truth, I don't care which job I do, but Izzy has warned me not to be too accommodating, otherwise I'll find myself being treated like the resident mug.

'Oh, such cold-hearted beauty, I can hardly bear it.' Dom holds his hands to his chest in mock pain.

'Shut up, Dom.' But I smile anyway.

'It's true; I reckon you could turn men to stone as a hobby.'

'Well, maybe you should stop staring then, or you might end up like one of those menhir statues.'

'God, don't remind me about Izzy's bloody history lesson again. Who cares that Corsican cavemen were making stone Mr Blobbys six thousand years ago?'

'It's art, Dom,' I say in my best superior voice, although Mr Blobby probably is a better description of Corsica's famous prehistoric statues, which Izzy took us to see on our last day off. 'Didn't you say you did art history at uni?'

'Hey, look at this!' Dom points over the side of the boat. I can't tell if he's changing the subject or has actually seen something in the water. But his eyes are wide enough to rouse my curiosity.

'What?' I say, edging towards him.

'Quick! It's massive! It must be a tuna or a grouper or something!'

I lean over the side of the boat, search for the chunky silver fish. But I can't see it. I stretch further.

A second later, a hot palm lands on my mid-back and I jolt forward. My limbs flail, trying to reverse the inevitable. Then I fall from the boat, splash into the salty water. I sink for a moment, my shorts and T-shirt dragging me down, then bob back up.

'You complete dick!' I screech, pushing my spikes of hair back, seawater spraying into the air. 'What did you do that for?!'

Dom is doubled over, howls of laughter spilling out of him. 'Oh man, I'm sorry,' he manages as he tries to catch his breath. 'Wow, you really fell for that fish story, didn't you? Hook, line and sinker!' Another burst of laughter explodes from his mouth.

I jerk my legs underwater, keeping myself afloat, but also kicking out in frustration. I have no idea if Dom uses this annoying practical-joker act with everyone, or if he's got something specifically against me. 'Well, I need to get changed,' I shout up. 'Which puts you on boat *and* kit duty, so it looks like your little joke backfired.'

I throw Dom a dirty look and feel a wave of satisfaction as his face slips towards remorse. Then I flip onto my belly and start swimming on a diagonal towards the shore, the sound of his laughter-laced apologies fading into the distance. When I get to the beach, I peel off my shorts and T-shirt, revealing my third item of uniform, a royal blue swimming costume with the hotel insignia – a spiky white flower – printed on the chest. It's past seven o'clock, so the beach is quiet, but as I wring out the sopping clothes, I sense someone behind me. I whip around, half expecting it to be Dom with another apology, but it's Salvo.

'Oh hi.' When Salvo offered me this job, I assumed that he'd be involved in managing me to some extent, but I've barely seen him since I arrived, and he now feels like a stranger. He goes out in his fishing boat most evenings, so I often get a fleeting view of him walking through the sea at dusk, but we haven't had a proper conversation. And the longer it goes on, the more awkward it feels. 'Sorry for looking like a drowned rat,' I continue, remembering a bit late that he is still – officially – my boss. 'Dom thought it would be hilarious to throw me off the boat.'

Salvo clicks his tongue. 'Young men. Always stupid. Especially young British men,' he adds with feeling.

I think about Izzy's description of Salvo as a gnarly old Corsican who hates everyone. 'Are you going to tell me I should find myself a good Corsican boy instead?' I ask, my tone light. I expect Salvo to smile, but his face grows serious.

'No, I wouldn't advise that either.'

'Oh, be careful,' I warn, making sure to keep the tease in my voice. 'Remember that's exactly what my mum did.'

'Pascal was different. He was a good man.'

'Different from who?'

Salvo looks out to sea, his expression hard to read. 'Corsica is a small, unforgiving island,' he starts. 'Always has been. For many generations, no one wanted to come here. Then people did, but only to invade us, to claim the island for themselves, just like the French are doing now. Corsicans learned to survive together, and then to fight together.'

There's an evening breeze, and my body shivers as it passes over my damp skin. 'Those sound like strong characteristics to me,' I murmur, wondering where this melancholy is heading.

'Oh yes, we're a strong nation,' Salvo says, nodding. 'But Corsicans can also be ruthless. In how we think as well as how we act. Sometimes we do things we know are wrong but that feel beyond our control in the moment. As though vengeance, violence are part of our destiny, as Corsicans.' He turns to look at me, and finally smiles, as though he's been brought back from the past to the present. 'Sorry, I'm scaring you. We can be nice too, I promise.'

I try to smile back, but it's hard. All this talk of vengeance and violence doesn't match my experience of Corsica so far with its sandy beaches, glistening blue sea and cocktail-glugging tourists. But I do know that Corsica has a dark side. 'Dad told me some stories about the Corsican mafia,' I say. 'How powerful they are. Is that what you mean?'

'Mafia?' Salvo's tone has changed again. Now he sounds guarded. 'Thankfully, your dad's memories are out of date. The mafia used to run the island, for sure, but they're part of our past now.'

'Oh, sorry, my mistake.' I pretend to look grateful for the correction, but in truth, I'm confused. From what my mum told me about Corsica before I left, I'm pretty sure the mafia still operate here, and I wonder why Salvo, the man who is happy to condemn his fellow countrymen, feels the need to gloss over the truth.

Frankie

13th June

I walk inside the accommodation block still thinking about my conversation with Salvo. His talk of vengeance and violence has unsettled me, and it doesn't help that I'm still only wearing my damp swimming costume.

But those thoughts melt away when I push open my bedroom door because Izzy is dancing around the small space between our beds, with a fifty-euro note between her teeth.

'What the hell?'

Izzy whips the note out and thrusts it at me. 'Where have you been?' she demands. 'I've been waiting ages.'

'For what? And what's with the cash?'

'I'm going to take you out for dinner, and I'm starving, so come on.' Then she pauses, narrows her eyes. 'Why are you carrying wet clothes?'

'One of Dom's practical jokes,' I explain grimly. 'But more importantly, why are you taking me to dinner?'

Izzy flicks the note. 'Got a nice tip, and before you ask, no, I didn't sleep with the kid's dad. But if you're not ready to go in ten minutes, I might have to find someone else to impress with pizza and house rosé.'

'Okay, okay!' Izzy's energy proves to be infectious as I race down to the shower block, wash the salt out of my hair in record time – silently thanking my grieving self for the dramatic hair chop – and throw on a white cotton dress that contrasts nicely with my deepening tan.

Exactly nine and a half minutes after Izzy laid down her challenge, I'm ready. But we pause when we bump into Jack and Archie in the doorway of the accommodation block on our way out.

'Oooh, you look nice,' Archie says. 'Going anywhere special?'

'An intimate dinner for two,' Izzy offers, looking at Archie first, then Jack. 'On me.'

'Izzy had a bit of a windfall.'

'Lucky Izzy,' Jack drawls, that now familiar smirk back. 'Well, have fun, ladies.'

Jack starts to move away, but Archie rests his hand on Jack's arm to stop him. 'Maybe we could all meet up after your dinner?' he suggests. 'At Henri's for a few drinks?'

'That sounds—' I start.

'You're not suggesting gatecrashing a girls' night out, are you, Archie?' Izzy interrupts, raising her eyebrows.

'Come on, Arch, we can have a boys' night instead,' Jack offers.

Archie sighs, then lifts his hands in surrender. I mouth an apology at him before Izzy whisks me away. It would have been nice to meet up with the boys later – one to chat with, the other to covertly ogle – and I also can't help thinking that if Izzy made more of an effort with them, they might be friendlier with her. But knowing that Izzy wants me all to herself tonight feels like a compliment too. 'Where are we going?' I ask.

'There's this pizzeria on the way to town,' Izzy explains. 'It's all open air – even the kitchen – and I really want to try it out.'

'Sounds cool.' I think about it for a moment. 'But if it's completely open, how do they deal with security?'

'That's just it, they can't. But nothing ever gets nicked. You know why? Because it's owned by one of the big Corsican mafia families. So no one dares.'

'I thought the whole mafia thing was consigned to history now,' I say, testing Salvo's claim.

'You're joking, right? The mafia are huge here. They reckon that percentage-wise, there are more mafioso in Corsica than in Sicily.'

I frown, wonder again why Salvo did such a whitewashing job. Or maybe Izzy is exaggerating.

'It's cool though, if you think about it,' Izzy goes on. 'Because instead of causing crime, they're stopping it. Like the police, but actually effective.'

'I guess the threat of a horse's head turning up on your doorstep is a pretty good deterrent,' I murmur.

Izzy bursts out laughing, and the sound makes me smile.

'Come on, let's get a cab. Then we'll be there in five minutes. My treat.'

Fifteen minutes later, we're sat at a table for two in a restaurant with no walls, just a collection of terraces on different levels and fairy lights strung like washing lines above our heads.

'Cheers,' Izzy says, clinking her glass of rosé against mine, the open bottle in an ice bucket at the side of our table. 'I'm so glad you came out to Hotel Paoli. I mean, I've tried to make friends with the others, but they don't want to know. I think it's a xenophobic thing, Brits sticking together, but it's different with you. I feel like we're destined to be best friends. Is that a weird thing to say?'

I think about my own mix of British and Corsican heritage, which I still haven't mentioned because that would mean talking about my dad, and I'm not sure I'm ready. In truth, I don't imagine the others care in the slightest about Izzy's nationality, but I can't help feeling grateful that she's singled me out for special attention. 'Not weird at all,' I say, taking a sip of wine, and then another. 'I feel the same way to be honest.' I twist the stem of the wine glass between my fingers, then take another mouthful – Dutch courage – and decide it's time to confide in Izzy. 'The thing is, finding you does feel like good timing, because I kind of need a friend at the moment.'

'Oh?' Izzy's face grows curious.

'My dad died three months ago, and I guess I've been feeling a bit vulnerable.'

I wait for Izzy to dish out the usual condolences, but instead she widens her eyes, and a grin spreads across her face. What the fuck? She quickly drags the corners down with her fingers, but the damage is done. I look away, my cheeks burning. Why the hell did I tell her? I've only known her a few weeks. And why is she grinning like the Cheshire cat?

'Shit, sorry,' Izzy says. 'It must look like I'm happy about your dad dying.'

I feel that familiar sting of tears again. I gulp down my wine and reach for the bottle. Ice-cold water drips on my arm as I refill my glass.

'Because that's not it,' Izzy goes on. 'Of course it isn't. I only look happy because it explains why we feel so connected.'

'You're not making any sense.'

'The thing is my dad died too.'

I look up. 'Oh. I'm so sorry.'

But Izzy wafts my condolences away. 'It was thirteen years ago, half a lifetime, but that will be why we feel like kindred spirits. We've been through the same thing.' She picks up her glass and clinks it gently against mine. 'We were clearly destined to meet each other.'

A waiter arrives with our pizzas, and I breathe in the smell of bubbling cheese as he lays down our plates. He gives me a pizza wheel, and after checking how Izzy uses it, I cut my pizza into eight slices.

'You know, you're the second person to talk about destiny this evening,' I say, after devouring my first two slices.

'Please don't tell me Dom said you were destined for each other. I swear that guy fancies you, and it would be just like him

60

to use the cheesiest line ever.'

'Dom? If he fancies me, he has a weird way of showing it. And no, it was Salvo actually.'

Izzy scrunches her nose. 'Why were you talking to that old dinosaur?'

I hesitate for a moment. But I've already told Izzy my biggest secret. 'Well, he was friends with my dad actually.'

Now it's Izzy's turn to look shocked. 'Really? How?'

'They grew up together,' I explain. 'I'm half Corsican, you see. But my dad moved to England when he was twenty-two, and didn't meet my mum until fifteen years later, so he was pretty much an anglophile by then.'

'But he stayed in touch with Salvo all that time,' she muses. 'They must have been really close at some stage.'

'No, they hadn't spoken for years, but they started writing to each other after my dad got his diagnosis. I only met Salvo at the funeral, and that's when he offered me a job.'

'Wow. Another "who you know" recruit,' Izzy mumbles.

'What do you mean?'

'Never mind. Did your dad know Raphael too?'

'No, I don't think so. I guess he knew *of* him through Salvo's letters. It's funny, finding out that my dad had this past that I was clueless about. And not being able to ask him about it anymore.' My chest tightens. I take a gulp of wine to loosen it.

'That's Corsicans for you. A secretive bunch.'

'Why do you say that?'

Izzy takes a long sip of her wine, her head tilted back for what feels like forever. Finally, she lowers her glass back down. 'No reason. But I'd steer clear of Salvo if I were you.'

'But you must have a reason,' I push, the Dutch courage still doing its thing.

But Izzy just sighs and gives me a sympathetic look.

'Sadly, not everyone is as trustworthy as you, Frankie. But don't worry; you've got me to look out for you now.'

Frankie

21st June

I feel hands on my upper arms, dragging me backwards. 'Hey!' I call out, stumbling as my feet try to catch up. Jesus, how much have I had to drink? Two cocktails? Four?

'Come and dance!' Izzy calls out. 'I love this song!'

Beyoncé's 'Crazy in Love' is blasting out across the beach. With a rush of euphoria, I twist out of Izzy's grasp, then take her hand and together we tumble into the beach bar, a square space with a thatched roof and four pillars in place of walls. The bar staff have moved all the tables and chairs out onto the sand, turning the main bar area into a makeshift dance floor. It's busy with guests, some swaying, others putting in bolder dance moves. Izzy and I find a spot in the middle and join the fray.

'Great party!' I shout, lifting my arms and pumping the air in time with the beat. Almost a month in, this hotel feels like home now, and that's mainly down to Izzy's friendship.

'Yes!' she calls back, nudging her hip against mine. 'Who would have guessed that Anna loves the summer solstice enough to put on a party to celebrate?'

'Or that she was capable of organising it,' I say, grinning. The more I've got to know Anna, the more accurate Izzy's description of her has turned out to be. Pointless. She clearly adores Raphael and hangs off his every word, but I've yet to hear her give an opinion of her own. And even worse, she seems to be equally nervous around her son. Maybe that's why Patrick's always hanging out with his grandparents.

I scan the crowd, looking for the others. Our whole waterfront team arrived at the party together – after sharing a couple of bottles of rosé in Dom's room – but Archie and Jack disappeared almost straight away, and now I can't see Harriet or Dom either. I wonder for a second if that means anything – the two of them going AWOL at the same time – but dismiss the idea almost instantly. Harriet has made it clear that she only fancies men who wear signet rings. And preferably ones with a family crest.

As the music changes to Kelis' 'Milkshake', and we wordlessly adapt our dance style in synch, I feel another wave of gratitude for Izzy. Since our dinner out, our friendship has strengthened, and we've confided in each other a lot.

As I've talked about Dad getting thinner, quieter, weaker, greyer, until he finally wasn't there at all anymore, Izzy has told me about the impact of her own father's much more sudden death. How the restaurant her parents ran in Nice's old town never reopened after his fatal car crash, and how her mum, still dealing with her grief five years later, moved north to her hometown of Lille as soon as Izzy finished school. After finishing her degree at Montpelier University, Izzy didn't want to live in a part of France she didn't know, so she travelled a little in southern Europe, and then went to live in London. She thought she might stay there for good, but she missed the beach. And that's how she ended up at Hotel Paoli.

The only subject that Izzy has been muted on is Salvo, and why she thinks he's worth steering clear of. She did finally admit that she'd seen him hanging out with a group of dodgy-looking men in the middle of the night, but wouldn't say any more than that. It's not enough evidence to condemn him – not nearly enough – but her warning has still left its mark on me, especially after our unsettling conversation on the beach. I'm always polite when I see him now, but I keep my distance.

When I think about how far Salvo travelled to pay his final respects to my dad, I feel bad for judging him harshly. But the fact is, I don't know him. And neither did Dad really – they hadn't seen each other since they were teenagers. And people change. My instinct is to trust Izzy, and Mum has always taught me to trust my instincts.

'Shall we get another drink?' Izzy says. 'Another Long Island iced tea?'

'Yeah sure, but do you know where Harriet is?' I ask. 'She owes me a drink.'

'She's waiting by the pool with Dom,' Izzy says, with an exaggerated booty shake.

'Waiting for what?'

'I said I'd get more wine. Then I heard Beyoncé, and saw you, and well, here we are.'

I burst into laughter, more raucous than Izzy's answer deserves, another clue to my drunkenness. 'They are going to be so mad with you!'

Izzy winks. 'Harriet is constantly mad with me. Dom is too desperate to be liked to be mad with anyone. But I guess I should probably make good on my promise at some point. Shall we go and find them now?'

The music changes to Steps, and that feels like a good time to leave. 'Yes, but I need to pee. I'll see you up there in a few minutes.'

Izzy nods, then weaves her way through the revellers. I jump off the wooden block of the beach bar, and onto the sand. The staff aren't supposed to use the guest toilets. The others regularly flout the rules, but I'm too fresh out of school for that, and anyway, a walk along the beach to the accommodation block might sober me up a bit.

While the gardens and top section of the beach are busy with people, it's quieter by the water's edge, and I enjoy the sense of privacy it gives me. Like nobody knows I'm here, except the tiny fish in the shallow water, darting away as my shadow looms over them. The view sways a little and I giggle. Wow, I am pretty drunk.

'Francesca.'

I gasp. 'Jesus! You scared me.' Why is my heart racing so much? It's only Salvo. I eye the beach bar. 'What are you doing down here?'

'I was out fishing, but I think the noise from the party has scared the fish away, so I came in.' He tilts his head. 'What's wrong, Francesca? You look nervous.'

'No, I'm fine,' I say, privately panicking that he'll guess he's the source of my fear.

'Has something happened? Are you not enjoying the party?'

I look towards the beach bar again. The music is still loud, but it feels distant now. Muffled. The exhilaration of my drunkenness replaced by a blurred anxiety. 'I was just going back to my room for a bit. But I'm meeting up with my friends again soon.' I burrow my toes into the sand.

He keeps staring at me, and I have a sense of him peeling back my skin and levering open my skull until he can read my mind. 'Raphael said you're sharing a room with the French sailing instructor,' he finally says.

'What? Yes, that's right, Izzy,' I whisper.

'And you get on?'

'Yes.'

He nods, and keeps nodding, as though he wants to say more.

'I should probably go,' I mumble, taking advantage of the silence. 'My friends will be wondering where I am.'

'Francesca …'

'I prefer Frankie, if that's okay.'

'Izzy hasn't said anything to you, has she? About me?'

'What? No, nothing.' Even in the darkness, I can see Salvo's face flood with relief, and it makes my stomach churn. I don't know what Izzy has against him, but it's clearly something. And now he's worried about what she knows too. 'I mean, why would she?' I hear myself ask.

Salvo looks away, towards the sea, and I follow his gaze. There are about ten fishing boats moored to buoys, swaying gently in the waves. One of those will be Salvo's, I think. Despite how much I love the sea, I can't imagine fishing at night, alone in the darkness.

'Maybe she doesn't know anything,' Salvo murmurs. 'She was there, but not involved at all. I hope, for her sake, that she's unaware.'

Izzy's warning comes back to me. How she saw Salvo talking to dodgy men in the middle of the night. 'I need to go,' I blurt out, not wanting to hear more. I turn towards the beach bar, my need to pee forgotten, but Salvo reaches for me. His fingers curl around my wrist and it makes me want to run even more. But my feet won't move.

'I didn't mean to scare you,' he says, his breath warm on my skin. 'I will always protect you, Francesca, for your dad's sake.'

'From what?' I manage.

'Hey! Frankie! Is that you?'

I look up. Relief floods through me. 'Dom!' Normally I keep Dom at arm's length on a night out. He always gets drunk and plays a stupid joke that only he finds amusing. But right now, I love the familiarity of his slurring voice. 'Over here!'

'You need to trust me, Francesca. I promise.' Salvo releases my wrist, then twists in the sand, his gnarled bare feet catching the moonlight as he disappears up the beach.

'I was looking for Izzy; she was supposed to get us some wine.' Dom pauses, a hiccup making his chest jump, as his eyes narrow. 'That looked a bit intense.'

'Huh?' My brain is stuck on a loop. Salvo's words spinning around in my head. *I didn't mean to scare you. I will always protect*

66

you. You need to trust me.

Suddenly a physical urge swamps me, a need to be distracted from the strange old man and Izzy's warning about him. Without thinking, I reach out for Dom, slip my arms around his muscular torso, pulls him towards me, rest my head on his chest.

'Well, hello,' Dom says, his voice somewhere between confused and thrilled.

'Don't talk,' I instruct quietly. Then I tilt my chin, lean in closer, and shut my eyes as our lips connect.

Frankie

22nd June

As my eyes open, I feel a rush of panic. Where am I?

I draw in a breath, and hold it, as memories from last night flash up. My conversation with Salvo. Dom appearing from nowhere. Wanting his physical reassurance. Kissing him. Saying yes when he invited me back to his room.

I turn my head, slowly, silently, against the pillow. Dom is fast asleep next to me. As quietly as possible, I peel back the sheet and slip out of bed. I inwardly cringe at my nakedness, but it's not a shock. It might have been the alcohol that made sex with Dom seem like a good idea, but I was sober enough to know what I was doing.

I pull my crumpled dress off the floor and over my head, then pick up my underwear and sandals, and tiptoe to the door. The lock makes a clunking sound as I turn it, and I freeze, my heart hammering. Of course it's ridiculous. Dom and I work together, spend up to ten hours a day on a boat that's less than three metres wide. I will have to face him at some point. But I need a shower and a fresh pair of knickers first.

I yank the door open, close it quickly behind me, and scamper down the corridor. Izzy starts squealing as soon as I walk into our room.

'Oh my God, Frankie! You minx. It was Dom, right? That's where you've been? Why the hell did you sleep with that loser?!'

I groan and drop onto my bed.

'I thought you found him annoying. Isn't he always playing stupid jokes on you?'

The mix of disapproval and confusion on Izzy's face makes my cheeks burn. 'It was kind of an impulsive thing,' I mumble, sliding my underwear under my pillow before she notices. I don't want to mention the role Salvo played in my decision to launch myself at Dom. Not because I don't trust Izzy, but sleeping with Dom because Salvo scared me isn't a great look.

'So it was just a one-off?' Izzy asks. 'A drunken mistake never to be repeated?'

'Yeah, of course,' I say, smoothing down my dress. I don't know why I feel uncomfortable about saying that. Dom is annoying, but he was a gentleman last night. Respectful, generous. I feel a bit weird about just brushing him off.

'Well, we've all made those in our time. Don't worry about it.' Izzy gives me a sympathetic smile, then leans over and kisses the top of my head. 'But you do need to make it clear to him that you're not interested. Men can be a bit slow when it comes to opinions they don't want to hear.'

I sigh, as silently as I can manage. I don't want to have to deal with the fallout at all, let alone address the issue head on. 'We need to work together though,' I say. 'So I can't be too harsh.'

'But you don't want to lead him on either,' Izzy presses. 'What's that English saying? You must be cruel to be kind?' She's wearing her usual wide smile, but there's a hardness in her eyes. It highlights our age difference, I think, how Izzy has eight years more life experience than me.

'I guess I should get ready for work,' I say, not wanting to think about Dom, or Salvo, or what I do or don't regret anymore. 'And I need a shower first.'

Izzy looks at her watch – a navy-and-white Swatch Scuba that I desperately wanted for my birthday but knew there was no point in asking for because it was too expensive. 'Well, you've got five minutes, so you better hurry up.'

Amazingly, I'm only a few minutes late for work, and there are no guests hanging around the waterfront when I arrive – clearly it wasn't just me who enjoyed the summer solstice party. I'm leaning on the desk, checking the water-skiing sign-up sheet, when someone taps me on the shoulder. I twist around.

'I got you this,' Dom says, holding out a hunk of French bread with a thin line of apricot jam oozing out from its middle. My favourite flavour. 'In case you didn't have time for breakfast.'

I doubt accepting a gift from Dom is the best thing to do after Izzy's advice, but he guessed right about breakfast and I'm starving. 'Um, thanks.' I take it from him and have a big bite. Keeping my mouth closed is tricky, but I don't care about looking stupid in front of Dom – I suppose it might even help.

'Listen, about last night.' Dom looks embarrassed, thank the Lord. I feel a swell of relief as I wait for him to row back, ask if we can forget it ever happened. 'I guess I wanted to say thank you,' he goes on. 'I know I do a shit job of showing when I like someone, so thank you for seeing through my idiot impersonation and taking the initiative.'

Shit. I need to say something. Explain. But I can't swallow the bread.

'Anyway,' Dom continues, filling the silence. 'You're awesome. So I'm going stop throwing you in the sea from now on. Unless there's an opportunity that's just too hard to resist.'

My face produces an involuntary smile and the bread dislodges. 'You're a dick, you know that?'

'What was that? I have a huge dick?'

I roll my eyes and shove Dom in the chest. His eyes light up with the challenge and he grabs my shoulders, twists me round. He pretends to put me in a headlock – his arm way too loose around my neck for me to feel trapped – and I jab backwards with my elbow, connecting with his torso. He folds at the waist.

'Argh,' he cries out with more than a hint of melodrama.

As he drops to the sand, I can't help laughing. But then I notice Archie watching us, a bemused look on his face, and I force myself to look serious. I'm supposed to be acting cool around Dom, cold even. And here I am, actively encouraging him. I turn to see if Izzy has noticed our playfighting, then breathe a sigh of relief when I realise she hasn't.

In fact, Izzy seems oblivious to everything around her – even the thunderous look on Harriet's face as she drags a sailing boat down to the water's edge by herself, a guest ambling along next to her. Izzy is deep in conversation with Jack, although on closer inspection, it seems more like an argument.

'How long 'til the first guest?' Dom asks, brushing sand off his shorts.

'Nine o'clock, so ten minutes.'

'I guess we should prep the boat, then. You coming?'

I look back towards Izzy. 'Sure. Just give me a minute.'

Dom nods and walks towards the hut while I wander over to Izzy and Jack.

'Everything okay?' I ask.

'Yeah, we're good,' Jack says, raising a smile. 'Isn't that right, Izzy?'

Izzy clicks her tongue but doesn't speak. I pull at my bottom lip, not sure how to handle the obvious tension between them.

'Anyway, I should probably get to work,' Jack continues. 'And if Harriet's face is anything to go by, I reckon you should too, Izzy.' Then his smile fades. 'And remember, no one likes being threatened.'

Izzy stares for a moment, then shifts her gaze away from him.

71

'I told you. I was drunk last night. Shooting my mouth off.'

'Is that an apology?' Then Jack sighs and his voice softens. 'Listen, I just want us to be friends, or at least not enemies. Is that too much to ask?'

Izzy's face tightens. 'I guess not,' she murmurs.

'There you go, that wasn't too hard. See you later, ladies.'

Izzy gives Jack a dark stare as he ambles away, then grabs my arm and pulls me up the beach.

She looks angry, but her hand is trembling against my skin. I've been so caught up in my own drama from last night that I hadn't thought to ask where she ended up. 'What was that about?' I ask. 'What happened last night?'

'That guy is so arrogant,' Izzy murmurs. 'Thinks his movie-star looks will always get him out of trouble.'

I look over at Jack who's now helping Archie carry windsurf boards down to the water's edge. 'What kind of trouble?'

'Take your pick. I just wish I didn't have to work with him. *Pauvre con*,' she adds, and it doesn't sound like a compliment.

I pause, trying – and failing – to reconcile the Jack that Izzy is describing with the one I've got to know over the last few weeks. He's quiet and does seem quite secretive. But he works hard and both Archie and the guests seem to love having him around. 'But he's good at his job,' I say carefully. 'And Archie was telling me about the charity that he did his instructor-training through, on a reservoir in north London. I get the impression that Jack didn't have the easiest start in life. Maybe we should cut him some slack.'

'You have no idea,' Izzy murmurs, shaking her head.

'So tell me then.'

Izzy closes her eyes for a moment, then opens them and tilts her face towards me. She smiles. 'I'm sorry. You're right. Maybe I'm grumpy because I didn't have passionate sex with a water-ski instructor last night.'

'Oh God, Izzy!' Heat explodes in my cheeks, and I cover them with my palms. 'What have I done?'

Izzy giggles, the tension evaporating. 'You've given us all something to gossip about. Now come on, before Harriet spontaneously combusts.'

Frankie

27th June

'How about truth or dare?' Harriet suggests, her voice already slurring despite it being the middle of the afternoon. It's the waterfront team's day off – always on a Sunday because it's the main transfer day for the hotel – and we've spent most of it either sleeping or drinking. A long lie-in followed by a rowdy discussion about what to do with our precious hours of freedom (while I mainly focused on not making eye contact with Dom). Dom wanted to go cliff jumping through waterfalls, while Archie suggested tennis and Harriet mentioned a visit to the local market. But there was no consensus until Izzy offered to get hold of a stash of hotel wine from Raphael for us to share.

We found a quiet stretch of beach out of sight from the guests and draped a collection of towels over the sand. Now we're sat in a circle with six wine bottles and three tubes of paprika Stackers laid out between us.

'I'm up for it,' Dom says, knocking his plastic cup against Harriet's then taking a swig. It's cheap rosé sparkling wine, like pink lemonade with a kick, and we're already on our fourth bottle.

'It's dangerous territory,' Archie warns, raising an eyebrow. 'You never know what secrets you might be forced to divulge.' I know he's trying to sound jokey, but I can hear the nervousness behind it, and it makes me wonder what his secrets are. Posh, Scottish, and with better listening skills than most – he seems like an open book to me.

'That's what the dare option is for, dumb arse,' Harriet throws back. 'Or are you scared of those too?'

'You Brits are so stupid,' Izzy says. 'You can just lie, you know. If you don't want to tell us your secrets, just make something up. That's the beauty of working in a place like this. You can be anyone you want.'

'So who do you want to be, Izzy?' Jack asks. He leans back, as though he doesn't really care, but his eyes scrutinise her.

Izzy gives him a tight smile. 'The queen of Corsica, of course.' She takes a gulp of her wine, stares at her cup for a moment, then turns to look at Jack. 'What about you? Ready to reveal your secrets?'

'Why don't you spin the bottle and find out?'

'Me first!' Harriet calls out. 'It was my idea.' She grabs one of the empty bottles, lays it on a smoothed-out section of towel, and flicks her wrist. The bottle spins three times, then slows to a stop, the neck pointing at Izzy. Harriet looks triumphant, as though she suggested the game for this very opportunity. 'Our lovely French Isobel,' she starts. 'Hmmm, let's see. Would you sleep with Raphael if he propositioned you?'

Izzy leans back, as though the idea has repelled her. 'What? Of course not! He's married for a start, and has a kid, and he's about forty.'

'He's thirty-four,' Harriet says defensively, put out by Izzy's unmitigated denial. 'And good-looking. And rich. And he gave you all this wine.'

'She could be lying,' Archie points out, raising his eyebrows and grinning. 'After all, she did suggest that option in the first place.'

Harriet's triumph partially returns. 'Come on, admit it. You fancy him a little bit.'

'Gross, no,' Izzy says, shaking her head emphatically, her eyes not quite keeping up. 'Now it's my turn to spin.' She winks at me, and it sends a lurch of panic through my belly – she seems even sassier than usual today, which is probably down to the wine – then twists the bottle. It spins on its axis, finally stopping opposite Archie. She looks at him for a few moments, as though weighing up what to ask, then takes a breath. 'Are you in love with Jack?'

Everyone seems to grow a bit taller as our backs straighten out. My eyes dart to Archie. Sure, I've always found him the easiest out of the three boys to talk to, but that doesn't mean anything. And yes, during the times we've chatted on the beach after a night out, there's never been a hint of sexual tension between us. But gay? And in love with Jack? It hadn't occurred to me. But the answer becomes clear when Archie looks at Jack with a Mayday signal clear on his face.

'That's none of your fucking business,' Jack warns, his anger dimming his good looks, while making his London accent more pronounced.

'He could lie,' Izzy offers with a dark smirk. 'If he was ashamed of it.'

'Ashamed of being gay?' Jack releases a bitter laugh. 'You homophobic bitch.'

'No, stupid. Ashamed of falling for someone like you.'

'That's not fair,' Archie says quietly. He shuffles sideways, closer to Jack. It's a small movement but one that shouts louder. 'Jack is stronger than any of us. He's had plenty to cope with back home, and he's dealt with it like an absolute hero. And I don't know about love exactly, but yeah, we like each other. Anyone have a problem with that?'

'Not me,' Dom says with a grin. 'Reduces my competition to zero.'

'As in, you're a couple?' Harriet asks, slow to catch up, although whether that's down to her traditional upbringing or the amount of wine she's consumed is hard to know.

'I think it's great,' I say, trying to ease the tension in the air. It's not entirely true. While I don't understand why Izzy dislikes Jack so much, there is something damaged about him. And Archie is too nice to be hurt. But then again, I slept with Dom to escape a scary old man, so I'm not really in a position to judge.

'What do you mean by plenty to cope with?' Harriet asks, leaning forward. Now she's digested the news, her thirst for gossip has kicked in.

Archie lays his hand on Jack's clenched fist. 'That's not really—'

'No, it's fine,' Jack interrupts, flashing Harriet one of his more attractive smiles, while the plastic cup crackles in his grip. 'You try being a gay kid on an estate like mine.' He reaches for Archie's wine and gulps it down. 'You get the shit kicked out of you for not supporting Spurs, so you can imagine what fucking boys gets.'

'Were you bullied?' Harriet asks, sounding uncharacteristically compassionate.

Jack shrugs. 'Given the cold shoulder at school. Knocked around by a few dickheads on the estate.'

'Jesus, that's terrible.'

Jack hunches over his empty cup. 'I don't want your sympathy.'

'Why not? You deserve it.'

'No I don't,' he mutters. 'Not after what I did.'

'Why, what did you do?' Izzy asks, her voice colder than Harriet's.

'He didn't do anything, not really,' Archie says quickly. 'Jack argued with his family. Said some cruel things to his mum and dad a few days before he came out here. You know, like we all do when we're angry. No one was hurt.'

'I don't,' Izzy says, staring down at her wine.

'You don't what?' Dom asks, reaching for a new bottle. He twists the cork, and I jump when it pops.

'Argue with my family. At least, I haven't for a long time.'

'What, you've never fought with your parents?' Harriet asks. 'You expect us to believe that?'

Izzy looks up, her expression clouding over. 'I promise it's not worth it. Arguments can have consequences that you'll never forgive yourself for.'

'So can staying silent,' Archie counters in a solemn voice. He doesn't say anything more, but I can guess what he means. Archie has told me that his family live on an estate too – except a very different one to Jack's. A Scottish estate with grouse shooting and garden parties. Extreme privilege, but probably not the easiest environment to grow up in if you're not following the rules of the establishment either.

'My mum has spent thirteen years wishing she'd stayed quiet and kept her opinions to herself,' Izzy finally says, in a quiet voice, without looking up. 'I tell her not to feel guilty but ...' Her voice trails off.

'What did you argue about?' Harriet asks quietly.

Izzy finishes her wine, then scrunches the cup in her hand, the flimsy plastic cracking in her fist. She looks up. 'No, it wasn't me. Mum argued with my dad. Just before he died. And now she can never take it back.'

'Jesus, Izzy, that's fucking awful,' Dom mutters.

'I don't like to talk about it.'

'Of course,' Dom says, his tone unusually respectful.

But Jack's tongue clicks with disapproval. 'So Izzy gets to choose which parts of her life we can talk about, but the rest of us have to bare our souls. That sounds fair.'

'Don't be a wanker, Jack,' Dom warns.

'He's got a point though, hasn't he?' Harriet says. 'Izzy had no respect for Archie and Jack's privacy when she forced them out of the closet, then made out like Jack doesn't deserve Archie's affection. But when it comes to her own private life, she wants to pick and choose what she tells us.'

'Maybe it's another one of her lies,' Jack says. 'Maybe Izzy's dad is alive and well, and she's just attention-seeking.'

I hold my breath in shock. How could Jack suggest such a thing after what Izzy has just shared? I turn towards her, ready to console her, but Izzy doesn't look like she needs comfort. She's staring at Jack like she wants to kill him.

Frankie

30th June

I shift my weight and slice through the wake, splitting the morning sun's reflection in the flat water. I take one hand off the rope and trail my fingers. When my outer thigh starts to shake, I straighten up – my leg enjoying the reprieve – and whip back through the wake to the other side. Staff are allowed to ski on three mornings each week, but only Dom and I can drive the boat, so I don't always get the chance to go out. But we had one spare slot this morning, and Dom said I could take it.

A few minutes later, Dom brings the boat as close to the beach as possible and drops into neutral. I fling the rope handle in his direction and sink into the water. After pulling the rope in, he navigates his way over to the pontoon while I swim the mono-ski to shore.

'Thanks for that,' I call out as Dom jumps out of the boat and moors up. 'I owe you one!' The words hover in the air, and I hold my breath, waiting for the inevitable inuendo. But Dom just lifts his hand in acknowledgement and disappears into the hut. I exhale, feeling like I've dodged a bullet.

I know I need to talk to Dom about our night together – tell him once and for all that it was a mistake. But every time I come close to it, he says something funny, and I laugh instead. Also, when he touches me – nothing sexual, but a hand on my back, or our shoulders brushing as we navigate around each other on the boat – I don't pull away. But Izzy would be horrified if we got together, and it's not fair on him to leave things ambiguous.

I step out of my beach shorts, rinse off the salt water in the outdoor shower, and towel-dry my body. Then I pull on my uniform. Wednesday morning is when the under-tens kids' club do their water sports – and it is always chaos.

An hour later, the noise levels are off-the-scale, and I'm getting a headache. My comment about owing Dom is proving painful in a different way – because he has used it to bagsy driving the boat while I manage four screeching eight-year-olds in brightly coloured surf suits and bloated buoyancy aids that make them move like robots.

'Now just grip tight onto the bar,' I say to the boy bobbing in the water, his arms high and fingers curled around the training bar that I've clipped to the ski pole. 'Keep your knees tucked up high and relax. The boat will do the rest.' I give Dom the okay symbol, and he gradually picks up speed. A moment later, the boy, Bertie, rises out of the water. His face is a mix of pride and terror – an expression I've seen countless times – and his knuckles are white with the effort of holding on.

'Wow, look at you!' I call out over the sound of his skis slapping against the churning water. 'What a superstar water-skier you are!'

The boy beams with happiness, and I smile back, but keep my attention on his form. His adrenaline will be surging, and keeping two skis under control is hard work for young legs. At some point exhaustion will kick in, and I need to spot it before it causes him to fall. A couple of minutes later, his left ski skids, and I notice that his knee is trembling more than it was. I give

Dom a thumbs down and he gradually slows the boat.

'That was brilliant. You're a natural,' I tell Bertie. 'Now you swim around to the back of the boat, and I'll hoist you up. Right, who's next?'

I turn towards the other three children as I drop the ladder for Bertie. But suddenly a noise out to sea makes me twist back around.

'What the hell was that?' Dom says.

'It sounded like someone screaming.' I lift my hand to screen out the sun and search the water. 'Look, I think something's up with the cat.' Izzy is sailing a few children on a catamaran, but the mainsail is flapping in the breeze. The children are huddled on the trampoline and one of them seems to be in trouble.

'Pull the kid in,' Dom instructs. 'I'm going over.'

I pull Bertie up, followed by the ladder. My voice has an authoritative edge as I tell the children to sit still, then I watch as we get closer to the sailing boat. When we arrive, the scene makes my stomach churn. 'Dom, radio through to reception,' I say as quietly as possible. 'Get an ambulance. And a container of ice.' Then I lie across the edge of the boat and reach for the catamaran.

'Frankie!' Izzy calls out. 'I told him to pull his hands in!'

I slide onto the boat.

'My finger!' a boy moans. Then he turns his head, spews up an acidic mix of croissant and smoothie. Three other children scream, crawl into each other.

A large patch of the navy trampoline is stained black with blood. My stomach flips again.

'I was tightening the mainsail,' Izzy shouts. 'I told them all to keep their hands away, but he clearly didn't listen because his finger got caught. I can't find the first-aid box!'

'Dom, throw me our first-aid kit!' I kneel by the boy, find his eyes. 'What's your name, honey?'

'Felix,' he whimpers. 'My finger … I'm scared.'

I look down, swallow some vomit of my own. Then I turn to the sound of Dom's call and catch the green plastic box he's thrown. I twist off a cap of saline solution, douse the tiny centimetre-long fingertip lying on the trampoline and seal it in a plastic bag. Then I repeat the process, using the new tube of solution to clean Felix's wound, and wrap what's left of his finger in a gauze dressing.

'Felix, you are the bravest boy I've ever met. But I need you to do one more thing for me.'

'I want my mummy,' he moans. His eyes roll back. 'It hurts too much.'

'I know you do. And I'm going to take you to her, I promise. But our boat is much faster than this one. And we need to get you to a doctor so he can fix your finger. Okay?'

'I want to come too!' a girl wails, her knees up by her chin, her teeth chattering.

'And me!'

'No, kids,' Izzy says, shaking her head. 'I know this has been really scary, but Frankie is going to look after Felix, and we're going to sail back to shore. I promise I'll make it fun.'

'No, I don't want to,' a girl with a French plait says. Her lip quivers, then she bursts into tears. 'I hate you!'

'Don't be silly.' Izzy tries to give the girl a reassuring smile, but her eyes darken.

'Why don't you radio for Harriet to bring the RIB out,' I murmur. 'It's not surprising the kids are freaked, and she can tow you back in.'

Izzy clicks her tongue, turns away. But when she turns back, there are tears glistening in her eyes. 'You're right, sorry. I'm not thinking straight.'

'Of course you're not – you're in shock,' I say gently. 'But I need to go. Good luck.' I grab the gunwale of the ski boat and pass the sealed bag to Dom. Then I usher Felix as close as I can to the edge, and together Dom and I lift him over. His face is ghostlike, and the other children watch on, whimpering.

'Bertie and Amber, move on to the floor please,' I say. As they slide off, I lower Felix into the cushioned seat and wrap a towel around his shoulders. 'What's your surname, Felix? I'm going to radio through to reception and they'll ask your mummy to come to the beach.'

'It's Drake,' he whispers.

'Thank you. Are you okay if I leave you for a second?' He nods, and I twist away from him. I walk to the front, where Dom is sinking into the driver's seat, and pick up the radio. 'Hello? Anna?'

'Fuck, Izzy is going to be in all sorts of trouble,' Dom murmurs under his breath. 'How do you slice off a kid's finger?'

'She didn't slice it off. It was an accident.'

'And then leaving it to us to save the day,' Dom continues like I haven't spoken. 'I mean, did she even check she had a first-aid kit on board before she went out? What kind of rookie mistake is that?'

The radio crackles to life and it feels like a reprieve until I hear Raphael's voice. 'What the hell happened out there?' he hisses. 'Please God don't tell me the ambulance is for one of the children.'

I take a deep breath. 'Felix Drake has lost the top section of his right index finger,' I explain. 'We have it. But he's asking for his mum, so can you find her and get her down to the beach?'

Raphael expels a deep sigh, but agrees and cuts transmission.

'She's the oldest of us all,' Dom mutters, shaking his head. 'She has supposedly been teaching sailing since she was sixteen, and she's acting like an amateur.'

'We haven't heard her side of it,' I mumble. 'Maybe we shouldn't jump to conclusions.'

'I reckon Izzy's going to get fired. And the way I see it, she deserves to be.'

I press my lips together. Part of me wants to defend Izzy, my best friend out here, but another part is reeling. Because Dom's right, she has made a huge mistake, and a young boy might suffer the consequences for the rest of his life. As I make my way back to Felix, I wonder how Izzy is feeling now, whether this incident will haunt her forever too. And how I'll cope for the rest of the summer if I lose my best friend here.

2025

Frankie

26th July

Lola is at Hotel Paoli.

How can she be there after everything I've done to keep us both away?

When I flew out of Corsica's Figari airport that August in 2004, numb with grief and guilt, I wasn't stupid enough to think that I was leaving it all behind me. I knew the memories of those two tragedies would haunt me forever, however far I ran. But I did believe that I would never have to set foot on the island again. That I could at least create a physical separation.

But now I need to go back. For Lola.

I slam my foot against the decking in frustration. Why did Mum keep those postcards? She knew I never wanted to talk about that place again. That I needed to lock it away in my past if I wanted to have a future. And then once Lola did find them, why didn't she come and tell me, ask me, rather than conspiring with her friends and taking a secret trip by herself?

I look at the date on my phone: 26th of July. Tears well in my eyes as I realise how close it is to the anniversaries. And in five days' time, it will also be the most terrifying night for me to be in Corsica. The 31st of July. Whatever happens, I need to get Lola off the island before then.

I push up to standing and my whole body feels weary. I've only slept for about three hours, but I think my exhaustion has more to do with the emotional toll of hearing Lola's news than sleep deprivation. Especially knowing who she's with now.

I sit at the table and pull my laptop towards me. Without letting myself think too hard about the consequences, I click into Skyscanner and look for flights to Corsica. There aren't any to Figari until Wednesday, which is the closest airport to Porto Vecchio, but it's not a big island, and I can get on a flight to Ajaccio Napoleon Bonaparte – named after Corsica's most famous resident – first thing tomorrow morning. It means that Lola will spend another night alone, but it's the best I can do. God, I hope she follows my advice to not ask any questions.

I book a seat on the plane, then look back at my phone. It's 10.30 a.m. I'll need to go home first, pick up my passport, then leave for Gatwick around three in the morning, but I still have time to kill. Really, I should try and sleep. But with Lola at Hotel Paoli, and all those memories resurfacing, I know that I'll see my friends' faces every time I close my eyes. Sometimes alive. Sometimes dead. And what will that do to me? Send me spiralling again? Summon up the worst nightmare of them all? I capture that terrifying dream on canvas to stop it coming for me in my sleep. But what will happen if I can't paint?

I'll do something constructive while I wait instead. A task to distract me. And if I'm going to get Lola out of Corsica before Thursday, I'll need to be as efficient as possible.

An hour later, I sit back and rub my eyes. From what I can glean from the Foreign, Commonwealth & Development Office website, Lola needs a crime reference number before she can apply for temporary travel documents – which means visiting the police station as soon as I arrive tomorrow. I hate the thought of going back to that place, but I need to remember that Lola's situation is completely different from mine. We'll be in and out in five minutes. And hopefully that misogynistic police officer will be long gone.

Then we need to contact the closest British consulate, which is in Marseille – on the French mainland – to apply for the documents. They take twenty-four hours to produce, and the consulate works seven days a week, so assuming they can send them next-day delivery, we can be on a flight home – or a ferry to mainland France if it comes to it – by Tuesday, Wednesday at the latest.

I don't have the energy to pack up all my stuff, but I've rented this place for two weeks, so I can come back once I've got Lola safely back to the UK. Instead, I shove my favourite clothes in my holdall – the cut-off denim shorts and white T-shirts, the Quiksilver sweatshirt and O'Neill windbreaker – and wolf down a big bowl of cereal. Then I lock the door on my refuge, and head back into the world.

It's hard to believe that I only left my house yesterday – so much has happened since – but its familiarity is welcome. The air is thick with July heat, so I head to the kitchen and push open the back door. I run the tap until the water finally turns ice cold, then pour a large glass. I sit on the back step to drink it, and as I stare at the lilac lavender wafting in the breeze, my eyelids grow heavy again.

I should go to bed. If I'm driving to Gatwick in the middle of the night, I owe it to myself – and Lola – to at least attempt sleep.

I head upstairs to my bedroom, pull the curtains closed, strip down to my underwear, and climb into bed. Sunlight is still streaming through the cracks, so I pull on my eye mask, and everything goes black.

But the darkness triggers my memories. I see Izzy in a bar, dancing wildly to Beyoncé. And then lying on her bed, the night air too hot for sheets, confiding in me about her father, and how losing him changed the trajectory of her life. I see Dom.

91

Laughing, sad, humiliated, bleeding. And I see Archie and Jack. Archie's glass of Long Island iced tea tipping against mine with a conspiratorial smile. Him looking at Jack, like he still can't believe his luck. And Harriet. *Fucking hell, Frankie! You're a shit friend!*

And then I see waves. And rope. And Salvo's wizened face. And then they're dead.

I push the eye mask off my face, catapult my body up to sitting, suck in air. My heart is pounding. The water I gulped down earlier sloshes in my stomach. Emotion swamps me and I burst into tears. Why did it happen? How could I have let it happen? And how the hell am I going to find the strength to go back there?

When I'm all out of tears, I push back the duvet and head into the bathroom. I run the shower and step inside – cold first, to calm my burning skin, then hot, another pointless attempt to scald my guilt away. The shower does its job of waking me up, but I know it will only be temporary.

When I'm dressed again, I head back downstairs and make myself a cup of strong coffee. If I'm not going to sleep, then I need to do everything possible to help keep my body awake. It's a three-hour flight to Corsica. Maybe when I'm buckled in, flanked by happy strangers heading off on their summer holidays, I'll finally be able to drift off.

A few hours later, I lock up for the second time in two days, this time with my passport zipped inside my jacket pocket and a new set of clothes in a cabin bag, and start the two-hour drive to Gatwick Airport.

Frankie

27th July

I glide slowly, silently, through the forest. Thin slivers of moonlight seep through the branches, providing just enough light to see. Its white glow is ethereal, ghostlike, and my body melts into it. I'm almost invisible as I move from tree to tree, calm, as though in a trance. But my mind is focused.

Searching for prey.

I drop my hand to my side, run my fingers over the cold metal of my dagger. A thrill surges in my chest, then ebbs away, leaving the smoking heat of a snuffed-out candle in my belly.

A dark shadow appears in the distance. I stop, crouch down, listen. But the sound of rustling fades, then disappears. Some might think it a lucky escape for whatever animal has moved away, a wild boar or perhaps a wolf, but I know that's not the case. Surviving was its destiny.

Just like mine is to hunt.

I straighten out my limbs but hesitate before moving again. I can hear something. Not the hushed crackle of leaves under an animal's step, but the faintest whisper of feathers. A bird. I look up. A soft glint of moonlight flickers down. There it is.

An eagle owl.

Perched high in a tree, its brown and tan feathers merging with the bark, but its fiery eyes vivid against the night sky.

I stare at the regal creature, knowing instinctively that I must kill it. It lifts its wings in protest, revealing the pure white feathers underneath. But it won't intimidate me.

I walk to the tree, reach for the lowest branch, pull myself up. The tree is tall. Perhaps fifty metres. But I'm not scared of falling. Branch by branch, I climb, the twigs and rough bark that scratch at me leaving no mark.

Whoo-whoo. Whoo-whoo.

The owl is warning the forest of a predator. But it doesn't fly away. It thinks it's got the power to repel me. It doesn't understand how much stronger I am.

I climb.

Finally, I reach its height. Our eyes catch. The owl tries to challenge me with its stare, but I hold its gaze and the energy shifts. I feel my dominance, and I know the owl senses it too. The imminent danger it faces. It lifts its huge wings, preparing to soar away.

But I'm too quick.

I grab my dagger, thrust it hard into the owl's chest, straight through its heart. The wings flare, then drop. Snowy feathers become stained by red, sticky blood as life seeps away.

I look at the owl's lifeless face, wanting to bask in the glory of my conquest.

But it's changed. The bird's features have gone.

Replaced by a human face.

One so familiar that it hits me like a lightning bolt.

I scream. My heart hammers in my chest. I rub frantically at my eyelids, trying to erase what I've just seen, but that final image is too strong, so I whip my eyes open instead. Try to adjust to reality. Light and darkness merge, blurring my vision. Think,

Frankie! I flail around with my arms, looking for clues. I find a door handle. A steering wheel. Of course, I'm in the car. I stare at the view through the windscreen. Concrete pillars and lines of cars on asphalt. Faded strip lighting.

The airport car park.

I remember now, how tired I felt, driving up the M3 from Lymington in the dead of night. And how relieved I was to finally arrive without falling asleep at the wheel, or veering off into a field and smashing into a tree. But the relief must have relaxed me so much that I fell asleep before getting out of the car.

And then I had the dream. The mazzeri dream.

And I saw Lola's face on a dying eagle owl.

The mazzeri legend goes that the person you see in your dream, their face imprinted on the animal you've killed, will die in real life soon after. It's a stupid fable – a Corsican myth – and of course I don't believe it.

I've never believed it, not really. What happened twenty-one years ago was just a coincidence. And it happening on the 31st of July – the darkest night according to the mazzeri legend – means nothing. Now, more than ever, I need to remember that.

I slam my hand against hard plastic. But if I know the mazzeri thing is all bullshit, why the hell won't it leave me alone?

When I had that first mazzeri dream in Corsica, it wasn't exactly a surprise – with the terrible trauma I was going through at the time, and Salvo's raspy voice like a worm wriggling into my brain, including my dad in his twisted claims, of course it would come while I slept. After all, that's what nightmares are – subconscious fears making their presence known.

But then the dream came true, and not even going back to England could help me escape that fact. Some nights I couldn't erase the dead faces of my friends from behind my eyelids, and sleep evaded me completely. But on others, I became so exhausted that I sank under, and then suffered that terrible dream again. Me hunting in Corsican forests, always with a weapon, always killing wild animals. And always seeing the face of someone I knew.

I couldn't bear it. That's why I started drinking heavily, and staying up all night partying. I found that catching a few chemically deadened hours, when I blacked out rather than slept, helped keep the nightmare away. But I could never repress it when the anniversaries got closer. To most Corsicans, the mazzeri legend is a cool story to spook kids and tourists, but to some old-timers – people like Salvo – it's unquestionably real. And he believed I was one of them, a mazzera.

I know it's not true. Not possible. But the bitter irony is that I did play a part in my friends' deaths. And so, when my insomnia is at its worst, and I'm half-dead with tiredness, the two things get mixed up in my head and I start talking crazy. It's why I've been sectioned twice – I tell people, usually medical professionals, that I can predict death, and they class me as delusional – without realising what a relief their diagnosis is to me.

But now I have seen my daughter's face on my prey.

The person whom I love most in the world, whom I am supposed to protect.

Except, of course the dream would come for me now. Knowing Lola is in Corsica. And at Hotel Paoli, meeting Anna and Raphael. These are the reasons why I had a mazzeri dream, not because it was ordained by some dark witchcraft. The mazzeri legend is nothing more than Corsican cult history and I need to let it go.

Lola is not going to die.

I push open the car door and step into the stifling air of the multistorey car park. I collect my holdall from the boot, hoist it over one shoulder, and slam the door. Then I look for the sign to departures and head inside.

Lola

27th July

Lola stares at the pale blue blind covering the window. The room isn't plush by any stretch, but it's a thousand times better than the one in that Airbnb. No loud men stomping around. A lock on the door. Lola stretches out on the single bed and dips her fingers into the carving on the dark wooden headboard behind her. She doesn't know what time it is – she's still phoneless – but from the strength of the sunshine leaking around the blind's edges, it feels like morning has been around for a while.

Which means her mum will arrive soon. And she's not sure how she feels about that.

She was mad with her yesterday, but maybe that wasn't fair. After all, it was Lola's choice to come to Corsica, alone, and in secret. Her idea to book a room without considering why it was so cheap. Yes, most mums would have their phone within three-second reach when their child goes on holiday without them for the first time, but her mum has always been different. At least, at this time of year.

When Lola walked up Hotel Paoli's long driveway yesterday

– palm trees and rolling lawns on each side of her, sun beating down – she didn't know what to expect. Her mum had lived and worked there, but it was a long time ago, and something bad had clearly happened that brought it to an abrupt end. The glass door had slid open automatically, so Lola didn't even have the chance to collect herself before she came face to face with the receptionist. A glamorous older woman with blonde hair and high cheekbones who eyed her suspiciously.

She wanted to tell her story gradually, but in the end, the words tumbled out. She was Frankie Torre's daughter. She needed help.

The receptionist had looked shocked at first, colour visibly draining from her already pale face. But she recovered quickly. She introduced herself – Anna Paoli, which told Lola that she was more than a receptionist – and asked lots of questions, like whether Frankie was in Corsica too (no), what she'd told Lola about her time working at Hotel Paoli (nothing) and finally, why Lola needed help. Once Lola had explained that she'd been mugged, that she was too scared to go back to her accommodation and couldn't get hold of her mum, Anna had ushered her into the office behind the reception desk, pushed the big phone towards her, and told her to take as long as needed.

When Lola re-emerged and explained that her mum was coming out, Anna's face had tightened for a moment. But then it had cleared, and she'd gone on to offer Lola a room in the staff accommodation block while she waited for her mum to arrive. Anna even said that her son Patrick would pick up Lola's things from her Airbnb that evening if Lola wanted him to. Yes, there was an atmosphere – Lola sensed Anna was keeping something from her – but she was too tired, and too grateful, to find out what.

Patrick hadn't returned to the hotel by nine o'clock last night, and Lola could barely keep her eyes open by then, so she hasn't been reunited with her bag yet. But she's desperate to change into fresh clothes, so she needs to track it down soon. She pushes back the sheets and climbs out of bed.

Her room is one of four in a concrete structure set back from the beach, with a shared bathroom at the end. When Anna showed her the room yesterday, she explained that they recruit most of their staff locally now, but there are two members of staff sharing the accommodation – a Spanish tennis pro and an Italian pianist – so Lola pulls the door open carefully in case they're around. But the only thing she sees in the hallway is her backpack, leaning against the wall. She feels a swell of happiness and says a silent thank you to a man she hasn't yet met.

After a deliciously long shower, Lola changes into a bikini and board shorts and walks down the beach towards the hotel. Her eyes are drawn towards the water shimmering in the sunlight. She has always been at her happiest in the sea. Especially whipping across it on a windsurfer, up on the plane, the board barely skimming the water. Tacking with bloody-mindedness, gybing with belief.

When she gets to the water sports area, Lola pauses. In those postcards to Grams, her mum describes working here as a water-ski instructor. It will have been her perfect job, Lola thinks, so what went wrong? As she stares, pondering the mystery, a man appears from a wooden shack. He's muscular and handsome in an older man kind of way, with spiky bleached-white hair and a deep tan. He's wearing coral beads around his neck and a faded Billabong T-shirt.

'Can I help you?' he asks in a London accent.

Lola eyes the brightly coloured sails hanging together neatly, then pans out to the glistening sea, the strengthening breeze lifting the water into champagne spray. Maybe this is exactly what she needs to wash away the bad start to her time in Corsica. 'How much is it to take a windsurf out?'

'Forty euros for an hour, seventy for two.'

'Oh.' Lola's face drops. She has never had to rent windsurf kit before – she's always had her own, courtesy of Grams' industry contacts and massive discounts – and that's more money than she can spare.

The man tips his head. 'Are you staying at Hotel Paoli?'

Lola wonders how to answer that. 'Why?'

'Because it's free of charge for the all-inclusive guests. At least, it's part of their overall package.'

'Right.' Lola bites her lip. She is staying on the hotel grounds, and she's kind of like a guest of Anna's. Does that count? Even though she's not paying a penny?

'Are you worried about managing the sail with the wind picking up?' the man continues. 'Because I can rig you up something small?'

'No, it's not that. I windsurf a lot back home; the more wind the better. It's just that while I am staying at the hotel, it's not as a paying guest,' Lola admits. 'It's complicated.'

'Oh?'

'They're helping me out because I was mugged,' Lola explains to the man's inquisitively raised eyebrows. 'Some guy took my phone and money; my passport.' She wafts her hand like it was yesterday's news. 'My mum used to work here, like twenty years ago, so I thought I would see if there was anyone here who remembered her. Turns out Anna did, and she kindly offered me a room in the staff block.'

Lola watches the man's face grow curious. 'What's your mum's name?' His tone carries a new weight, and Lola feels an instinct not to tell him.

'Why?'

'Because I was working here twenty years ago. I might know her.'

Simple words, a rational explanation. So why does it sound like a threat?

But that's ridiculous, Lola tells herself. This is just her own anxiety playing tricks after everything that's happened so far in Corsica. She shakes the tension out of her limbs. 'You were? That's crazy,' she says, because it's the right response. 'She's called

Frankie Torre. I think she taught water-skiing here.'

He nods but doesn't speak. Finally, he turns to the rack of windsurf sails. 'You can take a windsurf out on the house. A four-point-eight sail okay for you?'

'What? Oh, yes, that's perfect,' Lola says, struggling to keep up with the change in conversation. 'And thank you. For the freebie.' Lola watches him unhook a red-and-white sail from the middle of the rack, then disappear into the hut for a moment before coming out with a harness. He throws it to her, then attaches the sail to one of the shorter boards while she steps into the harness, pulls it over her shorts, and tightens it. Despite this man's weird reaction to her mum's name, a burst of anticipation swirls in her belly.

'You beach start?'

She nods.

'That figures: a child of Frankie's.' He proffers the sail towards Lola, and she curls her fingers around the boom. But she hesitates before carrying the rig into the water.

'You knew my mum well, then?'

'We worked together for a couple of months. Before everything went to shit. But I guess you know all about that.'

For some reason – to save face, she supposes – Lola nods. 'You stayed though,' she says slowly, maybe hoping he'll give her a clue as to what happened. 'But I guess it was worse for my mum,' she gambles.

It's one that doesn't pay off though because he lets out a bitter crack of laughter. 'I'm Jack.'

He says his name as though it's an explanation, but Lola doesn't know what of, or how to respond. 'Nice to meet you. I'm Lola,' she tries.

But it's another misstep. His face darkens. 'That name doesn't ring any bells?' he asks. 'Your mum hasn't bothered to mention me?'

Lola bites her lip, wishes she'd just taken the rig without asking him anything.

'The love of my life died, Lola,' Jack snaps. 'That's how bad it was. And the one person who could have saved him was your mum. But she didn't.'

Frankie

27th July

I sit motionless in the back of the cab, trying to stem the nausea and suffocating memories that are threatening to derail me.

'Miss?'

I was planning to tell the cab driver to drop me at the end of the drive, so that I could walk up to the front door of Hotel Paoli at my own pace, give myself chance to prepare. But as the cab got closer to the hotel, I found I couldn't speak, a solid lump of dread like a dam in my throat, and I watched dumbly through the window as the driver swept down the long drive.

'Um, twenty euros, miss,' he tries again. 'You have my fare, yes?'

I grasp for his voice, use it to drag me back to the present. 'Sorry,' I whisper. 'Yes, I have it.' I reach into my shoulder bag, open my wallet with shaking fingers, and pull out a crisp note. I bought the euros at Gatwick Airport along with a cheap phone for Lola. I bought a book too, a romcom to distract me. But I spent most of the flight in that familiar twilight between waking and sleeping.

I hand over the banknote and climb out of the cab. The heavy oak doors have been replaced by sliding glass panes. It looks better, I think, more welcoming, and I use this wisp of optimism to propel myself forwards. A few moments later, I drop my bag in the same spot as I did twenty-one years ago and turn to look at the familiar face behind reception.

'Hello, Frankie,' Raphael says. 'Anna said you were coming.'

I nod, wonder if I can trust my voice. Then I think about why I'm here and clear my throat. 'Thank you for helping Lola.'

Raphael gives me a stiff nod. 'I haven't met her yet. Anna gave her one of the single rooms in the staff block.'

'That's kind of Anna, of you both,' I manage. It sounds like Lola has kept a low profile like I begged her to, which is a relief, but their generosity is unnerving. Raphael was a nice enough boss for a while, until he denounced me as a killer. And Anna's opinion never veered far from her husband's.

'It's been a long time,' I continue. 'But you look well.' It's not completely true. Raphael's swept-back dark hair looks good with streaks of silvery grey, but his dark eyes have faded. His skin has sagged, and he's developed a small paunch. But of course he will have aged. The memories are still so vivid to me that I forget how much time has passed.

'Actually, life has been hard recently,' Raphael says. 'We buried Salvo on Thursday.'

I draw a sharp intake of breath. Salvo is dead. I feel a weird mix of relief and loss. As though I'm finally free of him, but it's still a bond broken. 'I'm sorry,' I manage.

'He's with my mother now. She died a few years ago. And he was eighty-five, so …' Raphael shrugs as his voice trails off.

Family is everything in Corsica, so I'm surprised by how dismissive he sounds. 'But life must feel strange here without him,' I try.

'Not really. My parents moved back to Sartène a long time ago, soon after you left in fact. Anna and I were so busy dealing with the fallout at the hotel that I barely saw him for the first few

104

years. And relationships need effort, even blood ties. We never quite managed it.'

I think back to my final conversation with Salvo, at the police station after my interview. How I despised his manner – accepting, calm, impassive. Like he didn't care at all. I can't imagine he moved away because of what happened.

'Can I go to the staff block?' I ask, suddenly desperate to get away from this conversation, to find my daughter and get the hell out of Corsica. 'Try and track down Lola?'

'Of course.' Raphael starts to gesture towards the back of the hotel, but then his eyeline shifts.

'Frankie, how lovely to see you.'

I twist towards the voice. Anna. Time hasn't reduced her like it has her husband. In fact, it seems to have had the opposite effect. She's kept her hair long and blonde and her skin is still smooth and pale despite the Corsican sun. But she was always beautiful; now she radiates confidence too.

'Hello, Anna,' I murmur. 'I really appreciate all your help with Lola.'

'You don't think we'd throw a young girl back out onto the streets, do you?'

'No, of course. It's just that …' How do I say it? That twenty-one years ago there was a double tragedy in this hotel, and life hasn't been the same since? That Raphael wouldn't look me in the eye after finding my friend's lifeless body in the sea, and things only got worse after that, so him helping my daughter now feels disorientating?

'And you should stay here too.'

'Me? No.' I shake my head. There's no way I'm spending a night here. 'Lola and I can find a room in town until we sort out her new passport. You've done enough.'

'Don't be silly,' Anna says. She glances at her husband's stony face, then turns back to me. 'And it's peak season now, so you'll struggle to find anything half decent at this late notice.'

'There must be somewhere,' I murmur, wondering why I didn't think to book a room before I came. Why I filled my head with memories of my friends dying, or me killing my own daughter in a Corsican forest, instead of doing the practical things like making sure we had somewhere safe to stay.

'And we've just had a cancellation, so you can have the room for free.'

'Anna, can I have a word?' Raphael is clearly as keen on me staying here as I am, but Anna doesn't even register that her husband has spoken, and miraculously, he doesn't push it, just looks away in surrender. It's a role reversal I would never have predicted. When I worked here, Anna lived in his shadow. Now she seems to be the one in charge.

'They cancelled too late for a refund,' she goes on. 'So we're not losing out.'

'I … I don't know what to say.' What I mean is that I don't know how to turn down the offer, but I realise that my words have the opposite effect.

'That's settled then. It's room 316. We'll get your bag taken up so that you can go and see Lola,' Anna says. 'She's on the beach by the way. I saw her talking to Jack.'

I catch my breath. 'Jack's here?'

'He never left,' Raphael says. 'We had to cut costs after that summer – funny how two sudden deaths aren't great for business – and not recruiting a waterfront team was an obvious way to save money. Jack was still hanging around, so I helped him set up his own business. He's been renting that section of the beachfront from us ever since. And he lives in my parents' old beach house too.'

As subtly as possible, I reach for the reception desk to steady myself. Any relief I felt about not bumping into Salvo is erased by the thought of seeing Jack again. I imagine Lola talking to him, what he might tell her, how he would react when he found out who she was. I crane my neck, try to look through the glass doors at the back of the hotel, but there are too many obstacles in my way.

'Dom lives on the island now too,' Anna continues. 'He bought a crumbling wreck in Sartène about five years ago. He's doing it up himself. Very slowly, it seems.'

'Dom?' I half-whisper, half-gasp.

'He did well in the UK apparently,' Anna continues. 'As an estate agent of all things. He was married, but no children. But then Brexit happened, and he had some sort of early midlife crisis – although he calls it an epiphany. He left his wife and moved out here while he still could.'

'I thought we'd all want to stay away,' I whisper.

'No, just you,' Raphael says.

I look away, towards the sea. 'I'd better find Lola.'

I turn and walk as quickly as I can without running. Past the hotel restaurant and out onto the terrace, trying not to think about what's coming – seeing Jack, staying in this hotel overnight. I zigzag through sun loungers spread across the lawn, almost all of them occupied by hotel guests, some holding books over their faces, others with their eyes closed, fat headphones covering their ears.

As I get closer to the beach, I see Lola talking to a man. It's clearly Jack. He hands Lola a windsurfing rig, and I watch her drag it down to the shallow water. She steps up on the board with one foot, angles the sail to catch the wind, then lifts up her back foot. She arches her back – which I know is her clipping into a harness – then flies out to sea, showing why she's always the one to beat in junior windsurfing competitions.

But today she's on a rig set up by the man who blames me for his boyfriend's death. A man who I also know is capable of murder.

Frankie

27th July

I don't take my eyes off Lola as I continue towards the waterfront hut. I can see from the white tips on the waves that the wind is strong out there, and Lola will be taking full advantage, pushing her body, taking risks, just like I did at her age. Lola is a very talented windsurfer – taught by my obsessed mother as soon as she was strong enough to pull up a sail – but right now, that's little comfort. Lola's sail is white and red, and it reminds me of the dying eagle owl's bloodstained feathers from my dream in the airport car park.

I turn my head away, exhale slowly. Remind myself that it was a stupid, meaningless nightmare.

Lola is not going to die.

I pause ten or so metres away from the hut. Jack is pulling another sail down from the rack while a young woman in a bright turquoise bikini and orange buoyancy aid hovers nervously by his side. When he and Archie worked together, Jack would sort out the equipment while Archie covered front of house, charming the guests with his smooth Scottish brogue. Jack has got no one to hide behind now, and I wonder if that has softened him at all. If such a thing is possible for a man like that.

I watch him slide a sail to the water's edge and attach it to a board. He gives the guest a demonstration – showing her how to stand up by planting one foot and using it to drag the board towards her. When she nods her understanding, he gives the board a gentle push into the shallow water and turns his back on her – his job done. I watch the woman clamber on, then tentatively rise up to standing. The board wobbles, but she stays upright. The first battle won.

I take a deep breath and walk up to the hut. 'Hey.'

Jack freezes for a moment, then slowly turns around. He assesses me, and I do the same to him. Age has damaged him, but not in the same way as Raphael. The coarse dyed hair and jagged crow's feet. More scarred than faded.

'Frankie Torre,' he finally says, his tone difficult to gauge. 'I didn't think I'd ever see you again.'

'I didn't think I'd come back,' I murmur, looking away, back out to sea, where Lola is still flying across the water. 'But my daughter needed me.'

'I heard. But still, it's brave of you.'

I turn back to face him. 'Brave?'

'You know,' he says, not looking at me. 'After everything you did. And didn't do.'

I catch sight of the catamaran in my peripheral vision, and suddenly a memory of Izzy flashes up. Her tearful face and frozen body as I did what I could to save a little boy's finger.

'She looks like you.'

Jack's comment snaps me back to the present. 'Thank you.'

'A natural on the water like you too.'

'I watched you put Lola's rig together.' I realise my tone is more accusing than grateful, and Jack's face sours.

'What, you think I tampered with it?'

'No, sorry, that came out wrong.'

'How dare you come back here after twenty years and start throwing accusations at me again?'

I swallow down the comeback that wants to spill out. That I know all about him, his past. And that he can blame me for Archie's death all he likes, but it won't change who's really responsible. I look back at Lola. She's still on her board, flying back out to sea now. The wind direction is clearly side shore, the best conditions. I hope she gybes soon, turns her nose back to shore. I want her back on dry land.

'It was a surprise, hearing that you never left,' I say, trying to sound civil.

He shrugs. 'I had nowhere else to go. And I wanted to help. The hotel barely survived that summer. Did you know that? Almost all the bookings got cancelled. Madly, it was Anna who saved it. Turns out she wasn't as pointless as Izzy liked to make out. Raphael was a mess – maybe being the one to find the body, or maybe … I don't know. Anyway, Anna took the helm. She had all these contacts in the UK, God knows how, and suddenly Hotel Paoli was popping up in lots of fancy travel magazines. It got things back on track.' He shrugs. 'And it feels like Anna's been in charge ever since.'

'I got that impression too,' I murmur. 'But I'm amazed Raphael allowed it to happen.'

Jack shrugs. 'He lost a lot that night. His hotel, his status, his father too because Salvo bought a vineyard in Sartène soon after. It changed him. Permanently. It changed us all, I guess.'

Jack looks out to sea, pretending to check on the smattering of guests on windsurfs. Most of them are floating on their boards, feet set, knees bent, hands gripping the rope as they try to pull the sail up without toppling over backwards.

'Does Lola know?' I ask quietly. 'Have you told her?'

'She said that you'd told her, but I worked out pretty quickly that she was lying. You're too ashamed, I suppose, to tell her the truth about your past.'

110

Heat burns my cheeks. I feel too weak to stand, so I lower myself onto the sand, feel its soft July warmth against the backs of my legs. God, I want to see my daughter. To hold her. For fourteen years, I have left Lola on her birthday. I've always thought it was for the best, that I was protecting her, but maybe that was bullshit. Because right now, I'm desperate to be with her. Is that how Lola has felt over the years? Abandoned. Longing for her mum to be there for her.

'So did you tell her anything?'

'No,' Jack says. 'But that doesn't mean I won't. I'm not here to keep your secrets.'

I feel tears threaten again, a mix of relief and fear. 'I know,' I whisper.

'Anyway, keeping things inside fucks you up,' he continues. 'Everyone knows that.'

It's an accepted truth, that you should talk about your problems. But it has never been that way for me. Every time I confess my darkest fears, I get labelled insane and locked up. It's better when I handle things in my own way.

'Lola was my therapy,' I say quietly. 'She wasn't planned, but when I found out I was pregnant, I knew she would save me.'

'So you leant on your kid from day one. That doesn't sound like something to be proud of.'

His words slap so hard that they sting. Because I know he's right. I should never have expected so much from my daughter. Especially when she was the one who ended up suffering for it.

'Anyway, it looks like you're about to have the chance to make it up to her.'

Jack nods towards the water's edge and I turn to look. Lola's board and sail are lying on the beach, and she is walking towards us.

But not with the welcoming smile I was hoping for.

Frankie

27th July

'Hi, Mum.'

Lola doesn't look at me as she unzips her buoyancy aid and drops it in the bin of fresh water. I stand up, then find myself wringing my hands in some pointless act of contrition. I want to reach out for her, but something stops me. A force field of unanswered questions. 'You looked good out there,' I say, trying to find a way in. 'How was the wind?'

Lola turns and I flinch under her glare. I can just make out Jack in my peripheral vision, a bemused smile playing on his lips. I twist my body away from him, and spread my shoulders, but it's a feeble attempt to block him out.

'Anna offered me a room here,' I continue. 'They had a cancellation, but I was thinking that we should find something in town instead, while we sort out your—'

'Why don't you want to stay here?' Lola interrupts, challenging me. 'It's paradise.'

'It is beautiful,' I admit. 'But—'

'Is it because someone died here? And you didn't save them?'

I draw in a breath. So Jack did tell her. The fucking lying bastard. I look at him, then quickly turn away.

'Or because you want to continue keeping this place a secret from me, like you've done for nearly eighteen years? Even though it clearly fucked you up and I suffer for that every birthday.'

I can feel Jack's stare boring into my back. He's not getting a ringside seat to this. 'Lola, I'm so sorry not to tell you, and I want to talk about this. But not here. Please. Let's take a walk down the beach. And I promise I'll explain everything.'

Lola hesitates for a moment, then gives me a curt nod – our bond frayed, but not broken, thank God – and starts walking. I scramble to catch up, then fall in step beside her. Our arms brush and I soak up the feeling of it, but I daren't risk trying it again.

'I'm sorry that I've kept so much from you,' I start. 'You're right that this place has haunted me, and it was selfish of me not to tell you, to explain. I want to make things right, so ask me anything you want, and I promise I'll tell you the truth.' What I really want is to slam the door on my past, grab Lola, and race back to the airport. Sleep in those hard metal chairs until Lola's new passport is ready. But I'm too late for that. If Jack has told her his version of events, I need her to know mine.

Lola stops walking and turns towards me. 'You know, it's weird. You're my mum, but I feel awkward around you suddenly. Like you're a stranger. I don't know what to ask.'

My throat tightens. 'I know I've kept things about my past from you, and it must have been horrible hearing it from someone else—'

'Why do you leave me?' Lola asks. 'I mean, I know it's because you can't sleep, and it drives you crazy, literally, but why is that? It's always around my birthday. And that horrible postcard that you sent to Grams, calling yourself a monster, was dated 1st August. My birthday. That can't be a coincidence.'

'It's complicated,' I whisper.

'Seriously?' Lola throws back. 'That's you telling me the truth?'

I wince at the accuracy of her words, then look out to sea. I need to do this. I won't tell her about the dreams, or Salvo, or his stupid, poisonous claims about me having mazzeri powers, but I will tell her about the real stuff. The guilt.

I take a deep breath. 'Something terrible happened on that date, around midnight, and yes, someone did die on my watch, a good friend. Every summer, the memories come back, disrupt my sleep, my mental state. And I'm not safe to be around.'

Lola bites her lip. 'Look, I'm really sorry that happened. And I see that it must have been truly awful for you at the time. But it was all so long ago,' she says. 'Isn't time supposed to heal everything?'

'Guilt doesn't come with a use-by date,' I whisper.

I feel the flutter of Lola's fingertips on my arm and then they're gone. 'Can you tell me what happened?' she asks softly.

I nod, just slightly, then force myself to think about that night.

I see Izzy's lifeless body, almost translucent in the sliver of moonlight that sneaked through the clouds.

'We were young,' I start. 'And stupid. We thought we were immortal.' I think about how excited Izzy and I were as we stripped off our dresses. 'Drunk too,' I admit quietly. 'It was really dark out there. We hadn't noticed when we decided to go for a swim, but the sky was thick with clouds, so there was barely any light from the stars or the moon.'

'You went for a midnight swim?' Lola asks. 'I can't imagine you being scared in the sea, even at night,' she adds, but it's an observation, not an accusation.

'The water was churning. A storm broke a couple of hours later, and we got the prelude to that. I was out there, by myself at that point, treading water. I was thinking that I wasn't having fun, that I should swim back in, when I felt something brush past my legs. It freaked me out, so I kicked at it. But then it got worse. Grabbing my leg, pulling me underwater. And that's when I realised it was a person, and my adrenaline went into overdrive. I just kicked as hard as I could to get away and swam for the shore.'

'Someone tried to drown you?' Lola asks, her pitch rising. 'So is that how Jack's boyfriend died? Someone pulled him underwater?'

'What?' My skin feels clammy suddenly. I shiver, despite the heat.

'Did they find whoever did it? Are they in prison here? Was it someone you knew?'

'No, you've got it wrong,' I mumble. 'It wasn't like that.'

Lola stops walking, turns to face me. 'Then tell me,' she pleads.

'It wasn't Archie, Jack's boyfriend, in the water with me.'

'Huh?' Lola's brow creases with confusion as shame smarts my cheeks. 'But Jack said ...'

'Archie did die that summer,' I admit. 'But that's not who I'm talking about. He committed suicide two days earlier.'

'Holy fuck.' Lola takes a step backwards. It's like she's repulsed. The death of one person a shock, but of two people, impossible to process.

'I was swimming with my friend Izzy.'

'And someone killed her?' Lola's voice is high-pitched, disbelieving. I feel my face crease. I drop it into my hands so that Lola doesn't see the hot wet tears that spread across my palms. 'Mum?' she presses.

'Nobody killed her. At least, not on purpose.'

'But I thought you said ...'

'They were Izzy's hands pulling at me,' I interrupt, whispering through my fingers, like the latticed divide of a confessional. 'I didn't realise at the time but ... She must have got into trouble in the water and was reaching out for help. I kicked her away, Lola, and then I left her to drown.'

'Jesus, Mum, no.' Lola shakes her head, a frenzied movement, and I know she's trying to clear the image from her mind.

'But I had no idea it was her,' I beg. 'I really thought I was being attacked. It was pure instinct. Only when the police explained it the next day did I realise what I'd done.'

Lola sinks down onto the sand, and after a moment's hesitation,

I join her. But I can't make eye contact, not yet, so I look out to sea. 'That's why people blame me. And they have every right to. But when I was out there, I was so certain that someone was trying to hurt me. I don't understand how I got it so wrong.'

'So how did the police know it was you?' Lola asks, her voice calmer, but still dejected. It breaks my heart that my daughter needs to process the enormity of my mistake.

'I guess they listened to my account and reached that conclusion because it was the only one that made sense.'

'It doesn't sound like it made sense to you,' Lola says. 'You thought someone was trying to drown you.'

'But I was traumatised. I wasn't a good witness.'

'But you were the only witness. Doesn't that make you the best one? Did you tell them how you felt? That you were scared for your life?'

'Yes, I did, but …' I pause, try to find the right words. 'But when the police officer suggested it was Izzy, I could see how I made the mistake. I was drunk. Scared. And I'd been having these crazy dreams. My imagination was in overdrive.'

'But there's also a chance that you didn't make a mistake,' Lola presses. 'Did the police investigate it as a potential murder at all? You know, like find out if anyone else was in the sea, check out if anyone had a motive to kill Izzy, those kinds of things?'

My mind travels back in time until I'm sat opposite that police officer with his thick moustache and air of superiority. Not a formal interview room. Just an office with a desk and a stack of paperwork, the window half open, but the breeze making no difference to the oppressive heat. He asked me lots of questions. And wrote the answers in his notepad, his eyebrows rising and falling with each new piece of information. But he'd been more interested in how many shots of tequila we'd drunk than my paralysing fear as someone dragged me underwater.

'No, they were convinced it was misadventure,' I say. 'A combination of Izzy being irresponsible, and me making a stupid, catastrophic decision.'

Lola leans back until she's horizontal, staring at the blue sky. 'A young woman not being listened to by an older man in uniform,' she murmurs. 'What a surprise.'

Lola

27th July

Lola dives into the cool, fresh water. She doesn't spend much time in swimming pools – she prefers the beach – but there's something about its chlorine smell that she needs right now. As though it might cleanse her brain, make her see things more clearly after the revelations her mum dropped on her earlier. Five days from now, she will officially be an adult. Eighteen years old. In her whole childhood, she has only spent three birthdays with her mum, and none that she can remember. And now she knows the reason.

Lola sinks under, and with her eyes protected by goggles, she stares into the illusion of blue water. Then she tilts forward, and cuts through it, her arms and legs powering her forward. As she nears the opposite wall, her lungs start tightening, sending early warning signals to her brain. But she ignores them. Her eyes focus on the horizontal red line ahead of her. One more strong stroke and she touches it. Her fingers land, and she holds still for an extra second, testing her willpower. Then she drops her feet to the floor and bursts above the waterline. She takes a long breath.

The pool area was rammed when she walked past earlier with her mum, on their way to get some lunch in the restaurant, but she's the only one in the water now. She flips onto her back and stares at the late afternoon sky. It has a light-wash look to it – faded, with wisps of white clouds. She reaches over her head with one arm, then the other, creating enough momentum to work her way down the pool.

Lunch was uncomfortable. She and her mum found a kind of truce on the beach, enough for Lola to suggest they get something to eat together. But as soon as they sat down, their plates filled with salads, chestnut bread, and different local cheeses from the buffet, her mum had reintroduced the idea of them moving to a different hotel. Lola doesn't get it. What's the point in trying to find someplace new? How will that change what happened twenty-one years ago?

Eventually her mum gave up trying to convince her, but then she started talking about Lola's new travel documents, and how they needed to get a crime reference number from the local police station to apply for them. She wanted to go there straight after lunch. Lola knows it's a task she needs to get done, but she wasn't in the mood, not after hearing about Izzy, and Archie, and her mum's possible involvement in both their deaths. Yes, she came to Corsica to find out about her mum's summer there, but now that she knows, a big part of her wishes she'd just gone to Ayia Napa instead.

Because it's made her see her mum differently. And created more questions than answers.

Like why did Archie take his own life? And why did Jack imply that her mum was involved?

And was it really Izzy in the water pulling at her mum as the police suggested, or were her mum's instincts right that she was being attacked? Was someone trying to kill both of them, and succeeded with Izzy where they failed with her mum?

Lola imagines being in the sea that night. Alone in the darkness.

A storm's energy building in the waves. Something grabbing at her legs. With all that going on, Lola can see how her mum might have got confused. But then again, her mum had lived by the sea her whole life. She qualified as a lifeguard when she was sixteen, just as Lola did years later, and she would have been first-aid trained. Would she really not know the difference between someone struggling and reaching out for help, and someone intent on dragging her under?

Maybe they didn't mean for Izzy to die. If they were all drunk, it could have been a practical joke gone wrong, a way of scaring both her mum and Izzy, making them look silly. And it had worked with her mum. But maybe Izzy had panicked. And the water was rougher than the joker had expected. Frankie lived, and Izzy drowned, and the person who really caused her death kept their mouth shut.

And all this time later, her mum is still beating herself up about it. Lola wonders if she can ask who else her mum worked with that summer without freaking her out.

'Hey, is it Lola?'

Lola tilts onto her feet at the sound of her name. A man is standing by the edge of the pool, a pile of tablecloths in his arms. Short dark hair, tanned skin, deep brown eyes. 'Um, yes,' she says, pushing her goggles onto her head.

'I'm Patrick, Anna and Raphael's son.'

Lola's eyes widen. 'Oh, you collected my stuff from the Airbnb! Thank you so much, and for dropping my backpack outside my room, I really appreciate it.' Now that she has stopped swimming, she realises that the air temperature has dropped. She wades towards the steps, climbs out, and grabs a towel. She can feel Patrick's eyes on her as she wraps it around herself.

'It was nothing,' he says, shrugging. 'I'm sorry I didn't get it to you earlier in the evening. I got distracted by an old friend.' He rubs the heel of his hand across his forehead. 'Been paying for it today.'

'Well, I hope it was worth it,' Lola says, grinning. She was late to the drinking phase compared to her schoolmates. When they were in the park sharing bottles of cider, she'd be catching the last waves, or getting an early night ahead of a race. But in her final year of school, she was invited to a run of eighteenth birthday parties in the first term. It was winter, so there was less to keep her head clear for, and she finally learned how much fun getting hammered could be.

Patrick gives her a sheepish grin, but then his smile fades. 'It was the first time I'd been out since my grandfather died. I got a bit carried away. And then when I got back here, I suddenly decided I needed to take his old fishing boat out.' He shakes his head, like he can't believe his own stupidity. 'It's barely been in the water for twenty years, but when my grandfather lived here, he loved to fish.' Patrick shrugs, then looks away, embarrassed. 'I thought it might be a way to get closer to him.'

'Oh, jeez, I'm sorry,' Lola says, wishing she could think of something better to say. She doesn't know what it feels like to lose someone – she's only got a tiny family for a start, a father who she FaceTimes barely twice a year, and no siblings. And the way Grams takes on a twenty-knot cross-shore wind shows that she's not going anywhere soon.

'Don't worry, you weren't to know.' Then he smiles, and the air temperature seems to recover a bit. 'I understand that your mum arrived today too,' he continues. 'How long do you think you'll be here?'

'A few days, I guess. Mum's keen to get away – I mean get home – as quickly as possible but we need to sort my travel documents out first.'

Lola eventually managed to convince her mum that she could visit the police station alone this afternoon, that all she needed was some euros for the cab ride. Her mum's eyelids were seriously drooping by that stage too, so Lola pointed out that she should get some rest. Her mum had reluctantly handed over fifty euros and gone in search of her room. Although in the end, Lola hadn't needed to go anywhere, and the euros are still in the back pocket of her shorts.

'I guess it's hard for her,' Patrick says. 'After what happened when she worked here. Seeing the people who remember it.'

Lola tries to work out how old Patrick is. Older than her definitely – he's broader than a lot of the boys at school and she guesses that he shaves more than once a week – but still young. Mid-twenties maybe. Which means he will have been a small boy when Izzy and Archie died. She wonders what he remembers.

'You know about what happened to Izzy and Archie then?' she asks.

'Kind of. I was only five, so I don't really remember it happening. But the story of Izzy's death particularly feels like it has seeped into the walls of this hotel over the years.'

'So you know my mum was in the water with her when she drowned?' Lola asks quietly.

He looks at her apologetically. 'I know it all.'

Lola feels her cheeks flare, like the shame of Izzy's death is contagious. 'Everyone has been very kind so far,' she says, trying not to sound defensive. 'Your mum's even given her a hotel room for free. Maybe I'm being a bit optimistic, but I'm hoping that my mum spending some time out here will make her realise that Izzy's death wasn't her fault.'

Patrick nods and their eyes catch. 'She's lucky to have you.'

'Thank you,' Lola mumbles, smiling back, wondering why she suddenly feels coy.

'And I also hope your mum finds she's able to enjoy her time here.'

Lola smiles. 'That's kind of you.'

He smiles back. 'Don't be too nice. My reasons might be a little more selfish than they sound.'

Frankie

27th July

I stare at my reflection in the full-length mirror and wonder if Raphael still likes his guests to dress for dinner. I'm wearing the nicest outfit I brought – claret red pleated midi-skirt with a fitted white T-shirt – but who knows if it's smart enough for him.

After my walk on the beach with Lola, my confession, I felt my whole body shutting down with exhaustion – a combination of barely any sleep over the last two days, and the trauma of taking myself back to that night – so when Lola demanded that she visit the police station alone, part of me even felt relieved. I dragged myself up to my room on the third floor – my bag was already inside, just as Anna had promised – then pushed my phone volume up to the highest setting and laid down on the bed.

Perhaps my body had hit rock bottom by then, or maybe telling Lola the truth released some of the tension inside me, but I fell straight to sleep, and didn't even dream. It was bliss. And when I woke up a few hours later, I felt more rested than I have for days. And with that came a kind of optimism. I'd told Lola the truth about Izzy. She was shocked, yes, but the world hadn't imploded.

And when I called her after my sleep to suggest she move her stuff into my room, she told me that she would do it after dinner because she was too hungry to pack, and that response was so default-teenager that it made me smile.

I add mascara to my eyelashes, run some gloss over my lips with my forefinger, and slide on my Birkenstocks. Then I pick up the room key and head downstairs.

Lola is sitting on a stool at the bar, her nails tapping a glass of Coke. 'Hey, Mum,' she says as I sink down beside her. Then she looks up at the barman as though she's going to ask for something, then turns back to me. 'You look better.'

'Would you like a drink, madam?'

Now it's my turn to look at the man in a white shirt and black trousers behind the bar. He reminds me of someone, but maybe it's just his Corsican looks that seem familiar. 'Yes, thanks.' I don't drink much alcohol these days, but I hear myself order a glass of rosé, like I've travelled back in time. As I watch the barman pour a pale pink wine into a glass, I feel someone coming up on my right. I expect it to be Anna, or Raphael, so when I turn, I let out a gasp.

'Hello, Frankie.'

'Wow.' I take a moment to settle my breathing. 'Anna said you lived on the island now, but I wasn't expecting …'

'Yeah, I'm sorry to ambush you like this. It's just that Jack messaged me, told me you were here. I live only about half an hour away, so I figured I couldn't miss the opportunity to come over and say hi. I hope you don't mind.'

'No, of course not, it's, um, it's good to see you,' I say, stumbling over my words. I can't believe how little Dom has changed. His face is a bit leaner perhaps, and there's the hint of crow's feet around his eyes. But otherwise, he has the same open face and quick smile that I tried hard not to fall for two decades ago. I notice the scar on his forehead, now just a thin white line, and remember how my heart thumped when I saw him with blood running down his face.

'Sorry,' I say, snapping back to the present, trying to find some equilibrium. 'This is my daughter, Lola. And Lola, this is Dom. He worked on the waterfront with me too, as a water-ski instructor. He lives in another part of Corsica now.'

Lola nods, but she's wearing a guarded expression, and it makes me think about her comment earlier, her suggestion that maybe my first instinct about what happened in the water that night was correct. Is she sizing Dom up as Izzy's killer? I think about her suggestion that it could have been a prank. And how Dom loved pranks. But no, he wouldn't risk people's lives like that. Even if he'd grown to hate both Izzy and me by then.

'Nice to meet you,' Lola finally says.

'And you too. Jack filled me in on what happened to you. Mugged in Porto Vecchio. Absolutely shocking. I promise that kind of thing is rare around here. Although I suppose you know that already. The local police like to do a PR job whenever a tourist reports a crime.'

'Actually, I haven't spoken to the police,' Lola says. 'So it is good to know, thank you.'

'You haven't?' I can't help blurting out. 'But I thought you went this afternoon? I gave you the money for the cab ride! You can't start the process of getting temporary travel documents without it, Lola, and we need to get home.'

I hate how manic I sound, and especially in front of Dom, but for all my bravado about the world not imploding, we need to leave before Thursday, the 31st of July. The Foreign Office website says it takes twenty-four hours to produce the paperwork. If they send it out on a fast service, we should still be able to get out in time if we apply tomorrow, but it's very tight.

'Hey, chill, Mum. I've applied this afternoon. And they work seven days a week apparently, so the papers should be here by Tuesday.'

'But I thought you needed a crime reference number as part

of your application?' I take a sip of wine, then another.

'You do, yeah. But when I went to reception to book a cab, Anna's husband was behind the desk and he said that he could get me one without me going to the police station, that he has a friend who works there who would do him a favour. He spoke to someone on the phone, and the reference number came through twenty minutes later.'

'Hah, typical,' Dom says. 'It's like getting planning permission. If you're foreign, it takes months. If you're Corsican, it takes a bottle of wine.'

I think about the officer who interviewed me as an eighteen-year-old and wonder if my nationality had any influence over his assessment of what had happened. He instantly dismissed my claims that there was someone else in the water and chose to blame me for Izzy's death instead. I was so traumatised at the time that I just accepted it – especially after the dream I'd had the night before – but Lola saw it differently this afternoon. And it's true that I was the only witness. Did the police officer not take my statement seriously because I was British?

'Hey, Dom,' the barman says. 'Do you need a drink?'

'Thanks, Patrick. Maybe a panaché? I'm driving back home later.'

My stomach lurches at the sound of the barman's name. Patrick. He must be Raphael and Anna's son – that's why I recognised him. He was a little kid when I worked here, but of course he'll be an adult now. And this is a family business, so it's not surprising that he's on the payroll.

Patrick must sense me working it out because our eyes catch for a moment, and his seem to carry some kind of message.

A shiver runs through me as I wonder if he can remember the night I found him, huddled under the sun lounger. The night of my dream. Maybe he even thinks that he owes me for taking care of him. When the truth is I was grateful for the distraction he provided.

I can see both his parents in him now – Raphael's colouring and Anna's bone structure – but there's a sadness in his eyes. Then I remember that he only buried his grandfather two days ago and look away.

'Shall we go to dinner?' Lola asks. 'I'm starving.'

I hesitate, then turn towards Dom with a mixture of reluctance and hope. 'Would you like to join us, Dom?' I don't know whether I want to spend my evening with him or not after everything that happened between us – and around us – but either way, it feels rude to abandon him when he's driven all this way.

'I'd love to, thanks,' he says, a grin spreading across his face. And despite everything, the sight makes me smile. A reminder that not everything that happened that summer was terrible.

Frankie

27th July

Five minutes later, we're seated at an outside table. The air is still warm, and I can hear the gentle lapping of the sea rolling onto the beach. 'I hear you've bought a house in Sartène,' I say to Dom. 'What brought you back?' What I really want to ask is how the hell could he set foot in Corsica again after that awful summer, but Raphael is right that Dom wasn't affected by the tragedies in the same way I was. Archie's suicide knocked him of course, but they were never that close. And there was no love lost between Dom and Izzy.

'It's an amazing place,' Dom says. 'Mountain views in one direction, sea views in the other. The architecture is stunning, and the whole town is one big history lesson. The wine's good too.' He pauses. 'You should come for a visit.'

'Maybe.' I know I should want to visit the town my father grew up in, but being in Porto Vecchio is challenging enough.

'I promise you'll love it. There's even an art museum.'

'Well, you're right there,' Lola says. 'Mum's an art teacher. She was always dragging me around museums and galleries when I was little.'

'Okay, guilty,' I say, forcing an apologetic smile. I find Dom mentioning art unnerving, but I know it's this place making me paranoid. An art museum is a draw for most tourists, not just art teachers.

'Have you been back to Corsica at all, since ...' His voice trails off.

I shake my head, don't quite trust myself to speak.

'Mum still feels bad about the way Izzy died, don't you, Mum?'

'Well, you shouldn't,' Dom throws back, then he clears his throat. 'Sorry, that came out wrong. It's just annoying. You blaming yourself when you did nothing bad. Unlike her. I'm not saying Izzy deserved to die of course,' he adds quickly. 'Just that you shouldn't be suffering for it.'

'She was my friend,' I murmur.

'She was a bitch,' Dom mutters, circling his wine glass and staring into the spiralling liquid. Then he looks up. 'Look, I know she was fun, always the life and soul of the party. But she was ruthless. It suited her to be nice to you because she wanted someone to adore her. But woe betide anyone who tried to cross her.'

'That's not how I remember it,' I mumble. 'None of you gave her a chance.'

'Us? What about the way she treated Jack?'

'She had her reasons—'

'And I suppose she had her reasons for talking to me like I was shit on her shoe too?' Dom sighs. 'And sorry, but she was a liability in that job as well. I mean, what would she have done if we hadn't rescued the situation when that kid lost his finger? She didn't even have a first-aid kit on board.' Dom shakes his head. 'And she still charmed Raphael into letting her keep her job. I think we can all guess how she managed that.'

The waiter appears at our table, and I breathe a silent sigh of relief at the distraction. We all choose *Aziminu*, a chunky fish soup that sounds delicious, and it only feels like a few minutes later when the waiter returns with three bulbous white bowls and a basket filled with chunks of baguette. As I rip off a piece of the warm bread and dunk it into the reddish liquid, I think about how different mealtimes were when I worked here. Staff food was served in a basement room with a TV and a couple of tatty sofas. Sometimes we were treated to a proper dinner – roast chicken and chips, or barbecue ribs and salad – but more often than not, it was a platter of curling cold meats, limp lettuce and leftover baguettes.

I look around the busy restaurant, humming with holiday chatter. When I left Corsica that August, I vowed never to set foot on the island again. But now I'm here, maybe I don't feel as scared as I thought I would. Salvo is gone. Anna has found her voice at Raphael's expense. Jack hasn't lost his hostile edge, but maybe he's more wistful than angry now. Less threatening.

And Dom. Tonight, here, Dom is reminding me that there are good memories from that summer too. Even that being forced to come out here, to face my fears, could possibly be restorative.

An hour later, Dom pushes back his chair. 'It was really great to see you, Frankie, and meet you, Lola, but I should be getting off. If you find you have time for a visit inland, I'd love to show you around Sartène.'

'Thank you,' I say, as graciously as I can without accepting anything, and then watch him walk out of the restaurant. 'I'm sorry about that,' I say to Lola. 'I didn't know he was going to show up.'

'Don't apologise,' Lola says. 'He seems nice. Actually, he seems like he's into you.'

I feel my cheeks getting hot and wonder if Lola can see it. 'Don't be silly. We haven't seen each other in twenty years. Anyway, shall we go over to your room and collect your stuff?' I ask, changing the subject.

'Um, about that,' Lola says, looking down at the table. 'I've decided that I'm going to stay where I am.'

'What? Why? No.' I shake my head. The serenity I was feeling earlier was clearly very flimsy because it has dislodged in an instant. 'I want you closer to me than that.'

'I'm practically eighteen, Mum. I don't need a babysitter.'

'Yes, I know, but …' I quickly run out of words. Because how can I explain? Say that I'm scared that some terrible fate awaits Lola because my friend drowned twenty-one years ago and I had a dream where I killed an eagle owl, and then saw my daughter's face? I have hidden that side of me from Lola for a decade and a half; I mustn't risk exposing it now. 'Never mind.'

'I just like having my own space. That's fair, isn't it?'

Of course it's fair. I just hate not being able to watch over her. I push my lips together.

'I am beat though,' Lola adds, filling the silence. 'So I might head off to bed now.'

'Me too,' I murmur, although I know I won't be able to sleep. One night, I think, then I'll try again tomorrow to persuade her.

We push back our chairs in unison, and Lola lets me hug her goodnight at the restaurant entrance. Eventually I slacken my grip, and she disappears through the glass doors towards the beach. I walk reluctantly over to the staircase.

'Frankie?'

My shoulders tighten at the sound of Raphael's voice. I turn around. 'Is everything okay?'

'I think I owe you an apology for earlier. It's a lot to take in, seeing you again, after everything that happened. But I think enough time has passed for us to at least be civil to each other.'

I try to hold eye contact with him. The last time I saw Raphael, he angrily accused me of killing Izzy. But he's right that it was a long time ago. Can I trust him now when he says he wants to move on? 'Yes, you're right,' I say carefully. 'And thank you again for the room. Lola's travel documents should be here on Tuesday, and I'll book a flight as soon as they arrive, so we won't take advantage of your hospitality for too long.'

'Actually, I thought you might want to stay for my father's send-off,' he says, his expression too blank to read. 'With Salvo being a childhood friend of your own father's. We're having a gathering to remember him on Thursday evening, in Sartène.'

I don't want to honour Salvo's memory at any time, but especially not on Thursday, the anniversary of Izzy's death, the mazzeri's darkest night. Does Raphael realise the significance of that date? Could he have arranged it on purpose?

'I'm sorry but I barely knew him really,' I say. 'I don't think it would be appropriate for me to attend something like that.'

'Didn't he travel all the way to England to pay his respects to your father?'

I stare at the tip of Raphael's ear until I blink. Salvo did make a big effort to come to my dad's funeral. But then he ruined my life. I don't owe him anything. 'I'll think about it,' I lie.

'Good,' Raphael says. 'By the way, you don't need to use the stairs anymore. We had a lift fitted.'

'The stairs are fine,' I mumble. There's no way I'm going to shut myself inside an airless metal box right now. I climb to the third floor, walk down the corridor to my room, and edge the key in the door. Finally, some peace.

Except.

I see the note before anything else. A white piece of cardboard lying on the light blue carpet. I hold my breath as I read the words, large and bold in black ink. Who the hell would write that?

Who the hell could know?

My vision feels fuzzy suddenly. I had convinced myself that the dream I had in Gatwick Airport was harmless, a sign of my stress, not a premonition of tragedy. But now a note? Clearly a real person is messing with my head.

I slowly reach down. My fingers shake as I pick the note off the floor. The nightmare feels so close that I can almost touch the sticky feathers of the eagle owl. Tears burn my eyes as I read the words again.

Hey, mazzera, did you dream about Lola?
Un, deux, trois …

2004

Frankie

14th July

'I thought today was about celebrating France's freedom,' Harriet muses. 'It looks more like a Halloween parade.'

'Bastille Day, Corsican style,' Dom murmurs, nodding. 'But I guess it wouldn't be a party without a man dressed up as a profusely bleeding wolf.'

I feel my face break into a smile, and I take another sip of my drink – warm beer isn't exactly my go-to choice but Raphael bought a can for each of us, and I'm not going to turn down free alcohol. It was Anna who mentioned that we should experience Porto Vecchio's Bastille Day celebrations together – even though it was blatantly Raphael's idea, him deciding we needed a bit of team bonding after the incident with Felix Drake's finger, then getting his puppet to suggest it because he knew it was his decision not to fire Izzy that was causing the tension. Personally, quietly, I'm relieved that Izzy managed to keep her job, but I know I'm in the minority. And it is true that she really screwed up that day.

Anna doing Raphael's bidding became even more obvious when, at the last minute, she decided not to come. Said someone needed to stay at the hotel, and she was happy to volunteer. The only other person missing from our outing is Izzy, but she's planning to join us later. She's meeting a friend from London who's out here on holiday for a drink first.

For an island that supposedly wants independence from France, they put on a good show for the birth of the republic. The parade has been moving along the blocked-off coastal road for at least half an hour. It started with groups of military personnel, then musicians carrying a selection of instruments, and now there are various people in fancy dress – Marie Antionette arm in arm with Madame Tussaud was quite a sight, especially when Raphael explained that Madame Tussaud made death masks from the corpses of the French nobility to save her own skin. Who knew she'd then make a career out of it.

And now the parade has introduced some macabre history that's more home-grown.

'I think the bleeding wolf is representing the mazzeri,' I explain. 'It's a Corsican legend. My dad told me about it when I was little, and I remember it freaking the hell out of me for a while.'

When I first arrived in Corsica, I didn't want to talk about my dad in case my grief spilled out. But confiding in Izzy eased the secret enough for me to gradually start bringing him up in conversation with the others too. And now both my dad's childhood friendship with Salvo and my Corsican heritage are common knowledge.

'Mazzeri?' Archie repeats. 'What's that then? A bunch of dying animals?'

Salvo is standing next to Raphael on the far side of the group, but I think I see him stiffen. Or maybe I'm imagining how my dad would react if someone spoke disparagingly about a legend that he was brought up to revere. It's nonsense of course, but still, I should tread carefully.

'The mazzeri are dream hunters,' I explain. 'The legend goes that certain people in Corsica have these special powers – they're

138

called mazzere if they're men, and mazzera if they're female.'

'And these mazzeri people hunt dreams?' Harriet asks. 'Because I've got a few I'd like to grab hold of.'

'Not quite.' I take a breath. 'The story is that the mazzeri hunt in their dreams, kill an animal, then just before they wake up, the face of the dead animal changes to that of a human being, generally someone they know. And the dream means that the person they saw is fated to die in real life.'

'Jeez, that is dark,' Archie murmurs.

'They sound more like dream murderers to me,' Jack says.

'They're not murderers,' Salvo grunts. 'They're prophets. And they deserve our respect.'

I look down at my feet. I expected Salvo to take the legend seriously, just like my dad did, so why am I struggling to keep the giggles inside? Perhaps it's because I can sense the same private tussle amongst my friends. It reminds me of Dr Smith's biology lesson when he was trying to work out who'd drawn a bra and tutu on his anatomy poster.

'So these mazzeri,' Dom finally says, and I hope Salvo can't see the smirk in his expression. 'Do they tell whoever they dreamed about that their days are numbered? I mean, I'd want to know if I was about to cark it, so I could go down in a blaze of glory. Wouldn't it be awful if you spent the entire rest of your life finishing a uni assignment or something?'

Archie is the first to giggle, and then I can't keep it in anymore either, followed by Harriet. Dom looks pleased with his altogether different kind of power.

But Salvo seems immune to our laughter. 'Well, that is a personal choice,' he answers. 'Maybe it's kinder to keep the victims in the dark. Knowing you're going to die might be more traumatic than dying itself.'

The mood instantly drops. I think about Salvo's choice of language – keeping the victims in the dark. When I first met him, at my dad's funeral, I thought he was a wise, insightful old man.

But since I've been out here, that wisdom seems more like bitterness, and his insight closer to manipulation. Izzy is convinced he's bad news, and from him badgering me at the midsummer party, it sounds like she did witness something he didn't want her to see. But what? Every time I ask Izzy, she just shrugs and clams up.

'Obviously it is just a folk story,' Raphael says, breaking the silence. 'Which is something my father doesn't always remember, hey, Babba?'

Salvo shrugs, but then jerks slightly as his phone rings. He pulls it out, stares at the handset for a moment as though it's an alien being, then answers the call. He doesn't say much – *d'accord, merci* – but the news can't be welcome, because his face turns to stone. He ends the call and pockets his phone.

'*Raphael, nous allons,*' he barks. Then he weaves through the crowd at speed, with Raphael hurrying after him, a confused expression on his face.

'What the hell was that about?' Dom asks.

'Sometimes it's best not to know,' Jack says.

'What do you mean?' Archie tilts his head. 'You think the Paolis are involved in something illicit?'

Jack rolls his eyes. 'No, I just meant that people deserve their privacy. Anyway, does anyone want another beer? My shout?'

Dom and Archie lift their empty cans, the international symbol for 'yes, please', while I shake my head. I need something colder, and tastier.

As Jack turns, I see Archie reach out to stroke his arm, but Jack jerks away to avoid it. Archie pushes his hand into his pocket and shifts his eyeline away, but I can see that the rejection has upset him. I wonder how I would feel if a boyfriend behaved that way with me. Generous with his affection in private but embarrassed to show it in public. Jack is relaxed enough when it's just the six of us, but maybe this more conservative Corsican crowd is too much for him.

I reach out and stroke Archie's arm myself, showing my

solidarity. He gives me a grateful look, then curls his arm around my shoulder and draws me in.

'I wouldn't want to know,' he says, looking at a group of teenage children running after the parade waving Corsican flags instead of French ones.

'Know what?'

'If I was going to die – I'd prefer to go in blissful ignorance.'

'Okay, noted,' I say, trying to inject some levity. 'If you show up dead in my dreams, I promise to keep it to myself.'

'What a good friend you are.'

I giggle and lean my head on Archie's shoulder. It's dark now, and the clear night sky is busy with flickering stars. 'Just for the record though,' I murmur. 'I would prefer it if you stayed alive.'

'Okay, noted,' Archie says, copying my words.

'Hey, guys!' I feel another body wriggle between Archie and me, Archie's arm sliding away until it drops.

'Hi, Izzy,' I say. 'How's your friend?'

'What? Oh yes, he's good. Anyway, what have I missed?'

I drain the dregs of my can. I thought Izzy said her friend was female, but maybe I heard wrong.

'Oh, just a discussion about dream hunters and whether knowing you've only got a few days to live is a good thing,' Dom says, shrugging with faux nonchalance.

'Wow. Well, it sounds like you need someone to lighten the mood then. Who fancies a Long Island iced tea on me?'

Frankie

14th July

Izzy drops her chin on my shoulder and rests her empty plastic glass in the crook of my elbow. A stage has been set up on the wide path in front of the Porto Vecchio marina, and a big crowd is gathering around us as four men in white suits belt out cheesy cover songs.

'What's the band called again?' Izzy asks, shouting into my ear to make herself heard above the noise.

'Eastlife,' I say. 'I think they're a Westlife tribute band.'

'Well, that explains a lot,' she says with a sigh. 'Shall we get another drink before the fireworks? Did you say they were starting at ten?'

I look at my watch. It's 9.30 p.m. I was the only one to accept Izzy's offer of a Long Island iced tea – the others preferring to wait for Jack to return with the beers – so it's just been the two of us milling around for the last hour. I wonder if I should suggest we find the rest of them. It is supposed to be a team night out after all, and I wouldn't mind checking on Archie. The more I see him and Jack together, the more I worry that Archie is going to end up getting hurt.

'Yeah cool. We might bump into the others around the bar area too.'

'Maybe,' Izzy says, shrugging while flashing me one of her light-up-the-sky smiles.

We push through the crowd towards the bar and I join the five-deep queue. As I shuffle forwards, I feel a tap on my shoulder, and turn around to see Archie, a couple of people behind me.

'Oh, hey,' I say, smiling. 'I was hoping to bump into you. Is everything okay?'

'Listen, is there any chance you could order drinks for Jack and me?' he asks. 'And I'll return the favour later? We don't want to miss the fireworks.'

I look beyond Archie, but I can't see Jack anywhere, and a flame of annoyance lights up in my belly. Him treating Archie like his skivvy. But that's not fair – I'm buying a drink for Izzy, and it doesn't make her my servant. 'Of course I can. Long Island iced tea?' It's a bit crazy that our default drink of the summer has five different spirits in it, but it's become so routine that its potency hardly registers.

'Brilliant, thanks,' Archie says, his smile strengthening a notch. 'Next round is on me.'

'Are you buying Jack a drink?' Izzy hisses in my ear.

I hadn't realised that she'd followed me into the queue and I sigh. I know Izzy doesn't like Jack, but she has never explained why. And the weird thing is, when everyone else (except me) was calling for her to be sacked after the Felix Drake incident, Jack stood up for her. Reminded us all – in his usual blunt way – that everyone makes mistakes and maybe we should cut her some slack. But when I relayed this to Izzy later, it seemed to make her more angry with him, not less.

'Yes. Because we work with him,' I say, as patiently as I can manage. 'And he's Archie's boyfriend. And I could hardly say no, could I?'

143

I reach the front of the bar and concentrate on catching the bartender's eye. When he looks over, I give him my order, then watch him mix the spirits and pour the liquid over four glasses of ice with Coke and lime. I hand over the money with a grimace – it's three times what we pay at the hotel – then hand two drinks to Izzy and together we snake back through the crowd.

We do a weird drink exchange where Archie takes one from me, then Izzy passes me one of her two, so Jack has to get his drink from me too. It's petty, and I don't blame Jack for swearing under his breath. He takes a couple of gulps without looking at any of us.

'Cheers,' Archie says, knocking his glass against mine and Izzy's, as though it might ease the awkwardness. But Izzy only manages a half-smile before looking away too.

'Where's everyone else?' I ask, wondering if a bigger group would make things easier, or if we should admit defeat and go our separate ways again.

'I haven't seen Raphael since Salvo marched him off after taking that call,' Archie says. 'Dom and Harriet are around though. We were with them until we came to get a drink.'

'Maybe they're getting friendly,' Izzy suggests, lifting her eyebrows. 'I mean, Dom's got form, hasn't he? And Harriet is so competitive. I bet she'd love to get one up on you, Frankie.'

'There's no way Dom would do anything with Harriet,' Archie says. He looks at me, as though I need the reassurance, which is crazy because Archie knows exactly how I feel about Dom – he's been my cover story on both occasions that Dom has quietly asked if I want to go for a drink with him.

'Sorry, was that Izzy making up stories again?' Jack mutters. 'You need to be careful, Izzy, don't want to get a reputation as the boy who cried wolf.'

Izzy stares at him. 'Don't worry, I can be deadly honest when I choose to be.'

Jack's face darkens and he pushes his lips together.

'Come on, Jack,' Archie says, pulling gently on his arm. 'Let's go and find a spot to watch the fireworks. Thanks for the drink, Frankie. We owe you.'

Jack resists for a few seconds, then shakes his head, and allows Archie to pull him into the crowd.

I turn to Izzy. 'Come on, you have to tell me what the hell is going on with you two.'

'Trust me, you don't want to know.'

'I do! One minute you're giving him the cold shoulder, then you act like you're scared of him. When he defends you, you treat it like an insult. And now he's accusing you of being a liar. Come on, Izzy, help me out here.'

Izzy takes a long gulp of her drink, then sighs. 'Look, I overheard something about Jack. It was by accident, and I really wish I didn't know. But sadly, that's not how knowledge works.'

'What did you hear?'

'I can't tell you.'

'Well, where did you hear it?'

'I can't tell you that either. It would give away too much.'

'Izzy, all this cloak-and-dagger stuff. I don't understand. It can't be that bad?'

'It is, okay?' Izzy throws back. 'And then I got drunk and shot my mouth off at that midsummer party. Jack told me to keep quiet, or else.'

'What do you mean, or else? If he's threatened you, you need to tell Raphael.'

Izzy shakes her head like I'm stupid. 'How can I when I need to keep it all a secret? And anyway, I'm not sure Raphael would listen.'

'Of course he would! You're one hundred per cent his favourite.' I don't add that the rest of the team think it's juicier than that, that Izzy and Raphael are sleeping together, and that's the sole reason she kept her job.

'I don't know,' she mutters. 'He seems to love Jack. Christ

145

knows why.'

'Maybe I could say something then?' I suggest, changing tack.

Izzy sighs again. 'No, it's fine. I don't want you to get involved. But it's for your sake though – you do understand that?'

'Yeah, I guess,' I say, trying not to feel offended that Izzy doesn't trust me to keep her secret.

'There you are!'

I look up at the sound of Dom's voice.

'Been searching for you everywhere.' He twists, shouts into the crowd. 'Hey, Harriet! I've found them!' Then he turns back. 'Are you coming to watch the band? I was thinking of attempting a crowd surf when they play "You Raise Me Up". Do you get it? Raise me up?'

Despite what Izzy has just told me, the corners of my mouth lift into a smile. Dom beams back.

'Hey, look who I spotted in the crowd,' Harriet says as she appears, arms linked with Archie on one side, and Jack on the other. 'The fireworks are starting soon, so we should head back to the marina, get the best view of them.'

'Not until they've sung "Flying Without Wings",' Dom says, shaking his head with mock seriousness. 'That's our special song, isn't it, Frankie? Damn, it gets me right here.' Dom punches his chest.

'Oh for fuck's sake, Dom!' Izzy pushes forward, turns to face him. 'I'm so bored of this! Frankie doesn't like you, okay?' she shouts. 'She slept with you because she was drunk, and then regretted it as soon as she woke up the next morning. Which isn't surprising because you're a fucking idiot. So stop hassling her!'

I hold my breath. Nobody moves. Izzy is just repeating what I've told her, at least the sentiment if not the words. But it sounds so much worse outside of our room. Am I mad with her for telling him? Or grateful?

'Is that true?' Dom finally asks, his voice suddenly quiet.

As I turn my head towards him, I take in everyone else's

expressions. Sympathy on Archie's face, curiosity on Harriet's, bemusement on Jack's. Only Izzy's is unreadable.

And finally, my eyes reach Dom. His cheeks are glowing pink and there's a moisture in his eyes that wasn't there before. Izzy's words were harsh, but their meaning was accurate, and I owe him the truth.

'I guess so,' I say quietly. 'But not about …'

But it's too late to finish the sentence. Dom has disappeared into the crowd.

Frankie

29th July

I walk along the uneven path and stare at the rucksack on Dom's back as he leads us towards the waterfalls. How can I have let things get to this? The last two weeks have been excruciating. We speak without eye contact, put on a show of camaraderie for the guests, but work in terse silence when they're not around. After Bastille Day, I tried to apologise, to explain, but Dom shut me down every time. Izzy told me to stop trying, that Dom just needed to grow up a bit. But it's hard. Even if I didn't want anything more, I miss our friendship.

After all the acrimony of the last few weeks, I don't really understand why we still spend our day off together as a group. But here we are. Maybe people cling to what's familiar when they're away from home, or it could just be habit.

'How much further?' Harriet whines from behind me. The sun is beating down hard, and the temperature must be at least thirty degrees despite the tree cover around us. We've been walking for nearly an hour, and the only thing that's keeping me going is the thought of diving into the promised pool of fresh water. It sounds like Harriet feels the same way.

'I'm pretty sure we're close now,' Dom calls out without turning around. 'Izzy, I assume you can't remember the route.'

'Correct,' Izzy calls back merrily.

It was Dom's idea to spend the day at the waterfalls. Dom and Izzy were the first of the waterfront team to arrive at the resort, back in May when the hotel was still quiet. On their first day off, Raphael brought them out here, along with two of his cousins who were visiting from the mainland. Izzy has never given the outing more than a passing mention, but Dom loved it, and he's been trying to get us all to visit ever since. I was the first to say yes when he suggested it this morning – another attempt to thaw his anger with me – but he didn't even register that I had spoken.

The path veers left, and Dom disappears for a minute. When Izzy and I catch up, he's standing still, staring at the view. And I can see why. The path has brought us to a stunning oasis of dark cliffs and plummeting water. A semicircle of tapered waterfalls splutter and dance towards the promised rock pool, and madly, a mix of pink and lilac wildflowers curl up through the cracks in the rockface. There's a border of conifer trees across the top with the sun shimmering through the branches.

'Pretty special, isn't it?' Dom says.

'It's beautiful.' I watch Dom start to smile at my words, then change his mind.

'Wow, what a view!' Archie says as he and Jack catch up with us. 'God, that water is calling my name.'

'Mine too,' Harriet says, dropping her bag on a flat section of rock and shimmying out of her shorts.

'Not so fast, kids,' Dom says, lifting his hand, a grin now returning to his face. 'You don't just get in the water.'

'What?' Harriet screws up her face. 'Why not?'

'You have to jump in; sorry, but it's the law. There are three levels. Easy, pulse-raiser and death zone. You're welcome to take your pick, but just so you know, I did all three levels last time.'

Dom flexes his biceps and winks.

'What about you, Izzy?' Jack asks. 'Did you enter the death zone?'

'If I remember rightly, Izzy didn't make it past easy, did you?' Dom's tone carries his signature humour, but there's a hardness in his eyes. She's not forgiven either.

'I don't need silly stunts to prove my worth.'

'Little defensive there, Izzy,' Jack says with a smirk. 'Well, I'm up for the death zone, mate, if you are?'

'Bring. It. On.' Dom gives Jack a high five and they both pull off their T-shirts. I've seen Dom's torso countless times over the last couple of months, so I should be immune to his tanned flat stomach, the faint shadow of a six-pack, but the sight makes me pause today. Is this about him taking on the hardest cliff jump? Am I that easily impressed?

'I'll do the death zone too,' I blurt out. This goes against everything my mum has taught me – every risk should be calculated, every challenge thoroughly assessed – but I've said it now. And I'm not taking it back.

'Arch?' Jack asks. 'You coming?'

Archie looks mortified, which makes me feel even worse. I don't want to make it harder for him to say no.

'Maybe later,' he chooses. 'Might warm myself up with the easy jump.'

Jack looks both disappointed and annoyed as he turns back towards Dom. 'So how do we get up there?'

'Follow me.' Dom turns to me and shrugs. 'You too, I guess.'

My heart is pounding when we reach the top of the cliff, and I don't know how much of that is down to the steep climb, Dom's hand reaching for mine as I faltered on the final stretch of rock, or the realisation of what I'm about to do. Apparently, the water is sixteen metres below, but it looks about six thousand metres from this angle. And to make things even more challenging, the cliff has a few protruding crags that I'll need to clear. I can see why Dom called it the death zone.

'Are you okay?' Dom murmurs under his breath. There's the smallest edge of concern in his voice and the joy of hearing it, of the thought that he might be on the path to forgiving me, makes me feel instantly better.

'Yeah, maybe a bit scared,' I admit in a whisper.

'You'll be fine,' he whispers back. 'You're the best athlete here.'

Tears shine in my eyes, but with gratitude, not fear.

'Fucking hell, what a ride.' Jack peers over the edge.

'Welcome to the death zone,' Dom says, his voice back to full volume.

'If I die, will you tell my mum I'm sorry?'

'What for?'

'Mate, you don't want to know.' Jack lets out a crack of laughter, then leaps off the rock. His jump isn't elegant, and his splash would have him banned from the Olympics for life, but he comes up whooping.

'You go next,' Dom says. 'Look out at the horizon, take a big step, and let gravity do the rest.'

I nod, because I can't talk, and edge into position. As I force myself to look at the cliff opposite, I wonder if Salvo ever brought my dad here when they were teenagers. If Dad balanced on this rock and felt the same mix of excitement and terror.

I jump.

And almost before registering that I'm dropping, I hit the water, and then I'm surging back up, a huge grin on my face. Archie claps, and I can see fraternal pride in his expression until Jack walks into my line of vision and sits down opposite him. I swim to the edge, push up out of the water, and turn to watch Dom jump.

He clears the crags easily, then drops into the water, and I wait for him to pop up.

Except he doesn't.

I check to see if the others have noticed. But Jack and Archie are deep in conversation now, and Izzy and Harriet are soaking

151

up the sun with their eyes closed. I realise with a clattering heart that this is my problem to fix. But just as I jump back into the water, Dom emerges, his hand holding his head.

'Fuck,' I exhale, my eyes widening. Bright red liquid is streaming down his face from an angry gash on his forehead.

'I'm fine, I think,' he says, wiping blood out of his eyes.

He looks awful. Like Bruce Willis in *Die Hard*. I tell myself that head wounds bleed a lot, and cold water makes it worse, but the rationalising doesn't help. 'Jesus, Dom. It looks bad. What happened? Does it hurt?'

More blood has dripped onto his cheeks, and without thinking, I reach out to wipe it off, but he jerks his head away. I retract my hand like a scared tortoise.

'Stop it,' he says quietly. 'Stop pretending you care.'

'But I thought …' My voice fades. Because what did I think? That Dom being kind to me up there – when all he was probably doing was making sure I jumped – means that he's forgiven me for humiliating him in front of our friends?

'It's just a cut,' he mutters. 'Cold beer will sort me out.' He swims to the edge of the pool, then climbs out. I wait a minute, then follow him and silently lay my towel next to Izzy's.

'Who's up for a drink then?' Dom says, wiping his face with a towel. 'And before you ask, no, I'm not dying.'

'Any rosé in that cooler box?' Harriet asks, lifting onto her elbows, and narrowing her eyes as she takes in Dom's injury without commenting on it.

'Sure is,' Dom says, pulling out a bottle and handing it to her. 'Jack? Archie?'

'Yeah, I'll go a cold one,' Jack says, pushing up to standing and wandering over, seemingly oblivious to Dom's bleeding head.

'Not for me,' Archie says, without even looking at Dom. 'In fact, I'm not feeling that great. I might head back to the hotel.'

Dom looks a little offended as he wipes his forehead again. 'You sure, mate?'

'Yeah, I just need some sleep.'

Archie does look pale. I try to catch his eye as he pulls his T-shirt on, but he keeps his head lowered, even as he lifts his hand into a wave. So I turn to Jack instead, who's wearing a stony expression as he downs a can of lager.

And it isn't until after Archie's left that I realise they didn't say goodbye to each other.

Frankie

29th July

I'm mildly buzzed when I get back to the hotel. Izzy, Harriet and I worked our way through two bottles of rosé at the water-falls, each cupful making us feel more confident until we finally persuaded Izzy to jump from the pulse-raiser. I tried to enjoy myself – forget about Dom's rejection and live in the moment – but my heart wasn't really in it, so I was grateful when we packed up and retraced our steps down the path.

'We should grab some dinner before showering,' I say. 'Chefs will clear it away soon and I'm starving.'

'Good idea,' Harriet says. 'Need something to soak up all that water I swallowed. Not to mention the rosé.'

Izzy looks at her watch, then turns to me. 'Sorry but I'm going to have to run. I'm meeting a friend in half an hour, and I need to get myself ready. I'll grab something to eat while I'm out.'

'A friend or a date?' Harriet asks, tilting her head.

Izzy gives her a sardonic smile, but her cheeks turn a subtle shade of pink. 'Let's call it a date with a friend,' she says. 'Anyway, I better go.' She lifts her hand into a wave, then scoots off before

I have chance to interrogate her further.

'That girl cannot be trusted,' Harriet murmurs. 'Always talking in riddles.'

'Because she's got a date with a friend?' I say, shaking my head. My default is always to defend Izzy, but inside, I can't help feeling hurt that she's out again without telling me who with. I thought we shared our secrets, but there's seems to be an increasing amount that she's not willing to tell me. Maybe our friendship isn't as solid as I thought. Except it's Izzy who's always talking about us being kindred spirits, not me.

'Come on, let's eat,' I mutter, then head towards the door to the staffroom.

Harriet scurries to catch up. 'No, Izzy can't be trusted because she won't tell us who that friend is,' she says. 'And she's happy for a little boy to lose his finger, and she manipulated you into humiliating Dom, and she's always such a bitch to Jack, and she talks about lying like it's a competitive sport.'

I sigh. 'Look, I'm tired and hungry, so can we just eat?'

Harriet shrugs, like she's got nothing more to say anyway. We reach the serving table, and stare at the offering. A bowl of radishes, the rind of a brie and a few baguette ends. We take what we can, then fall into one of the tatty sofas to eat.

Twenty minutes later, my hunger has abated just enough for drowsiness to kick in. It's only eight o'clock, but it's been a long day of exercise, alcohol and not enough calories, and I'm pretty sure I could sleep a full twelve hours if I closed my eyes. Harriet has started talking to one of the barmen who's on his break, so I just wave goodbye and head outside.

The sun is low as I walk along the beach, and the sea is glowing a pinkish orange under its mellow rays. The whole vista has a warmth to it, and I try to use it to buoy me. Whatever Dom said in the water, we *did* have a conversation before I jumped, and he *was* kind and thoughtful. Surely that's a sign of hope that he might forgive me.

155

When I get to the accommodation block, I realise I'm enjoying the beach too much to go inside, so I keep walking instead. Beyond the reach of the hotel, the beach gets quieter, and wilder, with pockets of scrubland and tangles of seaweed sprawled across the sand. As well as the salt in the sea breeze, I can smell something sweet and floral. Maybe there are myrtle bushes in the woodland beyond the beach.

I keep walking. It feels much more remote out here, and I jump when I hear the lisped screech of someone whistling through their fingers. It's hard to see who it is because the sun is so low that it's blinding, but I can just make out the silhouette of a man at the water's edge.

'Hey, Frankie!'

The silhouette waves but more than that, I recognise the voice. It's Archie. I pull off my flip-flops and pad towards him. But as I get closer, I slow my pace, because he's got a half-drunk bottle of Mirto Bianco in his hand – a local digestif that I've not tried – and he's swaying. 'Hey, Archie.'

'Want a drink?' He hands me the bottle and something in his manner tells me not to refuse, so I take a swig. It tastes bitter and herby and makes my eyes water, but I take a second gulp anyway, then hand it back.

'I thought you were ill?' I say carefully.

'Me? No, I'm not ill,' he says, the words slurring. He points at me with the bottle. 'I think you've been misinformed.'

'But you said—'

'That I wasn't feeling great?' he interrupts, his voice suddenly more clipped. 'It's amazing how we can twist words, manipulate people into thinking we're saying something we're not.'

'I don't understand.'

'No, you wouldn't,' Archie says bitterly. I watch him take another couple of gulps from the bottle.

'Can I have some more?' It feels like the best way to slow him down. I reach for the bottle, take a sip, and when I feel his eyes

156

bore into my cheek, I take another one.

'Can I have it back now?'

'Yeah, in a minute.' I drink again. It's not actually too bad, but my head is starting to swim. Rosé, and adrenaline, and not enough food. I shouldn't really be drinking at all, but I'm not going to leave Archie in this state by himself. 'So what made you feel not great?' I ask.

Archie sighs. 'Jack wanted to tell me something. He said it was time.'

I look at his distraught expression, remember Jack's disappointment in Archie at the waterfalls. 'Has he broken up with you?' I whisper.

But then I jump as Archie lets out a crack of laughter. 'If only it were that.'

Frankie

29th July

'Well, what then?' I try again. 'What was it time for?'

Archie sighs. 'I told Jack I loved him last night. It freaked him out, which freaked me out. Anyway, we had a long talk, and eventually he admitted that he felt the same way, just found it harder to say out loud.'

'Well, that's good, isn't it?'

Archie looks at me and there are tears in his eyes. 'I thought so, but then today he told me that if we were going to commit to each other, there was something I needed to know.'

I think about Izzy's words on Bastille Day, the information she'd overheard about Jack. 'And what was that?' I ask, not sure I want to hear the answer anymore.

'I wish I could tell you,' he says, dropping onto his haunches and staring out to sea. 'But the crazy thing is, I'm scared to.'

The sun is just a sliver on the horizon now. Any moment, it will disappear, and then darkness will follow. Izzy refused to tell me what she knew about Jack because it felt like too much of a risk. And now Archie's scared of confiding in me too?

'Did he do something?' I ask quietly, dropping down next to Archie.

'I thought I knew him.' He takes the bottle off me and pours more of the fiery liquid down his throat. 'I mean, we'd talked about his rough childhood. He'd been in trouble with the police when he was a kid, but nothing serious. Possession. Anti-social behaviour. Stuff like that. And he'd fallen out with his family, but that's nothing new for a gay kid coming out.'

'We're all running away from something, I suppose,' I say, thinking about my dad, and wishing I'd tried harder to get to know him when I still had the chance. I reach for the bottle, then realise it's empty. The sky is a faded shade of night now, the last of the day's light slipping away, but Archie must notice the disappointment on my face, because he crawls towards the water and pulls another bottle out of the sand.

'Where did that come from?' I ask with a mix of surprise and admiration. I take the bottle and drink a few generous mouthfuls.

'Sand keeps it cold. I was a Boy Scout once,' Archie says with a drunken, sheepish grin.

I smile, then giggle, then my body starts bouncing with belly laughter. A moment later, Archie is laughing too, and we collapse onto the sand on our backs like little kids, our heads touching. 'No one likes Izzy except me,' I finally say. 'Does that make me a bad judge of character?'

Archie tries to whistle, but it comes out like a wild wind. 'Jeez, you are asking the wrong person.'

'And she doesn't like Jack,' I continue. A tiny voice in my head tells me to shut up, but a louder one shouts that Archie should know this. 'She overheard something about him.'

Archie sits up, twists towards me. 'What did she hear?'

'She wouldn't tell me, but she thinks he's dangerous. But I don't know, maybe she's lying.' I curl my body up to sitting, register how hard the movement was. I feel dizzy again, and I wonder if I'm going to be sick.

'I don't think she's lying,' Archie says grimly.

I listen to the familiar glug-glug of him drinking from the bottle. I reach out, curl my fingers around the cool glass, and do the same. 'Has Jack done something to you?' I ask quietly. 'Has he hurt you?' Some movement out at sea catches my eye and I turn to look. It's dark now, only a few stars peeking around clouds, so the water looks black. It's a fishing boat probably, cruising across the water, the hum of its engine just audible above the lapping of the waves.

'No, something worse,' Archie murmurs.

'What could be worse than that?' The boat noise gets louder, and now I can see it, coming into shore, further down the beach.

'You promise not to tell anyone? Because I told Jack I'd take his secret to the grave.'

'Of course.' I take another gulp.

'Christ, I need a drink.' Archie grabs the bottle and keeps drinking until I pull it off him.

'Hey, easy!'

Archie looks so angry that, for a second, I think it's him shouting. But then I realise the noise is coming from further away. The fishing boat is up on the shore now, and there's a bunch of men walking towards it, squabbling like seagulls. One of them looks as drunk as Archie, being dragged along by his mates.

'Jack tried to kill his family, Frankie.'

My head spins round. 'What did you say?'

'They were arguing, and his dad said some things, and Jack stormed out. But he went back that night, put a petrol bomb through their letterbox.'

'Oh my God.' In my drunken state, his revelation struggles to land. But two words pound at my temples. Bomb. Family. I don't know what I expected – a fight maybe, a criminal record possibly – but not this. The attempted murder of the people he's supposed to love the most.

In the distance, there's a thud, another shouting match,

followed by the noise of the boat powering off. But I don't take my eyes off Archie.

'He regretted it instantly, at least that's what he told me, and woke them all up and got them out. No one was hurt, but their flat was ruined. All of their stuff gone.'

'But that's arson,' I whisper. 'Attempted murder. Why isn't he in prison?'

'Because his family kept quiet, and someone helped him get out of the country before the police could work it out.' Archie's voice breaks as tears start to roll down his face. 'I don't know who, but I don't really care either. What I care about is that I've fallen in love with a man who tried to kill his own family.

'And what the hell does that say about me?'

Frankie

30th July

The cold wakes me up. I shiver, my body jerking in its search for warmth. My stomach roils, and my body jerks again, but this time I'm retching. I twist onto all fours and spew liquid vomit onto the sand. I close my eyes to stop them watering, but all I can feel is my brain knocking against my skull. I throw up again.

How did I let myself get into this state?

And what the hell am I doing on the beach in the middle of the night?

Gradually, my stomach unclenches. I twist onto my backside and pull my knees up to my chest. I desperately want to go back to my room, to crawl into bed and sleep for days, but the accommodation block feels so very far away. Too difficult a feat. With blurred vision, I stare at the sea and take tentative steps backwards in my mind.

Archie was drunk. Upset. I drank that shitty local booze with him.

Why was he upset?

Jack. His rough childhood.

Bomb. Family. Suddenly I imagine a burst of flames, a family screaming in fear.

Adrenaline surges through me and I push onto my feet. I look around, but there's no sign of Archie. Where did he go? I screw my face up in concentration, but nothing comes. My memory of the night ends with him dropping that bombshell. It's hard to believe that Archie would leave me out here, but then he was more drunk than me, and distraught. He wouldn't have been thinking straight. Maybe he forgot I was here and wandered off to bed.

I look up the beach, towards the accommodation block. It still feels like an impossible task, but at least I'm on my feet now. Maybe I can make it. One step at a time.

Sometime later – who knows how long, I've lost all concept of time – I stumble up to the block's door and push down the handle. I expect the hallway to be dark and silent, and I'm desperate for sleep, so when I walk into blinding light, I close my eyes, and the next moment, I'm crying. I drop my face into my hands, then fold like a deflated balloon onto the floor.

'Oh my God, Frankie! We were so worried!' Izzy drops down next to me and curls an arm around my shoulder. 'Harriet said you were coming straight here from supper, but when I got back you were nowhere to be seen!'

'I got waylaid,' I murmur.

'Until four in the morning?!' Izzy wails. 'What happened to you? You look terrible.'

I find the strength to lift my head and open my eyes. Harriet is leaning against the wall opposite. Her face is ashen, like she was genuinely worried about me. It's more than I would expect from her, and I feel a stirring of gratitude. 'Is Archie here?' I ask.

'Archie?' Izzy repeats. 'I don't know. Why?'

'Were you with him?' Harriet asks.

I nod. 'I took a walk down the beach after supper,' I start.

'Towards town?' Izzy asks.

'No, the other way. It's really peaceful out there, and I guess I

163

kept walking. But then I found Archie, and he had some booze. We got talking and ...'

'You got hammered and fell asleep,' Harriet finishes for me.

'Except Archie wasn't there when I woke up. He was pretty drunk. I'm scared he's wandered off and got lost.'

'How far down the beach were you?' Izzy asks.

'Maybe half an hour,' I mumble, trying to remember. 'But it was really remote. We didn't see anyone.' I shake my head, and some vague memory of guys shouting slithers out. 'If Archie fell,' I go on. 'Hit his head or whatever, there'd be no one to find him.'

'Surely it's more likely that he stumbled back here, like you did,' Izzy says, curling my hair around my ear. 'I bet he's fast asleep in bed now. And you look exhausted. Let's figure out what happened in the morning.'

'But what if he hasn't found his way back? It's pretty cold out there.'

'Guys, this is an easy problem to solve,' Harriet says, pushing off the wall. She walks over to Jack and Archie's door and raps her knuckles against it. When no one answers, she does it again, louder. But still nothing.

'Try the handle,' I suggest. 'He was drunk enough to forget to lock it.'

Harriet nods, and it seems I'm proved right, because the door swings open. But Harriet doesn't walk inside. Instead, she turns and gives us a nervous look. 'It's empty. Archie isn't in there, and neither is Jack.'

A cold shiver runs through me. Archie's words, coming back to haunt me. *The crazy thing is, I'm scared to tell you.* Has Jack somehow found out that Archie confided in me? Has he done something to him?

'We need to go and look for him.' I push up to standing. The world shifts left and right and I swallow a wave of nausea.

'No way.' Izzy shakes her head. 'We all have work tomorrow, and Jack and Archie are big boys now. They can look after themselves.'

164

'But you said that Jack was …'

'Shut up, Frankie.' Izzy gives me a warning glare.

'I'll help you look,' Harriet says. 'Give me a sec to get my torch.' She pushes on her own bedroom door and disappears for a moment.

'Have you told Archie what I said about Jack?' Izzy whispers, her voice low but intense.

'No, of course not,' I lie, a tremor building in my spine. 'I promised I wouldn't.'

Izzy nods, satisfied, I think.

'Ready to go?' Harriet says, emerging from her room. 'Oh, and I thought you could use a jumper.'

I catch the Helly Hansen hoodie that Harriet throws at me and pull it over my T-shirt. It feels like a hug. 'Are you coming?' I ask, turning to Izzy.

'Of course.' She unfurls from the floor, and we set off, Harriet leading with her torch. We retrace my steps slowly, with Harriet constantly casting light across the beach, from the sea to the trees. Eventually we reach the indent in the sand where I slept.

'What now?' Harriet asks.

'I still think that Archie's with Jack somewhere,' Izzy says. 'It's the only thing that makes sense. Otherwise, where's Jack?'

'Maybe you're right,' I say. Archie was broken after his conversation with Jack, traumatised. But perhaps he was also drunk enough to go looking for him. 'There's no footprints in the wet sand, thank God, but can we walk home through the woodland? It's only up there.' I gesture towards the black mass at the top of the beach. 'Just in case he stumbled in there and fell over a tree root or whatever.'

Izzy rolls her eyes, but turns away from the sea, and we walk up the beach to the treeline. Harriet shines her torch into the dark woodland, and the spooky glow reminds me of that terrifying film *The Blair Witch Project*. I take a step closer to Izzy.

We walk through the woodland, close together, heads twisting over shoulders whenever we hear a noise. After ten or fifteen minutes, I start to relax a little. But then something in the trees lights up.

Harriet screams, drops the torch, stumbles backwards, falls on her backside.

My heart booms. What was it? I pick the torch out of the scrub, lift it with quivering fingers. The image stutters and shakes, but not enough to ease the horror of what I'm seeing.

Archie's limp body. Hanging from a branch by his belt.

Frankie

30th July

I haven't slept in over twenty-four hours. Have barely eaten. My body feels broken. But how can I possibly sleep now? When every time I close my eyes, I see Archie?

Izzy and Harriet handled everything. Got me back to the accommodation block. Woke up Raphael and Anna. Told Dom. Izzy eventually found Jack in the staffroom, asleep on one of the sofas. He told her that he'd been at a bar in town, hadn't seen Archie all night. Apparently, he broke down when Izzy told him the news, sobbed on her shoulder. I can't believe she let him – she's supposed to hate him and might even know what he did to his family – but maybe the suicide of a loved one transcends all that.

Suicide. That's what the police said. And it makes sense in a way. Archie was drunk, emotional. He'd just found out something terrible about the man he loved.

But choosing to end his life? He was only twenty-two. He'd just graduated from university. He was funny, kind, thoughtful, clever. A brilliant windsurfer and an even better friend. Wasn't that enough? Didn't all that cancel out the one mistake of falling for the wrong guy?

If Izzy knew what drove Archie to it, Jack's confession yesterday, I bet she wouldn't have offered her shoulder. But do I tell her the truth? Or has enough harm been done already?

And why didn't I do more to keep him alive?

I strip off my clothes and pull on a swimsuit. Then I grab a towel and walk out of my room. I head for the sea. The water sports hut has a sign outside – *due to unforeseen circumstances, there will be no water sports today* – in Anna's handwriting. While Raphael deals with the police, Anna is in crisis-management mode, working hard to keep the guests happy. I didn't think she had it in her.

I don't stop when I reach the shoreline, and soon I'm chest-deep in water. I pick up my feet and let my head drop under. I want the cold water to calm the burning grief inside me, but it has no impact. I reach forward with my arms and start swimming.

Why did I get so drunk? Archie was upset. He needed a friend, someone to look after him. But instead, I took his bottle and drank until I passed out. Of course he would feel abandoned after that. Lonely. The man he loved had just admitted to the attempted murder of his own family, and I'd left Archie to deal with that all by himself.

Does that mean Archie's suicide was Jack's fault? Or mine?

I dive underwater. Swim until my eyes burn and my lungs threaten to explode. Should I keep going? Apologise to Archie in the most genuine, unequivocal way?

God, I'm tired. I could just …

I feel a scratch at my back, and then I'm being hoisted up through the water. I splutter and flail as I reach the surface. I flick my hair and turn towards the shadow.

'Climb in, Francesa,' Salvo says. 'I'll take you back to shore.'

I blink, tread water, unsure what to do. Unable to make a decision.

He gestures with his head. 'Come on.' And the instruction is so clear and simple, and I'm so tired and broken, that I follow it, laying my hands on the edge of his little fishing boat, and letting him help me aboard. Its wooden bottom is dented and stained red from years of catching and gutting fish, and I stumble over it to reach the seat. I sit down and pull my knees towards my chest.

Salvo starts the engine, and we move slowly towards the beach. 'I'm sorry about your friend,' he mutters. 'It is a terrible business.'

'I was the last person to see him alive,' I whisper, not sure why I'm confiding in this old man who scares me. 'He was drunk, upset,' I go on. 'But I didn't think for a second …'

'You can't blame yourself, Francesca,' Salvo says softly.

'I keep replaying the scenes in my mind, you know? Sitting on the beach together, sharing a bottle of some dodgy local digestif, watching the waves. It was peaceful, just us.' I think about the men we saw, the boat. 'Well, almost just us. There were some fishermen arguing over a guy so drunk he couldn't stand up. But that felt right, somehow. Like it was a metaphor for how we were feeling.'

Salvo hesitates, like he's weighing up how best to respond. 'How was Archie when you parted ways?'

I look down at my feet, ashamed. 'I don't remember. I fell asleep on the sand, and when I woke up, he was gone.'

Salvo nods slowly. 'And how did you feel when you woke up?'

I remember my body retching, quickly followed by me vomiting. 'Terrible. And scared.'

'You were worried about your friend.'

I look up at Salvo, grateful, in the moment, for his compassion. 'It was like I already knew something bad had happened to him.'

'A sixth sense.'

The tension in my shoulders eases a notch. 'Yes, that's it.'

'You foresaw it, Francesca.'

'What?'

'You know, many years ago someone who I cared about deeply died,' Salvo continues. 'And I still feel guilty.'

'Oh, I'm sorry,' I say, my tired brain struggling with this new information. 'What happened?'

'I thought warning him was the right thing to do. And maybe it was, I'll never know. But I wish I hadn't. I wish I'd let fate run its course.'

'Fate?'

'I think you dreamed about Archie last night.'

'Maybe,' I murmur. 'I don't remember.'

'Francesca, did you know that your father was a mazzere?'

'Wait, what?' I look up, my eyes stretched wide. 'Do you mean the mazzeri legend?'

Salvo nods. 'He confided in me a long time ago. That's why he wanted to leave Corsica, to get away from its influence. When I had my mazzeri dream, years later, I thought about trying to find him, but I never did.'

'But the mazzeri aren't real,' I say, my voice raspy. I think about the stories my dad told me when I was little, the magical hunters gliding through make-believe forests. But they were only ever stories.

'They are real,' Salvo growls. Then he sighs and softens his voice. 'I can't know for sure if you've inherited your father's gift, if you are a mazzera and dreamed about Archie dying. But I know the mazzeri exist in Corsica. How could I not believe in them when I am one myself?'

My skin feels tight from the salt water, and my eyes sting. Dry land is only a few metres away now. I stare at it. I need to get away from Salvo, from the nonsense he's spewing. Because of course the mazzeri aren't real. And the foreboding I felt when I woke on the sand wasn't any kind of premonition. Was it?

Frankie

31st July

The sky is inky black, the air cool against my skin. I walk towards the forest. My feet are bare, but I feel no pain from the sharp stones or rough foliage underfoot. A cloud moves, exposing the full moon, its white light casting an ethereal glow, until the sky changes again, and darkness sweeps back over.

I walk deeper into the forest.

I'm here to hunt, I think, with a sudden, overpowering burst of desire.

To kill.

I slide my open palms down from my hip bones. There it is. The sheath, protecting the weapon hanging heavy against my leg. I curl my fingers around the knife's handle, grip hard. I close my eyes, imagine slaughtering an animal, feel a quiver of anticipation in my chest.

There's rustling between the trees. My eyelids flick up, just in time to see the deer. Small, and beautiful. Perfect prey.

Except I have the wrong weapon. To kill with a knife, I need to catch the deer, and that isn't possible. It will outrun me.

Except I know, deep inside, that it won't.

I edge closer. Even in this dense forest, my footsteps are soundless. The deer knows I'm near; it can smell me. But it doesn't move. As though it understands, accepts its fate.

Our eyes catch and I don't hesitate. I grab the knife, lift it high, sink it into the deer's chest. The animal whimpers, drops to its knees. Its head lolls, life ebbing away, then falls onto its side.

I wait. I don't know what for, but I remain still.

The deer rears back up, gasping for breath. The moon reappears, lighting up its desperate face.

Not a deer's face.

I sway on my heels, lose my balance, fall backwards. But the image remains vivid behind my eyes. The leaves feel softer now, the air warmer. But I can't lie here. I need to get away from the forest, away from what I've done. Who I've killed.

I open my eyes. I'm hot, sticky with sweat. My heart is pumping too fast.

What the fuck?

It took me ages to get to sleep, even after being awake for a full thirty-six hours. And now this.

A lurch of nausea rises as the image reignites, me sinking the knife into the deer's warm body, all the blood spilling out. Then I see Izzy's lifeless face again. Not Archie, like Salvo said. But my friend who's still alive.

A surge of adrenaline grabs me, and I push up to sitting. I look at Izzy across the room. She's lying on her side, fast asleep, her shoulder lifting and dropping with each breath. The sight calms me a bit, but not enough to erase the memory of that dream.

I need some air.

I climb out of bed – quietly so I don't disturb Izzy – and tiptoe out of the room. My feet are bare, just like in the dream. A shiver grabs hold of me, and my eyes prick with tears. It was just a stupid nightmare, so why am I so freaked out?

This is Salvo's fault for spouting nonsense. Archie's fault for leaving me in the most brutal way possible. This summer was supposed to be fun but it's turned into hell.

I stumble down to the beach, needing the soft whoosh of the sea. But as I fold onto the cool sand, Salvo's words come back to me. *Francesca, did you know that your father was a mazzere?*

But that's bullshit. Lies. The mazzeri legend is just a Corsican fable, a stupid story. No one can foresee someone's death, awake or asleep.

Of course it's no surprise that I had a nightmare that reflects the mazzeri story after Salvo's crazy claims this morning. This has nothing to do with prophesying Izzy's death, and everything to do with my trauma at Archie's suicide.

I look at my watch. But when I realise it's the early hours of 31st July, another wave of dread sets in. According to the legend, tonight is the darkest night for the mazzeri. A load of mazzeri warriors fight through the night as July becomes August.

But it's all crazy. A fantasy story. And I am not crazy.

I hear a noise. I whip my head around, away from the sea. 'Hello?' I call out. No one responds, but the sound continues. A snuffling noise. Like someone crying.

I push to standing and walk towards it. The sky is clear, but the shadowy moonlight makes me feel uneasy. My eyes fall onto a dark shape underneath a sun lounger. I crouch down. 'Patrick?' I whisper. 'What are you doing under there?'

Raw fear spreads across the child's face and he wriggles backwards. I've seen Raphael and Anna's son around the hotel enough times to recognise him, but have never spoken to him. It's natural for him to be wary of me. 'I'm Frankie,' I say gently. 'I work on the water-ski boat with Dom – you might have seen me around.'

Recognition edges onto his face and he shuffles a bit closer, but he still doesn't speak.

'It's very late for you to be out of bed,' I go on. 'Does your mummy know you're here?'

'Don't tell her,' Patrick whispers. 'I ran away. I don't want to go back.'

I nod, even though I don't have a clue what to do. My experience of kids is teaching them to bend their knees and straighten their arms. 'Why don't you want to go back?' I ask, playing for time.

'Mama and Papa. They're shouting. Really loud. I don't like it.'

It's hard to believe that Anna is capable of arguing with anyone, and especially Raphael, but I guess it's been a stressful day. 'What are they shouting about?' I ask.

'Someone called Izzy,' Patrick says solemnly.

'Izzy?' I repeat, not hiding my surprise.

Patrick shrugs. 'I heard them say the name.'

I sit back on my haunches. Why would Anna and Raphael be arguing about Izzy? Could the gossip about them sleeping together be true?

'Grandpa was there too, for a while,' Patrick goes on. 'I think he was cross as well but I'm not sure.' Patrick's little voice breaks. 'My grandpa never shouts.'

I imagine a quietly seething Salvo skulking along the beach and feel an urge to be back in my bedroom, behind a locked door. 'You know, Patrick, it's pretty late,' I say. 'And I bet you're getting cold under there.' Patrick hugs his knees into his chest and looks down at his feet. 'How about I take you home,' I coax. 'If your parents are still shouting, I promise I'll make them stop.'

'Are you sure?' Patrick asks.

'Oh yes, I have magic powers.' I regret the words as soon as they're out, the images of hunting they conjure up, but I manage to smile, just.

Patrick sighs and wriggles out from under the sun lounger. 'Okay, as long as you tell Mama and Papa not to be mad with me.'

'It's a deal.' I reach for Patrick's hand, and together we walk towards his home on the edge of the hotel complex.

It's quiet when we arrive, no voices spilling out, and I knock softly on the door. After a minute, Anna opens it. She looks perfect, as usual. The only sign that anything's wrong is that she's fully dressed at three in the morning.

'Frankie?' Then her eyeline dips and her pitch rises. 'Patrick?' She crouches down to her son's level, pulls him into her arms, then looks up at me. 'What going on?'

'I found him on the beach,' I say. 'I brought him home.'

'What was he doing on the beach?' But her face grows even paler than usual as she processes why he might have run away. 'Actually, never mind. Thank you for bringing him home.' She starts to close her front door, but then she pauses, takes in my pyjamas. 'What were you doing out at this time?'

'Me? Well, I couldn't sleep. It's been ... a lot.'

Her face tightens. 'Of course. I'm sorry about Archie.'

I nod. 'I was with him, in the evening before he ... I feel like I let him down.'

'It wasn't your fault, Frankie,' Anna says. Her tone is firmer than I would have expected and it causes a mad urge to tell her everything. What Jack did, how upset Archie was when he found out. That Jack's crime must have played a part in his suicide. But I promised Archie not to tell a soul.

'Thank you,' I murmur instead.

'Most things in life are beyond our control – you'll find that out soon enough. But now I need to get Patrick into bed.'

I nod, take a step backwards.

'Look after yourself, Frankie.'

Then she closes the door, and I'm left wondering why her words land on me like a heavy blanket of dread.

Frankie

31st July

'I just think we should go for a drink,' Izzy says, shrugging and looking towards the window. 'Say goodbye to Archie properly.'

We've all gathered in Izzy's and my bedroom. The water sports reopened today – apparently one day of mourning was enough – and we're all exhausted after eight hours of smiling at guests, pretending everything is fine. Izzy is on her bed, and I'm on mine. Dom and Harriet are sprawled on the floor between us and Jack is leaning against the door, his fingers curled around the handle as though he might leg it at any moment.

'I don't know,' Harriet says, biting her fingernails. 'Is it wrong to have a few drinks when Archie's body is cold on a mortuary slab?'

'Harriet,' Dom warns, dipping his head in Jack's direction. 'Easy on the imagery.'

'Sorry,' Harriet mumbles. 'You know, maybe you're right. I could do with a drink.'

'What do you think, Jack?' Dom asks with a kindness that makes my skin crawl. If he only knew what Jack had done, how undeserving of sympathy he is. But I can't blame Dom. This is my fault for being too spineless, too scared of the possible fallout, to tell anyone what I know.

Jack knocks the back of his head against the wooden door, like he needs it to think. 'Yeah, let's get fucked.'

'Uh, okay great,' Dom stutters.

I thought Archie's death might put our issues in perspective for Dom, and that the thaw he hinted at high up on that rock might continue. But things almost seem to be more tense. Except maybe this is me shrinking into myself. Too tired, too frazzled by losing Archie, and last night's dream, to see clearly.

'But shall we go to Henri's?' Dom continues as he pushes to standing. 'I can't face seeing hotel guests this evening.'

'Now that is a very good point,' Harriet says, uncrossing her legs and standing up. 'But I need a shower first, so can we meet outside in half an hour?'

Thirty minutes later, I take one last look in the mirror – dark circles; sad, bloodshot eyes – and pull the room door closed behind us. Izzy looks stunning tonight – too dressed up for a makeshift wake really. Her curly blonde hair is hanging loose over her shoulders and she's wearing a new dress – long sleeves and lacey, but super short with a steep neckline – and against her tanned legs, it looks incredible. I usually love the pale blue beach dress that I'm wearing with my Vans, but compared to Izzy, it looks plain and childish.

The others are already outside, and we walk down the beach in silence. Henri's is a busy locals' bar with live music and shabby decor. It serves beer, wine, spirits, and mixers if you're lucky – if you ask for a cocktail, Henri will show you the door. But we've been down a few times after the hotel bar has shut for the evening, and as gossip seems to spread fast around here, I'm hoping Henri will know not to ask where Archie is.

'Francesca?'

Shit. I stop, turn. Salvo is walking up the beach behind us, his hands clasped in front of his chest, like he's praying. 'We're going to Henri's,' I blurt out. I want to keep walking, but everyone else slows to a stop.

Salvo nods, eyes the others. 'Patrick told me that you helped get him home last night. I wanted to say thank you.'

'Oh, yes.' My shoulders relax slightly. 'No problem.' I turn to go, but Salvo reaches for my arm, takes two steps towards me.

'Patrick said that it was very late,' he whispers into my ear. 'I wondered why you were on the beach in the middle of the night?'

Acid forms in my mouth.

'Did you have another mazzeri dream, perhaps?'

'Hey, old man, let her go.' Izzy pushes Salvo's hand off my forearm, then wraps her arm around my shoulders. 'Come on,' she says. There's strength in her voice, but I can tell she's shaking. 'Are you okay?' she asks quietly. 'I hate that creepy old guy.'

I nod, but Izzy doesn't relax her grip on me until we arrive at Henri's.

Frankie

31st July

'What do we drink?' Harriet asks, resting her arms on the mahogany bar and staring at the line of bottles across the wall behind it. 'What would Archie approve of?'

'Tequila shots,' Jack mutters. 'Multiple.'

'Hey, guys,' Henri says, ambling over and spreading his palms across the bar. 'I'm sorry to hear about—'

'Ten tequilas please,' Izzy interrupts, and I wonder how much this is about settling her own nerves after confronting Salvo rather than complying with Jack's wishes.

Henri nods, understanding clear on his face. 'Sure.'

I watch him line up ten shot glasses and free-pour from a bottle of tequila. Then we all step forward. The last two days have been the worst of my life – discovering Archie's lifeless body, Salvo messing with my head, only sleeping long enough for that terrible nightmare to come – and the numbing effects of alcohol are exactly what I need, so I pick up a glass, rest its rim against my bottom lip, flick my wrist, and swallow the burning liquid.

'And another one,' Izzy says, reaching for her second glass.

I down the next drink without hesitation too. The alcohol races into my bloodstream, and I love how it floods me with a new energy. The promise of oblivion maybe. 'Shall I get us another one?' I ask.

'Do you think we should just take a moment?' Harriet says.

'I think we deserve to get wasted after what we've all been through,' Izzy counters, stroking my back. She lowers her voice to a whisper. 'Especially you.'

I flinch on instinct, but she's right. I am right at the centre of this. Tears threaten so I shout Henri's name to fight against them. It's loud and he comes straight over.

'Ten more,' I say.

He scans all our faces, and the others must look determined too, because he collects up the empty glasses and replaces them with fresh without questioning the speed of our drinking.

'How about we sit down for these,' Dom says. 'We haven't even raised a toast to Archie yet.'

My face smarts as I realise he's right, and I carry my two new shots over to an empty table in the corner. Izzy sits on one side of me, but I tense as Jack drops into the chair on my right. I close my eyes for a moment to ride the fear, but then I see Archie's face, hear his voice. *Jack tried to kill his family, Frankie.*

I open my eyes.

'A toast,' Dom announces. 'To Archie, a lovely bloke who—'

'Shut up.' Jack's caustic words make me jump.

'All right, chill out,' Dom says.

'He was my boyfriend. I should do the toast.'

'Yeah, of course, you're right,' Dom says, chastened, even though he's a far better man than Jack could ever be. He reaches for his glass – probably to avoid Jack's glare – and his fingers graze mine. A jolt of charge rushes through me, but it repels him. He spills some of his drink, swears.

'To Archie,' Jack says, raising his glass. 'Why the fuck did you leave me?' His voice breaks and he throws the fiery liquid into

180

his mouth, then reaches for the second glass and does the same. Anger rises inside me. How dare he play the victim? He as good as killed Archie with his confession. I shake my head, blow out air, and down a shot.

'What?' Jack asks. 'You didn't like my toast?'

'Why are you pretending that you don't know why he did it?' The words are out before I can stop them.

Jack's face contorts. 'What the fuck does that mean?'

My head is buzzing now. Henri has cranked up the music and Destiny's Child is blaring out of two huge speakers. 'It means that it's your fault, dickhead. And don't tell me you can't see it.' I drink the second shot. I wonder for a moment if it's going to come back up, but then my stomach settles.

'Jesus, Frankie!' Dom shakes his head. 'When are you going to learn to keep your mouth shut? The guy's just lost his partner. Where's your compassion?'

'My compassion?!' I'm slurring my words now. I need to stop talking. Dom thinks I'm a bitch, and fuck, Jack is capable of murder. He tried to kill his family. What will he do to me if I start spilling his secret?

'Listen, everyone needs to take a moment,' Izzy says, picking up my hand and squeezing it. 'We're all devastated by what Archie did. And confused. It's natural to lash out, but we should be supporting each other.'

'I didn't think I'd ever agree so wholeheartedly with something Izzy said,' Harriet picks up. 'But she's right about this. How about I get us some beers? Archie liked beer, right? Then we can take it slow, give ourselves time to make friends again and remember Archie properly.'

'I'll help,' Dom mutters, pushing out of his chair. The two of them disappear, leaving just Jack, Izzy and me.

Izzy leans in. 'Say sorry,' she whispers into my ear. 'Trust me, you don't want Jack as your enemy.'

I think about Archie. His lifeless body. Then I think about what

Jack's capable of. Izzy's warning must mean that she knows what he did too, so at least I'll be able to confide in her when we're next alone. Maybe that will be enough to get me through this. 'I shouldn't have said that,' I mumble, looking down at the table.

'No you fucking shouldn't,' Jack throws back. 'I loved him. I'm fucking broken. Why the hell would you blame me when you're the one he turned to for help and you clearly did fuck all?' He sighs and his volume lowers. 'Did he say something about me?'

Izzy squeezes my hand, and it helps me find the words. 'No, nothing bad anyway,' I stutter, feeling the weight of Jack's accusation despite everything. 'Archie was upset but he wouldn't tell me why. I guess I assumed it was to do with you, but that wasn't fair, so I'm sorry.'

Jack's expression stays impassive, but he gives me a small nod. Then we sit in silence until Dom and Harriet return with the beers.

Maybe it is the more mellow alcohol, or maybe we've said all there is to say, but gradually the mood settles, then improves. We start sharing stories about Archie – his pale skin always turning pink in the sunshine, the female guests who'd fall for his Scottish brogue, then wonder why their flirting got them nowhere. Hours pass, and the sky grows inky black.

'Hey look,' Izzy says, pointing to the clock on the wall. 'It's nearly midnight. Almost August.'

'God, is it really?' Harriet moans. 'That means I need to be up in seven hours.'

'Ah, stop being so boring,' Izzy says. 'Do you know what I think we should do?'

'What?' I ask.

'Make this a night we won't forget, for Archie's sake.'

'What are you thinking, Izzy?' Dom asks.

'Let's go for a midnight swim.'

I think about diving into the sea, my favourite place. How it would cool my skin, clear my mind. The dark water giving me the space to think straight. To believe I can get through this. I stand up, sway a little. 'Yes, let's do it!'

Frankie

31st July

'Come on,' Izzy says, tugging at the hem of my dress, her own now a crumpled mess on the sand. 'It's nearly midnight.'

I stare at the sea. Normally it feels like my second home, but it looks dark and unforgiving tonight. Clouds are blocking any moonlight, and the waves carry a menacing energy. When Izzy suggested a midnight swim, I jumped at the idea – literally jumped up and ran outside. But as my drunkenness fades in the fresh air, I can feel my enthusiasm draining away too. A wind gust whips up from the shoreline and I rub my arms. 'Where are the others?' I ask. 'Shouldn't we wait for them?'

Izzy scoffs. 'Harriet says she doesn't want to get her hair wet, which is the wettest excuse I've ever heard. Dom's coming, but he was deep in conversation with Jack when I left the bar, and I didn't want to interrupt.'

'And Jack?' I ask, desperately hoping the answer is no.

'Hmm, I don't think so,' Izzy says. 'He didn't seem that impressed with my idea to be honest. Which feels all the more reason to do it.'

I give her a half-smile. Wonder if now's the time to tell her that I know what Jack did too.

'Look, there's Dom.' Izzy nods up the beach. 'Let's beat him into the water, come on!' She tugs again, and I realise now's not the time for deep chats. I pull the halter-neck dress over my head and drop it next to Izzy's. Then I accept Izzy's proffered hand, and we run down the beach together, and through the frothing churn.

When the water reaches our hips, Izzy drops my hand and dives into the oncoming wave. She pops back up, flicks her hair away from her face and grins. 'Night swimming is the best!' she calls out. 'I know Archie would approve of this!' Then she twists onto her front and starts splashing out to sea.

I take a breath, then dive in too. The water is cold, and the salt stings my skin, but my senses react to the onslaught with a rush of adrenaline. I burst out of the water, any nerves I felt on the beach washing away with it. I wave at Dom who's walking into the water too now. He seems to be staring right at me, but he doesn't return the wave, so I flip over and start swimming. Clean arm strokes, strong kicks. The water is rougher than usual, but it's not dangerous. This is the Mediterranean after all.

I mistime a stroke, and a wave hits me in the face. As I pause to catch my breath, I look back towards the beach. I can't see Dom now and the dim lights of the hotel suddenly look miles away. I've swum farther than I thought. I tread water, scan the gloomy scene. I want to find Izzy, but it's so hard to see anything beyond the surrounding waves in the darkness. I feel the claustrophobic tug of fear.

Something grabs my foot. I gasp. Pull it up. Seaweed, I think. Seaweed vines spiralling in the churning water. But as panic grabs me, the dream tries to edge in – the dead deer, the blood. I shake it away.

It happens again. But this time it pulls me down. As I sink, I try to scrabble upwards with my hands, but it's like climbing an ever-collapsing mountain. The water swirls around me. I can't breathe. Can't reach the surface. Panic sucks greedily on my oxygen. The downward force gets stronger.

In desperation, I kick out with my free foot. Does it slam into something? A sea creature? A person? Or have I got it all wrong? Am I just drunk, and traumatised, and half-crazy with guilt and grief?

My head reaches the surface. Still struggling for breath, I throw one arm out wildly, then the other. I kick my legs chaotically, but finally they gain some purchase, and I start to move. To escape.

The waves are bigger now, the darkness closer. My lungs scream in agony, but I don't stop. I stare at the beach, focus on my only goal. Finally, my fingertips brush against sand. I pull my legs up and try to stand, but I'm shaking. I fall over, then right myself, and stagger to the shore. My heart is pumping like a jackhammer. But I've escaped, survived!

Izzy.

The thought smacks me in the face. Izzy is still in the water.

'Izzy!' I scream into the darkness. I whip my head left and right. Shit, where is everyone? I try to run back into the water, but I can't do it. The fear is like a forcefield, holding me back, my toes disappearing into the wet sand. Izzy is in danger, and I'm too scared to help her. The dream comes rushing in. The deer bleeding to death. Izzy's face.

What have I done?

'Frankie? Are you okay?' Dom appears, his curly hair dripping seawater.

'Where's Izzy?!' I scream.

'I … I don't know. Is she in trouble?' Dom's face twists as he tries to make sense of what I'm saying.

'Can you see her?!'

Dom scans the water, then a beat later, he starts running towards the water, his arms pumping as the emergency sinks in. 'Izzy!' he shouts, splashing and smacking into the waves.

I sense someone behind me and twist around. Harriet.

'What's going on?' she asks. 'Why is Dom calling for Izzy?'

'We went swimming,' I say, my voice cracking. 'I don't know where she is!'

'Fuck, really?' Harriet says, her eyes widening. 'Why aren't you in there looking for her?' She unzips her denim skirt. 'Are you coming?'

I open my mouth, but no words come out.

'Fucking hell, Frankie,' Harriet hisses. 'You're a shit friend!' She charges into the water, her strong arms whipping through the waves. My knees buckle and I drop to the ground. Why haven't I told them about the hand grabbing my foot? How close I came to drowning myself?

My body sways. Did that even happen?

A strangled cry rises up in the distance, followed by the smack of limbs on water. I push to standing, then watch as my friends surge back towards the beach. Dom, Harriet.

And Raphael. Carrying Izzy.

Where did he come from? How did I not notice him running into the water?

He lays her on the sand, turns to the others. '*Appelez les secours!* Call 112 someone!'

Harriet runs back up the beach. I imagine her scrabbling for her phone – the only one of us to have a mobile that works out here. But I don't turn to look. My body is rigid, staring at Izzy. Her eyes are open, but glassy. Her head has dropped to one side. I watch Raphael pump at her chest, breathe into her mouth. I listen to him call Izzy's name, then cry out in frustration when she remains lifeless.

I turn away. And Jack's there, standing a couple of metres behind me.

'Is she … Is she dead?' he asks.

I squint. Why is his hair wet? 'Where have you been?' I ask. His expression hardens. 'Why?'

I swallow. I want to scream at him, tell him what I know. But the memory of being pulled under the water, the sight of Izzy's body jerking under Raphael's desperate pumps, has stripped me of any bravery I might once have had. 'I don't know,' I whisper. 'I don't know if she's dead.'

But in my heart, I do know.

Frankie

1st August

The police officer's words bounce off my skull. No, I won't let them in.

When the paramedic officially pronounced Izzy dead on the beach as the storm broke and rain pounded down last night, I thought then that my emotions would overwhelm me. Shock, pain, loss, guilt. I'd swum away in terror from something that might just have been seaweed – turned into something deadlier by images from that nightmare – and left my friend to drown.

If the police had interviewed me last night, I wouldn't have mentioned being grabbed at all – a mix of self-hatred and self-doubt – but nobody asked me anything. Only one police officer turned up with the paramedics – the man sat opposite me now – and after speaking to Raphael for a while, he addressed the rest of us together. He said that he knew we'd all been drinking, so there was no point interviewing anyone until we'd slept it off. And I'd been too grateful for the reprieve to wonder why he wasn't treating the incident with more urgency.

I'd gone back to the accommodation block with the others,

all of us too shellshocked to speak, and taken a shower. I'd tried to burn away the guilt with scalding water, but it hadn't worked, so I'd shuffled back to my room and crawled into bed, making sure not to look at the empty one next to mine. The images had come on a loop for a while – Archie, Izzy, the deer, the churning black water, struggling for breath – but eventually I'd drifted into some state of unconsciousness.

When I woke up a few hours later, I went to the beach, like I needed to return to the scene of the crime. The clouds were still moody from the night's storm, and I'd stared out to sea. Salvo was there, heading out in his fishing boat, water spraying up behind him. That's when the sensation of being pulled under came back to me. And I knew then that it had happened. It was a real memory, not the by-product of a dream.

So when the police officer eventually got around to bringing me into the station for an interview this morning, and asked for my recollection of events, I told him everything, and he wrote my account down in his own language. At first, he didn't seem interested – typical stupid behaviour by drunk English kids, Izzy tarred with the same brush by association – but then I mentioned someone pulling me under.

And the way he has now made sense of my account makes me want to vomit.

'So do you think that could be it, mademoiselle?' he presses. 'That it was your friend in the water, struggling, reaching out for your help?'

The officer's words finally muscle their way in, and the room shifts around me. I see Izzy's lifeless body, feel the pull on my leg. 'Can I go home now?'

He sighs. 'You can, yes. We need a copy of your passport and your address in the UK. You may need to return for the inquest, but hopefully not. I believe we'll be recommending a verdict of *décès accidentel* – death by misadventure – which wouldn't require your attendance.'

189

I remember how I kicked out. Then I see the deer's face become Izzy's.

I push the chair back and stand up. The room is small and stacked high with files, and it's too oppressive. I lunge for the door handle and step into the corridor. But the relief I was praying for vanishes as I see three generations of Paoli family sitting in a line of chairs opposite.

Salvo is in the middle, with Patrick curled up next to him. Raphael gets up from his chair on the opposite side and our eyes meet. I want to see sympathy there, a bond built on shared adversity, but there's only a glare of hostility, like he blames me for Izzy's death too. It hits me like a sharp slap, and I turn away as he disappears into the police officer's room.

I look at Salvo and a burst of burning-hot rage engulfs me.

'This is your fault,' I hiss. 'I was only scared because of you! The crazy ideas you put in my head!'

'Scared? What do you mean?'

'I felt something out there, someone. I thought they were trying to kill me! I didn't think it could be Izzy!'

'Ah, I see.' His expression is serene, unaffected by my screaming. 'Don't hate yourself, Francesca. If you had a mazzeri dream about Izzy dying, which I am guessing is the real cause of your distress, then it was her destiny to die. You could never have saved her.' His tone is calm. I want to scratch his ice-blue eyes out.

How can he be so fucking accepting?

'No, this is on you,' I spit out. 'The mazzeri story is bullshit. You made me think that I had this terrible power, and that fucked my head up, and now a terrible thing has happened! But you did this, not me.' I point a shaky finger at him. 'This is your fault.'

Salvo taps Patrick, who straightens, and they both stand up. 'Go home, Francesca. Take your grief and your accusations far away from here.'

'You think I want to stay on this island?!'

A door slams and instinctively I turn towards the noise.

190

'So you killed her,' Raphael says, walking towards me.

I take a step back. 'What?'

'I've just read your statement.'

'Why did they let you …'

'I thought you were just too much of a coward to help rescue her. But it's worse than that, isn't it? She reached out to you, and you kicked her away.'

'No, I …'

'Izzy was a much better person than you'll ever be. She took you under her wing, and you repay her by leaving her to drown. Shame on you.' Raphael tuts loudly, shakes his head, then throws me one last look of disgust before marching out of the police station.

I stand rigid, hold my breath. Because if I let it out, I'll cry. And I can't let Salvo see that. Slowly I collect myself enough to walk outside.

And I don't look back.

2025

Frankie

28th July

Hey, mazzera, did you dream about Lola?

No violent words; no threats; no aggression. But enough to keep me awake all night, fighting the urge to run across the beach into Lola's room and check she's alive.

I haven't told a soul about my dream in Gatwick Airport car park, so the note can only be guesswork. But whoever slipped it under my door knows enough to taunt me with the mazzeri legend.

Defeated by the glare of morning sunshine, I push up, pull my knees into my body, and lean back against the oak headboard. This is how I've spent most of the night. Restlessly changing position, as though movement might provide the answers. My eyes feel gritty now, and my head is swaying on the inside. I lean over towards the bedside table and pick up my phone: 7.13 a.m. Lola will still be asleep. If I call her now, she might not pick up, and I'll panic. Imagine the worst.

Her face forever imprinted on a bleeding eagle owl.

I fling the sheet away and climb out of bed. It was a note, I remind myself again. Written by a human hand, someone who clearly wants to mess with my head. The mazzeri legend is a story, a fantasy, no different to Harry Potter or Hansel and Gretel.

But someone real did write it.

Dom had the time. He left the restaurant before Lola and I last night, and he always loved playing practical jokes. Maybe his sense of humour has become more depraved with age. But while he knows about the mazzeri legend – I remember talking about it at the Bastille Day parade in town – why would he associate it with me? I never told him about the dream I had before Izzy died.

It could have been Jack trying to punish me – if he still blames me for Archie's death, even though my failing was nothing compared to his. I never told him about my mazzeri dream either, but he's been here twenty years, plenty of time for Salvo to let it slip. Or Raphael, if Salvo confided in him.

But perhaps it's Raphael who wants to freak me out. He may have said last night that he wants to put the past behind us, but I still remember his angry accusation in the police station. *Shame on you.* Looking back, it was obvious he had feelings for Izzy, whether they were sleeping together or not. And he knows how intensely Salvo would have pushed his mazzeri beliefs onto me, so he could guess that they'd still be haunting me twenty years later.

I shake my head. The most important thing to remember is that it's just a note. A piece of paper. It can't hurt me or Lola.

And we'll be out of here soon.

I pad into the bathroom, turn the shower on, and step inside. I close my eyes, tilt my head, and feel the jets of cold water bounce off my face. An official in the British consulate in Marseille will print off Lola's travel documents today. He or she will slide them into an envelope and stick on a label with Hotel Paoli's address. The envelope will leave the building in a bag full of post, and travel to the port, or the airport, then cross the sea overnight. And tomorrow a whistling Corsican postie will pick it up in a little van and drive it to the front door of the hotel.

And Lola and I will go home.

Tomorrow.

I switch off the shower, reach for a towel, and hold it against my face.

I just have to make it through one more day.

Frankie

28th July

Fifteen minutes later, I pull the bedroom door closed behind me. It's past eight o'clock now, which feels late enough to venture over to the staff accommodation block and knock on Lola's bedroom door. But when I reach the ground floor, Lola is already there. Leaning on the reception desk, talking to Patrick.

'Lola?'

'Oh, hey, Mum. I was going to come up, see if you wanted to come for breakfast?'

The scene looks so normal. Lola is wearing her usual cut-off denim shorts with an emerald-green vest top over a navy swim-suit. The sun is shining through the glass doors. Guests are milling around, heading to the restaurant, or outside towards the pool or beach. It doesn't seem possible that I've been awake all night, wondering if my daughter is going to die.

'I'm not that hungry actually, but I'll keep you company?'

'You don't have to do that,' Lola says, wafting my offer away. 'I'll grab something and meet you on the beach instead?'

'No, I …'

'If you can wait a few minutes, I could join you,' Patrick says. 'If you want, that is. My mum will be back soon; I was just covering reception while she ate something.'

'Um, yes, why not, thank you,' Lola mumbles.

Despite my lack of sleep, I sense a new charge in the atmosphere. I narrow my eyes and look at my daughter. Is she blushing? I glance back at Patrick. His smile is also lingering. I feel my shoulders tighten. Never mind the age difference, this is a complication I really don't need. I jerk slightly as the telephone rings in the office behind.

'Sorry, back in a moment.' Patrick gives Lola another smile, then heads into the office, closing the door behind him.

'You two seem friendly?' I try to keep my voice neutral.

Lola shrugs. 'We chatted a bit at the pool yesterday. Then at the bar last night. Before you came down. He seems like a nice guy.'

I nod, trying to work out if I should say more. My instincts scream at me to warn Lola off him, Salvo's grandson, Raphael's son, but parenting is about choosing your battles, and my priority right now is getting Lola home. They're only having breakfast together. All being well, we'll be on a plane home tomorrow evening, and she won't see Patrick ever again. He's not worth fighting over now.

'Oh, and I heard we're staying until the weekend,' Lola continues. 'That's so great, Mum. I'm really proud of you for confronting your demons and putting your past behind you.'

The atmosphere sparks again. It makes me feel dizzy. 'What?' I shake my head. 'No, no, no. We're going home as soon as your documents arrive, hopefully tomorrow. We discussed this.'

Lola's face creases in confusion. 'But I was talking to Anna before you came down. She said you'd agreed to go to Raphael's dad's memorial thing on Thursday evening? I think his name was Salvo?'

My heart skitters. But I can't lose my head, not here. Not now. I take a long breath. 'We must have got our wires crossed. Raphael mentioned it to me last night, and I explained that we couldn't go. He clearly misunderstood.'

'You know, I'd quite like to go,' Lola says, her voice quiet but determined. 'It's in Sartène, where our family comes from. Wouldn't you like to visit too?'

'Lola, listen …'

'And Dom lives there,' Lola interrupts. 'So you could go and see his house, like he offered last night. Come on, Mum. Please?'

My mind goes blank. Of course we can't stay. And we especially can't go to a commemoration for Salvo on the mazzeri's darkest night. But on zero hours' sleep, I can't work out how to explain this rationally. 'No, we need to go home,' I mutter.

'God, Mum, can we not at least talk about it? It's my birthday week remember, my eighteenth. And Patrick was telling me about a windsurf competition that's held on a beach near here, Pian something. It's on Saturday and it sounds so cool. People come from all over the world to take part apparently, and there are still places in the women's heats; Patrick checked. I know it's hard for you, Mum, but Izzy died over twenty years ago. And sorry but don't you think you owe me? You have put yourself first on almost every one of my birthdays. Isn't it my turn now?'

'Um, is everything okay?'

I twist around. Patrick must have finished his phone call because he's back behind reception, looking at us.

'Yes, all good,' Lola say, switching straight back into happy mode. 'Sorry. I'm ready if you are? See you later, Mum.'

Patrick nods quickly, then avoids making eye contact with me as he walks around the front desk. Lola also won't look at me, but she finds a smile for Patrick as he falls in step beside her. I watch on helplessly as they walk into the restaurant together. And then I panic as I see Anna walking in the opposite direction – I can't deal with her right now. I almost trip over my feet in my effort to get away, then dive into the hotel shop before she notices me.

'Good morning,' the assistant says, with a bright smile. I nod dumbly, then shuffle down the aisle, as far away as possible. I feel sweaty and nauseous. I need to calm down. Find some space to think.

Yes, Lola deserves to choose what she does for her birthday. And I know the competition she means – it's been held on Piantarella beach for decades and would be an amazing opportunity for her. She's right that I should have moved on from Izzy's death too.

But she doesn't know about the mazzeri dream I had the night before Izzy died, or the one that Lola featured in, in the dark gloom of Gatwick Airport's car park. And she doesn't know about the note.

Should I tell her everything? If I do, I risk Lola thinking I'm crazy, just like all those doctors have thought over the years. But if I don't tell her, she'll never understand why I hate this place so much. She'll continue to believe I'm pathetic, or selfish, unwilling to do the work to put my daughter first.

My whole body feels weak and my stomach churns.

No, it's too difficult a decision to make when my brain is fried from a night of insomnia. I need to get some sleep first. Then maybe things will be clearer, easier to deal with. Lola is having breakfast with Patrick. It's daytime. Of course she's safe. If I take a sleeping pill, maybe two, I'll black out for a few hours. And then I can work out what to do for the best later.

I walk back towards the shop entrance. But then I stop. Stare. The shop assistant is talking to me but it's like her voice is underwater, stretched and muffled. All I can do is hold my breath. Stare at the picture on sale for fifteen hundred euros.

And wonder how the hell one of my paintings has ended up in the Hotel Paoli gift shop.

Lola

28th July

'So that conversation with your mum looked a bit intense,' Patrick says, pushing his empty bowl away. He only had fruit and yoghurt, much more restrained than her, but Lola guesses the breakfast buffet isn't a novelty for him. She had a healthy mushroom omelette to start, followed by two waffles covered in maple syrup.

'Yeah. I think it's hard for her being back here,' she says. 'I'm playing catch-up, because she didn't tell me about any of this until I came to Corsica, but she carries a lot of guilt about Izzy's death.'

'It was ruled an accident.'

Lola hesitates. Patrick said by the pool that he knows everything, which must include the police's theory that Izzy was reaching out to Frankie for help. But she feels weird about bringing it up. Disloyal to her mum. 'I think it's survivor's guilt,' she chooses. 'Mum getting back to shore when Izzy didn't.'

He nods. 'Strange though, that she still feels so guilty after all this time.'

Lola studies him, looking for any hint of accusation, but his face drops under her scrutiny.

'Sorry, I shouldn't have asked that. My dad has always implied that your mum was responsible. But he can be like that, full of shit.'

A few beats of silence thrum between them. 'Do you remember her? Izzy?' Lola finally asks.

Patrick turns his head towards the sea. 'I don't know. Maybe. But it's what happened after she died that I remember more.'

'I guess it was hard for everyone to move on from, not just my mum.'

Patrick smiles, but sadly. 'My grandpa moved away soon after it all happened, and I missed him a lot. I'm not sure if the two events were connected, but I've always put them together in my mind. And my parents seemed different after too. I guess it was the stress of dealing with the bad publicity, the lost bookings.' He looks embarrassed suddenly.

'What?' Lola asks, tilting her head. 'What's wrong?'

He smiles sheepishly. 'You know, seeing your mum last night reminded me of something that happened that summer, between my parents. I'd forgotten all about it until then. I think it might have been the night before Izzy died, around that time anyway and definitely not afterwards, because your mum was there.'

Lola swirls her fork in the dregs of maple syrup. 'What happened?'

'My parents were screaming at each other in the middle of the night. And my grandpa was there too at some point. I didn't like it at all, so I ran away. Well, a few hundred metres down the beach. And it was your mum who found me, curled up under a sun lounger. She took me back home and they'd stopped arguing by then.' He takes a sip of water then places the glass back down on the table. 'What's weird though is the other part of the memory.'

'Oh?'

'I think I remember telling your mum that my parents were arguing about Izzy. But why would that be?'

Lola frowns. She doesn't know why. But Izzy's death coming so soon after Raphael and Anna's argument about her feels significant. Lola's mum's words come back to her – *I was so certain that someone was trying to hurt me. I don't understand how I got it so wrong.* Could Raphael have been in the water that night? Or even Anna? Lola knows that Raphael has friends in the police – that's how she got a crime reference number without visiting the police station – so maybe he knew he'd get away with it too.

'Are you okay, Lola?'

'What?'

'You look really pale.'

Lola flicks her head, feels her hair swish around her shoulders. 'Sorry, yes. I was miles away. So, um, are you working today?' she asks, grabbing the salt pot to steady herself, then letting it go in case it spills.

'Not until later. I'm on the bar from five. But I'm heading into town this morning. Apparently my grandpa left a letter for me at our family solicitor's office to read after his death.' He takes a deep breath and smiles at Lola. 'You could come with me if you like? I mean, not to the solicitor's, but you could have a wander round town, and we could meet up afterwards for a drink at the marina?'

The last time Lola was in the centre of Porto Vecchio, she was exhausted, phoneless and broke. She couldn't wait to get away from the tourists and dusty streets. But right now, the thought of being away from this hotel – from her mum, and Raphael, and other people's memories – feels like just what she needs. 'Thanks, I'd love to.'

Lola

28th July

Patrick pauses outside a three-storey sandstone building with an oak front door and a golden plaque glinting in the sunshine. 'So this is the solicitor's,' he says. 'I only need to pick up the letter, but Marco is an old family friend, and I can guarantee that he won't let me leave without having a coffee with him, so shall we meet in about half an hour?' He turns ninety degrees and points down the hill. 'The marina is in a direct line from here, three streets down. There's a café on the seafront, Imelda's, that makes the best lemonade in town. Is midday okay?'

'Sounds great. And good luck in there.' Without thinking, Lola gives him a kiss on the cheek, then feels her face flush. But Patrick's smile helps to cool her skin. Then he presses the doorbell, and a moment later, disappears into the building.

Lola takes in her surroundings. This must be Porto Vecchio's answer to a business district. Most of the buildings are replicas of the one she's stood outside now, heavy doors bearing small plaques engraved with names like *Barre & Atonio Financiers* and *Notaire, Porto Vecchio*. Not a bar or tacky tourist shop in sight.

She decides to head in the direction of the marina and hope she'll find some shops en route to pass the time in. She might even pick up a few arty postcards for her mum – a peace offering after their falling-out this morning.

The next street down is more bustling. There are the same three-storey buildings, but with cafés and newsagents at ground level and more people milling about. There's a large building on one corner – the tourist information centre – and opposite is the *Bibliotheque Municipale*. Lola speaks enough French to know that means library, and it gives her an idea.

For eighteen years she didn't even know her mum had been to Corsica. And then in the last two days, she's found out that two of her mum's friends died within a few days of each other here. And more than that, her mum was with Archie a few hours before he took his own life, and then in the water when Izzy drowned, feeling like she was being pulled under.

All Lola really wants is to help her mum come to terms with her past. But to do that, she needs to figure out what really happened that night in the sea, and not just accept the opinion of a Corsican police officer as the truth. She's almost certain that libraries hold copies of newspapers from decades ago. If she can find out how the tragedies were reported back then, maybe she'll come across a clue that will help. It must be worth a shot anyway. She pushes on the glass door and enjoys the cold breeze from the air conditioning as she walks inside.

'*Bonjour, madam. Puis-je vous aider?*' A middle-aged woman with red-framed glasses and a hairstyle that reminds Lola of a pineapple gives her a professional smile.

'Um. *Parlez-vous Anglais?*' Lola asks in a terrible accent.

'*Bien sûr*, of course. We have a whole English book section. Would you like me to show you?'

'Actually, I was hoping you could help me find a newspaper article. From 2004.'

'Hmm, okay.' The librarian drops the smile. 'We might be

able to do that,' she continues hesitantly. 'Are you looking for something specific?'

'I am, yes,' Lola starts, trying to impress with her politest voice. 'A girl drowned from a local beach on the 31st July 2004. She was a friend of my mum's, and as I'm here on holiday, I thought I could find out a little bit more about it. For my mum,' she emphasises.

Suspicion is replaced by a wistful expression. 'Ah, I remember that. So tragic. Even though we're an island, drownings are quite rare here. Let me show you.'

Lola follows her to a desk at the back of the room with a large computer screen fixed against the wall. The librarian pulls the keyboard towards her and the screen lights up. She rattles out a username and password and a database opens. *Journaux Francais*.

She takes a couple of steps backwards. 'Everything is digitised now, across France, so you can access old print versions of local newspapers here. And there's an English translation option. As you know the date of the incident, it should be a simple enough task to find what you're looking for.'

Lola thanks the librarian then senses her back away as she turns her focus to the screen. She types 1st to 31st August 2004 in the date range, and Porto Vecchio as a location, and watches a list of newspapers appear. She clicks on the first one – called *Corse-Matin* – and then the 'translate to English' tab. And the librarian is right. There's an article about Izzy on the front page of the newspaper dated 2nd August 2004.

Woman Drowns at Hotel Paoli

Tragedy strikes for the second time in a week at one of Porto Vecchio's most popular hotels. In the early hours of yesterday morning, a woman lost her life off the beach predominantly used by the guests of Hotel Paoli. This follows the sudden death of 22-year-old Archibald Muir, a hotel employee, two nights previously. It's hard to accept that one establishment can suffer such a torrid time.

A statement issued by local police confirmed that a female French national, aged 26, was pronounced dead at the scene by attending medics. The family of the deceased has been informed and her name will be released in due course. While no further details have been provided, we understand from witnesses that the woman is assumed to have drowned in the challenging sea conditions preceding the storm that blew through the island yesterday.

Hotel Paoli is owned by Salvo and Raphael Paoli, who sadly also suffered a personal tragedy earlier this month with the lethal shooting of Jean Paoli in Ajaccio on Bastille Day in what is thought to be an organised crime group killing. However, we understand that Jean had been estranged from his surviving brother for many years, and there is no suggestion that Salvo Paoli has any links with organised crime.

The hotel was first opened as a beachside café in 1951 by two sisters, Marie and Teresa, following the post-war efforts carried out by the US army to clear the surrounding beaches of mosquitoes. The café was eventually passed to Marie's younger son, Salvo, who turned it into a restaurant. Salvo's son – Raphael – joined the business in 1992 and was the mastermind behind its most ambitious transformation. Hotel Paoli opened its doors in 1998.

With 48 rooms, a beautiful seafront location, and a high-quality restaurant, Hotel Paoli has become one of Porto Vecchio's most popular places to stay, but guests will be shocked and saddened by these tragic incidents. We asked the hotel for comment but have not yet received a response.

Lola clicks out of the article. Seeing the details in black and white makes it more real, but it doesn't tell her anything she doesn't already know about Izzy's death. While it's interesting to read that Raphael's uncle was part of the mafia scene, if they were estranged like the article says, that can't have had anything to do with Izzy's death. She checks the next day's paper, and the incident is still front-page news.

Drowning Victim Named

Local police held a press conference yesterday afternoon concerning the death of a 26-year-old French national in the stretch of water behind Hotel Paoli. Capitaine Bartoli confirmed that the victim had been swimming in the sea following a night out with friends and was found unresponsive in the water by a member of the public – widely quoted as being the hotel owner, Raphael Paoli. CPR was given but medics confirmed the death at 01.45 a.m.

Capitaine Bartoli also named the victim as Isobel Bassot, and confirmed that she had been employed by Hotel Paoli as a sailing instructor. He explained that they were still in the process of taking witness statements. However, they confirmed that Isobel had a significant amount of alcohol in her system when she went into the sea, and that they believe this – coupled with the difficult swimming conditions – led to her death.

Sadly, it seems that tragedy is not unfamiliar within the Bassot family. Isobel was born in Nice, to Luca and Nicole Bassot. Luca was well known in the 1980s as the talented chef behind *Sur Mer*, one of Nice's finest seafood restaurants. However, he was killed in a road traffic accident in 1991, when Isobel was

13, and the restaurant never reopened following his death. Forensic evidence showed that Luca Bassot was travelling considerably higher than the speed limit when he lost control of the car and veered off a mountain road. The coroner ruled the incident as death by misadventure, and it is very sad that, 13 years later, it appears history has repeated itself.

Lola sits back in the chair. Izzy's dad died in an accident too? That must have been terrible for Izzy, losing him when she was only thirteen. And what about her mum? How did she cope with losing her husband so suddenly, and then her daughter too?

Nicole Bassot. Lola conjures up a picture of a grief-stricken French lady. The phone ringing, a Corsican police officer on the other end. *I've got some terrible news.* How does anyone cope with that much tragedy in their family? The article didn't mention any siblings. Was Izzy an only child like she is? Has Nicole had no family to lean on for twenty-one years?

Lola eyes the Google Chrome icon at the bottom of the screen. She runs her fingers along the keyboard, listening to the soft crackle of the keys dipping. Then she taps on the icon, and types 'Nicole Bassot' into the search box. But that's not enough detail, so she adds 'Luca Bassot car crash' and a list of links appear that all seem to relate to Izzy's parents. Articles about the car accident. Restaurant reviewers missing *Sur Mer*. And then more links around the time of Izzy's death.

But it's a more recent blog piece that catches Lola's eye. Dated July 2024. *My battle with loss twenty years on*, by Nicole Bassot. That must be about Izzy. Lola's stomach lurches as she wonders what Nicole knows about that night, and if she holds her mum responsible too. She clicks on the link, but suddenly can't face reading it. Seeing her mum blamed in black and white.

The blog is hosted on a simple website for a yoga studio in Lille, so as a diversion tactic, she clicks on the About page. There's a photo of a petite woman in yoga pants and a long-sleeved Lycra top. She looks old – grey hair and faded blue eyes – but more than that, she seems haunted. That must be Nicole, Lola thinks, but is she haunted by grief, or a grudge against her mum?

She needs to be braver. The blog piece could even hold some clues that absolve her mum. She pulls the chair closer to the desk, clicks back into the blog, and starts reading.

Frankie

28th July

A siren explodes in my head. I jerk awake, ride a wave of nausea.
I flail out with one arm, find my phone, switch off the alarm.

Lola.

But thinking of my daughter brings in a host of horrible images
too – a bleeding eagle owl, the goading note, our argument, her
disappearing into the restaurant with Patrick.

I push up to sitting. It's hot in here – I didn't think to put the
air conditioning on when I crawled into bed – and my skin is
damp. I push clumps of sticky hair away from my face.

When I got back to my bedroom, I was consumed with the
shock of seeing my mazzeri painting in the hotel shop. I recognised how loose my grip on reality was, and knew I needed to
knock myself out. So I took too many sleeping pills and descended
into a black hole.

But now I'm awake, I need to check Lola's safe.

A knock on my bedroom door makes me jump. 'Hello?'

'Mum?'

I scramble out of bed and pull open the door. The sight of my daughter makes me feel instantly better. I want to reach for her, but I know she'll sense my desperation, so I take a step backwards instead. 'Come in, come see my room.'

'Were you asleep?' Lola asks suspiciously. 'Are you sick?'

'No, I mean, yes, I had a lie-down, but I'm fine. Anyway, what about you?' I ask, wiping my sweaty forehead. 'Are you having a good day?'

Lola nods and walks further inside. 'I love your cute little balcony. Is there a minibar? Can we sit out there and have a drink?'

I follow her outside. My room is at the front of the hotel, so there are no sea views, but the garden is in full bloom and it's more peaceful on this side. I rattle the railing to check it's sturdy. 'I'd love that. What would you like?'

Lola smiles. 'A Coke would be great, thanks.'

I take two cans out of the small fridge, then sink into the free chair opposite Lola. I try to stop my arm from shaking as I hand over the drink. 'So what have you done this morning?' I ask.

'I went into town with Patrick.'

'Oh?' I take a sip. The drink is cold and fizzy, and I like how it pirouettes into my stomach.

'He had to pick a letter up from his solicitor's. We were supposed to go for a drink after, but in the end, we came straight back because he wasn't feeling great.'

'Oh, that's a shame,' I lie.

'No, I didn't mind. It gave me time to think actually.' Lola leans forward in her chair. 'And what I thought was that I really need you to stop blaming yourself for Izzy's death. For your sake, and for mine. This holiday didn't start how I intended at all, but now we're here ... well, the sun's shining, the sea's inviting, and I think we should make the best of it. Because it's important for mothers and daughters to spend quality time together, don't you think? I mean we never know how long we've got, do we?'

'We've got ages,' I blurt out. 'I'm thirty-nine and you're seventeen. What's with the doom slaying?' I try to control my breathing.

'I'm not,' Lola says, offended now. 'It's just a turn of phrase. And I think you're missing the point.'

I take a long, silent breath. *The mazzeri legend is bullshit. Lola is not going to die. And the note is just a piece of paper.* 'I'm sorry, and you're right about quality time. But what you're asking for, staying here, it's not that simple.'

Lola leans her elbows on the glass table and knits her fingers. 'Mum, did you ever wonder if it could have been Raphael in the water that night?'

'Raphael? Why would you say that?'

'Patrick told me that he and Anna fought about Izzy the night before she died. And badly enough that Patrick ran away from home. You were there, so you know this.'

'I do, but …'

'And Raphael has contacts in the police,' Lola goes on. 'And his uncle was in the mafia apparently, so it's in his blood. And I heard he found her, so he was clearly close by.'

'What? No.' I shake my head, but my mind starts whirring. It's true that Patrick said Raphael and Anna were arguing about Izzy, but he was only five, so could easily have been mistaken. It does seem that Raphael has police connections, but so will most Corsican business owners. And Raphael lived near the beach, so him being close by isn't that suspicious. Maybe his uncle was in the mafia, but that doesn't make Raphael a killer. If it points the finger at anyone, it would be Salvo because Izzy always suspected that he was involved in something illegal – but of course he didn't write that note.

'No, that's crazy,' I say, finding my voice at last. 'We've been over this, Lola. I killed Izzy. Not on purpose, but I made a mistake, got scared when I shouldn't have, and left her in trouble.'

Lola leans back in her chair. 'What about Dom then?' she says, ignoring my explanation. 'He made it clear last night that he didn't like her.'

'That doesn't make him a killer.'

214

Lola goes quiet for a moment, and I can tell that she's thinking. 'You said that you and Izzy were pretty drunk when you went swimming,' she finally says. 'Why was that? What had you been doing?'

I turn to look towards the garden. 'We were holding a kind of wake, for Archie,' I say quietly. 'It was our way of saying goodbye.'

'By getting drunk and going skinny-dipping?'

I close my eyes, a futile attempt to shield myself from how disrespectful that sounds. 'We were young and thoughtless. Izzy suggested a midnight swim, and it seemed like a good idea at the time.'

'Did everyone go in the sea?'

I shake my head. 'Harriet didn't want to get her hair wet. And Jack. Well, I guess he was hurting too much.'

'Or maybe he thought it was out of line,' Lola points out.

I look away. With hindsight, yes, it was an insensitive thing to do. But Jack has no right to take the moral high ground. 'I'm not proud of any of it,' I murmur.

'No, I didn't mean that. Jack must have been half-crazy with grief that night. Maybe he wanted to punish you and Izzy for being disrespectful?'

Jack tried to kill his family, Frankie.

Archie's words, just hours before he died.

I tap my can of Coke. It's true that Jack was ruthless. I can't believe he'd attack us for the reason Lola suggests, but what if my outburst at Henri's bar made him decide that I was a threat to his freedom? I tried to backtrack, to apologise, but maybe it was too late. With Archie gone, Izzy and I were the two people who knew the truth about him. Is there a chance that he tried to get rid of us both?

And if it was him, does that mean the note is a genuine threat?

Either way, the last thing I need is Lola putting herself in danger by digging for the truth.

'Lola, you can't go around blaming other people because you

215

want me to be innocent.'

'But why are you so determined not to?' Lola snaps back. 'Why can't you at least consider the possibility that your instincts were right about there being someone else in the water?'

I take another gulp of Coke, feel a stab of pain as a bubble lodges in my chest. God, I just want to get her back to Lymington, away from this danger that I can't quite articulate. 'Have you heard from the British consulate yet?' I ask.

'Sorry?'

'I guess they'll email you with an update when your travel documents are completed?'

Lola shakes her head and slams her can down. 'That's your response? Ignoring my question and changing the subject? For fuck's sake, Mum! Why are you being so stubborn?'

'I just want to take you home,' I whisper.

'I don't want to go home! I want to go to Sartène on Thursday, and spend my birthday here so I can actually celebrate, with you! And I want to compete in that windsurf race on Saturday. I only have you, Mum. Dad is half a world away; I have no siblings. And you're treating me like I don't matter.'

'Of course you matter!' I call out. 'More than anything in the world.'

'Look, you leaving me every birthday, keeping secrets from me. These are the things that *are* your fault, Mum,' she says, the words harsh, but her voice softening. 'But you're still fixated on the one thing that isn't. Whether it was an accident, or someone else's doing, it happened over two decades ago, to a girl you knew for less than three months. It's Izzy's mother who should be grieving for eternity, not you. You're *my* mother.' Lola pushes her fist against her chest. 'You're supposed to put *me* first.'

Tears come. I think I am putting Lola first, but I have I got it all wrong? 'I'm so sorry,' I whisper.

Lola sighs. 'I don't want your apologies, Mum. I want you to look me in the eye and tell me that you can move on from

216

Izzy's death.'

I wipe my cheeks. I try to hold Lola's gaze, but I can't manage it, so I drop my eyeline and stare at my hands. 'I don't know how,' I admit sorrowfully.

A chair scraping on the tiles makes me look up. 'Lola?'

'I'm going on the water,' she snaps. Then she strides through my bedroom, whips the door open, and slams it shut behind her.

Frankie

28th July

I launch out after Lola, but when I call her name, she just lifts her hand and keeps walking. I recognise the gesture – give me space or my anger will grow exponentially – so I hover, unsure what to do. I hate the idea of her going out on a windsurf, especially with Jack's kit, but how do I stop her without admitting my suspicions? I listen to the soft clip of her sliders as she heads downstairs.

I'll go to the beach. Watch her from a distance. Make sure she stays safe. I have a thirty-second shower – conscious I must smell terrible after my sweaty, drug-induced sleep – then pull on my favourite Speedo bikini, swim shorts, and a T-shirt. I jam my feet into my Birkenstocks and grab the room key. With a burst of urgency, I race down the stairs, and only slow my pace to a fast walk as I make my way through the hotel.

I usually love this time of day on the beach – the midday heat gone but the horizon still a warm hazy blue – and I try to use it to lift my mood. The wind is lighter today, and the sea is almost glass-flat. I can see Lola now, tacking out with an enormous sail, using her skills to build up some speed despite the conditions. A speedboat appears from around the bay, sending ripples through the water, and I watch it streak across the skyline.

It's a beautiful boat. Sleek lines. Sparkling white with a wide navy stripe around the hull. As the boat gets closer, I hold my breath. Because I recognise the driver. Dom. He has a passenger with him, a woman with blonde hair. He turns towards the beach and instantly slows to a crawl. A few minutes later, he manoeuvres alongside the jetty, jumps out of the boat, and ties a mooring line to one of the thick wooden posts. His passenger climbs out too, and they walk up to Jack. He gives the woman a quick hug, then releases her. Who is she?

I stare for a few more seconds, and then the woman turns towards me, lifting her hand to her eyes to block out the sun's glare. Then she waves at me and starts walking over.

'Fuck,' I whisper, as recognition seeps in. 'No fucking way.' Then I stand up and prepare to greet Harriet.

'Frankie Torre, wow. I did not think I was going to see you ever again.' Harriet is a softer, rounder, but more polished version of her twenty-one-year-old self. Perfect make-up, her blonde hair still iron-straight but styled into a sharp bob, and her curvy body wrapped in a sea-green chiffon robe.

'Me neither,' I murmur.

'I bet you're wondering why I'm here.'

'Well …'

'Dom called me. I was at a meeting in Lyon, trying to get an acquisition over the line. A small French software company. But the owner was trying to renegotiate terms, and my client threw his toys, so the deal's off.' She shrugs, like she doesn't care whether I understand what she's talking about or not (which I don't). 'Anyway, I was kicking around with nothing to do, so when Dom told me you'd pitched up with your daughter, I jumped on a plane.'

'So you're a …' Why can't I finish a sentence?

'A lawyer, yes. Life's funny, isn't it? One day I'm a sailing instructor with big dreams, and the next I'm a stressed-out city

219

lawyer with sciatica and a butt too big for Whistles trousers. Anyway, enough about me, come on, let's go.'

I look at Lola out at sea. She's still cruising across the horizon. 'Go where?'

'Dom got the boat out of the marina specially. We're going water-skiing.'

'Wh-what? But I'm not sure I want to.'

Harriet's expression softens and she lets out a sigh. 'Listen, I know you're here because your daughter was in trouble. I don't have kids myself, but I've got Sidney, my black Lab, and I know how far outside my comfort zone I'd go for him. I'm figuring that being back at the hotel is pretty tough for you. And I remember what water-skiing did for your confidence all those years ago, and rightly so, because you were like a pro out there. So come on, let me do this for you.'

Harriet reaches for my hand, and I have a sudden memory of her throwing me her Helly Hansen hoodie. How much comfort it gave me as we searched the beach for Archie. I let myself be led along the sand to the jetty. I see Jack disappear into the water sports hut and feel a mix of annoyance that he's blanking me, and relief that I don't have to face him.

'Hey, Frankie,' Dom says, drawing my attention. 'This was all Harriet's idea, by the way. So if you hate it, blame her.'

'Ah, so noble,' Harriet says, giving him a sardonic smile.

'Nice boat,' I say.

'She's a beauty,' Dom agrees, nodding.

'Expensive, I guess. You must be doing well.' I crease my brow. 'What is it you do again?'

Dom suddenly looks awkward. 'I play the stock market. And she is my only indulgence.'

'Along with that sprawling bachelor pad of yours.' Harriet laughs, then throws a buoyancy aid at me. 'Ski's on the beach,' she instructs. 'You go first.'

Two minutes later, Dom and Harriet are sitting in the idling boat and I'm standing in shallow water close to the shore, but far away from the swimming area. The ski is on my left foot, floating, and my weight is all on my right, my toes digging into the sand for balance. I have the ski rope handle in one hand and a loop of rope in the other – which marks how long I've got to react when the boat starts.

Dom raises his hand to show that he's ready. I take one quick breath and fling the slack of the rope out in front of me. 'Go!' I shout. The tension pulls. I lift up my right leg and slide it into the rubber binding behind my left. It's a perfect start.

A grin spreads across my face as I cut through the wake and fly out wide. I lean over and run my fingertips through the glassy water. Harriet is right – this is my purest, simplest pleasure. Wind whipping past my face, my mind relaxing as my body grows tauter. Eventually I cut back in, absorbing the bumps with my knees, then straight out to the other side. I look at my sparkling reflection in the sun-kissed water.

Maybe Lola is right about me moving on from Izzy's death. And maybe I can forget about the note too – file it as a humourless prank, not a threat, and focus on building a better relationship with my daughter. I cut back in, fly through the wake's churning white water, take the impact, until I hit glass once again. Maybe this is the metaphor I need to live by. Find the courage to face the rough water – go to Sartène, be in Corsica on 31st July, look these people in the eye without feeling scared or ashamed – and then enjoy the feeling of reaching the other side, stronger. A better mother.

Fifteen minutes later, my arm muscles are burning, so when Dom gestures that he's slowing down, I give him a grateful nod. The rope goes slack, and I slide into the water. Dom circles around and I hand the ski to Harriet. Then I heave myself onto the boat, dragging the rope with me.

'That was awesome, thank you.'

'My turn now!' Harriet drops her robe to reveal a burnt orange swimsuit and matching shorts. Then she grabs the mono-ski and jumps into the water. She slides it on more deftly than I would have expected, then calls for the rope. A minute later, she's whipping across the wake, and I'm hovering next to Dom, tiny droplets of white water spitting on my arm.

'Just like the old days,' he murmurs with a smile.

I wrap the towel with its Hotel Paoli logo around me and sink into the cushioned seat. 'Listen, I think I owe you an apology. If it hasn't passed its sell-by date.'

He's quiet for a moment, staring out to sea. 'It wasn't you I was mad with,' he finally says. 'Not really. I knew she got inside your head that summer.'

His tone is so bitter that I find myself thinking like Lola for a moment, suspecting everyone of killing Izzy. 'She told me that you never gave her a chance. That all of you blanked her from day one. I believed her.'

'Well, it's bullshit. When I arrived, I tried to make friends with her, but she didn't want to know. She only cared about sucking up to Raphael or going partying with the locals. She must have decided she wanted a friend on the waterfront at some point, and you were the chosen one. It was a hard watch at times.'

My face smarts. Was Izzy really as fake as Dom makes out? Was I that naïve?

Dom must sense my discomfort because his tone softens. 'Listen, you were eighteen and had just lost your father, and she was a master manipulator. You had no chance. And more than that, it was a lifetime ago. Just file it under "past mistakes" and move on.'

'But you didn't move on,' I note. 'Moving out here. Staying in touch with Harriet.'

'Yeah well, that was the long tentacles of Facebook. When I posted about buying a place out here, she messaged me and suggested coming out for a visit. Though it was more of a state-ment than a request. She travels a lot with her job, and I seem to be a stopping-off place for her when she needs some R and R.'

I laugh. 'You always were too nice for your own good.'

'Yeah, I was, wasn't I?' Dom smiles, then looks away. 'But people learn, I guess.'

Lola

28th July

Lola fixes a new sparkly stud into her helix and tries to ignore the pounding in her chest. God, she hopes tonight is going to work. It's either a genius idea, or the stupidest thing she's ever thought of. She pulls on her favourite Urban Outfitters camo pants and a black sleeveless crop top, then pulls her bedroom door closed behind her and walks with purpose towards the hotel bar. Too quickly to back out.

She came up with the idea after she was introduced to Harriet, another one of her mum's old work colleagues, who has shown up after hearing Mum was in town. Because the more she considers it, the more Lola thinks that her mum was right in the first place; there was someone else in the water that night. And with so many of the suspects now at the hotel, it was too good an opportunity to miss. She would organise a dinner together. The perfect opportunity to grill them all – in front of her mum.

Raphael is her number-one suspect – the argument, his mafia and police links, him showing up in the water, it all makes sense. But Jack is a close second – grief can make people do crazy things.

And she's not ruling the others out either – Dom didn't like Izzy, and he was swimming too. And if Anna was arguing with Raphael because she suspected an affair – Lola knows it's just a guess, but why else do married couples argue about attractive single women? – then Anna might have killed her. And there's also Raphael's dad, Salvo. Patrick said he had a fishing boat, and his own brother was a gangster. She doesn't know that he even knew Izzy, but that's why she needs this dinner. To uncover more info.

She invited Jack first. She thought he might refuse – he and her mum don't exactly get on – but he just shrugged and said, 'Sure, why not.' Dom predictably jumped at the offer, and Harriet seemed to invite herself before Lola could get the words out.

Lola then asked Patrick to invite his parents on her behalf, using Harriet showing up as an excuse. And he messaged her an hour ago to say they would be there.

It's like an episode of *Death in Paradise*, and she's proud of herself for setting it up. Although her strategy might be a little more basic than those tropical detectives. She's just going to ask questions about the night Izzy died and watch everyone's faces for clues. Twenty-one years is a long time to carry around that kind of guilt, and she's hoping it will reveal itself if she prods hard enough.

She pauses to take a breath, fixes on a smile, and walks into the bar.

The first person she sees is Patrick serving drinks. He winks at her, and her stomach lurches. The second person is her mum, but she looks decidedly less happy.

'Are you sure about this?' she says quietly when Lola sidles up next to her. 'I'd prefer it to just be the two of us having dinner tonight.'

Lola rouses her best smile. 'I thought it would help you move on. A reminder that everyone else has got on with their life, so you can too.'

'Hey, Lola. Frankie.'

Lola turns at the sound of Dom's voice. 'Thanks for coming, guys. Mum's really pleased you could make it.'

Harriet smiles, but it's nothing compared to Dom's beam. Lola guessed last night that Dom still has a thing about her mum, and it's even more obvious now. It's a long time to hold on to those feelings – especially as it doesn't seem like her mum returns them – so he must have fallen for her hard that summer. But is that relevant to Izzy's death?

'The table is ready,' Raphael calls out from the bar entrance. 'Shall we go?'

'No need to be so rude,' Anna tuts, but she turns towards the restaurant, beating him to the door. There doesn't seem to be much love lost between them – which might be a sign that something happened between Raphael and Izzy all those years ago – but why didn't Anna leave him? Was it about marriage values? Patrick? Or because Anna got her revenge in a different way?

Lola frowns as she follows the others. Maybe this is going to be harder than she thought.

Lola

28th July

An hour and a half later, their plates have been cleared, and Lola calculates that enough wine has been drunk for her to turn the conversation towards Izzy.

'I guess it's not long now until the anniversary of Izzy's death,' she starts, her eyes flitting between their faces as subtly as she can manage.

'Thursday,' Harriet says, nodding. 'Two days after …' She looks at Jack. 'Never mind.'

'Why are you talking about Izzy?' Jack asks gruffly. Their eyes catch and Lola has the sense that he can see right through her. 'It's not like you knew her. Or were even born then.'

'I guess I like murder mysteries,' Lola says, flustered by the directness of his question.

'But it wasn't a murder,' Dom reminds her. 'It was a tragic accident.'

Raphael shifts in his chair and stares at Frankie. 'We all know how she died.'

Shit. This isn't going according to plan. Lola needs to steer the

227

conversation away from her mum. 'Isn't the anniversary the same day as the gathering you've organised for Salvo?' The question is partly to change the subject, but she has also been thinking about the coincidence, and whether it implicates Raphael. Except why would he draw attention to Izzy's death if he was involved in it? Is there any chance that Salvo killed her and confided in his son, and this gathering is some kind of macabre celebration of him getting away with it?

Raphael nods, crosses his forearms, and leans them on the table. 'The 31st of July is an important date in Corsican history,' he explains. 'It's just ancient folklore, but the old boys still like to believe in it.' He pauses. 'My father believed in it.'

'Ah, you mean the famous mazzeri legend,' Harriet says. 'I still remember that gruesome procession on Bastille Day. I read up on the myth after that summer.'

Lola notices how colour drains from her mum's face. Could Bastille Day be another difficult memory for her? She narrows her eyes in concentration. Didn't that newspaper article say that Raphael's uncle was shot dead on that night in another Corsican town?

'Hang on,' Harriet continues, turning to look at Frankie. 'You were the expert back in the day, I seem to recall. Didn't your dad used to tell you mazzeri stories when you were little?'

'Yeah, sometimes,' her mum mutters, threading her napkin between her fingers.

'So what is the mazzeri legend?' Lola asks, feeling left out.

'The mazzeri are Corsican sorcerers with the power to kill people in their dreams,' Jack says, with an icy tone. 'That's right, isn't it, Frankie?'

'Actually no, that isn't right,' Raphael butts in impatiently.

Lola tilts her head. Why is Raphael coming to her mum's rescue? She turns to look at Jack's taut expression. Is he the real villain here after all?

'You know, there's an amazing painting of a mazzeri scene in the shop,' Harriet says. 'Have you seen it? Do you know the one I mean, Dom?'

'No, sorry, I haven't been in the shop in a while,' Dom says. 'Anyway, I don't know why we're arguing about Corsican folklore.'

'I think some Corsicans use the legend to remind everyone how ruthless they can be,' Anna says, looking sadly at her empty wine glass, then reaching for the bottle. 'One of many excuses, that is.'

Raphael clicks his tongue and shakes his head, but he doesn't challenge his wife.

'What's the significance of the 31st of July?' Lola asks, trying to pull the conversation back to Izzy, the date of her death.

'It's the darkest night,' Jack says. 'When most of the killings take place.'

'Again, you're not explaining it right.' Raphael's voice rises a notch. 'The legend goes that the mazzeri are most active on the night of the 31st of July. But they are prophets, not killers.'

'Whatever,' Jack says, wafting his hand like he's bored. 'I'm going to the bar for a drink.' He pushes back his chair and stomps off without offering to buy drinks for anyone else around the table.

Raphael raises his eyebrows, then continues. 'Dom is correct that it's just a fantasy story, but Salvo saw it as more than that. So when Patrick suggested we have the gathering on Thursday, it felt like a good way to honour him.'

'Did Izzy believe in the mazzeri?' Lola asks. She knows it's a stupid question, but she wants to start talking about Izzy again.

'I told you,' Harriet says. 'It was your mum who knew most about the legend back then.'

'Oh, it's all so long ago,' her mum says, wafting her hand in the air. 'I haven't thought about that story in decades.'

Her mum's voice is light and dismissive, so Lola doesn't understand why no one except Harriet can meet her eye.

'Well personally, I'm looking forward to celebrating Salvo's life on Thursday,' Dom says. 'I'm done with that date being all about Izzy's death. Especially with it coming two nights after the anniversary of Archie's passing.' He shakes his head. 'I still remember how happy he looked the last time I saw him.'

Her mum looks up. 'At the waterfall? But Archie didn't look happy at all. He left because of how bad he was feeling.'

'No, not then: later. I couldn't sleep because that cut on my head was throbbing like hell fire. And when I went out to get some fresh air, I saw Jack and Archie down by the hut. They were playfighting like a couple of schoolkids.' He sighs. 'That's why the news the next morning was such a shock. But I guess people are past logic when they decide to take their own life.'

Her mum turns towards Harriet, and they share a look. 'What time was this?'

'I don't know. Maybe around two o'clock?'

'But that doesn't make sense,' her mum goes on, a mix of confusion and shock on her face. 'Izzy told me that Jack was in town all night.'

Dom raises his eyebrows. 'You mean Izzy the pathological liar?'

Jack returns to the table and drops into his chair, making everyone jump. He swirls an ice cube in what looks like a glass of whisky. 'Speaking ill of the dead again, Dom?'

'I don't remember you mourning her too much.'

Jack shrugs. 'I asked her not to go swimming and she ignored me. It's not my fault that karma got her.'

'That's why I didn't go,' Harriet says. 'I felt it was disrespectful.'

'I'm pretty sure you just didn't want to get your hair wet,' Dom murmurs.

'Did you go swimming, Dom?' Lola asks, pretending she doesn't know.

'Um, yeah. I took a bit longer to get in than the girls though, so I hadn't swum that far when it all kicked off.' Dom turns to Frankie. 'Do you remember? I was still in the shallow water when you started screaming. I can't remember when you got in, Raphael?'

'After you, for sure,' Raphael says. 'It's hard to remember exactly.'

230

'You were on the beach too, weren't you, Jack?'

Everyone, including Lola, turns to look at her mum, surprised by the hardness in Frankie's voice.

'When Raphael found Izzy,' she goes on.

Jack bristles. 'I came when I heard all the commotion. I didn't go in the water.'

'Why not?' Lola asks. 'Didn't you want to help with the search?'

Jack's face sours. 'There were heaps of people looking by then. And I'd just had a shower; I didn't want to get dirty again. Is that all right with you?'

Lola nods in response, then looks at her mum's stricken face. Maybe it is time to drop the conversation. But she can't help thinking that a shower gives Jack the perfect excuse for having wet hair.

Frankie

28th July

I swill the Amaretto around the cubes of ice in my glass. I haven't drunk neat spirits for years, but I need it this evening after that dinner. The old-fashioned way to knock myself out.

'That was intense,' Lola murmurs beside me, nursing her own alcoholic drink – a rum and Coke. 'But I guess it shows that there are multiple people who could have killed Izzy. Do you see that now too?'

I turn to look at Lola sitting next to me at the bar. She looks pale – shellshocked – and it reminds me that she's still a child really. From the moment I confessed, she's been desperate to convince me that someone other than Izzy pulled at my leg that night, but it seems that it's only now that she has realised what that means. That there might actually be a killer amongst us.

And Lola doesn't even know about the note. I can't tell her – it will freak her out for a start. But more than that, she'll want to know what it says, and that would bring questions I don't want to answer. I'm sane enough to know the note is guesswork, not magic. But after everything that happened with Izzy, how can I just ignore it? When the sun's shining, and I'm skimming across the sea on a water-ski, it's easy to think I'm strong enough to ride this storm. But now, with black skies, and the bitter taste of that dinner. I just want to go home.

'Mum?' Lola nudges, pulling me back to the question. 'What do you think?'

I sigh. 'Sorry, but I really don't know.'

'Dom was already in the sea,' Lola reminds me quietly. 'And Jack was lurking around the beach with wet hair. And no one seems to know when Raphael got in the water, so maybe he was already there. And where was Anna? Or Raphael's father, Salvo? His own brother was gunned down in some mafia feud apparently and he owned a fishing boat. From how you describe the scene, either of them could have got out of the water further up the beach without anyone noticing. There are so many suspects.'

I take a mouthful of the Amaretto, feel the bitter almond taste hit the back of my throat. 'It takes a certain kind of person to be a killer, a very rare kind of person.' My words bring an image of Jack. The man who set fire to his home with his family inside. He told Izzy that he was in town on the night Archie died. At least, that's what Izzy told me. But Dom said he saw Jack with Archie at 2 a.m., so that can't be true. I can't believe I only found that out tonight, but I guess Dom and I were past communicating by then.

If Dom's right, it means that Jack was the last person to see Archie alive, not me. All this time, Jack has blamed me for not giving Archie the emotional support he needed. And now I find out that it was Jack who let him down. And lied about it.

They were playfighting. But were they? Or did Dom witness a real fight?

Nausea swirls in my belly and I tense my muscles to contain it. The police called Archie's death suicide as soon as they found him. But the police clearly like to jump to conclusions. How hard is it to tell the difference between hanging yourself and being hanged by someone else? Panic starts to edge into my chest. There's only one person who links both Izzy and Archie's deaths: Jack. They both knew his secret.

And so do I.

Is twenty-one years long enough to prove that I can keep my mouth shut? That I'm not a threat to Jack's freedom?

'Maybe whoever it was didn't set out to kill Izzy, like I said before,' Lola continues, not hiding the hope in her voice. The need to believe we're not in danger. 'You were all drunk. It could easily have been a joke gone wrong.'

'It didn't feel like a joke,' I can't help whispering. The memory is too strong. Being dragged underwater. The absolute terror I felt in that moment.

Lola's face cracks for a moment, then straightens as she sits up taller. She reaches out, her expression now resigned, and I feel a gentle fizz as her hand touches my arm. 'I think someone tried to kill you, Mum,' she murmurs. 'They didn't succeed, but they did kill your friend. And because you've been so blinded by guilt, they've gotten away with it for all this time.'

I look at Lola. For years I've convinced myself that the intense force of that pull was a sign of Izzy's desperation. But in truth, how can a young woman struggling for her life have that kind of strength?

Someone else was in the water that night.

Then I think about the note. Someone is clearly trying to scare me away, and Lola has just asked a dozen questions about that night at dinner – in front of every one of the possible suspects. I need to get us both out of here. Urgently. But that means persuading Lola to leave.

'If that's true,' I say. 'Then we really shouldn't be here.'

Lola narrows her eyes, then looks away.

'If Izzy was killed, like you say,' I go on. 'Then that means it might not be safe for us here. Especially with you bringing up Izzy's death at every opportunity.' I reach out for Lola, but she has moved too far away. 'We could come back another time, to

234

a different hotel, visit Sartène, maybe bring Grams too.'

Lola clicks her tongue. 'But I don't want to go,' she says, her voice quiet but steely. 'It's not right that we should be scared away when we've done nothing wrong. I came here because I wanted you to realise that you shouldn't feel guilty, and now you're twisting things to get us to run away.'

'Lola.'

'Listen, my birthday is Friday,' Lola says, her voice suddenly needling. 'And the windsurf competition is Saturday. Your room here is free until Sunday, so let's just stay here until then. Please, Mum? I'll be careful and it's only a few days.'

I look at her imploring eyes. I love this girl so much and I hate disappointing her. But it's too much of a risk. 'No, I'm sorry, we can't. There could be a murderer here,' I say quietly.

'Yeah, or it might have been Salvo, and he's dead,' she whispers back. 'Or Dom and he only ever meant to hurt Izzy.' She takes a deep breath. 'Listen, I promise to keep my head down, not mention that night again. I came here so that you could put the past behind you, so let's do just that.'

'No, Lola. We are leaving tom—'

'Why do you never listen?!' Lola interrupts, throwing her arms in the air, then twisting off the bar stool. 'Do you know what? I'm done. I've got over a grand in my bank account. I might not have a working bank card right now, but I can make online transfers. I'm sure someone here will sub me some cash, and book a flight for me, if I give them the money for it. Which means you can go. Hide away again.'

'Lola, please don't.'

'Goodnight, Mum.'

I watch Lola walk away in anger for the third time in one day. Tears well in my eyes because this is the worst of them. No chance to make up before bedtime.

I finish my drink and lower the glass onto the bar.

'Can I get you another?'

I look at Patrick and manage a weak smile. 'It's very tempting, thanks, but I think I've had enough.' I hesitate, then continue, even though I don't know why I need to explain myself. 'I guess this is the second time you've seen Lola and I argue today. You must think we have a terrible relationship.'

He looks guarded, like he's already chosen his side. But then his features soften. 'Lola told me at breakfast how hard it is for you to be here. After everything that happened. She cares a lot about you.'

I can't speak, but I nod and manage a half-smile. Then I push off the barstool and head for the stairs. As I walk towards my room, I sense a shadow shift in my peripheral vision. It unnerves me and I twist to see who it is, but I'm too late – they've disappeared down the stairs.

But I'm being silly – it will just be another guest heading to the bar. And yet, my instincts know differently because when I open my door I look straight down at the floor. And that same intuition means I'm not completely shocked when I see a new note lying there.

But that changes when I read the words. I push my hand against my mouth to dull the sound of the scream escaping, and I drop to the ground. But I can't drag my eyes away.

Guess who I dreamed about last night, mazzera?
But who will die first? Mother or daughter?
Un, deux, trois, quatre ...

Lola

29th July

Lola murmurs a few swear words as she looks over towards reception. She was hoping that Patrick would be behind the desk, but it's Anna. Anna who Lola still can't imagine getting her hair wet when she swims, never mind dragging a young woman under water. Although for some reason, that doesn't make her any less scary.

She takes a breath and walks over. 'Um, morning. Patrick said I could use the computer in the office again. I was hoping to check my emails, see whether my travel documents have been sent yet.' While she wouldn't admit it to her mum in the bar, last night's dinner did rattle her. Not enough to convince her they need to leave Corsica. But knowing it's possible suddenly feels important.

Anna looks pensive as she glances at the closed office door. 'Yes, I suppose so. Just give me a minute.' She disappears into the office, then returns moments later, more relaxed. 'She's all yours.'

Lola slips around the reception desk and into the office, pulling the door closed behind her. The desk is clear except for an old-fashioned telephone made of yellowing plastic and a boxy computer and keyboard. When she used it on Sunday to apply for her emergency travel documents, she had Raphael watching over her. It's a relief to have the place to herself this morning.

She opens her email account. There are two official-looking messages from the British consulate in Marseille, both sent yesterday, the first confirming that her documents had been produced, and the second that they'd been posted out. That means they should arrive today. Relief settles over her and she turns towards the window, as though the postman might suddenly appear. But there's just a gardener digging up weeds and a topless man in too-short shorts doing shuttle runs up and down the drive. She turns her attention back to the screen.

There are loads more unread emails. Mainly marketing ones which she deletes without opening. There's one from her school about A level results day next month, and a good luck note from Southampton University. The emails from the various water sports clubs she's involved with make her pause. Home feels so far away right now.

She's just about to close her account down when a new email pops up in her inbox. She feels a burst of adrenaline as she looks at the name. Nicole Bassot. She's not sure why she filled in the yoga studio's contact form in the library yesterday. Maybe because she had time to spare before meeting Patrick. Or perhaps because the raw grief in Nicole's blogpost got to her. Either way, she hadn't expected a response. Why would Nicole care that a stranger wanted to pass on her condolences?

But it looks like she does.

Dear Lola,
Thank you for your kind message, and for giving me an opportunity to practise my English. I think of Isobel every day, and it is comforting to know that people are still finding out about her story. I had no idea that the hotel had a plaque made in her honour – although they do owe her that and much more. It sounds like

you are enjoying your sailing teacher job there, but please be careful.

Lola squirms in the chair. She didn't want to mention her mum in her message to Nicole – at the very least, the girl who survived when her own daughter didn't – so she had to make up a reason for knowing about Izzy's death. A plaque in the hotel was the first thing that jumped into her head. But then she worried that Nicole might have visited the hotel, so she put the plaque in the staff accommodation. Which meant giving herself a fictional job. Why she chose the same job that Izzy did is harder to explain. She pushes hair away from her forehead – already sticky with sweat – and continues reading.

I try very hard to find peace in Isobel's passing. I have learned to accept that she made the wrong choice that night – like we all have the capacity to do – and so was partly to blame for the tragic consequences. But there was another girl in the water with her who I understand put her own wellbeing before Isobel's life. I try not to blame her, but it is a daily struggle.

And as you mentioned that you've read my blog, you will know that I have an intimate understanding of blame. I lost my husband when Isobel was young, and there are two people responsible for his fatal car crash. I am ashamed to say that I am one of them. I will carry that guilt forever, and I only hope the person I share culpability with feels an equally heavy burden. But that is an episode I won't let myself dwell on for long.

Thank you again for getting in touch, and I hope you have an enjoyable summer. Please stay safe. Corsica has its own unique dangers.

Nicole

Lola leans back in the chair. *Corsica has its own unique dangers.* Of course Nicole would say that – her daughter died in the island's waters – but it still makes Lola shiver. Because her own mum could have written those words.

She looks back at the email. It's horrible that Nicole has blamed her mum all this time, just as Frankie has blamed herself. But Nicole will have been fed the official police line, so doesn't know to be suspicious of anyone else. Lola wonders how Nicole would react if she confided in her. Explained her suspicions about there being someone else in the water, an actual killer. Would Nicole be glad to have a real villain to remove Izzy's portion of blame? Or would dismantling her theory that Izzy had some control over her destiny shatter Nicole's search for peace?

Lola opens Nicole's website and clicks on her image. Nicole and her mum have more than a fear of Corsica in common. Grief and guilt threaded together like rope, always threatening to hang them. And both of them with the shadow of another person looming in the background. Lola wonders who Nicole is referring to when she talks about sharing the blame for her husband's death. Then she leans forward and hits the reply button. She's had enough of secrets. Nicole deserves to know everything.

As she hits 'send' on her email, the door opens, and she instinctively shuts down the website.

'Hey, Lola. My mother said you were in here.' Patrick closes the door behind him – an act that causes a weird clenching in Lola's belly – and perches on the desk. 'Have you got what you need?'

'What? Oh sorry, yes,' she says, still flustered by Nicole's email and now Patrick's proximity. 'My travel documents should arrive today.' Lola is pleased to see a hint of disappointment wash across Patrick's face. 'But they last six weeks,' she hears herself follow up with. She watches Patrick's eyes light up and pushes away an image of her mum's pleading face.

'It's my day off today,' he says. 'I wondered if you wanted to go for a picnic?'

'You and me?' Lola asks, her heart suddenly thinking it's got a one-hundred-metre race to win.

'We can ask your mum to come too if you'd like?'

'No, God no. You and me, that would be great.' She catches his eye, then looks away, hiding the grin that's spreading across her face. At least she knows that Patrick isn't dangerous.

'I'll take you to my favourite secret beach.'

'Secret?' Lola's excitement wanes slightly. She's grown to hate that word lately.

But Patrick nods, oblivious. 'Not a tourist in sight. Probably not another person. You'll love it, I promise.' He smiles again, then twists off the table and opens the door, his palm leaning on the handle. 'I'll get some picnic stuff from the kitchen. It's ten thirty now, so shall I meet you out front at eleven?'

'Sounds good. Do we walk there?'

'Oh, it's too remote for that.' He laughs. 'Twenty minutes in the car, then a half-hour hike around the headland. Does that sound okay?'

Lola looks at Patrick's hopeful face. He may be eight years older than her, but he looks like a little boy now. She feels her shoulders relax. 'It sounds perfect,' she says.

Lola

29th July

Lola feels a line of sweat drip down the centre of her back. It's approaching midday and the sun is bearing down on them. But she doesn't care about the heat. She is with Patrick in a beautiful, secluded part of Corsica with the whole afternoon stretching out ahead of them.

'What's that over there?' She points at a crumbling stone structure, one and a half walls with holes for windows and a doorway.

'One of Porto Vecchio's many ruins,' Patrick says, smiling. 'If I had to sum up Corsican history in one word, it would be invasion. Everyone has wanted this little island – the Greeks, the Romans, the Genoese, the French; even Mussolini tried his luck. I don't know whether Corsicans are brave or stupid, but they fought them every time. Some are still fighting for independence from the French. They've never won, but that doesn't stop them trying.'

'I guess that's impressive?' Lola says. After parking the car on a dusty side road, they walked through some woodland, and onto a steep path that took them above the treeline. They're now on a flat stretch of grassland with boulders ahead of them and distant views of the sea below.

'It made them tough, for sure. Although some might say too tough.'

'What do you mean?'

He blinks, smiles. 'You know what a vendetta is, right?'

Lola nods. 'When someone hates another person and wants payback for whatever they've done to them.'

'Officially, it's a blood feud. You do something bad to my kin, and I'll kill someone in yours.'

A gust of wind swirls around Lola's shoulders as the word 'kill' hangs in the air. 'I guess that's what I meant,' she mumbles.

'Well, Corsica is famous for its vendettas,' Patrick goes on. 'And they can last through multiple generations. For centuries, Corsicans considered it their duty to avenge any wrongdoing. There's even a specific type of knife for it – it's called a *vendetta corse*.'

'I hope you don't have one of those,' Lola says, pretending she's joking. They've reached the boulders, and she plants her feet carefully. Last night everyone was talking about a deadly Corsican folklore, and now it's vendettas. So much for Corsica's French nickname, *L'Île de Beauté*.

Patrick smiles but doesn't answer her question. 'Do you need a hand?'

Lola shakes her head and moves on to the next boulder. It's smooth but sturdy, and she silently swears at herself for hesitating. It's not like Izzy's death had anything to do with Corsican vendettas after all.

But it could be linked to another element of Corsican culture, she thinks as she speeds up. If Salvo was involved with the mafia like his brother, maybe Izzy saw something she shouldn't have and got killed for it. And at least if Salvo's the bad guy, it means they're not in any danger now.

'Will there be any other family members at Salvo's memorial on Thursday?' she asks, digging for clues.

'No, I don't think so. He's got four nephews, my dad's cousins. But they live in Marseille, and they were only here last week for the funeral.'

'Four brothers, wow.'

'Yeah. I was told that their dad was desperate for a daughter so kept trying. But it wasn't to be.'

'That's your grandfather's brother, right? Did you know him well?'

'No, I never met him. He died when I was little.'

Lola wishes she could see Patrick's face, but he's ahead of her and she can only see his back, the almond tan of his neck against the white T-shirt. 'That's sad,' she says. 'How did he die?'

Patrick doesn't speak for a few moments and Lola worries that she's blown it. But then he coughs and starts talking. 'He was shot. The thing is, my uncle was involved with some bad people. Mafia. So yeah, he died when I was five, but I doubt I'd have met him even if he hadn't. My grandpa hated everything to do with the mafia, so he always kept us well away from Uncle Jean.'

'Oh, right.' Lola doesn't know whether to feel pleased that Patrick has no criminal influences, or disappointed that she might have to cross Salvo off her list of suspects.

'Anyway, it's not far now,' Patrick continues. 'Once we get over these rocks, the path takes us down to a footbridge, and we can access the beach from there.'

They clamber over the final boulders and pause to look at the view. They're high up now and the wind is swirling. Lola holds her flying hair back from her face. The sea looks magical, a mass of sparkles as the sun hits the crest of every wave. 'It's beautiful,' she says. 'And you're right about it being remote. I see now why you get the beach to yourself most of the time.'

'One of the benefits of being born here, I guess. Salvo used to bring me here before he moved away. We'd bring fishing nets and look for crabs in the rocks.'

'I bet you missed him when he left. Why did he go?'

244

Patrick looks out to sea. 'He grew up in Sartène, but I'm not sure why he went back there when he did.'

Lola thinks about the article she read, how it said the hotel was passed to Salvo by his mother. 'He still owned the hotel though?'

Patrick sighs, then eyes the footpath. 'Part-owned it, with my dad. I think they fell out over something, probably to do with business. My father wanted to modernise everything while my grandfather was a traditionalist. It's not a great combination.'

The path is wide enough for two now and Lola falls in step beside him. 'Did you go and stay with your grandparents in Sartène?'

'Yeah, in the school holidays. In fact, I was packed off there for most of the summer break for about ten years running.'

'That must have been fun?'

Patrick falls quiet again, as though he's considering the question. 'It was good to get away from here. But Salvo had changed by then, at least that's how it felt. He worked such long hours on the vineyard, like it was some kind of penance.' He blinks. 'I wish I'd known then what I know now.'

'And what's that?' Lola probes.

Patrick looks embarrassed. 'I'm sorry, but I don't really want to talk about it, if that's okay?'

Lola's cheeks flare. Why is she prying? Salvo's only been dead a couple of weeks. 'Of course.'

Patrick smiles his thanks. 'Look,' he says, pointing ahead. 'There's the bridge. Beach is just the other side. Come on.' He starts walking again and after a second of hesitation, Lola follows. She needs to forget about Izzy, and who might have killed her, for a while. She's here to enjoy a picnic with the most gorgeous man she's ever met.

'Coming,' she calls out, then picks up her pace to catch up.

They cross the wooden bridge over an inlet of water and finally arrive at the beach. And it's worth the journey. It's a small cove, formed by rocks and lined with yellow and lilac flowered shrubs.

The sand is soft and white, and the stretch of water in front of the beach is glistening bright aquamarine in the sunshine.

'This is amazing,' Lola murmurs as Patrick unstraps a picnic blanket from his backpack and lays it out on the sand.

'Are you hungry?' he asks, kneeling down over his bag. 'Because I brought loads.'

Lola smiles, nods, and drops down next to him. She watches him pull out a collection of fresh foods. Then he takes a knife from a separate pocket of his bag and starts slicing the cucumber and tomato. It reminds her of the knife he mentioned – *vendetta corse* – and she wonders how Corsican Patrick feels. He's lived here all his life, but his mother is English, and Lola can't imagine Anna has much time for Corsican traditions.

Lola pulls off a hunk of bread and rips it open with her fingernails. She fills it with a soft cheese that she remembers is called Brocciu, a local goat's cheese, and shoves in some salad. 'My grandfather is Corsican,' she says, suddenly realising they have that in common – a mix of Corsican and English blood.

'Oh really?' Patrick looks surprised for a second, then his face settles. 'On your mum's side?'

'Yeah.'

'So you're officially half as crazy as me then?'

Lola starts to laugh, but then she thinks about her mum, and how she's spent time on a psychiatric ward. Her face drops.

'What's wrong?' Patrick asks. 'I don't really think you're crazy, you know.'

Lola shakes her head. 'No, it's not that. It's just that my mum has struggled with her mental health over the years and …'

'Oh God, I'm sorry. And you're right, it's not something to laugh about.' He falls quiet for a moment. 'That must have been tough for you.'

Lola shrugs. 'Not really. I was sheltered from it mostly. But that's why Mum takes herself off for a few weeks every summer, just in case she loses it again.'

'Why the summer?'

'I think it's to do with Izzy's death. She gets nightmares, and insomnia, and it all spirals, I guess. It means she misses my birthday, but her mental health is more important.'

Patrick leans over, pushes a strand of Lola's hair away from her eyes. His face is only a few centimetres away from hers, and Lola can feel the electric charge sparking in the trapped air between them. 'She's lucky to have you,' he murmurs.

Then he leans further, closing the gap.

Frankie

29th July

'Oh my God, Lola, where have you been?!' Adrenaline is threatening to overwhelm me. I feel an urge to grab Lola's shoulders, but I don't know whether I want to hug her until she suffocates or shake her until she breaks.

'All right, Mum, chill out.' Lola lifts her hands.

'But I haven't seen you since first thing this morning! I've been so worried. Why didn't you tell me you were going out? Or answer my calls?'

'I've been on a picnic with Patrick, okay? And I didn't get any calls.' Lola pulls her phone out of her back pocket with a look of injustice. But then her expression changes. 'Oh,' she says, her voice deflating. 'It's out of juice. It's this stupid, cheap phone you got me. The battery only lasts five minutes. But why didn't you ask Anna or Raphael where I was?'

'I did! Both of them said they didn't know.'

'Really?' Lola tilts her head. 'That's weird; I'm sure Patrick told them.'

I blink away tears. After getting that terrifying note last night,

248

I ran straight out to see Lola. But I found I couldn't knock on her door, not after our argument. So I pulled a sun lounger up to the staff accommodation block entrance instead, grabbed a couple of towels from the water sports hut, and curled up on that. I didn't think I'd sleep at all, but the dawn birdsong woke me around five o'clock so I must have dropped off at some point.

When Lola emerged a few hours later, I pretended I'd been out for an early morning walk. I desperately wanted to convince her of the danger we're in, but I couldn't bear another argument, so I kept quiet and promised myself that I'd bring it up when I found the strength. I hoped we'd have breakfast together, but Lola said she wanted to check on the progress of her travel documents first. That was such welcome news that I let her go without arranging to meet up afterwards. And when I came down from my shower fifteen minutes later, I couldn't find her anywhere.

'No one knew where you were,' I say, my voice breaking.

'I'm sorry, okay?' Lola says, dropping down opposite me and leaning forward over the small table. 'I should have told you. But I'll be an adult in three days, Mum. I went for a picnic with a friend, we ate, swam, chatted, and then I came back to the hotel. No drama, no danger. Just usual holiday stuff.'

I nod. I need to let this go. Remember that the only thing that matters right now is that she's okay. 'So have your travel documents arrived?'

Lola lets out a long sigh and leans back. 'I haven't checked at reception yet, but yes, I guess so. I got an email from the consulate.'

'Great.' I try to hide the relief dripping off me. 'Shall we go pick them up now?'

Lola looks away. 'There's no hurry. I need a shower, and I want to charge my phone. I also think I might have run out of credit.'

I push my lips together. Last night Lola threatened to stay in Corsica by herself if I insisted on leaving. But she was angry then and I hoped it was just her lashing out. After last night's note, there's no way I can let her stay, but if I push too hard, I risk her storming off again. 'I can buy the phone card while you're in the shower. And we may as well pick up your documents now,' I coax. 'As we're so close to reception.'

'I know what you're doing, Mum,' Lola says quietly. 'You think that once I have them, I'll suddenly want to go home. But it doesn't work like that.'

I feel my eyes grow hot. I don't know who is sliding notes under my door, or what they know about my dream in Gatwick Airport car park. The first note could just about be described as harmless goading, but there's no sugar-coating the second one. That was a threat to kill. I need to change Lola's mind, and maybe there's only one way I can do that.

'I need to tell you something.'

'Oh?' Lola stiffens.

I scan the room. The bar area is empty, but not private. Anyone could wander in. 'Will you come for a walk with me?'

Lola looks away, then back again, and sighs. 'Okay.'

We push out of our chairs and walk through the sliding doors in tandem. We skirt silently around the pool and head in the direction of the sea. When we reach the beach, I veer left, until I reach an empty stretch of sand.

Here goes.

I turn away from Lola and look out to sea. 'Last night you thought I was overreacting about the danger we're in.'

'Yeah, I guess.'

'Well, I haven't told you everything.' I listen to Lola's breathing become shallower as she prepares for yet another secret.

'Oh?'

'I've been getting these notes,' I continue. 'One on Sunday night, and then again last night.'

'What notes?' Lola's tone is part disdain, part fear.

I reach into the pocket of my shorts and pull them out – as though I always knew, eventually, that I'd have to show them to her. I watch as Lola starts reading, but seeing her hand begin to

250

shake drags down the corners of my mouth. 'I'm sorry,' I murmur. 'I didn't want to scare you.'

'What do they mean?' she finally asks, looking up. 'Calling you a mazzera, talking about dreams.'

I've never confided in anyone about my mazzeri dreams, at least not when I've been thinking straight. But I need to try now. 'Do you remember us talking about the mazzeri last night?' I start.

'Yeah, of course. But what has that got to do with you?'

I take a breath. 'I ... I had a dream about Izzy. It was grotesque, but vivid,' I say, trying to find the right words. 'And I had it the night before she died. It was Salvo's fault, putting crazy ideas in my head the morning after we found Archie's body, saying my dad was mazzeri so I probably was too. I knew the dream wasn't really witchcraft or anything, but it was horrible. Me killing a deer, then seeing Izzy's face on the carcass. I can still see it now, clear as day. And then Izzy died, just like the dream foretold.'

'So you started to believe it?' Lola asks, but her voice is soft, not judgemental and it allows me to look at her. My skin feels taut as I hold it in place.

'Not really. At least, not during the daytime,' I say. 'But when I went to bed ... I was scared it might happen again. It was safer to stay awake, but then I'd get so tired.'

'And you've been dealing with this for twenty-one years?'

I shake my head. 'I really struggled in the beginning, but then you came along, and I had something else to focus on. Something amazing. And now most of the time I can treat it as what it is – a creepy story to scare kids around campfires. But then the anniversary comes around, which happens to also be the most powerful night for the mazzeri. And the doubt starts to take over again.'

'Which is the real reason you hide away,' Lola says. 'Why your mental health suffers so much.'

'I never wanted to leave you. But when I nearly killed us both in that car accident when you were three, and then I lost my mind in the hospital and didn't leave for nearly a month, I knew

I had to take precautions.'

'And then I came out to Corsica in secret, and you were forced to come rescue me.'

'I'll do anything for you, I promise. But it was scary. Coming to this hotel, at this time of year.'

'And someone here knows about your vulnerability and is using it against you. To stress you out, or scare you away.'

'I hope that's all it is,' I whisper.

Lola looks back at the notes and takes a long breath. 'You dreamed about me, didn't you?'

'I'm so sorry.'

'That's why you're so desperate to take me home. You think some dark magic is going to kill me.'

I look out to sea. 'I have been fighting it with every ounce of sanity I have. But now someone is sending me these notes. I thought the first one might just be a nasty joke, but look at the words of the second one: "Who will die first? Mother or daughter?" That's a clear threat. And there's a countdown.'

'A count up, you mean.'

'Sorry?'

'One, two, three, four. And the first note only counts to three.'

I look down at the notes in Lola's hand. 'Yes, you're right. Look, I don't know what it means, but I do know it's threatening.'

Lola furrows her brow. 'The first note only mentions me, the second talks about both of us.' She scrapes her bottom lip with her teeth, then looks up. 'What if it's a body count? I'm the third, which is why the first note counts that far, and you're the fourth.'

'But that means ...'

'There have been two before us.'

The waves lap against the shoreline. Cloud has gathered around the mountain peaks in the distance, and it reminds me of a childhood film, a magic kingdom in the sky.

Two before us. If Lola is right ...

'Izzy and Archie,' I whisper.

Lola

29th July

Lola puts down her newly charged phone and sucks on the straw. Keeps sucking until her nostrils burn with carbon dioxide gas. She can't believe this used to be her mum's staple drink; it tastes like rocket fuel.

'Another Long Island iced tea?' the barman asks. Not Patrick, but a young man with blonde hair cropped so short that he looks bald until his stubble catches in the overhead light.

'Sure, why not.' She probably shouldn't be drinking. Not now she knows someone's sending menacing notes to her mum. Threatening to kill them both. But that conversation on the beach, it was a lot. A little numbness is required.

While she hates to admit it, when she thought she was solving a two-decade-old crime, it was almost fun. Playing the detective, cracking a cold case like she was leading a Netflix docu-drama. But things are different now. She might be in real danger, and more than that, so might her mum. The woman who has lived in the shadow of a crime for more than half her life.

Un, deux, trois, quatre. Does the fact it was written in French mean anything? Is it more likely to be Raphael than Jack or Dom or Anna because he's a native French speaker? But they've all been living in French-speaking Corsica for years, and anyway, everyone over five knows those numbers. It doesn't tell her anything. The only thing she knows for sure is that it's not Salvo because he's dead. And for some reason that makes her feel relieved – Patrick's beloved grandfather being innocent.

The barman slides the potent drink towards her, and she sucks on the new straw. She had such an amazing day with Patrick. The picnic, the remote location, the sea lapping into rock pools; it was all perfect. They ate and swam, chatted and made out. How can that have only been a few hours ago? Now she's scared, half-drunk, and grappling with what to do next. Of course she should go home – her mum is desperate to, and there is clearly a risk here. But that means leaving Patrick, the man she is falling for hard. And it also means that whoever wrote the notes will have won. And possibly got away with double murder.

But also, possibly not. The notes are just words. It could all be fake news, some fantasist's bullshit.

She stirs her drink with the straw, then swallows another large mouthful. She has sailed in winds other people consider dangerous, swam in rivers with stronger currents than most swimmers would tackle. She's been flung around the sea on a mono-ski at fifty kilometres an hour. Is she really going to be scared off by a couple of notes and a mystery scribe?

She's so lost in her thoughts that when a hand lands on her arm, she jumps, her thighs smashing against the underside of the bar.

'Shit, sorry,' Patrick says. 'I didn't mean to scare you.'

'No, it's my fault,' she says. 'I was … someplace else.'

Patrick nods. 'Want another drink?'

'Sure. But maybe a glass of wine this time, otherwise you'll be carrying me out.'

'Oh, I wouldn't mind that.' He smiles, and his eyes shine, and despite everything, Lola smiles back, but it's a weaker one than he deserves.

'Hey, Vincent, can I get two glasses of rosé?' he calls out.

They watch in silence as the barman prepares their drinks, then when he puts the glasses in front of them, Patrick clinks his against Lola's.

'Listen, is everything okay?' Patrick asks. 'You look …'

'I'm fine,' Lola interrupts. She knows she sounds abrupt and winces slightly, but Patrick nods.

'I texted you a couple of times.'

'Sorry. I've been busy.' Why is she being so short with him? Whatever the truth is about what happened twenty-one years ago, none of it is Patrick's fault. She looks down at her hands in her lap, and with a swell of horror, realises that she's about to cry.

'Shall we go for a walk?' Patrick asks gently.

She nods, but jams her lips together. She loves that he's picked up on her fragile mood. But also, his thoughtfulness has brought her tears even closer to the surface.

'Come on, let's go.' Patrick curls his fingers around hers, then leads her past the swimming pool and onto the sand. He sinks down, pulling her with him. Lola wonders if he's going to kiss her, and if he does, whether she'll return it. Whether his touch can make her forget about the notes, or even that one of his parents could have written them. But instead, he pulls his trainers off and waits for her to do the same. When they're both barefoot, he pulls her up again and guides her down to the water's edge.

Lola digs her toes into the cold sand.

'I don't want to pry, but if something's wrong, I hope you feel you can trust me with it,' Patrick says quietly. 'I saw your mum earlier and she looked upset too. I want to help.'

Lola stares out to sea. The sun has disappeared behind the mountains, but it's casting a fiery pink glow across the sky and the colourful light is reflecting on the rippling waves.

She wants to confide in Patrick. She needs to talk to someone, and at least there's no way he could have been involved in Izzy's death. But he is also Raphael and Anna's son. If she tells him about the notes, will he talk to them? Where would his loyalties lie? He has nothing good to say about his father, but blood is thicker than water – isn't that how the saying goes?

'Do you believe in the mazzeri legend?' she hears herself asking. Patrick was close to his grandfather. Maybe he can explain why Salvo insisted that her mum was a mazzera.

Patrick shifts his face towards her. 'You mean the folklore about dream hunters?'

'I heard your grandfather believed in it.'

'Yes, that's true. Salvo was a proud Corsican who was born during the ravages of wartime. He had a lot of respect for many aspects of our culture including the mazzeri. But what's that got to do with whatever's upset you?'

Lola sighs. 'Salvo told my mum that she was mazzeri, back in 2004.'

Patrick's eyes widen. 'What? Why did he think that?'

Lola sinks onto the sand and draws her knees up to her chin. She senses Patrick drop down next to her. 'I think he thought she'd inherited it from my grandfather. But it freaked my mum out. And then she had one of those dreams about Izzy,' she admits in a whisper. 'The night before Izzy died.'

'Wow.' Patrick stares out to sea, as still as a mannequin.

'But it's just a fantasy story, isn't it? Like *Stranger Things* or *The Gruffalo*?'

Patrick turns towards her. 'Of course it is. Corsicans love their gruesome stories, but there's no actual truth to it.'

'And Izzy dying the next night is just a coincidence, right?'

'One hundred per cent. You can't cause someone's death by dreaming about it.' He looks at her quizzically. 'But you know that, so why are you so worried about this?'

Lola blinks. The tears are threatening again. Without speaking, Patrick shuffles towards her and she feels breathless in the rising heat between their bodies. 'Mum had the dream about me too,' she finally whispers. 'The night before she flew out here.'

She feels Patrick's torso stiffen. 'You need to forget about it,' he says. 'The mazzeri aren't real. You're not going to die.'

Is this when she tells him about the notes? Explains that her life might actually be in danger in the real world? She feels his arm wrap around her shoulder and leans in. 'Are you sure?' she chooses instead. Maybe this is all she really wants. Reassurance.

He picks up a strand of her hair and moves it behind her ear. 'Yes I'm sure. Because while you're here, with me, I won't let anything bad happen to you.'

Frankie

29th July

Both my friends were murdered. That's what Lola read in the notes, and it makes sense to me too now. Archie didn't kill himself, and I didn't leave Izzy to drown. Someone was in the water with us. Was I supposed to die too; did I fend off the killer? Or was I always meant to be the scapegoat?

I kick at the sand. It flies up, catches in the breeze for a second, then settles a few centimetres closer to the sea. It shows there's an offshore wind, the most dangerous type, the threat of being blown further into treacherous waters.

I know I should go back to the hotel. Check on Lola again. But I can't help wondering if I'm giving myself more credit than I deserve. That in fact, Lola can look after herself better than I can. She's already proven that she's smarter than me by figuring out what the notes mean, and she's been suggesting someone else was involved in Izzy's death right from the start. She trusted my gut instinct more than I did. I'm her mum; it's my job to protect her. But it's also my job to raise her into a capable young woman. And the last few days have shown how I've managed that at least.

I pull out my phone and send her a text. She was heading to the shop after our talk on the beach to buy a new phone card, and she promised to put her phone on charge as soon as she got back to her room, so I'm hoping she has both credit and power. A moment later, I get a text back.

Yes, all good. Meeting Patrick soon. Don't worry about me.

I send a quick response, feeling a mix of relief that Lola's fine, and unease with who she's meeting. Lola getting involved with Patrick is not a good thing, but I know I need to tread carefully. She's not a child anymore; I can't tell her to stop doing something and expect her to follow my rules. And the irony is, Patrick does seem like a nice guy. Nothing like either of his parents. He's older than Lola, yes, but my dad was eighteen years my mum's senior, so I can't hold that against him. Maybe him being around Lola until we get off this island might even be a good thing.

I pick up my pace again. This anniversary never hits as hard as Izzy's, but it always comes with some fallout. Except I'm hoping it won't tonight. I want to sit on the stretch of sand where Archie and I shared those two bottles of terrible digestif and find some kind of peace at last.

For years I have picked apart our conversation, looking for what errors I made, the missed opportunities to pull him back from the brink of hopelessness. But now I know that's not how it was. Yes, Archie was upset. But according to Dom, he was with Jack later on that night. Playfighting or just fighting, he clearly still had some life in him. And now I find out that it could well have been murder, not suicide. After years of hating myself for not doing enough, could the truth be something entirely different?

I pause, assess the view. I think this is where we sat. There's a new hotel set back from the beach that wasn't here in 2004 – although it's a small boutique one, suggesting Corsicans still guard their island against overtourism with the same passion. The sand has been cleared of the scrub that sprouted through it back then, but otherwise it looks the same. The headland with a dirt track that snakes down to the edge of the beach, the woodland behind – where we found Archie's body – and the wide expanse of empty sea in front of me. I drop down onto the sand and stare at the waves.

I don't know how much time passes, but I watch dusk turn to night. It's a clearer sky than I remember it being in 2004, and there is also light from the new hotel, so it's brighter and I can see all the way to the headland. My mind goes back to that night, and amazingly, I find myself smiling. I remember how pleased Archie was with himself when he pulled that bottle of Mirto Bianco out of the sand. And how we collapsed, giggling like little kids.

I lie down. I'm wearing long jeans and a thick hoodie, so the cold sand doesn't infiltrate. And I'm so tired, I wonder if I might drop off, just like I did all those years ago. I close my eyes and go back there. Our heads touching, us sharing our worries – Archie's about Jack, mine about Izzy.

There was a fishing boat that came right up onto the sand. A group of men walking down to it. One of them, so drunk he couldn't stand, being carried by his mates. At least, I assumed he was drunk at the time, but maybe he was ill, or even injured. They were angry, I remember now. Shouting at each other. I wonder why they were going fishing in that state. Were they even fishing? I also wonder why I'm only remembering this now. But that's stupid. That night was the start of the worst two days of my life. Of course I wouldn't remember something unconnected, however strange it was.

The images start to fade, grow darker until there's only blackness behind my eyelids. I'm drifting now, deeper into the sand.

Suddenly I hear a man's voice shouting. *La vengeance est douce!* I whip open my eyes, gasp, push up to a crouch. Volts of adrenaline pulsate through my limbs as images crackle through my mind.

But then I see a child, maybe eight or nine, running towards the water's edge, squealing. A man my age – his father probably – is chasing him, his hands up and fingers splayed like he's ready to tickle the child into submission.

Tears of relief sprout in my eyes. Not everything in this place is bad or dangerous. I straighten up and start walking back to the hotel. It's dark now, and when I see the lights of Hotel Paoli, I breathe a sigh of relief. But the feeling is only fleeting – because the real danger is in there somewhere.

I look at my watch. It's past eleven o'clock, which means I've missed dinner. I don't want to go to my room in case there's another note waiting for me there, but I'm also nervous about going to see Lola if she's still with Patrick. She's a young woman now and deserves her privacy. I could go to the bar, but I'm too wired to risk drinking alcohol, and too scared to abstain.

Reception used to stay open until midnight when I worked here. If there's someone manning the desk now, it will be quiet, and I doubt Anna or Raphael would work the late shift. I could collect Lola's travel documents for her. And with those in my possession, I might even be able to get some sleep.

My prayers are answered when I get to the desk, because there's a young woman behind it whom I don't recognise. 'Can I help you?' she asks. She's wearing a name badge. Gwen.

'Hi, yes, thanks,' I mumble. 'My daughter has some post to pick up. She asked me to grab it for her.'

'Sure. What's the name?'

'Lola Torre.'

Gwen searches the desk for a few moments, then looks back at Frankie. 'It must be in the office. If you could wait a moment.'

I nod, smile. My eyes sting in the overhead light and I blink to ease them. But as Gwen pushes the office door open, I notice Anna in there, talking to someone I can't see, but she's speaking English, not French. I lurch to the right before she spots me. A minute passes, and I fight the urge to rest my burning cheeks on

261

the cool smooth surface of the reception desk.

Finally, Gwen reappears. 'I'm sorry, there's no post for Lola Torre. Perhaps check back tomorrow?'

'But it was due today. My daughter got an email. Official travel documents, sent recorded delivery.'

Gwen shrugs. 'Maybe check with the sender? They haven't arrived.'

I think about Anna behind that office door. Has she intercepted Lola's post? Is there a reason she doesn't want us to leave? Or one of the others – Raphael, Jack, Patrick even?

I shake my head. This is nonsense; I'm being paranoid. Maybe Lola has already collected them. Or she could have read her email wrong, and the documents are not due until tomorrow.

The office door opens, making me jump. Then I suck in a breath. 'Dom?'

Dom's eyes widen. He looks so guilty that instinctively I know he's done something bad. But what? Pushed notes under my door? Stolen Lola's travel documents? Killed our friends? My vision blurs and I blink again.

'Um, hi, Frankie,' he stutters, weaving his way around the reception desk, his eyes darting in different directions. 'Yep, here again.' He laughs, but it sounds forced. He must recognise it too, because he stops abruptly. 'Harriet wanted to come back for dinner again,' he says. 'For old times' sake.' He rolls his eyes. 'It's costing me a bloody fortune in petrol, all this driving back and forth.'

His fake whimsy doesn't fool me. But I don't know what the truth is.

'So Harriet's here too?' I ask.

He nods. 'In the car. We're heading back home now, but I needed to have a quick chat with Anna.'

'Oh?'

'About Thursday night,' Anna says smoothly. 'Salvo's gathering. Dom has kindly offered to go to the bar early to help set things up.'

'And I hear you're coming,' Dom says. 'You and Lola. Which

is great news.'

'No, we're hoping to leave tomorrow,' I say.

'Oh really?' Dom's face drops, and it's the first time his expression looks genuine. 'Are you sure I can't persuade you? As I said before, I think you'd love Sartène.'

'Lola wants to be home in time for her birthday,' I lie.

He stares at me, then leans in slightly and lowers his voice to a whisper. 'I think you need to come to Sartène.'

I catch my breath. What does he mean by that?

But before I get chance to figure it out, he turns, says a quick goodbye to Anna, and walks outside. I watch him stride towards the car park and open the driver's door of his car.

It's dark, but I'm pretty sure there's no one in the passenger seat.

Lola

30th July

Lola lies in bed and stares at the sun leaking around the edge of the blind. *While you're here, with me, I won't let anything bad happen to you.* That's what Patrick said to her last night, but does she believe it? At least enough to convince herself that it's safe to stay until the weekend? She knows it sounds fickle with everything that's going on, but she's never taken part in a wind-surfing race outside the UK before and the one on Piantarella beach sounds amazing. More than that, Patrick has already paid the entry fee for her.

Patrick. She knows her urge to stay isn't just about windsurfing. *Who will die first? Mother or daughter?*

She should get up. Her mum will be freaking out. She pushes onto her elbows, then twists and reaches for her phone. Sure enough, there are four missed calls and two texts from her mum. She sends a holding text back, then flops back down on the bed.

Last night, lying on the beach with Patrick, everything seemed simple again. Mazzeri dreams are just fantasy, so there's nothing to worry about there. And Patrick would keep her safe from whoever wrote those notes. But can he really protect her from a killer or is that just fantasy too? And what about her mum? She pushes back the sheet and climbs out of bed. One thing is for sure, she can't hide from her any longer.

Fifteen minutes later, she's showered, dressed, and walking along the beach towards the hotel. The sun is in its usual spot, projecting its warmth over guests lying on sun loungers in angled lines down the beach. The sea is producing lazy ripples, and a few kids are splashing around in the shallow water. How can she possibly be scared for her life in a place like this?

She hasn't eaten since the picnic yesterday and her stomach is full of acid after those Long Island iced teas, but there's a big chance her mum is waiting for her in the restaurant, and she knows her first question will be whether Lola has picked up her travel documents. If she collects those first, at least she'll have some good news for her. With her stomach growling in protest, she veers away from the restaurant entrance and heads to the reception desk instead.

She slows a little when she sees who's behind the desk, then shakes herself down and walks up. 'Hi, Anna, I think my new travel documents arrived yesterday. Is there some post for me?'

Anna looks agitated. 'No, Lola. I'm afraid there isn't. Just as Gwen, who was on duty last night, explained to your mum. More than once, as I understand it.'

Lola bites the inside of her cheek. Her travel documents should be here. And even though she hasn't decided whether to leave Corsica today or not, their absence makes her feel uncomfortable. Trapped even. 'The email from the British consulate in Marseille said they would arrive yesterday.'

Anna's smile tightens. 'This is Corsica, I'm afraid. Not France, and certainly not the UK. It works to a different concept of time. I'm sure they'll arrive soon.'

'But the paperwork was sent on twenty-four-hour recorded delivery,' Lola says as politely as she can. 'Surely twenty-four hours is the same everywhere?'

Anna gives her a hard stare but then her eyes glisten and she lets out an unsteady sigh. 'Look, all I know is that they're not here. You're welcome to use the computer again if you'd like to contact the consulate.' Anna gestures towards the office door. Lola gives her a halfway grateful smile, then sidles behind the reception desk and into the office.

Lola soon realises that contacting someone at the consulate is not very easy. Every hyperlink takes her to another list of frequently asked questions, or an online contact form – which she does complete, but without much hope for a response. The delivery status on her account doesn't help either because that's marked as complete. And the only phone number she can find starts with 0800, which, if it's anything like the UK, will gobble up her new credit in seconds. Feeling defeated, she notes down the number and closes the website. She'll call the consulate from her mum's phone instead.

But before she leaves, she decides to check her emails, and when she sees a new one from Nicole Bassot, her face burns crimson. Shit. She'd almost forgotten about the email she sent to Izzy's mother, listing all the suspects in her very own 'who killed Izzy' true crime drama. She feels so stupid now. She turns her head slightly, as though that might help lessen the impact of the email, then clicks to open it.

Dear Lola,

Thank you for owning up to who you really are – I try not to hold a grudge against your mother, and I definitely don't hold one against you. Thank you also for confiding in me about your suspicions, although they were quite shocking to me. You see, one of the names you mention is familiar. There is a chance it is a coincidence, or unrelated to Isobel's death, but if you have your doubts too, perhaps not.

I would love to talk to you about this. Could you call me when you get a chance? My number is 00 33 4 48 20 16.

Thank you, Lola.

Nicole

Lola leans back in the office chair, her head buzzing. Does Izzy's mum have a clue that will tell her who Izzy's – and possibly, probably, Archie's – killer is?

And if so, which one of the suspects on Lola's list is Nicole referring to?

A burst of adrenaline rushes through her and, without giving herself time to question it, Lola taps the number into her phone and presses to call. But as she listens to the flat European ringing tone, the thump of her heart grows louder. This is Izzy's mum she's about to speak to. The grieving mother who has blamed Lola's own mum for nearly a quarter of a century.

The call clicks into voicemail, and she experiences a storm-level wave of relief. 'Oh, hi,' she mumbles. 'This is Lola, from Hotel Paoli. Sorry not to reach you,' she lies. 'Anyway, I probably shouldn't have called. Never mind.' She quickly ends the call, then closes down her email account. She feels exposed suddenly. As though the killer – whoever it is – is going to burst into the room with a *vendetta corse* and stab her. She pushes out of the chair with sweaty palms and half-runs towards the door.

When she opens it, she sees Patrick behind the reception desk. Her heart rate slows, then races again as he turns to face her. 'Hey.'

'Hey,' she returns, trying to act normal, even though her head is about to explode.

'Everything okay?'

'Yes, no, I think so.' She breathes. 'My travel documents haven't turned up. I'm trying to make sense of it.'

'Sorry, Corsican post isn't known for its reliability.'

Lola nods. 'That's what your mum said. I guess that's what it is.'

'How about I take your mind off it? I'm free from eleven 'til five today. Do you fancy coming out on the catamaran with me?'

'Won't the guests want to use it?' She's playing for time. On one hand, sailing with Patrick is exactly how she wants to spend her day. On the other, her travel documents are AWOL, her mum is getting threatening notes, and it seems that she's opened a hornet's nest in a yoga studio in Lille.

'I checked the log; no one's booked it. And their loss ...'

'Is our gain,' Lola mutters on autopilot.

But Patrick grins, taking that as her acceptance. 'Meet me on the beach at eleven thirty?'

Lola smiles back. His enthusiasm is contagious. 'Okay, yes, great,' she hears herself say. Then she gives him a quick wave, steels herself, and heads into the restaurant.

She sees her mum before Frankie notices her. Her face is pinched, and there are dark circles under her eyes. She's drinking a cup of coffee, with both hands on the white porcelain and elbows resting on the table, like the cup is too heavy for her to hold without support. Guilt flares up. Lola knows her insistence on staying is making things a hundred times worse for her mum. But Frankie's life has been messed up for over twenty years. Is running away again really the answer?

And anyway, what choice do they have without Lola's new travel documents?

She walks over to her mum's table and sinks into the chair opposite. Frankie squeezes her hand, and she gives her a smile in return. Then she tells her.

268

Frankie

30th July

I know there are things I should feel grateful for. The floor of my room was bare when I went back there at dawn this morning, no new note to greet me after spending another restless night on a sun lounger outside the staff accommodation block. And while Lola is hanging out with Patrick again today, at least I know where she is this time. Sailing, something she's very good at, and in light winds. She's even given me permission to contact the consulate about her missing travel documents, which didn't turn up in today's post either.

But I feel no gratitude.

I'm too tired, too scared, too suspicious of everyone around me, for that.

After a thirty-minute wait in a telephone queue, I finally got hold of someone at the consulate, but that only strengthened what I've come to believe. Lola's papers have been stolen. Of course the woman I spoke to didn't say that exactly — she just confirmed that the papers had been posted out, and that *La Poste* had marked them as delivered yesterday. Then she gave me a consignment number and said that if I wanted to check further, I'd need to contact *La Poste* directly.

I haven't called them. What's the point in going through the motions of pretending there's an above-board explanation when I know it's bullshit. Someone at the hotel has received Lola's new travel documents – signing with her name probably – then hidden them.

Which can only mean that they want to keep us here.

Who will die first? Mother or daughter?

At first, I thought the notes were just about messing with my head. Then after the second one arrived, I thought they were about scaring us into leaving. But that doesn't make sense if whoever wrote them is hiding Lola's documents. So do they actually want to go through with it? Kill us both?

The whole thing could still be about freaking me out of course. Scaring me half to death and then forcing me to stay for the anniversary of Izzy's death and the mazzeri's darkest night to really test my sanity. But what if it's not? If someone really is responsible for both Archie's and Izzy's deaths, does that mean two more wouldn't faze them?

I push off the bed and walk out onto the balcony. I try to use the sun – its warmth and brightness – to clear my head and feed me some energy, and it works to an extent.

I guess there always the possibility that the notes and the theft of Lola's travel documents aren't connected. Perhaps Patrick took Lola's post as some creepy romantic gesture. Although he doesn't seem the obsessive type.

And there's Dom acting weird too. He looked so guilty last night and then – I'm pretty sure – lied about why he was here. But why would he take Lola's documents? Is this about wanting to get me to his house? *I think you need to come to Sartène.* What the hell was that about anyway?

I'm too tired to make any sense of this. And hungry.

I missed dinner last night and couldn't face more than coffee at breakfast this morning. My body – and my brain – needs sustenance if I'm going to get through this. I throw some cold water on my face, then pick up the key and leave my room.

The main restaurant is busy with chattering families and clinking cutlery, and I can't face it, so I walk past the entrance. At the end of the hallway, there's a side door that will take me outside the hotel and around to the beach shack selling pizza slices. It's a new addition to the hotel – all distressed wood and Café Del Mar soundtrack – but it's small and relaxed and has its own outdoor terrace.

The memory of seeing my picture in the shop makes my palms sweat, so I look away as I walk past its entrance. But I'm so focused on the door ahead of me, that I almost collide with a couple coming out of the shop. The woman drops her large parcel with a thud.

'Shit, sorry,' I mutter.

'Oh no,' the woman calls out, sinking down onto her haunches and grabbing it.

'Is it okay?' the man asks, like their package is a small child. He lifts it off the floor carefully.

'God, I hope so.'

And that's when I realise from its shape what it is. A painting. I smile at them both, manically I think, then shuffle away. But when I get to the door that will lead me outside, I can't help pausing. And then – like a car crash you can't drag your eyes away from – I turn and watch.

The woman runs her fingernail down a royal blue Hotel Paoli sticker, then folds back the tissue paper. And just as my instincts warned me, it's one of my pictures. But not the one I saw in the shop on Monday. I remember painting the one they're inspecting now. It was my final night away last summer, and I was feeling relieved to have survived another year, and excited to see Lola again. I left clues in the painting too – the mazzera looking upwards, serene, a hint of dawn arriving in the night sky.

271

'Thank fuck for that,' the man says. 'That cost a small fortune.'

'It's beautiful though, isn't it?' the woman counters. 'And spooky. That mazzeri story is wild.' She folds the tissue back over and lifts the picture up. Then I watch them walk the length of the hallway, his arm around her shoulder, until they disappear into the lift.

I don't feel hungry anymore, but when I reach the pizza shack, I buy two slices of Napoli pizza, and a bottle of fizzy water, then find an empty table and sit down. The smell of creamy cheese and salty anchovies does something to my tummy, because I manage to munch through the first slice. I'm considering the second when a hand rests on my shoulder. I jerk around.

'Hey, Frankie! Can I join you?'

I suck in air. 'Harriet,' I breathe out. 'What are you doing here?' My eyes flit left and right. 'Is Dom with you?'

'No, not today. He had to work so I convinced him to lend me his jeep. Sartène may be beautiful, but there's no beach, and those mountains hug the clouds. It's much nicer here. Are you going to eat that?'

I shake my head and watch Harriet try to navigate the now drooping pizza slice into her mouth. 'What work does Dom do?' I ask. Harriet points at her mouth, and I wait for her to finish chewing.

'Well, I'm not exactly sure,' she finally says, taking a gulp from her pink Chilly water bottle. 'He's always pretty cagey about it. When I asked him once, he said import, export. And I'm a lawyer, so I was not going to risk delving further into that hot potato.'

'You think Dom's into something dodgy?'

She holds her hands up. 'Far be it for me to speculate. He makes an amazing bouillabaisse and that's enough for me. But he's not short of cash.'

I lean back against my chair. Import, export. Is Dom a drug dealer? No, he can't be; not Dom. This is my wired brain in over-drive again. Not helped by seeing yet another one of my paintings.

Import, export.

A fear creeps over my skin as those words settle. I only paint fourteen pictures a year – one per night for the fortnight I spend hiding away – and the shop has displayed two of them in the time I've been here. Someone at the hotel must know my art dealer, Nick.

Import, export.

I lean forward again. 'Do you think that Dom could be an art dealer?'

Harriet scrunches her forehead. 'I don't think so. I've never seen any pieces around his house, other than what he's bought himself, and why would he keep that under wraps?'

Then I find a rusty fact from somewhere deep inside my brain. 'Didn't he study art history at uni?'

'Well if he did, you have a better memory than me.'

I shrug, like I'm not really interested, even though my heart is clattering at the thought of Dom knowing about my paintings. 'So how was dinner last night?' I say, testing Dom's assertion that Harriet was with him.

'Not as juicy as the night before sadly. Dom had to go out somewhere, so I stayed in with some stinky cheese and binge-watched three episodes of *Gossip Girl*.'

I take a gulp of fizzy water. Dom looked so guilty last night and Harriet has just confirmed that he lied to me. At the time I thought it meant that he'd taken Lola's documents, but it could have been anything. Like dropping off one of my paintings, pretending to be someone he's not.

I think about what it would mean if Dom was my art dealer. The secrets I've shared with the faceless person I know as Nick Daniels on those lonely summer nights, waiting for dawn for arrive. Dom would know all about my mazzeri dreams, the fears I carry with me.

But is this just another crackpot theory I've come up with because I'm too tired? Harriet knows Dom much better than me and she's more willing to suspect him of drug dealing than being an art dealer.

I've barely slept and I'm starting to not trust my judgement. I know where that leads.

I need to get off this island.

Frankie

31st July

My heart booms in my chest. I'm dog-tired but also fizzing with the energy that fear creates. Am I really doing this? Prowling the hotel in the dead of night? Especially after spending the last few hours alone in my room, my mind going to darker and darker places after Lola made it clear that she feels safer with Patrick than me.

But I can't think of a better plan. I need to get away from Corsica – from this hotel, from Dom and what he might know. From whoever is threatening us. And that means finding Lola's travel documents.

I know there's only a slim chance they'll be in the office. If Dom has them, they will be hidden away in his house in Sartène. And if Jack took them, they will probably be in Salvo's old house where he lives now. But if one of the Paoli family took them – Raphael, Anna, Patrick – then there's a chance they'll be hidden in the office, especially with the postman delivering them to reception. I know it's a long shot, but I need to try.

I edge down the last few stairs. There are security guards

who work through the night, but hopefully they'll be outside, protecting the perimeter rather than checking what's happening inside the hotel. I wait at the corner of the reception area with my excuses ready, but it's deserted, and my heart slows a beat. The lights in the area are switched off but there's enough ambient light to see by. I tiptoe over to the desk then slip behind it and push on the office door handle. I allow myself a silent sigh of relief as it opens.

There's one window in the office overlooking the front driveway, but the heavy oak shutters are closed, so I turn on the desk lamp. Its weak beam gives me just enough light to search by. My hands shake as I open each of the three desk drawers in turn. The top drawer is full of office staples – pens, paperclips, Post-it Notes – and the bottom drawer is empty except for a half-drunk bottle of Pastis.

The middle drawer takes longer to search. It is full of paper-work – loosely filled cardboard wallets in pastel shades – and I flick through them, searching for Lola's envelope. By the time I get to the last wallet in the pile, I've run out of hope, but my fingers slow when I realise what I'm reading. A legal document from a solicitor's firm in Porto Vecchio, the words *testament authentique* written across the top. As I scan for words I can translate, I realise it's a copy of Salvo's will.

This is not what I came for. Salvo's final wishes are none of my business. But this is the man who fucked up my life. Who made me think I was crazy, and somehow responsible for my friend's death. Alive or dead, I don't owe him anything.

It's written in French, so I can't understand most of it. But there are some names I recognise, and numbers too. It says that Salvo owned thirty per cent of Hotel Paoli when he died, which is less than I might have expected. But it's who he's leaving his share to that's the real surprise. He has bequeathed it all to Anna. Why would he do that? And how does Raphael feel about it? Twenty-one years ago, Anna was like Raphael's puppet – or puppy. Now she acts like she's in charge. And according to Salvo's will, she now owns a major share of the hotel. Is this all because she took the reins after Izzy's death or is there more behind his loyalty to her?

I look back at the document, scan more writing I don't understand, then turn the page. On the second sheet, there are handwritten scribbles in the margin next to one clause. Scrawling black ink with three exclamation marks at the end. I concentrate on the words I recognise. It looks like Salvo owned a one-half stake in a vineyard in Sartène, and he's leaving it all to one person. But the benefactor is no one in the family – which means neither Raphael nor Patrick have inherited anything significant.

I squint at the name for a second because it looks familiar. Then I gasp.

Nicole Bassot.

That's Izzy's mum's name.

It can't be a coincidence. Salvo has left his share of a vineyard to Izzy's family.

Why would he do that?

I drop the document on the desk and lean back in the chair. I only saw Salvo once after Izzy drowned, for a few minutes at the police station, but I will never forget our conversation, or his demeanour. He didn't seem upset about Izzy's death at all – just acted as though it was simply her fate – so why did he leave this part of his estate to Izzy's family?

I look back at the document. I don't know what Raphael's handwriting looks like, but I wonder if those angry scribbles are his, and what his father leaving him nothing might do to his mental state.

With shaking hands, I tidy up the document, slip it back into the folder, and return all the paperwork to the desk's middle drawer. But there's a filing cabinet against the wall with four square-shaped drawers that I should search too. I push onto my feet and pull open the top drawer. But as I'm rifling through more files, my mind keeps wandering back to Salvo. I knew him for less than six months. And in that time, I only spoke to him four or five times. And yet I've let him become this invisible but omnipresent force in my life, a constant thorn in my side.

But Salvo remembered Izzy in his will. Was he more human than I gave him credit for?

Twenty minutes later, I've checked all the possible hiding places for Lola's travel documents and accepted that they aren't in the office. I've achieved nothing.

I switch off the light, edge open the door, and return, defeated, to my post outside the staff accommodation block. And I pray for at least a few hours of dreamless sleep.

Lola

31st July

'You did what?' Lola asks, sucking on the straw of her breakfast smoothie. Her mum looks like a ghost, her insides clawed out by insomnia.

'Someone has stolen your travel papers, Lola,' Frankie says, her voice gravelly. 'The *Poste France* website lists them as delivered, so someone signed for them, and took them.'

'But you broke into the hotel office in the middle of the night to search for them?' Lola still can't get her head around it. When she planned her secret trip to Corsica, she was excited to visit Hotel Paoli, to find out her mum's secrets. Now a big part of her wishes she'd left them well alone.

Except that means she wouldn't have met Patrick.

'The door wasn't locked, so I wasn't breaking in,' Frankie says quietly. 'And I looked everywhere, so at least we know your documents aren't there.'

Lola shrugs. 'But how is that helpful? You still don't know who's taken them – if anyone has,' she adds, remembering how Patrick's views on the Corsican postal service aligned with Anna's.

'You're right, I don't know who's got them,' Frankie admits. 'But maybe it makes Raphael less of a suspect.'

'Same for Anna,' Lola muses.

'And Patrick.'

'What?' Lola sits back in her chair. 'You can't think Patrick took them?'

'To keep you here,' Frankie mutters. 'And it was just a thought.'

'Oh.' Lola wonders if it could be true. And why on earth a tiny part of her feels pleased at the idea.

'I think it might be Dom who's taken them,' Frankie murmurs, then shakes her head. 'But I don't know why. I want to ask him.'

Lola's nose crinkles in confusion. 'Why do you think it's Dom?'

Frankie opens her mouth to talk, but no words come out.

'Mum?' Lola nudges.

Frankie sighs, then leans forward over the table. 'It's complicated. And I might be wrong. But I'm going to hire a car, drive to Sartène this morning. If he has them, I'll make him give them back. And then I'll book a flight. I checked on my phone and there are seats on the three thirty Air France flight. It means a stopover in Paris, but that would be fun, right? We'll be home early tomorrow.'

'Mum, I don't think ...'

'I just need to know that you'll come with me.' She takes a long inhalation. Her face cracks, then straightens. 'Today. No more arguments.' Her mum's eyes look vivid in the bright sunshine. Deep brown, stark white, red-rimmed.

'First off, I don't think you should go to Dom's house by yourself,' Lola starts carefully. It's partly to avoid talking about leaving, but she genuinely doesn't think her mum is in a fit state to go anywhere by herself, and especially not drive on mountain roads. 'What if he is the killer? Do you really want to take that risk?' She waits to hear her mum scoff at her concern, but instead Frankie looks away, towards the sea.

'I'm not scared of Dom.'

Lola pulls at her napkin. When she was sailing with Patrick yesterday, she felt on top of the world. Like nothing bad could happen to her. And then he convinced Vincent to cover his bar shift that night so they could spend the evening together. Her mum didn't like it, but when Lola pushed for an explanation, Frankie couldn't come up with a good one. They both knew that Patrick would do a better job of protecting Lola from any would-be attacker than Frankie could.

Patrick took her into town for moules marinière. They ate from big metal bowls, pulling out a never-ending supply of black shells and dunking fresh bread in the creamy white wine sauce. Lola told Patrick how she dreamed of visiting her dad in New Zealand one day and windsurfing in Taranaki or on Lake Wakatipu near Queenstown. He countered that by saying he wished his father lived on the other side of the world, and how his dream was to get away from him.

At the end of their meal, she asked him to walk her back to her room. And then she invited him to stay over. They didn't do anything more than kiss, but having him with her through the night was exactly the comfort she needed.

And she must remember that her mum didn't have that same safety net. While she was sleeping next to Patrick, her mum was prowling around the hotel on Lola's behalf.

'Listen, I know tonight is a big thing for you,' Lola starts, with as much compassion as she can muster. 'The anniversary of Izzy's death, and the significance of the date in the mazzeri legend. But it is just one summer's night, the same as any other.' She wants to believe this more than anything, and saying the words out loud takes her one step closer.

'And what about the threatening notes?' Frankie asks. 'And someone stealing your papers?'

Lola swallows. 'If Dom did take them, maybe he did it for the same romantic reasons that you accused Patrick of.'

'No way. It's not that.'

Her mum says it with such conviction that Lola doesn't challenge her. She tries a different approach instead. 'Mum, you look exhausted. You're not in any fit state to be driving on unfamiliar mountain roads right now. Why don't you get some sleep today, then come with me this evening – Patrick has offered to drive us. There's still a chance that the post is just late, and that my documents will arrive today. And if they don't, we can ask Dom about them at Salvo's gathering. It's a public place, and you'll have me and Patrick there as backup. I know there might be someone out there who wants to hurt us, and we need to be careful, but we will be.'

Lola leans over the table, reaches for her mum's hands. 'Please, Mum. Trust me on this.'

Frankie gives her a watery smile, but then her lips shift downwards and her eyes glaze with tears. She rubs the heel of her hand across her forehead. 'I don't know.' Then she shakes her head. 'No, we can't go tonight. Being with them all, in Salvo's hometown, it's too dangerous. But maybe I shouldn't go to Sartène this morning. I'll find us another hotel room instead, away from here. We can apply for new documents. That must be possible, right?'

'Mum, stop it,' Lola warns. 'You're making this worse than it is. My documents might just be late, an admin error. You've been here for four days, and nothing bad has happened to us, which must mean that whoever is writing these notes is bluffing, like online trolling in paper form. All I'm asking is that you see it for what it is. Let us spend my birthday together in the sunshine, and then let me kick arse in that windsurf competition. And we'll figure out my travel documents along the way.'

Her mum's face is so twisted, it looks like she's in physical pain. 'I'm scared that if we go tonight, it will be too powerful, that you won't make it to your birthday.'

'What?' Lola pulls her hands away. 'What will be too powerful?'

'The mazzeri.'

'What the fuck?' Lola says, her voice rising. 'The mazzeri story is bullshit!'

Frankie looks away. 'I don't know,' she mumbles. 'Maybe. I'm not sure anymore.' She blinks three, four, five times, like she's closing down a set of images. 'The dreams feel so real; they must mean something.'

Lola's heart thuds faster. She needs some air. She pushes back her chair and stands up. 'I'm going to Sartène tonight, with Patrick, to see the town my grandfather grew up in and say goodbye to his. I would like you to come with me, but if that's too much to ask, I'll go by myself.'

'No, you're not safe there!'

'For fourteen years you've left me with someone else on my birthday because you don't think I'm safe with you.' She pauses, swallows back tears. 'I'm starting to think that maybe you were right.' Her mum looks like she's been punched and Lola instantly regrets her words. 'I'm sorry. I shouldn't have said that.'

But Frankie doesn't look at her. She drops her napkin onto her plate – still laden with the food she hasn't eaten – and pushes her chair away. Then she turns on her heels and, with a shaky gait, disappears out of the restaurant.

Frankie

31st July

Maybe you were right.

Lola doesn't feel safe with me.

I close my eyes to shut out the pain, and zone in on the whip-whip of my hair against my cheeks. I should tie it back – the journey in the back of Patrick's open-top jeep is giving me no protection from the wind – but I like the sting of it flying around my face. And I don't care what I look like.

After all, I'm not going tonight out of respect for Salvo. Or to see the town my father grew up in.

I'm going to watch over my daughter. To prove to her that I am her protector, not Patrick nor anyone else. Never mind that I can barely see from tiredness.

Maybe I'll find out who took Lola's travel documents too, but I'm not sure how much I care about that anymore. It's too late.

When I flew to Corsica on Sunday morning, I had one job. To get Lola home before the anniversary. But here I am, heading to the town most indelibly linked with the mazzeri, on the legend's most important night. Lola is barely speaking to me, someone is

284

threatening to kill us, and Dom – the one person I thought I might be able to trust – might have been lying to me for years. And for what reason? An obsession? Or to find out what I remember about that night?

When I think about the online conversations I've had with my dealer, Nick Daniels, the details I've confided, it makes me feel sick. Because it has to be him. Dominic. Nick. How could I have not seen it before?

Does that also mean he slipped those notes under my door? It would explain how he knew to use the mazzeri legend to scare me. But I've also told Nick how much it felt like an assault in the moment, how forcefully I was pulled under the water. Have I put myself in danger?

'You okay, Mum?'

I open my eyes. Lola has twisted around in the front passenger seat and is looking at me. I gather my hair off my face and force a smile. I need to pretend I'm in control of myself for her sake.

'Did you get some sleep earlier?'

'Yes, some,' I lie. 'I'm feeling much better.' The intense relief on Lola's face makes me want to cry.

'That's good. The views are spectacular, aren't they?'

I turn my head to take in the scenery. Patrick has started climbing the mountain road to Sartène and I can see for miles. A patchwork of pea green fields, craggy rocks, and darker woodland, with peaks and valleys that blur in the hazy evening sunshine. Lola's right, it is stunning. But it's also frightening. A rugged, alluring landscape that is full of promise, but only for those strong enough to face down its threats.

'Did you ever visit Sartène when you worked here?' Patrick asks without taking his eyes off the road.

'No, I never got around to it,' I mumble. The truth is, his grandfather put me off exploring my heritage, but I'm not going to tell him that.

'It's an impressive town. And you'll be able to taste some of

285

this season's wine fresh from the barrel. I promise, you'll love it.'

Patrick's comment takes me back to Raphael's office, and Salvo's will. 'Is that from your grandfather's vineyard?' I ask.

'Yes,' Patrick says, nodding. 'I spent my summer holidays at my grandparents' house when I was growing up, so I hung out at the vineyard a lot. When I was older, Salvo taught me how to harvest the grapes, and I'd watch them being pressed. One day I'd like to have a vineyard of my own.'

I bite my lip. Does Patrick think he'll inherit Salvo's share of the vineyard? Maybe Raphael hasn't told him what's in the will. I wonder how he'll feel about his grandfather leaving it to someone outside the family.

'Like your grandfather?' Lola asks.

'Yeah, exactly. Although he only owned half his vineyard; he had a business partner.'

'Don't tell me, it's your dad.'

Patrick laughs. 'No, for once my father didn't get his greedy fingers on my grandfather's assets.'

Lola laughs along with him, so this dislike of his father can't be news to her. But it jolts me. Family is everything in Corsica, so seeing him so blatantly criticise Raphael is a shock.

'He's not really built for Sartène though; it's too authentic for him. He belongs in Porto Vecchio with its flashy tourists and their corrupting euros.'

Despite myself, my mouth lifts into a half-smile at the image. 'So who is Salvo's business partner?' I ask. I don't add that whoever it is, they're going to have to get their heads around working with a grieving French mother in her sixties.

Patrick looks into the rear-view mirror and our eyes catch. He looks conflicted, and I wonder why. Then he shifts his gaze back to the road. 'Can you keep a secret?' he asks.

'I guess.' I look over at Lola, try to read her expression. But she's facing forward now.

'Salvo's partner is Jack, but my father doesn't know, so keep it to yourselves.'

'Jack?'

'Yeah, I know. It is odd.'

'Did they buy it together?' Lola asks.

Patrick shakes his head. 'At the start, Salvo owned it by himself. But when I turned eighteen, I asked if I could get a job there, full-time. I wanted to get away from the hotel and I'd loved my summers working there.'

'And your grandfather said no?'

'He said he needed to check with his business partner, and he said no, so I pushed to find out who it was. My father and Jack are pretty tight, so Jack would have known that me leaving the hotel wouldn't have gone down well. And we can't upset the great Raphael Paoli, can we?'

I lean back against the leather seat and let my hair fly free again. Jack was Salvo's business partner? How could he afford to invest in a vineyard? It doesn't make sense, but then nothing makes sense in this place. I lift my arm to check my watch. It's almost 8 p.m. which means there's only an hour or so more daylight. I've done everything to stop this happening, but now it's too late. A swell of fear tightens in my chest, and I try to breathe through it.

Finally, Patrick pulls up alongside a town square and cuts the engine. The square is lined with palm trees and there are pockets of tables and chairs spilling out from the restaurants.

'Where's the event being held? In one of these bars?' Lola asks, nodding towards the line of restaurants facing the square.

Patrick smiles. 'Locals wouldn't be seen dead in these places during tourist season. It's at a more hidden away kind of place. We'll toast Salvo with his own wine, and then we'll all get chance to tell a story about him.' He turns to me. 'Will you say something?'

There's no way I'm telling anyone about mine and Salvo's story, but I manage a watery smile. 'I don't think I have one.'

Patrick nods, then reaches for Lola's hand. I follow them across the square. We walk through a narrow archway in a stone wall, and into a covered alleyway. Only a tiny chink of light in the distance shows that it's not a dead end, and the noise of my sandals hitting the flagstones bounces around my head as I stumble onwards. The narrow alley eventually opens out onto a small stone courtyard with shuttered-up buildings and one bar with a faded blue canopy. Condensation drips down the window.

The bar is narrow but deep and we wind through small groups of people until we reach a larger room at the back of the space. There are about thirty people sat on benches with carafes of wine and glasses dotted along the tables. Most of the guests are strangers but I can see Raphael and Anna sat with Jack. Harriet and Dom close by.

I take a few steps towards them. I need to find the strength to confront Dom.

But then I see a large poster stuck to the wall. A close-up of Salvo staring directly into the camera lens. I stare at the lies or truth etched into his deep wrinkles, the kindness or cruelty glowing from his eyes.

Then exhaustion engulfs me, and I slump onto a bench.

Frankie

31st July

Harriet is talking about her day trip to Ajaccio, how she visited Napoleon's birthplace, and the cathedral he was baptised in, but she's exhausted and needs her bed. But it's just white noise to me as I scan the room for Lola. This is how the evening has gone. Me prowling, keeping my daughter in sight. Lola slipping away, then reappearing, like a game of cat and mouse she doesn't know we're playing. I spot her coming back from the toilet and breathe a sigh of relief.

I check my watch. It's eleven o'clock already. One hour until midnight. In this cavern-like room at the back of the bar, with Salvo's friends telling stories about the old man in a language I don't understand, time has felt suspended, but now it's all too close – the anniversary, Lola's birthday – and I'm not ready.

I haven't even confronted Dom yet.

I spot him at the makeshift bar area at the back, alone, filling up his wine glass. I have to find the strength to do this. 'Excuse me, Harriet,' I mumble, backing away before she can resume her monologue. I snake through the swell of old men, their pungent scent of sweat and earth making me dizzy. Dom looks up as I approach, then his eyes dart away as though he's looking for an escape. But he doesn't move.

'We need to talk,' I murmur.

Dom looks nervous, and sweat is beading on his forehead, but he nods and sinks onto a wooden bench close by. 'So what's up?'

'Why did you do it?' I ask.

He gives me a weak smile. 'Do what?'

I hesitate for a moment, then sit down beside him. My eyes burn. God, I'm so tired. Tired of the secrets, and the regrets, and the questions that never get answered. 'I didn't think it could be you, writing those notes,' I say. 'Because how would you know about the mazzeri? But you do know, don't you?'

He shakes his head. 'I don't know what you mean. What notes?'

'Five years I've been emailing, then packaging up my paintings, dutifully sending them off to that storage facility. I thought I was the one hiding my identity. But it was you really, wasn't it, Nick?'

Dom blinks. 'I really don't—'

'Please, stop lying.'

He stares at me for a long moment, then sighs and drops his gaze. 'You were never supposed to find out,' he whispers.

'That makes it worse.'

'I didn't plan it,' he says. 'My life was … boring. I was an estate agent, selling big pads in Surrey to feed my ex-wife's spending habits. But I couldn't stop thinking about this place. Remembering our season.'

'But that summer was hell, Dom! Losing Archie. Then Izzy. God, what I would give to forget it all.' I fall quiet and wonder if I mean that. The truth is, I don't know what my life would look like without those memories.

'Yes, I know,' Dom says. 'But it was a shared hell. We went through this thing together – and there was good as well as bad, you know that – and I guess I felt less whole without it.'

'So you moved out here.'

'Yeah, when I could. But before then, I started a side hustle selling Corsican artwork – I've loved art since my university days – and that's how I came across this article in an online magazine. I promise it was the pictures that grabbed my attention at first.'

I think about the interview I gave and how I insisted on the magazine only using my initials. I thought it would be enough, but of course it would be a shiny clue for Dom. Especially with all the other details I shared. Spending time in Corsica as a teenager, coping with a personal trauma. 'You worked out that it was me,' I say.

'I suspected. Enough to look for you online. When I found out that you were an art teacher, it all fell into place.'

'But instead of contacting me in a regular way, like Harriet did with you, you catfished me.'

Dom flinches. Then he pushes his palms together and looks down, like he's praying. 'I didn't think of it like that.'

'You manipulated me, Dom. I trusted you with my deepest, darkest secrets.'

'I'm sorry. It just never seemed like the right time.'

'That's bullshit! There were loads of opportunities to come clean!' I take a breath. 'Is it because you wanted to find out what I knew about Izzy's death? Whether I'd remembered something incriminating over the years?'

His face screws up. 'What? Why would I do that?'

'Because you …' My words float away. Dom didn't kill anyone. Of course he didn't. 'Did you want to punish me for humiliating you?' I ask instead. 'Did you put notes under my door because you knew it would freak me out?'

Dom's face softens. 'I moved on from that night a long time ago, Frankie. Yes, I was hurt in the moment. But I preferred to remember you for the hundreds of good moments we shared instead of the one bad one.' Dom opens his palms. 'And I still don't know what notes you're talking about.'

I want to read his expression, to be sure he's telling the truth, but the lighting is low, and there's a fog of body heat in the air. 'Someone is putting notes under my door,' I finally say. 'Calling me mazzeri, threatening to kill me and Lola.'

Dom's eyes widen. 'Fucking hell. You can't think I'd write that?!'

I rub my palm against my forehead, then sigh. 'I guess I don't – not really. But you have been lying to me for six years.'

Dom winces. 'I didn't mean to hurt you. I didn't admit who I was because I valued our new friendship too much. And it always felt like you needed a faceless confidant whose opinion didn't factor. It's the same reason I think you needed to come tonight, to Sartène, to this gathering for Salvo. To face your fears head-on, not hide away from them.'

I look away. It's true that writing those emails felt like the difference between sanity and insanity some nights.

'And I was making sure your art went to people who really loved it, and at a good price,' Dom goes on. 'When Jack called me, told me that you'd shown up at the hotel with your daughter, I nearly didn't come. I was scared that you'd read the truth on my face. But I also couldn't give up the chance of seeing you.'

'So you could gloat in secret?' I ask, but there's no strength in my anger now.

'So I could find a way to tell you the truth.' He sighs. 'But you seemed so on edge. Looking over your shoulder the whole time. It never felt like the right moment. I understand why now.'

I stare at him. He sounds so genuine. Lola has me to protect her, and Patrick now too, but I have no one. And I feel so alone. I wish I could lie down, sleep, hear someone tell me that everything is going to be okay, and believe them. 'It's the darkest night tonight,' I murmur.

'The anniversary of Izzy's death, you mean?'

I nod. Why do I keep bringing up the mazzeri stuff? Why do I keep forgetting it's not real?

'I think someone's stolen Lola's new travel documents too. I'm worried that whoever's doing these things wants to trap us here.'

Dom's expression shifts to concern. 'Where's Lola now?'

Frankie

31st July

'Is she there?' I ask, my voice trembling. Why the hell did I let myself get distracted? My eyes flit across the room, powered by panic and guilt. But the crowd has thinned to a few groups of people finishing up their wine.

Dom shakes his head. 'I've searched the whole bar, and the courtyard at the front. Maybe she's out the back?'

'I already checked out there. And the toilets. She's not here.'

'Can you check her location on your phone?' he asks.

I shake my head, dig my nails into my palm. Why did I buy her such a cheap phone with no option to download apps?

'Can you call her?'

'Yes,' I breathe. I fumble for my phone, press on her number. It rings out. Has it run out of battery again? Or is she in trouble? 'No answer.' The words catch in my throat as I think about the narrow alleyway we walked through to get to the bar. How threatening it felt. I imagine Lola lying on the cold flagstones, her chest oozing blood like the eagle owl in my dream.

But I need to hold it together. 'Is Patrick here?' I ask. 'He'll know where she is.'

'Patrick?' Dom looks confused.

'They're …' I struggle for the right words. 'Having a holiday romance.'

'Oh right. Well, he's a good kid. Came and visited his grandfather loads when Salvo got sick. And you're right, I'm pretty sure he's not here either. But that's good news, right? Them just having a little private moment somewhere close by?'

'Yes,' I whisper, desperately hoping he's right. 'That will be it.'

'Look, there's Anna. Let's see if she knows where they are.'

I let Dom guide me past the dwindling group of mourners. Anna is standing with Raphael. His ebony hair is swept away from his face and his eyes have narrowed, like two black slashes on a sallow face. He must sense me staring because he turns slightly. Our eyes catch and his shine with hatred.

Maybe there was something going on between him and Izzy all those years ago. It's difficult to believe she had strong feelings for him; she was such a free spirit. But maybe he fell hard for her. Could all this be about a broken heart?

But Raphael is in here, I remind myself. Not outside hunting my daughter.

Does that mean Lola is safe? Or are my instincts wrong again?

'Hey, guys,' Dom says. He's trying to be cheerful, and it sounds so out of place, but still, I try to match it with a smile. 'We're looking for Lola,' he goes on. 'Have you seen her?'

Anna nods. 'Yes, she and Patrick left together. Lola wanted to tell you, so that you wouldn't worry, but apparently you two were having a pretty intense – her words – conversation and she didn't want to interrupt.'

I want Anna's words to soothe me, my daughter's thoughtfulness, but I won't feel better until I find her. 'Where did they go?' But before Anna gets chance to answer, a phone bursts into life, making me jump.

Raphael pulls out his phone and squints at the screen. Then

he backs away a few feet and twists around as he puts it to his ear. I look back at Anna.

'I think he's taken Lola to the vineyard,' she says. 'It's only ten minutes away in the car, and Patrick probably wanted to show it off. He loves that place, poor kid.' She sighs – it sounds like Anna knows more about Salvo's will than Patrick does – then looks up. 'Anyway, it seems that Raphael is otherwise engaged, so I better go and settle up with the bar, if you'll excuse me.'

'A car journey away,' I say, as Anna glides off with her usual elegance.

'I can take you,' Dom cuts in. 'But I'll need to ask Raphael for directions; I've never been there.'

'No, not him.' But as I shake my head, an idea spills out. 'We can ask Jack.'

'Jack?'

I know Patrick asked me to keep it a secret, but this is an emergency. 'Jack owns half the vineyard.'

'He does?' Dom looks at me in confusion.

I turn, grab his arm. 'Can we just find him?'

'Sorry, Jack left about half an hour ago, in a foul mood too. Harriet asked him for a lift back up to my place and he point-blank refused.'

'Jack's gone?' I mumble, tension spreading across my back.

Dom narrows his eyes. 'Wait. You can't think Jack would hurt Lola?'

In all those years of confiding in Nick, I never told him about Jack or what he did to his family. I was too busy blaming myself for everything. 'Oh my God, Dom, you have no fucking idea! Can we go now?'

'Of course. My car's parked on this side, so it's quicker to use the back door.' He grabs my hand, and we race out of the bar together.

Lola

31st July

Lola stands at the top of the hill and stares at the view. Navy grapevines cut into the hillside in neat lines. The black snake of a river hums in the valley below, and mounds of pale boulders on the riverbank glow in the moonlight. She wants to reach for Patrick, wrap herself up in him as she soaks it in. But he's a few metres away, on his phone.

'So this is it,' he says as he returns to her side, his voice a mix of emotion and pride. 'My inheritance.'

Lola's eyes widen as she turns to look at him. 'Your grandfather left you his share of the vineyard?'

'We're going to the lawyers next week for the official reading of the will, but do you remember that letter I picked up the other day? He as good as promised it to me in there.'

'So Jack will be your business partner.' Lola thinks about the brusque man with sad eyes who lends her his windsurf kit but snarls when she asks him a question. 'How do you feel about that?'

'He and Salvo had an understanding. We can have one too.' Then he turns and smiles. 'Do you want to have a look around?

Maybe I can even sell you the Corsican dream.'

He raises his eyebrows, and she smiles in response. Then she curls her fingers around his and lets him guide her down the path between two sets of vines towards the river. It's dark, but the sky is clear, and the moon provides enough light to see by. 'What grapes are these?' she asks, trying to sound grown up – which she will be in a matter of minutes.

'They're Sciacarello grapes,' Patrick explains. 'Which is why the domaine only makes rosé wine. I suggested to Salvo that he should try planting something different, but he wouldn't hear of it. Native Corsican grapes. Traditional viticulture methods. The unique Corsican climate to protect the vines instead of pesticides. The old guy was obsessed with his culture.'

'Will you change things when you start working here?'

Patrick considers her question. 'Maybe at some point. But I want to honour my grandfather's memory for a while. Make him proud from beyond the grave. Is that crazy?'

'Yes,' Lola says with a grin. Because she doesn't want to say what she really feels. That Patrick is becoming more and more perfect with every passing second. She promised her mum that she'd leave Corsica after the windsurf competition on Saturday, but will she really be ready to go? She'll be eighteen with the whole summer ahead of her; she could stay. Then she feels a jolt of frustration as she thinks about those notes and imagines her mum's reaction.

They reach a low fence where the land drops away to the river and Patrick points to the path going left. 'The winery is up here. How about we sneak a bottle off a shelf to toast your birthday? There's thousands so no one's going to miss one.'

Lola frowns. 'Won't the winery be locked up now?'

'That's not the Corsican way,' Patrick says with a smile. 'This is Salvo's place. Everyone in this town either loved him or feared him. Some did both. And him being dead doesn't change that very much. Which means there's no need for locked doors.'

'It's like I've stepped back in time,' Lola muses. 'I think it was like that in England a hundred years ago.'

Patrick laughs. 'It's what comes from living in remote places like this, I guess. Yeah, it's insular, but I like it this way. Proud Corsicans defending their territory from a tourist invasion. People here believe in a higher purpose than just making loads of money.'

A minute later, they reach the edge of a large stone building with a line of windows hidden behind wooden shutters. There's a traditional arched doorway in the centre of the building with a thick oak door, and Patrick pulls it open. But as he disappears inside, Lola hesitates, suddenly scared of the black hole in front of her – she's never liked the dark. Then she hears a soft click and the room floods with light. Lola smiles and walks inside.

The room is open plan across the width of the building. There's a shop to Lola's left, and a café to her right, with tables and chairs and a long bar across the back.

'They host events here,' Patrick explains. 'It's not busy like in Provence or Bordeaux, but they run tours twice a week in the summer, and it always ends with a wine tasting. It's usually held outside on the terrace, but they've got this space in case it rains.'

'And where is the wine made?' Lola asks, suddenly curious about the process.

'Through here, come on.'

As Lola follows Patrick, her phone rings in her pocket. She is used to having her iPhone on silent, but she doesn't have that option on the old Nokia her mum bought her, and the shrill electronic sound makes her jump. Her signal has been patchy since she's been in Sartène, so she's relieved to see her screen showing three bars. She assumes it will be her mum calling, so when she sees a number instead of a name, she automatically cancels the call.

'Who was that?' Patrick asks. 'Your mum?'

'That was my first thought, but amazingly it's not. Must be a misdial because no one else knows this number apart from you.'

Her phone buzzes in her hand twice – whoever called has left a voice message – then falls silent again.

Patrick looks at his watch. 'Looks like we've got some celebrating to do.'

Lola's eyes widen. 'Wait, is it my birthday?'

Patrick grins. 'Welcome to adulthood. Let me show you something cool.' He reaches for her hand and leads her through a doorway at the back of the shop into narrow rooms separated by solid stone walls. Each room has a line of wall lights on one side, and a stack of wooden barrels on the other, shadows dancing everywhere. Lola shivers.

'Are you cold?' Patrick asks. 'I know this place looks like something from the eighteenth century, but the temperature is centrally controlled. I forget what at, but it's chilly.'

'No, I'm fine,' she says, rubbing her arms, while secretly wishing that Patrick would warm her up. Her thoughts must show on her face because he edges closer to her until their shoulders are touching.

'Do you want to see the cave?' he asks.

'This isn't the cave?'

'It's downstairs. Kind of a half-cellar, cut into the hillside.' He floats his arm around the room. 'All the wine in these casks is still fermenting but there are thousands of finished bottles downstairs. And definitely a spare one for us to raise a toast with.'

Together, they snake their way through more narrow rooms – all identical in their layout – until they reach a staircase. Patrick gestures for Lola to go first, but she pauses at the bottom, waiting for him to lead again. He guides her down a corridor until he reaches a heavy wooden door, then pushes it open. The place is like the cellar of a castle. Granite floor tiles, bare brick walls, all lined with bottles of rosé in rows up to the ceiling.

'Impressive, hey?' Patrick says, reaching for a bottle. 'Shit, I should have brought glasses from the bar.'

'Oh don't worry,' Lola says, smiling. 'We can drink straight from the bottle.'

But Patrick shakes his head. 'We can't raise a toast that way. And we could do with some ice. I'll only be a second, wait here.' Patrick kisses her cheek and disappears out of the door. There's no furniture in here, and all the walls are stacked with bottles, so Lola stands awkwardly in the middle of the room. The way each wall looks the same, and the mottled bulge of the protruding bottles, makes her feel a bit claustrophobic.

A feeling that gets a lot worse when the lights go out.

Lola

1st August

She mustn't panic. She's in darkness, not danger. A bulb has blown and tripped the switch. Or the centralised system Patrick was talking about has malfunctioned. He'll sort it, then come back for her. She just needs to wait it out.

But damn, it's dark. Actually, more than dark. Pure, perfect blackness, the type that makes you wonder if you really exist. Are those wine bottles still lining the walls? Or is she floating in space, or some other unknown dimension?

A noise brings her back to earth. Rustling. She flicks her head left and right, sees nothing. She imagines rats scurrying across the floor. Spiders crawling. Her breath judders inside her chest.

Shit. She needs to hold it together.

Patrick will be back soon, she reminds herself. The lights will come back on.

She feels unbalanced in the darkness, so she lowers down to sitting. She runs her hands down her legs. The soft material of her dress, the slight rise of the hemline, then the smooth flesh of freshly shaved skin. She pulls her knees into her chest, curls into a ball.

In her new position, she can feel the hard mound of her phone in her jacket pocket pressed against her thigh. God, she wishes she had a phone with a torch function instead of the stupid relic her mum got her. Then realisation hits. It might not have a torch, but it will light up if she turns it on, which is a hundred times better than the black hole she's in now. And more importantly, she can call Patrick. She pulls the phone out of her pocket and feels around for the on button.

The screen lights up with a dim green glow. She looks around, but the light ebbs away quickly – she can't make anything out beyond a metre or so – so she looks back at the screen. Then sighs at the now missing bars. Patrick called it a cave. And there are thick stone walls. No wonder there's no signal. The screen does show that she has a voicemail – it must have downloaded when she was still upstairs. Maybe she should listen to that, something to distract her while she waits for Patrick to come back.

She presses the button to play the message, then pushes the phone against her ear. She tenses as she realises it's from Nicole.

Thank you for your phone call, Lola. I'm sorry I missed you because I really want to talk to you. You know, I've been processing Isobel's death for a long time now, but the names you mentioned in your email came as a shock. When Isobel died, I broke. My doctor gave me pills that kept me alive, but I didn't know night from day. I couldn't travel to the boulangerie, never mind go to Corsica, so the local police organised her repatriation. Perhaps you're wondering why I'm mentioning all this. Well, it's to excuse me. My stupidity. Because it's so obvious now, what she was doing. Who she was with.

Lola swings around. She was sure she heard something, the door pushing open. But no, a false alarm. Just Nicole's words messing with her head. What is so obvious? What was Izzy doing? Lola forces herself back to the message.

Isobel's father was Corsican, you see. He was born there, in Porto Vecchio, then moved to Paris for university, which is where I met him. He missed the sea, the fishing, so we set up the restaurant in Nice. Luca's parents – Teresa and Nicholas – moved to Nice too, but there was an aunt who stayed in Corsica, Marie. And she had a son called Salvo. Now I know that's quite a common name in Corsica, but his son was called Raphael. And it's harder to believe that was a coincidence.

The crackling, tinny voice swirls around in Lola's head and it makes her feel nauseous. Izzy was related to the Paoli family? That's why she was working for them? But why would they keep that a secret? Lola swallows hard, focuses on Nicole's voice.

I didn't want Isobel anywhere near Salvo with his mafia links, the drug trafficking that he was involved in. But she promised me that her job in Corsica had nothing to do with the Paoli family. She said she'd been offered a sailing instructor job by a hotelier she met in London, and I believed her. And as far as I knew, the Paolis had a restaurant, not a hotel. But now I realise that wasn't true. That Isobel spent her final days with her father's cousin, who also happened to be a ruthless criminal ...

Nicole's voice trails off, and for a few seconds there's just breathing. Lola feels the sound crawl over her skin. If Nicole's right, then Salvo *was* involved with the mafia; it wasn't just his brother Jean. She thinks about the picture of him in that bar, his weather-hardened face and all-knowing eyes. Patrick is so certain that Salvo was one of the good guys. Did Salvo keep the truth from him? Lola feels the creep-creep of darkness closing in on her. Could Patrick have been lying to her? Lola focuses on the voicemail again.

... As well as culpable in my husband's death. You know, Isobel

knew that Luca and I had argued before his car accident, but I always kept the substance of that argument a secret from her. But if she found out from Salvo, or his son, it would have made her angry. She inherited Luca's passion, his sense of justice. But if she confronted someone like Salvo, maybe he would have killed her? You see, Salvo called Luca the morning he died to warn him about some crazy dream he'd had. Salvo believed he had this special power, bestowed on him by a Corsican legend, and this dream had told him that Luca was going to die. I know it sounds crazy, and when Luca confided in me, I told him that. But he was scared. He said we must close the restaurant for a while, and he suddenly wanted to go to church. I told him he was being overdramatic, silly, and we argued.

Then he stormed out, and that's the last time I saw him alive. So yes, I'm to blame for his death, for starting the fight, but so is Salvo for what he said to Luca that day.

Will you call me, Lola? Please?

The voicemail clicks out. Lola lowers the phone. Salvo was part of the Corsican mafia. Izzy had a reason to hate him. And it was Salvo who made her mum feel responsible for Izzy's death, who broke her resolve and self-belief with stories of strange powers and violent dreams. It's all so obvious now. It must have been Salvo in the water that night. Of course he could have swum out and back from his fishing boat without anyone noticing.

Patrick adored his grandfather. Has he been wrong about him all this time?

Lola thinks about the notes under her mum's bedroom door.

Or has she been wrong about Patrick?

Suddenly the weak green light disappears and total blackness returns. Lola pushes on the phone's start button. And again. But nothing happens. She closes her eyes, feels the slow trickle of salty tears down her face. Her stupid phone has run out of power. And in her black hole, all she can see are horrible images. Salvo slipping underwater. Izzy's death-white face. Wild animals being chased through forests by hooded warriors.

There's that noise again but coming from a different direction. Actually, no. It's a different noise. Rustling, but louder, like a person. 'Hello?' she calls out, her voice breaking in that one word. 'Who's there?'

Patrick

31st July

'Papa, it's me.'

Patrick listens to his father grunt, then shuffle. He will be moving out of somebody's earshot in the bar, maybe his mother's, more probably one of Salvo's old adversaries. As he waits, Patrick stares out at the beautiful view of the vineyard below him and thinks about that letter from his grandfather. *If I want to rest in peace when I die, I need to unburden my soul.* Is this vineyard Patrick's reward for taking on that burden? He hopes so.

'What is it?' his father finally says. 'Anna said you left with the British girl?'

'I did, yes.' Patrick pauses. He knows this is a gamble, a risk; but a calculated one. And with everything it promises if it works, he needs to give it his best shot. 'She told me something, about you. I … I don't know whether to believe it.'

For a while Raphael just breathes. 'What did she tell you?' he finally asks.

'That her mum said you killed Archie.'

Raphael sucks in a breath. 'What? That's bullshit,' he spits out.

'You didn't believe her?'

Patrick shifts his eyeline to Lola. She's staring out at the same view as him. Her arms are wrapped around her body, like she's cold, and he wants to pull her in for a hug, warm her up. But he needs to do this first. 'She was quite convincing,' he says.

'So you're trusting a dumb English girl over your own father? How could you be so stupid? Not to mention disloyal. Okay, maybe I'm not the perfect dad, but I'm not a killer, Patrick. You must know that.'

Patrick grinds his heel into the soft soil. 'She said that her mum saw you carrying a dead body down the beach when she was there drinking with Archie. The same night he died. That you dumped the body in Grandpa's fishing boat and took it out to sea.'

'This is all lies,' his dad growls. 'She's a crazy bitch, just like her mother.'

'And that Archie saw it too,' Patrick goes on. 'And you killed him for it.'

Raphael releases a bitter laugh. 'Your grandfather thought Frankie was mazzeri. Now I know why. She's good at making up fantasy stories.'

'Listen, I just wanted to warn you. Lola said that her mum is going to tell the police, tomorrow, and not the local force, but the National Guard up in Bastia.' Raphael doesn't respond. Patrick takes that as a good sign and keeps going. 'Is Frankie still there in the bar with you?'

'Yeah, she's talking to Anna.'

'I mean, I don't want to tell you what to do, Papa. But maybe you could talk to her, alone. Convince her not to go to the police. You know, just in case they believe her.'

Raphael clicks his tongue down the phone. It reminds Patrick of a cork popping from a wine bottle, and it buoys him. He has come up with a good plan – not failsafe, but good – and so far, it's working just as he'd hoped.

Raphael clears his throat. 'Maybe I should. Not because I'm

guilty of anything; I assume you know that?'

'Of course.'

'But I don't want anyone delving into our past. That's our family's business, no one else's.'

'And family is everything,' Patrick murmurs, partly to his dad, partly as a reminder for himself.'

'Shit,' Raphael mutters. 'I think Frankie's gone.'

'What? Already?' It's a deviation from the plan. Patrick feels sweat trickle down his neck. He looks over at Lola, thinks about how protective Frankie is of her – guilt perhaps, for dreaming of her daughter dying.

'You said she's going to the police tomorrow?' Raphael says, failing to hide his growing fear. 'It's fine; I'll find her. Anna will know where she's gone.'

'I better go,' Patrick says. A burst of adrenaline, maybe anxiety, is making him itch to finish the phone call.

But Raphael won't let him. 'Hang on, what about Lola? If she knows all this stuff too …'

'Don't worry about Lola,' Patrick says quietly. He thinks about his grandfather again, what the old man asked of him before he died. His eyes begin to burn, and he closes them until they cool down. Then he flicks up his eyelids, looks at the tangles of vines, the winery in the distance. 'I know what to do with her.'

Frankie

1st August

I drop my phone into my lap – Lola's number is still going straight to voicemail – and silently scream at Dom to speed up. He's already chosen the wrong road twice, and I'm struggling not to let my frustration show. I need to remember he's doing me a favour. And more than that, if I lose my grip now, I might never get it back. The car dips into another pothole and I tip forward.

'Sorry,' Dom says. 'Road maintenance isn't really a thing in Sartène.'

'Are we close?' I ask. I am still praying that Lola is fine, just doing something romantic with Patrick. But someone has threatened to kill her. And Jack's disappeared. And that fucking dream. The bleeding eagle owl. I drop my head into my hands, scratch my forehead.

'Yes,' Dom says. 'The vines run all the way down to the river, but the main entrance is at the end of this road up here.'

I stare at the lines of grapevines, their mangled branches twisting and coiling around each other, and it makes me shudder. Finally, we reach a set of iron gates. Dom jumps out of the car and pushes them open. Then he climbs back in and drives down an even narrower road towards a big stone building.

I get out of the car so fast that I almost fall over, but then I pause. Where first? There are no signs of life in the winery – the shutters are all closed and there's no light seeping between the cracks. But the vineyard is vast.

'Do you want to try calling her again?' Dom asks, the enormity of the task clearly evident for him too.

I shake my head, trying to hold the tears back. 'No, I've tried too many times. Her phone must be out of power.'

'Do you have Patrick's number?'

Fuck, why didn't I think of that? Why didn't I get his number from Anna? 'They left just before us,' I say instead. 'They can't be that far away.' I look back at the winery. 'You check in there,' I say. 'And I'll start walking through the vines.'

'Are you sure?' Dom asks. 'I don't know how I feel about you being out there on your own.'

'Yes, I'm sure. Call me if you find them.' I set off down the path. With the sky clear, the moon gives me enough light to see by, and I walk quickly. There are vines on one side and a fence on the other, the river beyond. I want the sound of the water to calm me, but I'm too tense, too panicked.

'Lola!' I call out. 'Lola!'

A sound echoes back, but it's not human. The call of a bird. I look up and see a huge bird of prey flying overhead, each of its wings a metre long, their underside pure white. I can't catch my breath as I watch it disappear into the distance. Was that an eagle owl? No, it can't be. I'm too tired, too scared. I'm seeing things that aren't there.

Suddenly I sense movement between the grapevines. I whip my head side to side. 'Lola?' I say again, quieter, less certain. 'Is that you?'

The sound stops. I swallow, take a few steps into the vines. My heart is pounding so much that it's ringing in my ears.

Suddenly the sky darkens. A cloud must have passed in front of the moon. Out of some instinctive fear, I lower down onto my haunches, let the vines hide me. My breathing is short and ragged, and when the light returns, I almost cry with relief.

But the feeling is short-lived when I stand up.

'Hello, Frankie.'

Frankie

1st August

'Raphael,' I say, taking a step backwards, trying to pretend I'm not petrified. 'What are you doing here?'

'Looking for you.'

I wonder if I should run. He's older than me, less fit. Maybe I'd be faster.

'I heard you've been making up stories. Telling your daughter that I killed your friend.'

'Wh-what?' I stutter. Fuck. Lola must have said something to Patrick about our suspicions. Why would she do something so naïve? Surely she'd know that Patrick would take his father's side over hers? I only ever said it could have been Raphael in the water that night, just like it could have been Jack or Dom. Or Anna or Salvo. But gossip and whispers always become more entrenched as they travel.

'I didn't say that,' I mumble, flicking my eyes right and left. God I hope Dom has found Lola, and that Patrick hasn't hurt her.

'Bullshit,' he spits out. 'You think I don't trust my own son?'

'No, I just … It was only after …' Do I mention the notes? Will

312

that help explain why I was suspicious, or make him angrier?

Raphael's eyes narrow and he lets out a snarl. Then he reaches behind his back and suddenly there's a gun pointing at me. My legs go weak, almost buckle, and my breathing stutters. I should have run when I had the chance.

'Well, maybe I don't give a fuck anymore,' he says, pointing the weapon at me. 'Because you're not going to be talking to anyone soon. So yeah, I killed Archie.'

Despite the gun in my face, and Raphael's angry expression, his words jolt me. 'Wh-what?'

'And you were supposed to die too. But somehow – some fucking how – you survived, and Izzy didn't.'

'I don't understand,' I whisper.

'I didn't want to kill Archie, or you, at least not at first. In fact, I never wanted to move that snitch's body in the first place. I was supposed to be the money man, that's all. They could give me all the dirty notes they wanted, and I'd flush it clean. I never let Uncle Jean down, not once in thirteen years. And in return, he kept me away from the enforcement side of the business. But then Uncle Jean was murdered. And my cousins were too angry to plan their retribution properly. So suddenly there's a screaming match in their car, and then a dead snitch, and they've got nowhere to hide the body. So of course they call me, the local man with access to a boat.'

He clicks the catch on the gun, reaches up with his second hand to steady his aim. 'No one ever goes on that stretch of beach at night. Except you were there, weren't you? You and that Scottish lord. He asked me about it later that night – straight out, like he wasn't scared of me, even though he was accusing me of something that could get me a ten-year stretch. He didn't even hesitate when I suggested a walk. Dumb, fucking posh drunk. Life had been too easy for that boy; he hadn't learned to read the danger signs.'

'So you killed him,' I say. 'And then found out I'd been with Archie, and realised you needed to kill me too.'

Raphael shrugs. 'I knew you were with him, but I didn't know what you'd seen, not until Salvo told me about your conversation in the boat the next morning.'

There were some fishermen arguing over a guy so drunk he couldn't stand up.

I see his ice-blue eyes again. 'And Salvo told you to kill me?'

Raphael snorts. 'That man wouldn't kill a fucking fly. At least, not after his epiphany or whatever that change of heart was. No, he told me he'd already solved my problem for me, that he'd filled your head with mazzeri nonsense so that you wouldn't remember what you'd really seen. That started an argument. First with Salvo, then my darling wife suddenly decides she's got an opinion worth listening to. Both of them trying to convince me that a fucking mazzeri tale would save my skin, that you didn't need to die.' He shakes his head.

My eyes widen, then crease in confusion. 'So Salvo thinking I was mazzeri, that my dad was too, it was all a lie? Just a story to distract me?'

'Of course it was. It's all just a story, isn't it? Although Salvo was always adamant that the mazzeri legend was true. That's probably why he thought it would work with you.' Raphael takes a step forward. 'But it wasn't enough for me; I've never liked loose ends.'

'So you tried to kill me, that night. But you fucked up and drowned Izzy instead.'

Almost before I see him move, I feel the pain of the pistol whip – cold metal burning my cheek. I stumble, sink my face into my hands, then drop to my knees.

'I would never hurt Izzy,' he hisses, looming over me. He lowers the gun so it's aiming at my forehead. Like a mafia execution. 'She was my flesh and blood.'

I look up. The gun seems to have grown in size, the barrel now a canon, the muzzle lion's teeth. My whole body shudders in response. 'What did you say?'

'Mine and Izzy's dads were cousins. Salvo always told me that

314

family means everything, but when Izzy turned up at the hotel that first time, he didn't want to know her. He wouldn't even look her in the eye, and she hated him for that. So it fell to me to help her. Not that I minded. She was a Paoli in all but name.'

Raphael's face softens for a moment, then he remembers where he is, what he's about to do, and it hardens again. 'Izzy was desperate to work with me, to help me launder the money, but she needed experience first. So I hooked her up with a business partner of mine in London, asked him to show her the ropes. I owed him a favour after that – which is why Jack ended up as my windsurf instructor. He'd got himself into a sticky situation at home – I didn't want to know the details – and had all the qualifications he needed. It worked out too; Jack's a good man.'

'He tried to kill his family,' I whisper, the words out before my sluggish brain can process the consequences of riling Raphael. 'The man you've been friends with for twenty years. Who owns half this place.'

Raphael kicks my knee. A jolt of pain runs up my thigh. 'God, I'm going to enjoy killing you,' he murmurs. 'Even if it is twenty-one years too late. And do you know who else I'm doing it for?'

'Salvo,' I murmur, seeing his face again. Those eyes.

'No, not him. For some reason Salvo always wanted to protect you.' He puts his finger on the trigger. 'I'm doing it for Izzy, because she died trying.'

And he shoots.

Lola

1st August

Lola arches her back. Her heart is pounding, her body quivering with an overload of adrenaline. The noise is still there. A busy rustling with intermittent loud thuds. The longer she listens, the less she thinks it's a person. It's too frenetic. But it's nothing small like a rat either. Why is she so scared? Blind people deal with this all the time. Hearing noises, seeing nothing. They don't freeze with fear.

Slowly, she uncurls her legs until she's standing. She pauses for a moment to ground herself, then starts shuffling towards the noise, her limbs shaking with fear. She doesn't think the creature is in the room with her, otherwise surely she'd have felt it by now, so it must be the other side of a door, or maybe a window. Which means, if she's brave enough to get close, there might be a chance for her to escape.

It's hard to believe her heart can beat any faster, but it manages to as she edges closer. She holds out her arms, teetering forward like a zombie, both scared and hopeful of what she might find. The noise gets louder. Her heart pounds.

Finally, she touches something cold and coarse. Brickwork. It's a wall. The relief makes her knees weak, and she leans her hands against it for a moment, her palms cooling. When she first walked in, it seemed like every wall was stacked high with wine bottles, but she wasn't paying much attention then. She was too excited about toasting her birthday with Patrick.

Patrick. Where is he? Why didn't he come back for her? There could be an innocent explanation – maybe he fell in the darkness and hurt himself. Or maybe he hasn't been gone very long at all, and it's just fear stretching time. But then Lola thinks about the voicemail from Nicole, Salvo's mafia crimes, those threatening notes. And the strong chance that Patrick locked her in this terrifying cellar on purpose.

That thought spurs her into moving again. Using the wall as her reference point, she works her fingers towards the noise. Slides left and right, but only finds more brickwork. She stills, concentrates. The noise is coming from higher up, she realises. She reaches towards it. With her arms straight, and on her tiptoes, she feels a bump. She creeps her fingers further along. Thin slices of wood. It's a shutter, she realises. Which means there's a window behind it. A high window. Too high to climb through. But something to give her light.

Suddenly excited, she scrabbles around, stretching further until she finds the locking mechanism. A metal latch. With a small jump, she manages to lift it and both shutters sway forward. She curls her fingers around the edges and swings them wide open.

Then she screams.

Moonlight floods in. Lighting up the biggest bird she's ever seen.

A huge owl. Brown and tan mottled feathers. Piercing orange eyes. It lifts its wings, revealing a pure white underside, and the sight is so magical that Lola's scream freezes in her throat, her mouth gaping open in wonder and horror and shock. The owl holds its position for a moment, staring straight into Lola's eyes, then it lifts off, flying into the night.

317

Frankie

1st August

BOOM.

The sound of the gun ricochets off the mountains. I collapse on the ground and wait for my heart rate to slow, for the pain to flare. But neither of those things happen. No pain, no blood loss, no injury.

Raphael missed his shot.

The huge bird from earlier swoops overhead and I look up, suddenly mesmerised by its size and aura. But then I hear a click. A reloaded gun. Of course the danger isn't over. I flick my head, looking for an escape, but it's a reflex action. I might be faster than Raphael, but the range of his pistol would outpace me in this vast sloping vineyard. I stare up, like cornered prey.

'Stupid fucking bird!' Raphael shouts, swinging the gun towards the sky in frustration, the owl just visible in the distance, then back to me. 'But I won't miss this time.'

I wait for a few seconds, but nothing happens. So I slowly, carefully, rise to my feet. Dom is somewhere in the vineyard, and he will have heard the shot. If I can keep Raphael talking, maybe there's a chance I can survive this. 'What do you mean by Izzy died trying?' I ask, forcing myself to make eye contact, to hold his attention. 'Trying what?'

His sudden crack of laughter makes me jump. 'You still haven't worked it out, have you? It was always only Izzy in the water with you that night. But she was there to kill you, not swim with you. She worked for me, remember? And that meant getting her hands dirty if I asked her too, not that she showed any reluctance when it came to killing you. She said you'd become too needy.'

His stare sharpens. 'But you killed her instead. I don't know what went wrong out there in the sea – she took Salvo's mini-oxygen kit out of his boat, just like I told her to, so she should have had the upper hand. But she wasn't wearing it when I found her, and it never showed up. I do know you got her drunk on tequila though, and judging by the mark I saw on her forehead when I found her, you also kicked her in the head. You knocked her unconscious, Frankie. You caused her to drown.'

My breathing stutters. I'm there in the water again. Fear giving me a strength I didn't know my muscles were capable of. Kicking out, slamming my foot into something solid. Was that Izzy's head? After all these years swerving between guilt for her death, and the trauma of escaping a predator … was it actually both?

'If you kill me, you'll go to prison for a long time,' I say, my voice quivering. 'Your life will be over too.'

'I doubt it,' Raphael says. 'You're roaming my family's private land. I'll say that a wild boar had been spotted trampling the vines and I came here to deal with that. I always keep my gun in the boot of my car, so no one will question it. And if a Brit is stupid enough to trespass on agricultural land in the middle of the night, those are the risks.'

'Especially when you've got friends in the police,' I throw back.

'We do what we need to get by.'

He raises the gun again. My body convulses with fear.

'Lola will make sure you get justice!' I shout, like a final call to arms. 'She'll go to France, to police beyond your reach.'

'Hah! Lola won't be talking to anyone; Patrick will make sure of that.'

His words are worse than bullets. I fall silent, slump forward, close my eyes, wait for the pain. I see Lola, waving at me from a podium, a gold medal between smiling teeth.

A muffled sound cuts through the night. 'Help me.'

My eyelids flick open. My head swings, in perfect synchrony with Raphael's.

'Please, help me.' A pained, low voice wafts over. But it's a man's voice, thank God. Not Lola. 'I've been shot.'

I watch Raphael's face morph from confusion, to understanding, to horror. Then he sprints towards the voice.

Calling out his son's name.

Salvo

7th July

7th July 2025
Sartène

My dearest Patrick,

I am an old man now and my time is drawing to a close. I have had a long life, and I should be ready for this next chapter. But I'm scared. I have too many secrets. And if I want to rest in peace when I die, I need to unburden my soul.

I am sorry to pass this weight to you. But you are a man now, a good man, and I know you're strong enough. All I really hope is that you use this knowledge to escape your destiny. Because I've spent too long not believing that's possible.

Over the years I have tried to keep the worst of my discord with your father from you, but I'm sure you're aware of how difficult our relationship is. Now, I will tell you why.

You will know that your Uncle Jean was the leader of a mafia gang in Ajaccio before he was killed in 2004. What you don't know is that, to my shame, I used to work with him. It was the 1970s and 1980s and the heroin trade with America was blossoming. Jean ran the factories in Marseille while I negotiated with our American partners. But I'm making it sound like a legitimate business. It wasn't. We were ruthless, violent. It was the only way to survive in that world, although I know that doesn't excuse what we did. I even lost my best friend Pascal to England because he couldn't stand by and watch me live the cruel life I'd chosen.

Then in 1991, something happened. Something that meant I needed to walk away – I could not be responsible for any more suffering.

I killed my cousin. At least, that's how it felt.

It was no gang fight, or family feud. But I had a mazzeri dream and saw my cousin's face on a wild boar as it lay dying in the forest. Young people call the mazzeri a fantasy, a mystical legend. They ridicule its power. But two days after my dream, my cousin died in a car accident. The mazzeri power is real, Patrick. Please never forget that. And while I knew I was merely the prophet; I couldn't shake the feeling of responsibility that came with it.

Jean agreed that I could leave the firm, but unbeknown to me, it came at a price. Your father was twenty-one at the time, and he filled my shoes. The FBI had shut down our American trade by then, but there were other opportunities, and your father laundered Jean's dirty money. It paid for the hotel expansion and other businesses in Porto Vecchio that you no doubt never knew he owned. I'm not proud to admit it, but I benefited too.

I turned a blind eye to Raphael's criminality, convinced myself that laundering money was an improvement on what I was doing at his age. But I was lying to myself, and that became evident when Jean was murdered by one of our rivals. Of course Jean's boys, my nephews, wanted to take revenge against the killer, and when things went wrong, they needed a *local man to get rid of a body. Perhaps I could have accepted that, even with Raphael stealing my boat to take the man's body out to sea – I'm sure the man had blood on his hands too, and as you know, we Corsicans love a vendetta. But then your father crossed a line.*

A young man witnessed the body being carried down the beach. One of your father's employees, Archie. He was drunk, and I'm not sure he even realised what he was bearing witness to. But accepting the balance of probabilities is not the mafia way. Your father used his position as Archie's boss to draw the poor boy into the woods, then wound his own belt around his neck and strung him up on a tree branch.

You father killed an innocent man, Patrick. But it gets worse.

I was brought up to believe that family is everything. So when I realised that another employee had witnessed your father taking a dead man's body out to sea, my first instinct was to protect my son. And I used the death of my cousin to do that. It worked. I filled the girl's traumatised mind with too many macabre possibilities for those real memories to ever surface. Then I told your father what had happened, to reassure him. But my solution wasn't enough for him. However passionately your mother and I argued for her salvation, he wanted her killed too. You mother never forgave him.

Except it didn't work out. The girl survived and another young woman died in her place.

And do you know who that woman was?

My cousin's only child. So first I had Luca's blood on my hands. And then I stood by while his daughter died too. I felt numb after that. Too guilty to even allow myself to feel.

It ruined your father too. Your mother worked to save the hotel – a generosity I'm finally able to compensate her for – and Raphael never worked with his cousins again. But it was all much too late for redemption. I gave Jack half the

323

vineyard to assuage my own guilt, but Raphael needs to pay for his crimes.

I am asking you to take revenge against your father for me, Patrick. But without bloodshed – I know you're clever enough to find a way. Then get away from your Corsican family. Make the choices Pascal made, go to England, find a British bride. You are half British after all.

And one last thing before I sign off forever. I am bequeathing you the thing I have loved most in my lifetime. It came to me in the embers of my life, but I have treasured it ever since, and I know you will too.

Your loving grandfather, Salvo

Patrick

1st August

Patrick can hear his dad's voice. Muffled and distant. Speaking French. '*Oh mon fils, qu'ai-je fait!*' Oh my son, what have I done.

You've killed your only son, Dad. That's what you've done. Because Patrick can feel his life ebbing away.

But it wasn't supposed to end like this. Lola's mother should be dead. And Raphael should be in handcuffs, arrested for her murder – one anonymous phone call to the police would have ensured that. And it's exactly the kind of revenge that Salvo had wished for in his letter.

A wish that can't come true now.

And the worst thing is, that mazzeri witch surviving means that Lola is still in danger.

Salvo was right that Patrick had picked up on the tension between his father and grandfather. But there was tension everywhere, and he hadn't questioned what caused it. So reading Salvo's letter had been a shock – discovering the extent of his mafia heritage was bad enough, but finding out that the suicide of their windsurf instructor twenty years ago had been murder, and at his father's hand. And also that he was related to the girl who drowned.

And it was so much worse because he'd met Lola by the time he read it.

The daughter of the woman his father tried to have killed.

At first, he felt terrible for them both, especially when Lola explained how tough the last twenty years had been for her mum. Just as Salvo asked for in his letter, Patrick was determined to find a way to get justice for them both. As he got closer to Lola, he even began dreaming of following another one of Salvo's wishes and making her his British wife. Maybe. One day.

Then Lola told him about her mum's dream.

And it sparked a memory. Patrick sat on a cold plastic chair in the corridor of the local police station, leaning on his grandfather, his father on the other side, the air thick with something invisible that made him want to cry. Then Frankie walked out of a room, and his mood suddenly made sense because she'd been crying too.

You had a mazzeri dream about Izzy dying. That's what his grandfather said to Frankie that morning, and her wild stare was enough to answer the question without words.

And Izzy did die.

The mazzeri power is real, Patrick. Please never forget that.

Salvo's letter warned him too. And how could he trust his grandfather's words, that his own father had killed Archie, and not trust his other warning? Yes, his grandfather described the mazzeri as prophets, not killers. And by that logic, Lola's fate was already sealed. But how could Patrick ever forgive himself if Lola died and he'd done nothing to try to stop it? Surely if the mazzera is extinguished, then so is her power?

That's when the idea formed. A chance to keep Lola alive and make his father pay for killing Archie and letting Izzy die. But it couldn't happen in the hotel – too many witnesses, his mother over everything.

He always hoped that Lola would go to Salvo's gathering with him, but he couldn't leave it to chance anymore. So he took Lola's travel documents from the pile of post and kept talking about how special it would be for Lola to begin her birthday in both their grandfathers' hometown.

And things started well tonight too. Lola agreed to go to the vineyard with him, meaning that he could keep her far away from any crime scene. And when he phoned his father and pretended that Lola had accused the older man of killing Archie, Raphael took the bait. But that's when things started to go wrong. Raphael was supposed to take Frankie down one of Sartène's medieval stone alleyways, the perfect setting for an undetected murder. But he was too slow, or she was too protective a mother perhaps.

But as soon as Raphael told him that Frankie had left the bar, he knew where she was headed. So he adjusted his plan, locking Lola in the cellar to make sure she didn't witness her mum being killed. He didn't know how Lola would react when she found out her mum was dead – he has no strong bond with either of his parents, so he's got no point of reference – but when he allowed himself to dream, he saw her turning to him in her grief.

Now he'll never know.

Why did he get so close to the scene? He didn't need to be right there. But he couldn't miss seeing his plan succeed. So in the end, it was his thirst for retribution that killed him. Perhaps he's more like his father than he thought.

The pain was agonising when the bullet ripped through his stomach. He knew instantly that it was a pain he wouldn't survive. He's only grateful that it doesn't hurt anymore. He's just cold. Bitterly, freezing cold.

Something soft lands on top of him, his father's jumper maybe, and he wonders if it might warm him up. He thinks perhaps that it does too. Just a little.

And he hopes the jumper softens his landing, because he's falling now. Sinking into the Corsican soil.

I am bequeathing you the thing I have loved most in my lifetime.

It came to me in the embers of my life, but I have treasured it ever since, and I know that you will too.

Suddenly Patrick knows what his grandfather was passing on to him. Not this vineyard. Something that came to him much later, courtesy of the letter.

A clean conscience.

God, he wished he'd paid more attention.

Frankie

1st August

'No, no, no, no,' Raphael moans. 'Don't you dare die on me!'

I look at the gun by Raphael's side. He flung it there when he found Patrick, his son's torso shredded by the bullet meant for me. I want to grab it, but it's so close to Raphael's hand. And I'm shaking so much I'd probably drop it.

Raphael crouches down, puts his ear by Patrick's mouth, his face reddening with shame and anger. Then he pulls back and shakes his son. As the body flops in his grasp, he releases a strangled scream, like the bray of a wild animal rising into the night sky. Then he picks up the gun and pushes to standing. His hands are trembling but he's only a couple of metres away, too close to miss.

'Get up!' he screams. 'This is your fault! My son is dead because of you!'

I rise slowly to my feet, but from somewhere deep in my belly, injustice rises too. Twenty-one years of hating myself for something this man caused. This man who's about to kill me. 'No, he's dead because of you, Raphael!' I shout. 'You shot your own son, just like you strangled Archie with his own belt and then hanged him from a tree! But all I care about is whether Patrick is like you, a monster. Has he hurt Lola, Raphael? Has he killed her?'

'You think I care about your daughter?!' Raphael screams back. His face is contorted; tears stream down his cheeks. He's still enraged, but bewildered too. Like he's out of his depth.

A sudden realisation hits me.

Patrick orchestrated this. It was Patrick who brought Lola to the vineyard, not Raphael. And Patrick who has charmed Lola into staying in Corsica, and persuaded her to visit Sartène tonight. Did he draw Raphael here too? To kill me?

'Who called you tonight in the bar?' I demand. 'Was it Patrick?'

'He called to warn me; to tell me you were going to tell the police about Archie. He came through for me when it mattered.'

'I didn't know anything about you killing Archie until you told me,' I hiss. 'I've never talked about going to the police.'

'Bullshit.'

'Your son played you. Getting you to come here and kill me. I don't know why he wanted me dead, but he clearly wanted you to do his dirty work.' Silently I wonder if that means Lola is alive, if I can hope.

'He wouldn't!'

'Why was he here then?' I go on. 'Spying on you?'

'No.' Raphael shakes his head, but manically, like he's trying to rid his mind of my logic. 'He's my son. He loves me.'

'But he was closer to Salvo, wasn't he?' I say, things starting to fall into place. 'And Salvo hated you for what you did. That's why he moved away, isn't it? He couldn't bear to look at you. And it's why he gave Jack half his vineyard, and left Izzy's mum the rest.'

'My father?! Hah! He was the most ruthless of us all!'

'And Patrick hated you too,' I finish.

'You need to shut up now.' Raphael releases the catch on the trigger, takes a breath.

I look at the barrel. I suck in air, but I can't release it. This is it.

A gun sounds. A thud. Raphael drops to the ground, blood spreading from his head. I spin around and my eyes widen.

'Jack?'

'Fucking arsehole! I've known the guy for over twenty fucking years. I have cried on his shoulder; he's listened to my guilt spill out on drunken nights too many times to count. And the real truth is that he killed Archie?' He kicks Raphael's still torso, and the momentum snaps the dead man's head back. The moon catches his glassy eyes, blood pooling in the crevices. 'He deserves more than a bullet in the head!'

'Like a petrol bomb through his letterbox?'

Why the fuck did I just say that? Jack has just saved my life! The adrenaline is making me crazy.

But Jack's anger instantly deflates. 'You know about that, then. I did wonder.'

'Um, yes,' I stutter. 'Archie told me on the night … the night Raphael murdered him. But I haven't told …'

'Two seconds,' Jack says. 'That's how long it took for me to regret it. I couldn't save the flat, but I got them all out. And I paid for all the repair work. Yeah, it was drug money, but none of us are perfect. I told Archie all this, and he got it too. After a while.' He releases a sad sigh. 'He pretended to beat me up for it, that night, but we were laughing in the end. That's why I couldn't believe it when Izzy told me he'd killed himself. God knows why I made up that bullshit story about being in town. I was scared, I suppose. Of telling the police I'd been with him only a couple of hours before he died. Old habits.'

'Izzy knew what you'd done in London too, I think. She was scared of you.'

He shakes his head. 'Not as scared as I was of her. Swaggering around Achille's nightclub like she owned the place. She was in much deeper than me in London. I thought we'd be friends, both of us coming from the same scene, but she hated that I knew who she really was. Even though I never said a word.'

I look at the gun in his hand, his composed expression, and wonder whether I'm still in danger. 'And are you still involved with those people?' I ask in a whisper.

'What? God, no.' Jack looks down at his gun and it's as though he doesn't recognise it. 'Archie made me see things differently. I've only got this to scare off the wild boar that like to munch on the vines in this place. Amazing that I made my shot really, but I guess rage and adrenaline can go a long way.'

'But how did you even know to come down here?'

'I had an alert on my phone that the winery's door had been opened. Salvo's reputation meant that we never had to worry about thieves, but with him gone, and me close by, I thought I should check it out. The place was quiet when I arrived, but then I heard the gunshot and screaming. I grabbed this out of my boot and came running. I thought I was going to save someone, but then I heard what you said about Archie.'

'That Raphael strangled him.'

'He didn't even try to deny it.'

'Mum!'

My heart stops, then surges. I twist around. 'Lola?!' I breathe out, not quite believing my eyes. 'LOLA!' I stumble towards my daughter. My knees start to give way, but someone holds me up. Dom.

'Oh my God, Frankie. I thought …' Dom looks around him, eyes skittering over the two dead bodies. Father and son. 'We got here as fast as we could,' he says, breathless, his words rushing out. 'I heard the first shot, started running towards it, but there was a noise from the winery, someone banging on a window and screaming for help. I had to get Lola out.'

'I'm sorry, Mum,' Lola sobs, folding into my outstretched arms. 'This is all my fault. I should have listened to you.'

'Don't even think about blaming yourself,' I say, my voice so much stronger than the swirling flotsam in my brain. 'I have spent over two decades blaming myself for a tragedy. I won't

332

have you do the same.'

'Izzy's death wasn't your fault, Mum,' Lola gulps between her tears. 'I don't know what happened, but she was part of this horrible family.' Lola looks around the scene with a mix of fear and disgust.

I gently pull her closer. 'Yeah, I know that now,' I murmur. 'Maybe if I'd known to be wary of her then, none of this would have happened.'

'Who knows,' says Jack, his voice gritty. 'Every choice we make, big or small, changes the trajectory of our lives to some degree.'

'No such thing as fate then,' I murmur.

Jack gives me a half-smile. 'I think I'd need a few tequilas before answering that one.'

2026

Lola

1st August

'So are you ready for this?'

Lola smiles at her mum, then lets her knees drop until she's sitting cross-legged in the warm sand. She looks at the expanse of sea in front of her. Shades of blue from aquamarine to cobalt. A strong easterly wind darting across the water, creating hundreds of tiny white peaks in the otherwise flat Piantarella lagoon. And fluorescent buoys marking out the one-kilometre course. 'Yeah, I'm ready.'

Her rig is waiting for her down by the windsurf centre, painstakingly adjusted to give herself the best chance of winning the race she was supposed to take part in last year. That didn't work out – there were other things to do that day – but the race admin honoured her entry for 2026. There are fifty windsurfers taking part – forty men and ten women, room for improvement, as always – with ten staggered start times. She's in the penultimate race, which will begin in about half an hour.

'This view is beautiful, isn't it?' her mum murmurs. 'A bit different to what we were doing on your birthday last year.'

Lola doesn't take her eyes off the sea – the five male competitors out there, up on their fins, bright sails catching the wind as they aim for the next buoy – but she nods and smiles.

Her last birthday – her eighteenth – was mostly spent in a police station in Sartène, giving a statement about the two deaths. Dom was the first to think about calling the French equivalent of 999 as they stood, shellshocked, in the vineyard that night. The emergency services had turned up soon after, a red-and-blue flashing convoy. Both Patrick and Raphael had been pronounced dead at the scene. Jack had been arrested and taken away in handcuffs, but it hadn't taken long for them to let him go. Once he explained what happened – that Raphael had killed Patrick and Jack had shot him to stop him doing the same to Frankie – they'd released him without charge.

Lola's travel papers had been found under Patrick's mattress in his bedroom, and she'd flown home with her mum the day after her birthday, on the promise that they would cooperate fully with the police investigation from the UK. There were inquests into both deaths, but no official asked them to give evidence. It seems that Corsican pride extends to not wanting to draw too much attention to the country's darker side.

A shadow looms over Lola, and she looks up, her hand at her forehead to block out the sun. 'Oh hey, Jack.'

'Hey, guys.' He nods at them both. 'And happy birthday. Nice to do this on the beach rather than in a police station.' He looks out to sea for a few moments, then sinks down next to Lola. 'You know, I entered this race a few times myself when I was younger. But I have a feeling you're going to do better than me.'

She smiles her gratitude, then punches him lightly on the arm.

'No Dom today?' he continues.

'He had a painting to deliver,' her mum says. 'He's on his way.'

This is something new. Throughout her childhood, Lola never questioned why her mum had no partner. Even though most of her friends had dads, she knew her own father lived in New

Zealand, and it never occurred to her to wonder why her mum hadn't married or even dated. Now she knows. Her mum couldn't get that close to anyone with the thick cloak of guilt that she constantly wore. But that finally slipped off a year ago. And now her mum visits Corsica every school holiday. She pretends it's to help Dom with the new art gallery he's opened in Sartène, but Lola's not that dumb.

Personally, she's not ready for a relationship yet. It's not like she and Patrick were together for long, but she did fall for him hard, and she's still reeling from what happened. Although that doesn't mean she's not making the most of university life, joining clubs, making friends. Yes, the scars of her experience in Corsica are permanent, but she won't let them rule her like they ruled her mum for so long.

She looks at her dive watch. 'I guess I better get going,' she says, pushing up. She pulls the tight rash vest over her head and wriggles it down to the hem of her bikini bottoms. She checks her plaits are still tight, then grabs her harness.

'Fly like a bird, sweetheart,' her mum says.

Lola raises her eyebrows and grins. 'Like an eagle owl maybe?'

A slight waft of fear crosses her mum's face, but then it vanishes, and she smiles.

'It was a good omen in the end, wasn't it?' Lola reminds her. 'You were saved by the flight of that bird.'

'Which you scared away from the window.'

'I like to think of it that way, yes. My guardian owl.'

Frankie

I watch my beautiful daughter stride towards her rig. Shoulders back, eyes watching the windsurfers, picking up any last-minute clues about the wind. This time last year I was scared she might be dead. Today she's full to the brim with life.

'She's fucking awesome, your daughter.'

I laugh. 'Yeah, she is. I just wish I'd been more present when she was growing up. This is only the fifth birthday I've spent with her.'

Jack shrugs, unfazed. 'We all do things we regret. Me more than most. The only thing that matters is how we remedy them.'

His words make me think of Anna. How I caught a glimpse of her from the taxi window as we left the hotel. She was barely recognisable – no make-up, hair scraped back, the carefully constructed bravado gone. The crushing devastation of losing her husband and only child in one night radiating from her like a dark mist. I wonder if she'll ever be free of her regrets.

I never told the police about the notes. I convinced myself that it was because there was no point – three generations of Paolis were already dead – but that wasn't really it. For all Raphael

340

confessed to, he didn't mention them. It could have been Patrick of course, but I've never been able to quell the suspicion that Anna slipped them under my door. She knew what Raphael had done, and how Salvo derailed my thoughts. So she understood the damage I could cause – to the hotel she'd worked so hard to get back on track and had just inherited a third of – if my memories returned. I think that was why she offered me a room when I arrived too. Keep your enemies close.

And I figured she had suffered enough.

'I mean, look at Salvo,' Jack continues. 'He had plenty to regret. But now I own a vineyard with Izzy's mum, Nicole. Salvo wasn't responsible for either Archie's or Izzy's deaths, but Raphael was his flesh and blood.'

'Family is everything,' I whisper.

'He felt responsible. And he did what he could.'

'You know, I always thought Salvo was my nemesis. And now it turns out he might have been the best of them.'

'Yeah, well. That's life, I guess. Never goes quite how you think.'

I watch Lola carry her rig towards the sandbank where the race starts. A bird flies overhead and disappears into the haze of the horizon. And if it wasn't the brightest, sunniest part of the day, I'd swear that it was an eagle owl.

A Letter from Sarah Clarke

Dear Reader,

Thank you for reading *Someone in the Water*. Just a quick warning, there are spoilers in this letter.

Frankie always knew that the mazzeri was a mystical legend rather than a real phenomenon, but at times she struggled to accept that truth. Within her circumstances, could you sympathise with her mindset, or do you think she was a fool to pay the legend any heed?

Frankie preferred to deal with her mental health problems by hiding away rather than addressing them in therapy. Do you understand why she did this? Do you think it was a mistake?

Even after Frankie showed Lola the threatening notes, Lola wanted to stay in Corsica. Do you think this was more about wanting her mum to resolve her issues, or her burgeoning relationship with Patrick? Was it selfish of Lola to behave that way, or justified? Or both?

The concept of family is a thread that runs throughout the novel. Do you think Raphael and/or Patrick might still be alive if they had felt less family loyalty? Or was it just an excuse for their bad behaviour? Salvo spent a long time trying to atone for his mistakes, but ultimately, he lied to protect his criminal son, damaging Frankie in the process. Could you forgive him?

I'd love to know what you think about all these questions. You can reach me by email at sarah@sarahclarkeauthor.com or on Facebook and Instagram as @sarahclarkewriter. And if you enjoyed *Someone in the Water*, I would be very grateful if you could leave a review. It really makes such a difference.

You can also join my mailing list to download my short story *The Morning After*. And follow my publisher @HQstories for more book news and great giveaways.

Happy reading,
Sarah

Twitter: @SCWwriter
Instagram: @sarahclarkewriter
Website: sarahclarkeauthor.com

A Mother Never Lies

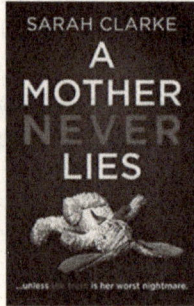

'Brilliantly tense, with an unexpectedly dark heart – a totally compelling read.' Sophie Hannah, *Sunday Times* bestselling author

SOME TRUTHS CAN'T BE TOLD.

I had the perfect life – a nice house, a loving husband, a beautiful little boy.

But in one devastating night, they were all ripped from me.

It's been fourteen years, and I'm finally ready to face the past.

I'm taking my son back.

He just can't know who I am … or why we were torn apart.

A nail-biting thriller packed with twists and turns, perfect for fans of Lisa Jewell and Shalini Boland.

Every Little Secret

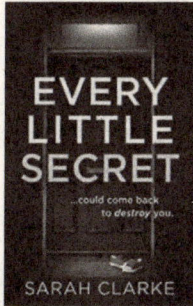

'A fast-paced, twisty story … A thrilling read' Catherine
Cooper, bestselling author of *The Chalet*

From the outside, it seems Grace has it all. Only she knows
about the cracks in her picture-perfect life … and the huge
secret behind them. After all, who can she trust?

Her brother Josh is thousands of miles away, and he and Grace
have never been close – he was always their parents' favourite.

Her best friend Coco walked away from her years ago, their
friendship irreparably fractured by the choices they've made.

And her husband Marcus seems like a different man lately.
Grace can't shake the feeling that he's hiding something.

But when her seven-year-old daughter makes a troubling accusation, Grace must choose between protecting her child and
protecting her secret … before she loses everything.

My Perfect Friend

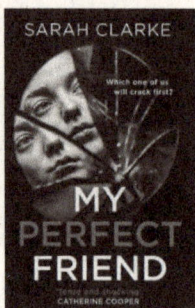

'An intensely gripping thriller' Philippa East

Beth has the perfect life. She has constructed it carefully over the last eighteen years. But one night she makes a choice that risks everything.

When **Kat** sees an article about that night online, buried memories begin to surface. She and Beth were friends once. Things ended badly then, but now she has a chance to make them right.

Kat introduces herself to Beth. Not as her old friend, but as a stranger. Beth has no idea Kat isn't who she says she is.

But then neither is Beth.

The Ski Trip

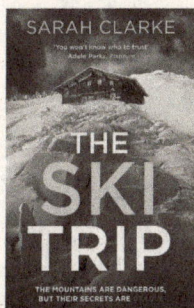

'You won't know who to trust' Adele Parks, *Platinum*

When four friends embark on a boys' skiing holiday in the Alps, they anticipate a weekend of fun, drinking, and some healthy competition on the slopes. But their trip is cut short when one of them falls to his death.

A TERRIBLE ACCIDENT …

Tom's widow, Zoe travels to France with her friend, Ivy to collect his body. While Zoe is consumed by grief, Ivy starts to question everything.

OR COLD-BLOODED MURDER?

The slope Tom fell from wasn't dangerous, and tensions between the group were at breaking point in the days before his death.

But if Ivy's suspicions are correct, Tom was killed by one of his closest friends. And they are still in the chalet …

The Night She Dies

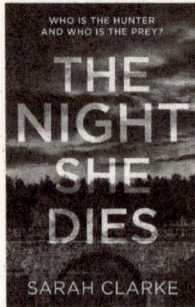

'Tense and tightly plotted with a killer twist'
Louise Jensen, author of *The Intruders*

Bullied at school, Rachel's teenage daughter Lucy
is a shadow of the sweet, happy child she once was.
So when Rachel returns home one night to find
Lucy gone, she fears the worst.

Rachel searches through the night with her husband
and Lucy's older sister, desperate to find her child safe.

The following morning, a body is found in the woods.

But the nightmare is only just beginning.

Acknowledgements

In the summer of 1998, I worked as an aerobics instructor at a Mark Warner beach resort in Corsica. Not only did I meet my husband there, but I had one of the most raucous, fun and memorable summers of my life. And all this amidst the backdrop of beautiful beaches, snowcapped mountains and rumours of mafia influence. AKA the perfect setting for a destination thriller!

But while I may have pulled some scenes from memory, I should point out that this story is not autobiographical. All the Corsicans I met were gracious, welcoming and not in the slightest bit ruthless …

My first thank you must go to all the amazing people who made that summer so worthy of a twisty thriller – especially Abi, Kate, Lisa, Scotty, Steve, My, Sam, Rory, Tom and Oli, Ben, the many Wills, 'Mum and Dad' Ali and Hamish, and of course my now husband Chris. Thank you especially to Will Ellwood for sharing his vast sailing knowledge. And I must also thank my friends in New Zealand who taught me enough about windsurfing to write this book.

To extend my knowledge of the mazzeri legend, I read *The Dream Hunters of Corsica* by Dorothy Carrington, which is a fascinating book that covers centuries of Corsican history as well as explaining the mystical legend in detail. For the last few years, I have created content for a wine decanter brand, so I also want to thank Dina and Tom at Eto for inspiring the location of my final showdown (and paying for my "research"!). And thank you, Josh and Sophie, for 'lending' me *The Wolf Den* for those early chapters.

Thank you to everyone at HQ. To Georgia and Lou for your PR and marketing support and Francesca for answering all my queries. And to my amazing editor Cicely Aspinall. This is the sixth book we've worked on together (how is that possible?!) and was the most challenging to get right – but I am grateful for your high standards, and for pushing me to do better.

Support from fellow authors is one of the best things about this job. A special thank you to Jacqueline Sutherland, Catherine Cooper and Diane Jeffrey for reading an early copy of *Someone in the Water* – your suggestions (and reassurances) were invaluable. And thank you to every other author who I now consider a friend, especially Alex, Emma, Katy, Sarah and Sophie. Thank you to my friends and family for continuing to ask about my books and get excited on my behalf. And thank you to all the bloggers who shout about my books – I will always be so grateful for the time you spend championing authors like me.

Ultimately it is readers who make it possible for me to spend my day writing stories, so thank you to everyone who has bought or borrowed my books, and a particular thank you to those who have taken the time to write a review, and to recommend my books to others.

And finally, my family. For various reasons, this book has been written in the early hours, at weekends, in evenings, and on holiday. So thank you, Chris, Scarlett and Finn, for your patience, your understanding … and your cooking skills.

Dear Reader,

We hope you enjoyed reading this book. If you did, we'd be so appreciative if you left a review. It really helps us and the author to bring more books like this to you.

Here at HQ Digital we are dedicated to publishing fiction that will keep you turning the pages into the early hours. Don't want to miss a thing? To find out more about our books, promotions, discover exclusive content and enter competitions you can keep in touch in the following ways:

JOIN OUR COMMUNITY:
Sign up to our new email newsletter: http://smarturl.it/SignUpHQ
Read our new blog www.hqstories.co.uk

𝕏 https://twitter.com/HQStories
f www.facebook.com/HQStories

BUDDING WRITER?
We're also looking for authors to join the HQ Digital family!
Find out more here:

https://www.hqstories.co.uk/want-to-write-for-us/

Thanks for reading, from the HQ Digital team